For my real parents; they know who they are.

ACKNOWLEDGEMENTS

Thank you to my family and friends for their unstinting support throughout this exciting process, in particular my husband Marc, my daughter Héloïse and my friend Nicola Davis, without whose benevolent chivvying this book would forever have remained a work in progress.

To my beta readers for their patience and precious feedback: Emilie Altot, Joan Coutts, June Davies, Judith Hunt and Tamsin Jeffrey.

To Maya Jevans for her fabulous artistic input: she immediately grasped the spirit of the book and was able to translate it visually in the cover art.

And to my readers – past, present and future.

RELATIVE ERROR

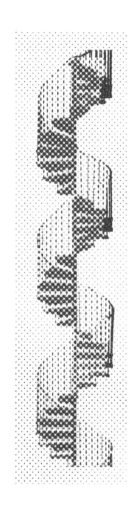

Susan Turbié

Cover illustrated by Maya Jevans

Author photograph by Maraki Studio (Malak Laraki)

Kavanaugh
Family Tree

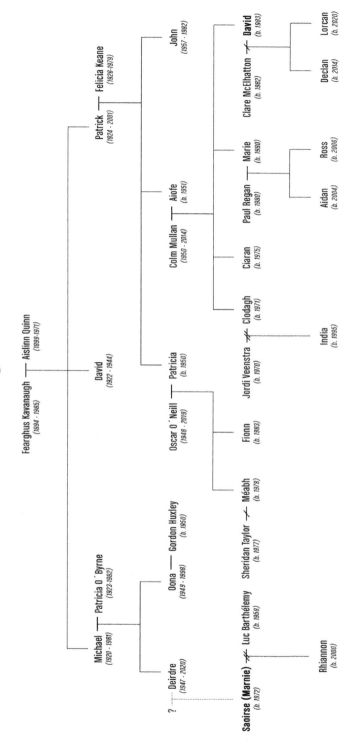

If a son of a paramour or a prostitute say to his adoptive father or mother: 'You are not my father, or my mother,' his tongue shall be cut off.

The Hammurabi Code, c 1754 BC

- It's an alternative culture now, sir. People are asking questions; they want to know who they are.

-Well they should damn well look at their passports!

The Thin Blue Line, BBC sitcom, 1996

PROLOGUE

Marnie had been in the throes of an absorbing dream when the phone rang. It was *the* Dream; the recurring one she had had for years: she was wandering around a large, rambling, labyrinthine house and exploring it, room by room. As usual, she felt no fear, only a burning curiosity – one which was invariably doomed to be frustrated. On this particular occasion, the house was more capacious and complex than ever, with hidden doorways, secret passageways, priest holes and *The Lion, the Witch and the Wardrobe*-style backless wardrobes.

The bedside clock showed it was 6:30am. Groping for her mobile, she saw it was Dave. She answered and, clamping the phone between ear and shoulder, slipped on her bathrobe and tiptoed out of the bedroom.

'Dave. What's up?'

'Hey. Sorry to wake you. Listen… It's Deirdre. She's gone. She passed away a few hours ago.' After a few seconds of silence, he prompted: 'Marn? Are you there?'

She nodded, then realised he couldn't see her.

'Yes. Yes, I'm… OK. I see.'

'Her partner just called my Mam to tell her. It was the cancer; it came back. She'd been in a hospice for the past few weeks. None of us knew. Apparently, she didn't want anyone to know.'

'Right,' her voice was cracked. She cleared her throat. 'Well, thanks for letting me know.'

'Of course.' He paused. 'Listen, I don't know what's happening about the funeral, but…'

'Oh, don't worry,' she said quickly. 'Even if I wanted to come, I couldn't: I'm stuck over here for now.'

'Actually, I was going to say, none of us could go anyway, what with the stay-at-home order and the travel ban –'

'Right, of course. Listen… I've got to go. Thanks for letting me know.'

1

'Marn…' She hung up and sat down on the top stair. She was stunned at how little she felt. Further sleep unthinkable now, she arose and padded downstairs to make coffee. After drinking two cups and having a shower, it was still only just after seven. She waited until eight before calling Luc.

'It's me. Did I wake you?'

'Of course not. What's up?'

'She's dead. My… Deirdre. The biological… that woman.'

A sigh on the other end of the line. *'Je suis désolé. Comment tu te sens?'*

'That's just it. I don't feel anything. Why should I? She was nothing to me. I just happened to come out of her womb forty-seven years ago.'

'Sure. But still…'

'I'm fine,' she said briskly. 'I'm sorry. I don't know why I called you. I just, I immediately thought of you, I mean, you were with me when –'

'Of course. I'm glad you did.'

She cleared her throat. 'Anyway… How's Rhiannon? How's it going? Are you driving each other crazy?'

'Not at all. It's great being able to spend all this time with her – albeit under rather unpleasant circumstances. What about you? How are things over there? When do you think you'll be allowed home?'

'God knows. Soon, I hope. It's pretty scary here: I literally can't leave the house. But it's all right. Listen, I've got to go. Give Rhiannon my love.'

'Will do. And I'm sorry. Will you be OK?'

'I'm fine. Thanks.' She hung up and, for the first time in days, switched on the news. The usual footage of people in Hazmat suits spraying disinfectant around the streets, the usual deluge of statistics: Italy had recorded an increase of 919 deaths since the previous day, making it the highest single-day death toll recorded by any country since the outbreak began, and bringing their total death toll to 9,134.

Her thoughts returned to Deirdre. What was one more death, on top of so many thousands?

CHAPTER ONE

Bristol, 24 June 2016

Marnie awoke that morning with an eerie sense of foreboding that was soon to be justified as she switched on the television and was confronted by the sight of a group of men in three-piece-suits, each with one fist thrust triumphantly in the air whilst the other waved a Union Jack.

So that was it: they had actually voted Leave. As she looked with horror and disgust at the ugly spectacle, the faces twisted grotesquely in jubilation, she was reminded – bizarrely – of a documentary she had recently seen on the *mani pulite* investigations in Italy in the nineties: she imagined members of Cosa Nostra celebrating with similar spiteful euphoria upon hearing of the assassinations of Judges Falcone and Borsellino.

A wave of nausea suddenly engulfed her and she stumbled into the bathroom and retched. After flushing the toilet, she remained crouched on the floor and began to weep, her head buried in the crook of her elbow that rested on the toilet seat. A few seconds later she heard her phone ringing. Gathering a handful of toilet paper, she got up, blew her nose, tied back her hair, splashed water on her face at the sink and went into the living room to retrieve her phone. It was Luc.

'Tu n'as vraiment pas de chance, ma pauvre.'

'Oh, fuck off!' she sobbed.

'I'm sorry,' he said. 'Come on. Look, it'll be OK.'

'How is it going to be all right?' she wailed. 'In what fucked-up, Dystopian parallel universe could this situation be deemed OK? We've just signed our death warrant. Well, those stupid Leave bastards have. Listen, Val's calling, I've got to go.' She hung up on her ex-husband's apologetic protestations and took the call from her friend.

Val and Marnie had met at boarding school in 1984. A mediocre public school housed in an impressive Palladian mansion set in extensive grounds in the depths of the West Sussex countryside, St. Ursula's had catered essentially for untalented young girls who, whilst not distinguishing themselves academically, were either not quite stupid or not quite rich enough for finishing school. How Val and Marnie had ended up there was a mystery. According to Val's father, the headmistress of Val's prep school had endorsed the establishment in the most animated terms. However, it soon became clear that a place such as St Ursula's simply did not know what to do with bright, curious, lively girls like them. Second-rate education notwithstanding, both girls had managed to secure some good A-levels and whilst Marnie had studied Modern Languages at Exeter, Val had gone on to study Chemical Engineering at Imperial. She was now a Process Engineer and lived in London with her husband Jolyon, an Environmental Lawyer, and their two teenaged children.

'Oh, dear,' she said. 'You picked the wrong time to move back here.'

'You think?' Marnie shrieked. 'Thanks, Luc just very helpfully pointed that out to me.' She sighed. 'I'm sorry… I'm just wretched.'

'I know, we're in shock. Well, I am; Joly is actually only half-surprised. Thank God I work from home on Fridays; I'm a total basket case. I just can't face people.'

'Same here. I'll be hitting the gin once the clock hits double-digits.'

'Isn't it the sun over the yardarm?'

'What are you, a bloody sailor? Crisis, Val. We're in mourning. Drastic situations, and all that.'

Val laughed. 'Fair enough. So, what drastic measures do you intend to take – other than getting wazzed at ten in the morning?'

'Well, there's only one thing for it. I need to get European nationality.'

'Oh, you mean French? Well, that would have been a whole lot easier if you were still married to Luc… Oh. Sorry.'

'Again, very helpful. But in point of fact, I wasn't thinking of French: evidently, that ship has sailed. I was thinking Irish.'

'Irish? How are you eligible for –? Ah. Right, of course.'

'It's worth a try. I'll have to look into it but from what I hear, they dish out passports to anyone with a shred of Irish ancestry.' She was interrupted by the sight of Rhiannon appearing in the doorway, in her pyjamas, wide-eyed, white-faced, equally white knuckles clutching her mobile.

'Hey. Morning, Honey Bee,' she said, forcing herself to sound jovial.

'I can't believe you made us move here for *this*!' she wailed, with a withering, accusatory glare at her mother.

('Val, I'll call you back.') Hanging up, she looked up at her daughter. Whilst favouring her father physically, for she had his amber-flecked hazel eyes, dark brown hair, as straight as Marnie's was wavy, and olive complexion, and having inherited Luc's strong social conscience and political awareness, she had her mother's fiery temperament and penchant for withering sarcasm.

'Look, love, I know it's a terrible blow, but…' and then she found herself trotting out the same feeble, (and surely totally unfounded), assurances the girl's father had been proffering just moments before, and which she had so vehemently scorned. And Rhiannon reacted just as she had:

'*How* is it going to be all right? *You* brought us back to *this country*,' (she said these last two words as though it were Syria or the Democratic Republic of the Congo), 'you uprooted us and brought us to this reactionary little island with its pathetic, post-imperial inferiority complex, its stupid nostalgia for the Taj…'

'I think you mean the Raj….'

She ignored her. 'Its crappy, biased press, its pebbly beaches and grey water, its *compulsive queuing*…' Marnie breathed deeply while her daughter reeled off her catalogue of indictments against the British Isles.

'….It's like George Bernard Shaw said: never trust a civilisation that upholds autolysed yeast as a culinary delicacy.'

Marnie frowned. 'No, he didn't. Pretty sure no one said that.'

Privately, she thought it was a bit rich Rhiannon slagging off Marmite when she had grown up in a country where eating exploding songbirds under a tea towel, cirrhotic goose liver and tripe sausage were considered the ultimate gastronomic experiences. However, she took another deep breath and simply said:

'Look, I get it, it's far from ideal. But at least you already have dual nationality. You can go back to live and work in France – or anywhere else in Europe, for that matter – once you graduate from university, whereas I'm stuck with this useless, embarrassing passport. I was actually just saying to Val, I'll have to find a way to stay in the European Union.'

However, having vented her spleen, Rhiannon, with the self-absorption and limited attention span of the adolescent, had no further interest in the exchange and wandered into the kitchen in search of breakfast – but not before she had delivered her final, stinging blow:

'I wish I'd stayed in France and lived with Papa.'

Marnie sighed and dialled Val's number.

'Hi again. Sorry about that. Rhiannon having histrionics. I should have known she'd find a way to blame me for this. Anyway, fuck ten o'clock: I am going to start drowning my sorrows in about…let's see… *now*. Catch you later. Give my love to Joly and the kids.'

She hung up and exhaled slowly. *For Christ's sake*, she wanted to scream at her daughter, *get some perspective, you ungrateful, self-involved, precocious, melodramatic brat.* Honestly. The future of Great Britain was now, admittedly, uncertain and bleak. But they were at least in a country where they had free healthcare, some of the world's greatest seats of learning; they personally had no material worries. Not to mention that, as a woman, and a feminist, Rhiannon should remember that she was living in a country whose track record where women's rights were concerned was far more progressive than France's. French women didn't get the vote until World War II; abortion wasn't legal until 1975 (thank you, Simone Veil!), and up until the late seventies, a woman couldn't open a bank account without her husband's permission. Even in the early nineties, when Marnie had first arrived in France, she was shocked by some of the attitudes to gender parity that even women themselves had had. At the time she was working as a *lectrice d'anglais*, a part-time English lecturer as part of a university programme whereby language graduates could spend a year at a European university teaching language students part-time whilst devoting the rest of the week to studying for a Masters. Thus Marnie, having graduated from Exeter, obtained a post at a new university in the western suburbs of Paris, whilst enrolling for a Masters in Contemporary French Theatre at another university, Nanterre. Among her students there were a number of young upper-middle-class Catholic women from nearby Versailles, and one afternoon, when teaching English to a class of law students made up essentially of this particular demographic, she raised the topic of women's rights and perceptions of gender and was half-amused, half-dismayed by their reactions. Some of them seemed to think of feminism as some quaint import from what the French infuriatingly (and inaccurately) insist on calling the *'le monde anglo-saxon.'* One rather supercilious young woman even said:

'This is good for you, but we don't need it here.'

Not knowing how to respond to this, Marnie tried another tack: what about equal pay? Did they not think it was unfair that when they graduated, for example, they would be paid less as lawyers or judges than their male counterparts? At this they merely frowned and exchanged doubtful glances with each other, before one piped up:

'Are you really sure this is true?'

Just when Marnie started stuttering incredulously, she was saved by one of her brighter, more sensible students, who conceded:

6

'Of course, you are right. It's important for women to have a career, to be independent. Me, for example, I study law because my mother said: you must have a diploma. Just in case. You know, if I don't get married…'

Yet even this depressingly archaic admission was positively progressive compared to that of one of her classmates who said she was studying law not with a view to exercising any of the legal professions, but so she would be able to keep up with the conversation at the dinner parties she would one day host for her future husband.

And forget France, (which, admittedly, had come a long way where gender perceptions were concerned in the twenty-odd years since then): what about certain African and Middle Eastern countries? Christ, Rhiannon should just consider herself fortunate to be living in a country where she was entitled to have an education and keep her clitoris and labia intact!

Anyway, Marnie fumed internally, that was not the point. She deeply resented being in a position whereby she felt she had to defend her country of birth in the first place. After all, she hadn't moved back there after twenty years in France because of some dewy-eyed nostalgia for vinegar-soaked chips and cricket on the village green. She had no illusions about the UK. But, after the divorce, she had felt the need for a fresh start, and realised that her love affair with France had waned long before her marriage had. And going back to the UK seemed like a logical move, and one which would involve considerably less upheaval and adjustment – for both her and Rhiannon – than starting from scratch in an entirely foreign country.

But of course, that was before the referendum. For since the events in the past twenty-four hours – indeed, those of the months leading up to it, the media coverage, the ugly tactics employed in the Leave campaign – her country of birth suddenly felt alien, hostile, utterly incomprehensible.

As the rolling news showed excerpts from Cameron's tearful resignation speech for the twentieth time that day, she helped herself to a stiff measure of Tanqueray from the drinks cabinet and went into the kitchen in search of tonic water. Just as Marnie was opening the fridge, Rhiannon looked up from her bowl of cereal and her glance fell upon the crystal tumbler in her mother's hand. She opened her mouth, but was stopped by Marnie's sharply raised hand:

'Not. One. *Bloody*. Word.'

Her daughter meekly obliged. Returning to the living room, Marnie picked up her laptop, and, taking it and her drink over to the sofa, went onto the website of the Irish government's Department of Foreign Affairs. After a stiff drink and just fifteen minutes on the DFA website, She already had a strategy for maintaining European Union citizenship.

According to Irish law, she was not automatically an Irish citizen as this required having an Irish parent who was born on the island of Ireland. Deirdre fulfilled the first of these conditions, but not the second: her parents had emigrated to the UK in the forties, and Deirdre and her sister had been born there. Marnie was, however, eligible to apply for Irish citizenship, fulfilling both the requisite conditions (having one grandparent who was born in Ireland, and having one parent who was an Irish citizen at the time of her birth – regardless of whether they were born in Ireland). All she had to do was apply for citizenship through Foreign Birth Registration, and she would be entitled to apply for an Irish passport. Easy.

Except, of course, it was anything but easy. For if the administrative procedure seemed fairly straightforward, it involved submitting, among other documents, the Irish parent's original birth certificate and a copy of their ID.

Which meant getting in touch with Deirdre.

CHAPTER TWO

Killiney, Co. Dublin, 18 March 2019

The day after St Patrick's Day, Dave Mullan left the marital home for the last time beneath a torrent of pejorative epithets and chill March rain.

As he strode briskly along the street towards his car, Clare's screeching recriminations were gradually drowned out by the drone of traffic and rain. The last words he could distinguish clearly were 'whoremongering bastard' before he hurled himself into his brand-new BMW X5 (which, he would soon reflect ruefully, he would no doubt be forced to sell to pay for maintenance and solicitor's fees and take the DART to work every morning), and shut out the rain, Clare's bitter reproaches and the tattered remains of their six-year marriage.

As he pulled away from the kerb, he glanced at her diminishing figure in the rear-view mirror, standing on the doorstep of the three-bedroom house they had bought together, in a blue dressing gown, her strawberry-blond hair already flattened against her head by the rain. And Declan, his wee man, at her side, sucking his thumb that way he had since he was a baby, with his index and middle fingers curled around his nose, and the other hand clutching at his mother's hem.

'*Fuck!*' he shrieked, pounding the steering wheel. 'Fuck, fuck, fuck!' As he joined the stream of commuters crawling along the rain-drenched streets into town, he reflected on the past twenty-four hours, possibly the worst in his thirty-six years on earth.

The weekend – Round Five of the Six Nations – had started innocuously, even pleasantly enough: they had even had sex. On Saturday morning, he had awoken with a hard-on and, despite the bickering and cold, monosyllabic exchanges that had come to characterise his and Clare's marriage over the past four months, the physical side of their relationship at least was far from moribund. He had taken her briskly and without ceremony, spooning her, bringing them both to a swift, effective climax and gently biting her freckled shoulder as he did. She had arisen almost immediately afterwards, hastily pulling her night-shirt down, and padded downstairs to tend to Declan's breakfast whilst Dave remained in bed with the papers for another half-hour. When he had finished reading everything that interested him in the paper, he began idly flicking through Clare's *Grazia* and came across an article on make-up techniques. It was not the sort of thing that would normally attract his attention, but when he read the tip on smiling in order to raise the cheekbones when applying blusher to the apple of the cheek, it occurred to him that the only time he saw Clare smile these days was when she applied her blusher in the morning.

It was briefly uncharacteristically dry, so after breakfast he had taken Declan down to Bullock Harbour for a run around and bought him a lemonade then dropped him back at home for lunch with Clare before heading off to the pub with Andy and the others to watch the rugby.

It was then that a series of cataclysmic disasters began to unfold – beginning with Ireland getting thrashed by Wales 25-7. It seemed doomed from kick-off – before then, even: for Joe Schmidt's decision to keep the Principality Stadium roof open proved very ill-judged: it had pissed it down for most of the match. Then there was Ireland's performance: a series of poor decisions and general sloppiness. At half-time, after yet another Irish penalty, Wales were leading 16-0. The second half was scarcely better (Sexton was kicking like a mong); honour was finally just about saved when Larmour scored a try, but it was still a disaster. Dave tried to tell himself that if anyone other than Ireland had to win the Grand Slam, he would rather it was the Taffs than the Sassenachs. But still: such a crushing defeat, and on the eve of St Paddy's Day! It was too much to bear. Thank God they hadn't made it over to Cardiff to watch the fiasco live, as they had originally planned – before the WAGs had put a stop to the plan.

Needless to say, Dave, Andy and the boys were inconsolable, alternately enraged and despondent, cursing Joe Schmidt, and had spent the rest of the afternoon and evening on a pub crawl. When he rang Clare about an hour before closing to tell her he was too far gone to drive and would be crashing at Andy's, she was even frostier than usual.

'We need to talk,' she said. 'You get back here.'

'No can do,' he half-said, half-belched, nodding his thanks to Ben as he deposited another pint of Guinness before him. 'We're all fuckin' wasted, drownin' our sorrows, I mean did you see that match? Jesus –'

'I don't give a fuck about your bloody match!' she hissed. 'You get back here now or so help me, you'll never set foot in this house again!'

'Yeah, look we'll talk tomorrow, all right?' and with that he hung up and raised his pint to the others.

'Trouble in paradise?' inquired Chris with mock concern.

'Don't fuckin' ask, mate,' said Dave grimly. 'She'll get over it. Cheers!'

10

He didn't remember stumbling back to Andy's or cracking open the bottle of Bushmill's 10 Year, but awoke on the sofa just after eleven with a gruesome hangover. Too depressed and hungover to participate in the parade, he and Andy decided to go out for a fry-up and when Andy said he was heading to Dundrum Shopping Centre to buy a birthday present for his new girlfriend, Keira, Dave decided to tag along. It was not a desire to shop that prompted this decision so much as a wish to avoid a confrontation with his wife, for he had had an acute sense of impending doom ever since their frosty exchange the night before, and Dave, as was his wont, chose the path of cowardice and procrastination.

Whilst Andy went to Harvey Nichols in search of some scent for Keira, Dave had a wander around the shops and by the time they met up for a latte at Costa Coffee half an hour later, he had acquired a pair of skinny jeans from Superdry (50% off), a Ben Sherman T-shirt from TK Maxx and a couple of pairs of boxer briefs from Diesel.

Agreeing that coffee and Advil weren't making a dent in their hangovers, they concluded that hair of the dog was the only solution. They texted the rest of the gang but only Ben was up for it, the others demurring on the grounds of either their hangover or watching the parade. And so it was that the three of them met up at the Almshouse on that Sunday evening for more rounds of Guinness, (although no whiskey this time). As the bell rang for last orders, Dave checked his messages and saw five missed calls from Clare.

Perhaps if he had gone home after the pub that night, things would have turned out very differently. But alcohol, far from fortifying Dave, merely made him even more fainthearted and determined to defer the inevitable. His only concession to facing his family responsibilities was texting Clare to check if Declan was all right. Having received a curt, two-word reply confirming his son's safety and wellbeing, he concluded that there was nothing to rush home for and, after asking Andy to extend his hospitality for another night, he texted Clare informing her that he would be back early the next morning.

After another night on Andy's sofa, he awoke just before seven on Monday morning, at last ready to face the music. Thirty-five minutes later he was back in Killiney, turning the key in the lock of his front door. The usual morning odours of coffee and toast failed to mask the overpowering stench of imminent disaster that hung in the air.

He was momentarily softened by the sight of his son, standing in the kitchen doorway in his Star Wars pyjamas with a piece of toast and jam in his hand.

'Daddy!' he shrieked and tore across the hall into his father's arms.

'Hey, little man,' Dave managed to croak, sinking to his knees and putting his face up to receive a jammy kiss.

'Declan, come back and finish your breakfast.' Clare appeared in the kitchen doorway. Declan clung defiantly to his father.

'*Declan.*'

'Do as your mammy says,' urged Dave gently, ruffling the child's dark curly hair. Once Declan was settled back at the kitchen table before his toast and Nesquik, Clare closed the kitchen door and strode up to her husband. She looked pale and haggard.

Dave sighed. 'Look, I'm sorry about last night, but I feel like shite and I'm late for dropping Declan round at my Mam's so why don't we talk about this later –'

Without a word, Clare walked calmly up the stairs and descended a minute later with a rucksack and a large leather hold-all.

'This is Declan's stuff,' she said evenly, holding up the rucksack, 'but *I'll* take him to *my* Mam's today before my shift. And *this*' – she let the hold-all fall to the floor with a heavy thud, 'is some of your stuff. Some clean shirts, underwear, that sort of thing.'

Dave rubbed his forehead for a few seconds. 'OK, I don't know what the fuck's going on, but I'm in bits. If I could just get myself a painkiller…' He went upstairs to the bathroom, helped himself to a couple of ibuprofen from the medicine cabinet and knocked them back with a tooth-mug of water. Clare followed him, and then it all came out: how last night she had talked to Maura, whose cousin had somehow found out about Dave and the barmaid from the Black Horse. That interfering bitch Maura had then gone on to say that, now she thought of it, she'd heard rumours about Dave and other women. He had begun by making a half-hearted attempt at denial but it then occurred to him that he no longer cared enough to maintain the pretence, that he even resented having to. And then came the screaming and mutual accusations and threats, culminating in Dave's rather undignified ejection from the conjugal nest.

It was only as he parked outside his office – surprisingly easily, for once – forty-five minutes later that he remembered it was a Bank Holiday. Still, he had nowhere else to go: there was no point worrying his family – or providing them with gossip fodder – when he was almost certain Clare would have calmed down by the end of the day. Besides, he had work to do: contacting customers was of course out of the question today, but he had some admin to catch up on – contracts to draw up, the customer database to update. So, he let himself into the office, which occupied the ground floor of an elegant Georgian townhouse in Fitzwilliam Place. As he hurried inside and shook off his coat, he discovered to his surprise and dismay that his co-worker, Mike, had also come into work. A model of equanimity, Mike was his usual affable, serene self.

'Morning!' he called out pleasantly from the kitchenette. 'Coffee?'

Dave grunted a negative response and thanked the God he had long ceased to believe in when his colleague proceeded to inform him that he was just picking up some paperwork then he'd be back home for lunch with his in-laws: he would not have to endure Mike's offensively good humour for long.

Cheerily oblivious to his colleague's bilious mood, Mike emerged from the kitchenette with a mug of coffee in his hand and made further valiant attempts at conversation.

'So, did you see the game on Saturday?'

Dave clutched the edge of his desk.

The rugby. He had *to mention the fucking rugby!* For the third time in forty-eight hours, Dave experienced an irrepressible desire to commit violence. Retreating to his office and closing the door, he sat down at his desk, put his head in his hands and cursed his life.

CHAPTER THREE

On the day of the referendum results, Marnie stayed in her pyjamas all day, doing no work other than occasionally checking her inbox. She kept the rolling news on: not due to some perverse, masochistic urge, but because some part of her was clinging to the hope that it was all some monstrous hoax, or that a recount would result in a Remain victory. After two stiff gins she felt drowsy and nodded off on the sofa, to be awoken an hour or so later by Roger, her Chinchilla Persian – then still a kitten – gently prodding her cheek with her paw.

A lifelong cat lover, Marnie had had to renounce any hopes of owning a pet when she married Luc, an asthmatic with an acute allergy to cat hair. Her decision, within weeks of moving to Bristol, to acquire a kitten from a breeder just outside Bath was not a gesture of defiance, an assertion of her independence as a newly divorced woman, nor was it a substitute for male company or an antidote to loneliness, but merely the fulfilment of a need – long-since denied – for a feline presence at home. The kitten, which Marnie had christened Roger the Shrubber, despite its being a female, would be joined a year later by a scrappy, flea-bitten tabby Rhiannon had brought home from the local rescue centre. The cat – also a spayed female – was named Tim the Enchanter and its age, according to the estimations of the woman at the rescue centre, was between a year and eighteen months. Rhiannon claimed at the time that introducing an alley cat into a home hitherto occupied by a pedigree animal was a demonstration of her commitment to inclusion and social integration. Yet despite her well-meaning – some might say, utopian – intentions, the two animals never bonded, divided as they were by issues of territory and caste, although the fighting had eventually subsided and their mutual antagonism cooled into indifference.

Gently prying Roger off and setting her on the floor, she rose from the sofa and wandered into the kitchen. After making herself a ham and pickle sandwich and a cup of strong tea, she thought about the Irish nationality issue and Deirdre.

It must have been nearly fifteen years since Marnie had been in touch with her: it was a few months after Rhiannon was born. For that was what had started it all in the first place: her quest for identity – biological, at least. Up until then she had been supremely indifferent to her origins: as far as she was concerned, her life had begun when she was six weeks old and Fay and Martin Wade had adopted her. Indeed, she had never understood the apparently universal assumption that biological parents have innate moral superiority and rights – whatever their treatment of their offspring. She was also invariably exasperated by the many film and soap opera plotlines in which adopted children who, having sought out, or being sought out by, their birth mother, suddenly threw over the people who had raised them, fed and clothed and loved them, and went running into the arms of their biological progenitors. Even her beloved Dickens romanticised – beatified! birth mothers. His orphaned heroes and heroines, be they the illegitimate products of forbidden, passionate idylls, like Esther Summerson or Arthur Clennam, or the offspring of loving married parents who came to tragic, untimely ends, like Pip or David Copperfield, were invariably raised by tyrannical, abusive foster or stepparents, heartless Tartars who resented the child's very existence. This assumption – that it was impossible for a woman to show genuine love and affection for a child that she had not physically brought into the world – provoked in Marnie a surge of indignation and outrage on behalf of the loving, nurturing, devoted people who had raised her – the only ones she had ever and would ever deem worthy of the term 'parents.' Surely for every Miss Barbary, Mrs Clennam, Mrs Joe Gargery, Miss Havisham or Edward Murdstone, there was a Martin and Fay Wade?

Of course, in calmer, less emotional moments, she was able to consider the matter more objectively, placing it in the socio-economic context of Victorian England, and understand that the aim of Dickens, a tireless advocate for children's rights, was not to denigrate foster parents so much as highlight the plight of children. For in those pre-contraception, pre-Welfare State times, long before such modern-day phenomena as the child-centric culture and the rise in infertility, it was a simple, sad fact of life that the combination of mass poverty and its consequential health issues, rampant, unchecked birth-rates and the lack of an official state body dedicated to children's welfare and protection meant that there was inevitably a glut of orphaned children who either ended up in the workhouse or were foisted upon reluctant guardians with neither the inclination nor the aptitude for parenthood. (In another life, she sometimes pondered, she would have liked to write a thesis on adoption and parenthood in literature.)

At any rate, she had never, neither as a child nor an adult, shown the slightest interest in tracing her birth parents, unlike her younger brother, Guy, who had also been adopted and had searched for – and found – his own biological parents as soon as he was legally of age. Both parents had been teenagers when Guy was conceived and after giving him up for adoption they had emigrated to the States and, after separating, gone on to pursue successful careers in their respective fields. A decade or so later, their paths had crossed again, and, improbably, they had resumed their relationship, married and had another child together – a girl – before divorcing. Guy had met all three members of his birth family and formed a bond of sorts with them (fortunately for all concerned, his parents – Vince and Heidi – had always been completely transparent with their daughter as to Guy's existence and the circumstances of his birth and adoption). Marnie herself had met Heidi and her daughter, Madison once, many years ago, when they had come to the UK. They were pleasant enough, although she had had to suppress a gasp of shock upon seeing Guy's sister for the first time, so uncanny was the physical resemblance between the siblings.

As pleased as she was for her brother and his obvious satisfaction at finding and becoming acquainted with his biological family, Marnie herself still had no desire to follow his example.

However, when she herself became a mother some years later, everything changed. She had tried to imagine giving up a child: a child one had chosen to grow in one's womb for nine months. She had tried – and failed.

She still vividly remembered that day all those years ago. Luc had just brought her and the baby home from the hospital; she was breastfeeding Rhiannon and suddenly a disconcerting thought occurred to her and, exacerbated no doubt by sleep deprivation and plummeting hormone levels, degenerated into a near panic attack, crystallising into this one, sobering observation: *a complete stranger gave birth to me.*

And so it was that, like an atheist who had been temporarily converted, Marnie had been briefly convinced of the supremacy of nature over nurture: her brother's tireless, well-meaning proselytising over the years had finally worn her down – partly, but only partly – due to her weakened emotional state as a new mother. And thus she had agreed to undertake her own research. Guy had offered both emotional support and practical assistance in abundance. It turned out there were all sorts of ways for adopted children to trace their birth parents: on the one hand, the 'official' route, involving applying to the relevant administrative bodies and an interview with a social worker, and on the other, undertaking independent research – consulting electoral rolls and the like. All these processes, of course, as Guy pointed out, were considerably quicker and easier now with the advent of the Internet than when he himself had embarked on his search back in the early nineties.

She had begun by applying for a copy of her original birth certificate through the official channels. Some weeks later she was summoned by letter for a meeting with a social worker, in Paris: she was surprised that such processes could be managed locally, via a French organisation, without her having to go back to the UK.

The case worker, a sensible, efficient-looking Antillean woman in her early forties, was suitably patient and sensitive as she explained the process, the resources available, but also made inquiries about Marnie's intentions (Why this? Why now?) Then there were the inevitable caveats: be prepared that the parents might not want to be found, that they might have hidden Marnie's existence from their loved ones, might be married with other children. After this preamble, Marnie was presented with a copy of her original birth certificate: it showed that Saoirse Patricia Kavanaugh had been born on 9 August 1972 to Deirdre Philomena Kavanaugh.

It was no surprise to see her original name: her parents had told her long ago that her mother had given her a name at birth, and which they had subsequently decided to change – not least because it was simply unpronounceable for the average non-Irish person. Martin Wade, a Hitchcock fan, had chosen Marnie.

What did shock her, however, was the brutal blank space under 'father.' She had always known her paternity was something of a mystery: her parents had been unable to give her any information about this. But seeing that blank space had been like a punch in the stomach. That afternoon whilst taking Rhiannon for a stroll in the park she suddenly stopped pushing the buggy, lifted the baby out and, clasping her to her chest, wept. She scolded herself for this irrational reaction. After all, why did she care, or was even surprised, that the man who had impregnated her mother had subsequently left her and wanted no part in either of their lives, when her own father had chosen her, given her a home, lavished her with love and affection?

And yet, that blank space haunted her. After returning home and putting Rhiannon down for her second nap of the day, Marnie had called Guy and debriefed him on the day's events. He had comforted her and asked if she planned to contact Deirdre directly. She expressed reservations but said she needed to know more about her father. How should she go about it, she wanted to know? Guy said to leave it with him. The next day he called her back. He had checked the electoral roll and found two Deirdre Kavanaughs, both of whom were based in Greater London. He recommended writing to both, adopting a casual, non-invasive approach: introduce herself, give her date and place of birth, and make a vague allusion to 'researching her family,' suggesting they 'might be related,' and inviting them to get in touch if they wished to. She had written that very day and posted both letters. Just two days later, having fallen asleep in the afternoon whilst nursing Rhiannon, she was awoken by a phone call.

Clearing her throat, she said her name.

And then those words: those seven words, spoken in a soft, slightly breathy voice, with a middle-class, educated Southern-English accent – much like Marnie's own – that made her feel as though she had swallowed her heart and was choking on it:

'It's Deirdre Kavanaugh.' A pause, and then: 'Is it really you?'

After a few seconds of silence, Marnie propped herself up on her elbow, gently shedding Rhiannon from her breast and laying her on her back in the middle of the bed.

'Yes,' she had finally managed. Leaving the baby sleeping soundly in the bed, she slipped quietly out of the bedroom. 'Yes,' she repeated, 'It's me.' And then, somewhat absurdly, 'Is it... *you?*'

'Yes! I can't believe it! I never expected...'

'No, I can imagine it was a bit of a shock.' Suddenly Marnie no longer recognised the sound of her own voice.

'No, I mean... Look, I didn't think you could... They told me at the time, that you'd never be able to contact me.'

'Oh.' Marnie felt her spirits plummet. 'Well, I believe they've changed the law since then. I'm sorry if –'

'No! I'm so glad you did!'

And then, after this initial stilted exchange, the words began to gush forth from them both, irrepressibly, insatiably, feverishly: what did they each look like? What did they like doing? What had their lives been for the past thirty years? At one point, Marnie forced herself to steer her questions to more practical matters, such as Deirdre's medical history: for years, when various medical specialists had asked Marnie whether there were cases of heart disease or cancer in her family, she had naturally been unable to answer. Deirdre replied that her sister had died from breast cancer at the age of forty-eight. She also learned, among other things, that Deirdre had never married, nor had she any other children, that she had recently retired after a career in HR management, and that she lived with her partner of twelve years, who was ten years her junior and was, more significantly, the only person other than her late sister who knew of Marnie's existence. She was lactose intolerant, a defiant, committed Luddite who shunned all forms of digital communication technology, and she had enjoyed those nine months carrying Marnie.

18

When she eventually hung up half an hour later, amid the tangle of thoughts and emotions that whirled around Marnie's head was the realisation that Deirdre must have telephoned her almost as soon as she received her letter. She could only imagine what a shock it had been for her. And yet, she had apparently not hesitated.

At the end of their conversation they had agreed to correspond – necessarily by snail mail, as Deirdre was not on email. After hanging up, Marnie cried uncontrollably for several minutes: not so much for sorrow or joy as the sheer emotional shock of this overwhelming and wholly unprecedented experience. She longed for Luc to return home from work so she could share it with him. In the meantime, she composed herself and called the one person in her life who could truly understand what she was going through. She called Guy.

As she scrolled though her contacts for Guy's number and waited for him to answer, she thought of the last thing Deirdre had said to her before they said goodbye, just after promising to write to one another:

'Please try to… don't expect too much,' she had urged. 'I mean, I wouldn't want to let you down a second time.'

A few months later, Marnie would remember these words ruefully and think: *well, I can't say she didn't warn me.*

CHAPTER FOUR

Monza, 18 March 2019

Amedeo Di Meglio had always felt like an outsider in his family: when he was growing up, even his brothers had called him *il diverso*. Indeed, Orazio, the eldest, had followed their father into the army where he had enjoyed a moderately successful career and lived in Turin. Cesare, the youngest, meanwhile, had gone into local politics and was currently the Deputy Mayor of Città della Pieve, his wife's hometown where he had moved to fifteen years ago. A prominent figure in the community, the *vicesindaco* inhabited an eight-bedroom neo-Gothic castle on the outskirts of the town (mortgaged to the hilt), was on the boards of various cultural institutions and charities and claimed to be on first-name terms with Colin Firth and his Italian wife, who famously had a holiday home in the town. Both brothers regularly attended Sunday Mass in their respective parishes, invariably accompanied by their impeccably groomed wives and copious progeny (two girls and a boy for Orazio, four sons for Cesare). Cesare also had a longstanding mistress in the town, a sculptor and potter in her late thirties who ran art workshops for foreign tourists in the summer.

Amedeo, the middle sibling, on the other hand, had trained as an engineer, graduated with distinction, then pursued a career that combined his passion for technology and innovation with his profound need for human interaction. But his professional achievements, including developing a number of ground-breaking software programs and holding a series of senior management positions, had always failed to impress his father as much as the military or political accomplishments of his brothers. He still remembered when, all those years ago, he had proudly shown his father his very first patent (for a firewall), which he had framed and hung on the wall of his study. Massimo Di Meglio knew nothing about new technologies and had no idea what a firewall was, and upon hearing Amedeo's concise, highly simplified explanation, he had merely observed that it was hardly the internal combustion engine and computers wouldn't lead to any great advancements for the human race.

As for his mother, despite having a more indulgent attitude towards her second son than her husband (for Amedeo was her favourite), she nevertheless despaired of his single status. Indeed, he could have been a millionaire tech mogul and world-famous philanthropist but no end of professional achievements could ever come close in her eyes to his brothers' ability to procreate.

But it was not merely his failure – or, as it happened, merely a disinclination – to wed or beget children that made Amedeo stand apart from his siblings. There was his lack of religious faith – for his love of rationality and science had caused him to reject Christianity along with all other theological doctrines at the tender age of eight, much to the mortification of his entire family. His veganism; his political beliefs; his love of poetry and his other intellectual and cultural pursuits, which he suspected were somehow perceived by his family as vaguely effeminate; his introverted nature, in stark contrast to his brothers' and father's volubility and swaggering confidence. Hence, the moniker his brothers had adopted for him as children: *il diverso*. The interloper. The odd-one-out. The cuckoo's egg in the nest, as Cesare had once rather spitefully put it.

Then one day, stung by this particular metaphor, Amedeo, who, at the age of ten, already had a voracious curiosity and a tendency to seek reassurance and solace in facts and science, had spent an afternoon in the municipal library reading about Edward Jenner's pioneering research into the nesting habits of the cuckoo in the late eighteenth century. For in addition to being an eminent physician and the father of immunology, Jenner was also a keen natural historian and had studied cuckoos to try and understand why it was that after the parent deposited its egg into a nest of another species of bird, only the intruder cuckoo survived, whilst all the other eggs and fledglings in the host nest perished. At the time, it was widely believed that it was the parent cuckoo that rid the nest of its original and rightful young occupants so that its own usurping offspring could benefit from the entire food supply provided by the foster parents. Jenner, however, discovered that it was the newly hatched cuckoo itself that eliminated the other eggs and fledglings, by pushing them, one by one, up the side of the nest and out over the edge.

This discovery had a profound effect on the young Amedeo. For if he truly was the cuckoo's egg, he would one day prevail over his foster siblings, cast them out of the nest and henceforth bask in his parents' exclusive and undivided love and attention! He had briefly contemplated sharing his ornithological discoveries with his brothers later that day, but wisely refrained, intuiting that they would respond by beating (Orazio) and mocking him (Cesare).

So he said nothing, resolving instead to keep his head down, bide his time, and wait for the propitious moment when he would supplant his brothers in the family nest and in his parents' affection.

However, this was not to be: Orazio and Cesare continued to rule the Di Meglio nest for years to come and Amedeo never succeeded in graduating from intruder to autocrat: it turned out he lacked that ruthless, single-minded instinct for survival and domination. He was a Beta male surrounded by Alpha males.

His attitude towards the English doctor and naturalist, whom he had initially so revered, soon cooled – all the more so when he learned that, in the course of his experiments in immunology, Jenner had used his gardener's eight-year-old son as a guinea pig, purposely infecting him first with cowpox and then with smallpox to see if the first would provide immunity against the second. Fortunately for the little boy in question – and subsequently, for mankind – this turned out to be the case. But still…

And yet, despite the failure of the cuckoo theory, Amedeo survived and, in his own way, thrived. He eventually discovered that, once one ceased trying to conform to other people's expectations, one was free. When his father died at the age of seventy, Amedeo not only felt no great sadness but no bitterness or regrets.

It was Sunday morning and he was just beginning his usual dominical routine: a trip to the local farmer's market followed by a run or bike ride in the park before a leisurely late lunch with friends which, more often than not, lasted for most of the afternoon and merged seamlessly into an *apericena*.

This Sunday there was a new greengrocer's stall run by a swarthy man who vaunted the merits of his wares with a thick Apulian accent. Amedeo wandered over to the stall, greeted the stallholder and began squeezing aubergines and sniffing melons. His eye then fell upon some okra. Not accustomed to cooking with it, he asked the stallholder for advice on how to prepare and serve the vegetable, to which the Apulian smiled broadly and suggested Amedeo ask his wife. When he retorted good-naturedly that he had no wife, the greengrocer proceeded to recount, with excruciating (and completely unsolicited) candour a heart-rending tale of how, twenty-seven years ago, he had been engaged to a young lady from Bari who had perished in a road accident, from which he, the driver, had escaped relatively unscathed. There then followed two decades of (presumably solitary and pathetic) bachelorhood, until five years previously he had married his current wife who, though eight years his junior, was past childbearing age and thus he found himself today, fifty-eight, without issue.

Profoundly embarrassed by any sort of intimate confidences from strangers, Amedeo was horrified by this outburst and at a complete loss as to how to respond. To compensate for his inadequacy as a confidant, he ended up buying far more produce than he had originally intended: he hurriedly filled bags with aubergines, courgettes, chicory, sweet potatoes, okra – he'd ask Siri to find a recipe for that – pears and walnuts, thrust some notes into the man's hand and, muttering 'keep the change,' scuttled away.

It was only as he was putting the groceries into his fridge fifteen minutes later that it occurred to him how brilliantly the Apulian had scammed him: the man was a sales genius! He laughed out loud and went upstairs to change for his run.

CHAPTER FIVE

Dublin, 23 March 2019

```
Fifteenth Amendment of the Constitution of Ireland
Article 41.3.2
A Court designated by law may grant a dissolution of marriage where, but
only where, it is satisfied that -
    i. at the date of the institution of the proceedings, the spouses have
lived apart from one another for a period of, or periods amounting to, at
least four years during the previous five years,
    ii. there is no reasonable prospect of a reconciliation between the
spouses,
    iii. such provision as the Court considers proper having regard to the
circumstances exists or will be made for the spouses, any children of either
or both of them and any other person prescribed by law, and
    iv. any further conditions prescribed by law are complied with.
```

Barely a week had passed since Clare had thrown Dave out. He was currently sleeping on the sofa at his sister Marie's in Newbridge where she lived with her husband, Paul, and their two teenaged sons, Aidan and Ross. It was Saturday night and his mates had taken him into town for a pint to cheer him up.

The spouses have lived apart from one another for a period of, or periods amounting to, at least four years during the previous five years.

Fuck. They *had* to be taking the piss.

Dave knew, of course, objectively, that the Fifteenth Amendment represented a huge step forward in Irish social and legal history. Why, the very idea of divorce had been simply unthinkable until just two decades ago. He cast his mind back to the Referendum: he had only been twelve at the time, but he vividly remembered the Papist propaganda, the billboards depicting family photos ripped in half accompanied by some trite yet effective emotional plea not to tear families apart. His parents, of course, had voted No, as had his brother Ciaran. His elder sister Clodagh, however, had voted Yes, much to the outrage of almost the entire family: certain aunts and uncles had refused to speak to her for months. Although, this was nothing compared to the deluge of censure reserved for Clodagh nine years later when she had availed herself of this legal landmark and divorced her feckless husband Jordi.

But the idea that he and Clare would have to be Mr and Mrs Mullan for at least another *four years*… But then, he reflected, as he got another round in, things weren't uniformly bleak on the horizon: workwise, he had reason to celebrate. He had just signed an eight-figure deal with the pharmaceutical company he had been prospecting for months: a four-year contract for desktops, laptops, tablets and servers, plus services. At this rate he would easily exceed his target for this month. But then, there was this damned legal separation to sort out, custody of Declan, finances.

And then there were his living arrangements: Marie was being great but she had her own family to worry about and he couldn't impose on them forever. Besides, his brother-in-law was a bit of a prick and he'd rather not stay under the same roof as him longer than was absolutely necessary. He was fond enough of his nephews and they in turn idolised him – much to their father's chagrin.

And, of course, there were the reactions of his mother and brother to this new turn of events in his domestic life to contend with; although his mother, oddly enough, seemed more concerned that Declan would end up an only child than anything else. His brother Ciaran had been far more disapproving: the most fervent Catholic in the family, his sanctimony had known no bounds, leading him to stoop so low as to play the 'What-would-Dad-have-thought' card. Self-righteous dick. His sisters, on the other hand, had been fantastic, especially Clodagh, who, of course had been through a failed marriage herself.

He was just contemplating the varying degrees of family solidarity when Chris elbowed him in the ribs. Looking up, he saw a short but cheaply attractive buxom brunette heading purposefully towards him through the crowded bar. She had milk-white skin, bee-stung lips, dark, wavy hair and wild, dark, kohl-rimmed eyes. She was wearing a tight black miniskirt and black leather jacket over a low-cut white peasant blouse against which her copious bosom strained. He was just thinking he wouldn't mind giving her one, when recognition dawned and he realised he already had: for it was Tina, the barmaid from the Black Horse.

Once again, he was gripped by that feeling – all too familiar of late – of foreboding.

She strode up to Dave's table and declared baldly in her broad Northside accent:

'I'm pregnant. It's yours. I'm having your baby.'

'La famille,' said the portly, jovial old man, 'c'est tout ce qui compte, pas vrai?'

For the first forty years of his life, Luc Barthélemy would not have agreed with this statement, would barely have understood what the man was talking about. For he was the only child of parents who had told him, from an early age, that he was the result of one of the many ineffective contraceptive methods that abounded in those pre-Pill days in the fifties, and that the only reason they had kept him was that Luc's father had believed – erroneously, as it turned out – that having a young child would exempt him from going to fight in the Algerian War. In the end, Victor Barthélemy had gone off to fight after all, Luc's mother had to get a full-time job, and Luc was mainly raised by his paternal grandmother, Edith, a warm, affectionate woman, a diligent homemaker and devout Catholic who doted on her grandson. Luc in turn adored her and was heartbroken when she passed away when he was thirteen.

As for his father, he barely saw him at all during the first few years of his life; shortly after Victor returned from Algeria, he and Luc's mother divorced, and he married an heiress and went to live with her in a lemon chiffon-coloured Belle Epoque villa in the hills above Nice.

In his teens, Luc had become closer to his mother, although they were more like friends than mother and son. Certainly, she was nothing like his friends' mothers: she was barely twenty years his senior and treated his friends like peers, not teenagers. She never nagged him about his schoolwork or tidying his room, rarely cooked and never baked. The closest thing he had to family in his teens and early twenties was the Party. That was how he had met Chloé, his first love: they had met at a *Jeunesse communiste* meeting in the spring of '74, when he was sixteen and she fifteen: a few months later they had gone on a summer camp organised by the Party, where they had lost their virginity to each other. He remembered that summer vividly: the other kids at camp had thought he and Chloé were brother and sister in an incestuous relationship on account of the striking resemblance they bore to one other. The rumour going round was that they had come to camp to escape their family and live out their clandestine love free from judgement and censure – a theory they made no attempt to refute, due essentially to a childish desire to shock.

Their passionate relationship was, however, to be short-lived: at the end of July, he and his friend and comrade Eric Mesmer had decided to go to Portugal for the Carnation Revolution, and Chloé had declined to join them. Of course, neither he nor Mesmer had the funds to undertake such a voyage, but after two weeks detasseling corn just south of Clermont Ferrand, they had earned enough for the train fare to Hendaye in the French Basque Country, near the

26

Spanish border. Here they had crossed the border on foot and hitchhiked the rest of the way – for reasons both pecuniary and ideological: they had resolved not to spend as much as a single peseta in Franco's Spain. Having crossed that country – hitchhiking, camping and sleeping rough – they finally reached Porto, and thence went on to Nazaré, where, sunburnt, grubby and starving, they had scraped together a few escudos and purchased and devoured some grilled sardines down at the harbour. Thus fortified, they had set off, armed with their letter from the French Communist Party to an address in the town centre – a house requisitioned by the Portuguese Party – where they had approached, and were subsequently taken in by, their comrades.

What an adventure it had been! However, their initial youthful euphoria and idealist fervour were soon to collide with reality: the looming menace of the PIDE – Salazar's secret police – the infighting, the many evenings spent in endless sterile discussions with the comrades, the atmosphere laden with paranoia and Definitivos smoke.

After about a month, tired, disillusioned and entirely broke, Luc had called his mother asking her to wire the train fare home to the local Post Office – money which he and Mesmer had subsequently blown on chocolate bars, fags and beer and hitched back to Paris.

Two years later, he had resigned from the Party, following the French Communist Party's highly controversial and much maligned decision at the 22nd Party congress in '76 to abandon the dictatorship of the proletariat.

But it was not until he had met and married Marnie and had Rhiannon that he had learned what family was in the traditional sense – no doubt in the sense that this kindly old gentleman was referring to. Before that, he had had no desire for children, not even all the time he was married to Philippine; especially not then.

He looked now into the old man's grey eyes – cloudy with cataracts and dewy with sentiment – and said yes, indeed, there was nothing like family.

The old gentleman in question was a potential client, a wealthy former *charcutier* who had spawned a chain of lucrative pork butchers which he had eventually sold, allowing him to retire to a well-appointed apartment in the fashionable sixteenth *arrondissement* which was littered with assorted pig ornaments. It was into this extraordinary home that he had invited Luc to view some merchandise: his beloved late wife had evidently been something of a bibliophile, and since her passing, he was looking to sell her collection of books. He himself had no use for them, he explained to Luc as he led him down a long corridor; he had never been much of a reader. He had arrived at the matter in hand – the possible business to be transacted – after a lengthy and effusive panegyric on the manifold virtues and accomplishments of his offspring, cumulating in his remark about the joys of family.

With his genial, parochial demeanour, upwardly mobile aspirations and ostentatious – and a tad *nouveau riche* – taste in interior decoration (gilded furniture, Louis XV headboards, Zuber wallpaper, marble bathroom), he rather put Luc in the mind of Nicodemus Boffin from *Our Mutual Friend*. Except, of course, the latter's fortune derived from refuse, not pig's trotters, *andouillette* and *rillettes*, and was entirely inherited. It was Marnie who had introduced him to Dickens: for his fiftieth birthday she had bought him the entire collected works, translated into French, a series of handsome, leather-bound volumes which he had spent a couple of years working his way through.

After his offers of coffee and *eau de vie* had been politely declined, the host led Luc into a cluttered drawing room, a wall of which was lined with bookshelves, each one inevitably adorned with porcelain anthropomorphised pigs.

'Here are the books,' said M. Pinçon, waving a chubby hand towards the bookshelves. 'I'll let you have a look. I'm not entirely sure myself what there is.'

Luc thanked him and began perusing the books. There were about fifteen in total, all nineteenth-century works, in folio format, on religion, astronomy and some more esoteric subjects. The condition varied from shabby to fair; some of them would certainly be of interest to specialist collectors, although he saw nothing sufficiently rare or well-illustrated to fetch any significant price. As he flicked through one book, a postcard fell out. Picking it up, he saw that it was Dante Gabriel Rossetti's *Proserpine*, which reminded him of Marnie, as did all Rossetti's paintings of Jane Morris, although she bore a particular resemblance to Morris as Pia de' Tolomei, the auburn hair and green eyes much closer to Marnie's colouring than the model's usual dark brown tresses and grey eyes. Otherwise, the two women had the same pronounced chin, square jawline and rosebud lips, although Marnie's nose was slightly shorter.

After a cursory look at these last books, he called M. Pinçon back, informing him that there were no particularly rare or valuable pieces but he would be happy to take them off his hands and named a price. Despite the old man's professed lack of interest in books, Luc expected him to haggle – after all, he could hardly have built a flourishing ham and sausage empire without being a shrewd businessman – and haggle he did. They eventually agreed on twelve hundred euros, and Luc piled the merchandise into the carriers he had brought with him and, after several journeys, loaded them into the boot of his car.

Back at the shop that evening after closing, he fired up his Mac and began cataloguing the newly acquired batch of books. He had just finished inputting the data on some works on freemasonry and hunting when he stumbled upon a treasure: for one of the works turned out to be none other than a first edition of Manoel Carlos de Andrade's *Luz da liberal e nobre arte da Cavallaria,* the definitive work on Portuguese equestrianship, first published in 1790. The binding was more recent – probably from the nineteenth century – but the illustrations, including a frontispiece engraving of Joao VI of Portugal and over ninety engraved plates, were exquisite. Luc calculated that this book alone could fetch around eight times what he had paid for the entire collection: the equivalent of a year's tuition fees for Rhiannon!

Bless you, Gaspard Pinçon, the pork tycoon, he said to himself as he finished inputting the details of the last book and closed his laptop. It was time to shut up shop and head home to get ready for his date: he was meeting a woman – one of the shop's regulars – for drinks.

Fundamentally monogamous by nature, Luc had never once throughout his seventeen-year marriage to Marnie been tempted by the many female customers who came in and flirted with him, both during his years in real estate and more recently running the bookshop. Now he was single again, he had to admit that it was almost preposterously easy to meet women for conversation, a shared meal and sometimes, sex, and thus occasionally availed himself of the many opportunities that presented themselves. It was just as well, for the idea of online dating filled him with horror. Was it a generational thing? Surely not, for dating agencies had existed for decades, long before the advent of the Internet; besides, that was how his first wife had apparently met her current husband, or so he had heard. If he knew Philippine, she had almost certainly opted for one of those highly selective, elitist dating apps he had seen advertised that allowed you to narrow down your search for a mate thanks to a number of extremely specific criteria. Philippine would no doubt have cherry-picked a business school-educated, jazz-loving, vegetarian cat lover with centre-right political leanings – in short, everything he, Luc, was not. Indeed, no algorithm would ever have matched such fundamentally incompatible people as he and Philippine. Although, for that matter, the second Madame Barthélemy was hardly his ideal mate, on paper at least: for Marnie was from a different country, a different social background, a different generation. And yet, they had had the same passions and pleasures: books, travel, good food and wine, wandering around old ruins, museums and art galleries. They also shared an indifference to status and, indeed, money – beyond its capacity to provide the aforementioned pleasures.

But that relationship too had eventually run its course. There had been no infidelities, no bitterness, no recriminations; they had merely agreed that the best was behind them and it was time to move on.

At home, he took a quick shower and dressed in black jeans and a lavender Paul Smith shirt Marnie had given him years ago; she had bought all his shirts. He combed his closely cropped dark hair, only sparsely mingled with grey, splashed *Bleu de Chanel* on his neck, and, gathering up his wallet, keys and a few condoms – it seemed rather presumptuous to him but experience had taught him that women were generally more favourably impressed by this initiative, seeing it as responsible and prudent – left the flat.

CHAPTER SIX

If fiction abounds with examples of the felicitous reuniting of adopted children with their biological parents, there are no notable happy endings in which the protagonist realises, after a disastrous or at least fruitless and disappointing meeting with their progenitors, that they were quite happy and fulfilled as they were and did not require the acknowledgement of their blood relatives to feel complete and whole.

And yet, this is exactly what had happened to Marnie Wade.

For the honeymoon period that followed her tracking down Deirdre was soon to give way to frustration, bitterness and regret. As promised, they had regularly exchanged letters after that initial phone call, and this enthusiastic burst of correspondence had yielded a great deal of information, on both sides. Marnie gave the other woman a potted history of her life thus far – her education, her parents' divorce, her move to Paris upon graduation, her job as a lecturer then translator, meeting and marrying Luc, the birth of Rhiannon. Deirdre, for her part, had recounted her childhood and youth: she had grown up in an affluent, leafy suburb of Manchester with her Irish immigrant parents (solicitor father and housewife mother), and her younger sister, Oona. She then moved on to the circumstances leading to her pregnancy, saying how she had met and fallen in love with an unnamed young man who was entirely unsuitable as a mate, being married – to the daughter of some acquaintance of Deirdre's father, incidentally. For this reason, she had kept their relationship a secret from everyone except Oona. When Deirdre discovered she was expecting Marnie, her lover promptly broke off their affair. For aside from being married with a one-year-old son, he was evidently a highly ambitious young man: he planned to become a successful businessman, and neither his family circumstances nor his lofty professional aspirations allowed for a mistress and an illegitimate child.

The subsequent events in Deirdre's life seemed to Marnie to belong to another century: Deirdre had told her parents that she had enrolled on a secretarial course in London, and then, accompanied by her constant companion and confidante, Oona, travelled down South to stay in a rented cottage in the north of Hampshire for the remaining seven months of her pregnancy, then gave birth at a local nursing home and arranged for baby Saoirse to be adopted.

Marnie was dumbfounded: that a young woman in England in the early seventies, when the Pill was widely available and abortion had been legal for nearly five years, should be forced to lie to her parents and sneak away to the country for her 'confinement,' (for in these extraordinary circumstances, that particular term, so redolent of Victorian novels, seemed entirely appropriate), beggared belief.

But the Kavanaughs were Roman Catholics: Deirdre would never have entertained the idea of terminating her pregnancy (although, Marnie noted, the woman's religious principles did not apparently baulk at having carnal knowledge of a married man).

It was at this point that Marnie and Deirdre's relationship reached its first stumbling block: for whenever Marnie prompted the other woman for more details about her father – what was his name? Had he never attempted to get in touch with Deirdre after Marnie's birth, inquired after their wellbeing? – Deirdre immediately became reticent and guarded, even defensive. It soon became clear that Deirdre feared Marnie would bother her biological father – how, exactly, Marnie dared not inquire: did she think she would demand money, blackmail him even? Astonishingly, despite the shoddy way said nameless man had treated Deirdre, she not only never once criticised his behaviour but, to this day, seemed determined to protect him – his privacy, his reputation, whatever comfortable, privileged life he had forged for himself.

And thus, the blank space on Marnie's birth certificate remained: her father was as elusive and enigmatic a figure as he had ever been. When it became clear that no further information about her birth father was forthcoming, Marnie dropped the subject and asked for some photographs. With this request Deirdre complied, sending her various snapshots of her parents, her sister and herself at various stages of her life. Looking at the ice-blue eyes, broad forehead and patrician nose, Marnie concluded she must favour her father – although she did not dare ask for confirmation of this supposition. Marnie reciprocated by enclosing in her next missive pictures of her adoptive parents and Guy, her husband, and herself – as a child, teenager, bride – as well as some of the better shots of baby Rhiannon.

Deirdre's reaction to these photos was thoroughly unexpected and utterly disheartening. Proud, fond mothers in general – and new mothers in particular – invariably expect effusive, unadulterated praise when presenting likenesses of their offspring, and are thus disappointed – if not downright offended – on the rare occasions on which such compliments are not forthcoming.

But Deirdre's only response to seeing pictures of her long-lost daughter and the granddaughter she had not even known existed until a couple of months before would remain with Marnie forever: 'I've looked long and hard at the photos of you and your daughter and I must say, neither of you look anything like me.'

It was this apparent indifference to her own flesh and blood, with its undercurrent of profound narcissism – on top of her obstinate evasiveness about the birth father, that had hardened Marnie's heart towards Deirdre forever. She had subsequently ceased all contact with her mother, without informing her or providing any reasons for breaking off the acquaintance: she felt sure that any explanations would surely be lost on such a cold and self-absorbed woman as Deirdre apparently was.

It was also around this time that Marnie had first started having The Dream.

And thus, the two women were estranged for the next fifteen years, and would probably have remained so forever had it not been for the results of the Brexit referendum.

Indeed, Marnie would often reflect in the years to come on the bizarre twist of fate, the perverse conjunction of circumstances that had brought about one undesirable event – her being obliged to get in touch with Deirdre again – and one more felicitous one: meeting Dave.

CHAPTER SEVEN

At seven-fifteen am, Clare Mullan, née McElhatton, arrived in the orthopaedic paediatric surgical ward for her shift and hastily pulled on her uniform, along with the other nurses, both male and female, and healthcare assistants in the small, stuffy, windowless room near the toilets that served as a changing room.

The ward was warm and she was already sweating, and her loins ached from the previous night's vigorous intercourse. As she rummaged through her bag for her fob watch, black pen, scissors, tape, ID badge, pen torch and water bottle, she reflected on the monumental lapse in judgement that had led to her having sex with her legally separated husband the night before.

By seven-thirty she was in the break room, which doubled up as the handover room, waiting for the night nurse to come in to give the team the handover. A couple of the other nurses were chatting animatedly on their phones, but most of them, like Clare, were still half-deadened by slumber. There were a couple of new student nurses who looked exhausted and nervous.

Her thoughts drifted back to the previous evening's events. Her shame was compounded by the fact that she herself had initiated it. She did not even have the excuse of inebriation, for she had been stone-cold sober – as had he, (although, in her defence, she had not had sex for months). He had come to pick Declan up but was early; their son was still at a friend's birthday party down the road, and she had invited him to make himself a cup of tea while she finished changing the bed linen. When she came back downstairs five minutes later, she found him sitting at the kitchen table with his back to her, his hands cradling the IRFU Supporters Club mug. And as her eyes fell on his fingers clutching the mug, she was suddenly reminded of their first meeting all those years ago at her cousin Rob's wedding (he and Dave used to play rugby together). He was at the bar, chatting to some bloke – she couldn't remember whom – and she had of course been struck dumb by his looks. But oddly enough, as striking as his chiselled features, athletic physique and those blue eyes were, it was his *hands* that had really bewitched her. One was clutching a pint of Guinness, whilst the other absent-mindedly stroked his tie: they were peasant's hands, strong, sturdy, with thick fingers, but the nails were spotlessly clean and neatly cut. She suddenly found herself imagining those hands cupping her breasts, the thick fingers sliding deep inside her. She thought: *I would fuck him right now in the toilets, only he'll never marry me if I do,* (which is why, through a Herculean feat of self-restraint, she had waited until their second date).

Seeing his hands holding that mug of tea the night before had triggered that memory and, with it, the same primal surge of lust. Standing behind him, she had tentatively placed a hand on the back of his neck and, when he had not flinched, ran her fingers upward through his hair, at which point he had suddenly stood up, grabbed her by the wrist, turned round to face her and kissed her roughly. Within seconds, his hands were reaching up her skirt, pulling down her pants as she fumbled with his belt buckle, and she bent over the kitchen table as he entered her from behind. Both had come hard and fast; but for her part, the pleasure had evaporated by the time she had wiped herself. It was like gorging on fast food: momentary gratification followed by guilt and self-loathing.

It was seven-fifty by the time the night nurse finally deigned to arrive, twenty minutes late, and began the handover. Patients had started arriving, some of whom did not have a bed. As some needed pre-meds by eight, Clare and her team began frantically dashing around to get them ready for surgery. The handover seemed interminable: the ward was full, with two extra patients, which meant that, in addition to allocating patients to nurses, Clare also had to take on a few herself. She quickly filled up the whiteboard with nurses whilst racking her brain to work out where and when she was going to get beds for the extra patients. Fortunately, the bed manager would be arriving soon.

She had patients coming back from the High Dependency Unit that day, so she began checking how many patients she could discharge in order to free up some beds. Meanwhile, the students were hovering, staring at Clare, looking forlorn and utterly clueless.

Christ, she thought: on top of not having enough nurses to treat patients or enough beds to put them in, she had to assign nurses to babysit the students as their mentors were not in that day. Some nurses asked her to check premeds with them, but she also had to contend with an anaesthetist and a Senior House Officer who were both asking her to put EMLA cream on two small children, and an agency nurse who could not lay her hands on her patient's notes. Then a harried-looking mother came up to her and informed her that her daughter was vomiting. And thus began a frenzied sprint around the ward as she looked for notes, prescription charts, med cupboard keys, nurses, healthcare assistants. She barely had time to greet and introduce herself to patients and their families, some of whom were visibly anxious, and as usual, she wished she had more time to talk to them, reassure them. She got their meds, took their observations, asked about their night, welcomed the new arrivals, explained what was going to happen.

At ten o'clock it was time for the ward round with the paeds consultant and the SHO. By eleven she was in desperate need of a coffee, something to eat and a pee, but there was no question of her getting away. Resolving to make it to the ladies' before the bed meeting at noon, she tended to one of her patients, a four-year-old boy whose dressing needed changing. It was very sticky and he immediately began screaming. After distracting him with some bubbles, she went to another patient to start her IV antibiotics and then prepared to administer an enema to a terrified teenaged girl.

'I don't want to… go in my bed!' she wailed.

'I know, darling, it is a bit gross!' sympathised Clare. 'But you have to do it; you'll feel much more comfortable afterwards, I promise you.'

Within a few seconds of having the enema administered, the girl said she felt it coming out already, so Clare held her hand and started singing. The teenager began simultaneously laughing and crying.

'There's a good girl. When this is over, I'll give you a lovely bed bath. How does that sound?'

The girl sniffed back her tears and nodded, smiling.

As she finished giving her the bed bath, Clare thought resentfully of Dave, his beauty, and her ungovernable desire for him. She hated it; she hated him for it. It was gut-wrenching, it clawed at her loins, making her feel weak-kneed and nauseous.

Yet if his beauty had initially drawn him to her, it was his carnality, the animality of Dave that had subsequently fascinated her. Perhaps it was because of her chosen profession: for as a nurse and then a ward sister, she dealt with birth and death and blood and guts and bones and flesh on a daily basis and had, over the years, developed a mistrust of all things spiritual and insubstantial. And Dave was the most unapologetically – almost offensively – sensuous, physical being she knew. His appetite for life was insatiable: he devoured life, let its juice drip down his chin. He loved to feel the sun on his bare, unanointed skin, eat bloody, rare meat with his hands, drink to excess. Sunscreen, cooking meat thoroughly, condoms: all these were seen as tiresome and entirely unnecessary precautions, impediments to his raw, unbridled pleasure.

And sex, obviously. He loved sex. She was sure some poor women had romanticised his philandering, attributing it no doubt to some deep-seated existential malaise, some restlessness of the soul, resulting from a lonely, loveless childhood.

But Clare knew better. There was nothing desperate or nihilistic about Dave's relentless womanising: he was no cynical seducer, no Pechorin from *A Hero of Our Time*. Not even a Don Draper/Dick Whitman from *Mad Men*. He wasn't trying to fill a void. He had had an idyllic childhood, growing up in a rambling cottage in County Cork, the baby of the family, doted on by his three older siblings, cherished and adored by his parents, whose marriage had been harmonious and loving.

No: he just really liked fucking. The more the better. It made him feel happy and alive. Quantity over quality. It was as simple as that.

At the bed meeting at noon, Clare expressed her need for more nurses – a request, which, as usual, was met with amused looks. They were the only paediatric ward and should have had a nurse/patient ration of one to four, and yet, she was told her team was spoilt.

At one pm she took a thirty-minute break to heat up and eat the remnants of last night's lasagne and finally emptied her bladder. She winced as the urine seeped out, stinging her enflamed vulva – another unwelcome reminder of Dave's energetic attentions of the previous evening.

At one-thirty, patients started coming back from theatre and required observations every fifteen minutes. Clare asked for an update from all the nurses. TTAs needed to be ordered from the pharmacy and there was the discharge paperwork to be done.

At two o'clock she went to see her patients, then at three there were the patients back from the High Dependency Unit to attend to. She welcomed them back, took a handover from the HDU nurse and educated the patients on how to use their patient-controlled morphine pump (some tended to be a tad trigger-happy with it).

She spent the rest of the afternoon going from patient to patient, checking discharges, assisting parents, supporting nurses, liaising with the multidisciplinary team. She checked medications, changed beds, wrote notes, took a thirty-minute break and updated the handover for the night shift. She then gently told a patient who had not passed urine since before his surgery eight hours ago that he couldn't go home until he had done so. When this ultimatum failed to move him, she escalated the threat, and, as was usual with patients, the prospect of having a tube inserted into his penis had him reaching for the water jug in a panic.

By the time she had written up her notes, it was seven-thirty pm and time for handover. At twenty past eight, she finally thanked her team for their hard work, left the ward and returned to the stuffy, windowless room to change. Another thirteen-hour shift was over – just three more to go that week.

She was supposed to be meeting the father of one of Declan's schoolfriends, a widowed social worker, for drinks later, but texted him to cancel, pleading tiredness after her shift. Although this was true – God knew she could do with an early night – she was also looking forward to an evening in by herself; besides, some vague and obscure scruple made her baulk at going on a date with one man just over twenty-four hours after another man had been inside her.

It was a pity though, she reflected as she walked wearily to her car. Not because she was in need of any sort of romantic attachment – not yet. But it would have been nice to remind herself that it was possible to spend time in the company of a man and not come across as a shrew. For that seemed to be the only facet of her that Dave brought out.

For the hundredth time in six months, she cursed her future ex-husband.

CHAPTER EIGHT

Stow-on-the-Wold, Gloucestershire, 16 May 2019

Marnie couldn't remember the last wedding she had attended. Her generation was in that in-between marriage vacuum: too old to get married, whilst their children were not quite old enough. As thrilled as she was for Guy – she had been telling her brother to marry Nova practically from the minute they had started going out together four years ago – she was still mildly annoyed at the circumstances of their wedding. For, having originally said they were planning to marry in September, they had suddenly brought the event forward five months. This in itself was inconvenient enough as it was: it was on a weekday, meaning she had had to take a day off work, and at one of her busiest times of year as she was in the middle of organising an international in-house marketing seminar. And Rhiannon was unable to attend as she couldn't get away from university: Warwick was only thirty miles away from Stow, but she was in the middle of exams.

But it was the reason for rescheduling the wedding that really rankled. Guy had learned, just a month ago, that Heidi and Vince, his birth parents, along with their daughter, Madison, her partner and their young son, were planning a month-long trip to Europe in May, at which point he had decided to alter his and Nova's wedding date to accommodate them (whilst promising Marnie that they would have a second, unofficial wedding party at a later date, when Rhiannon and various other family members and friends could attend). She knew how much it must mean for Guy to have both sets of parents and siblings present on the day he married the woman he loved. And yet she could not help slightly resenting the fact that she and her parents had had to rearrange their schedules – she taking time off work, her mother flying back from Spain – to fit in with the plans of *those people*. Marnie knew she had to stop resenting them: after all, technically, they had not done anything wrong (apart from abandon her brother as a baby), and they had never asked to be tracked down by Guy. She also realised by now that any 'rivalry' between Guy's biological and adoptive families existed essentially in her head. She had to let it go – especially on such a day as today.

And as she turned the car off the tree-canopied lane onto the drive of Braeburn House, she briefly forgot any residual negative feelings she was still obstinately hanging on to: for the sight of the handsome Georgian manor house, built from the ubiquitous honey-coloured Cotswold stone, nestling in gently undulating, cedar-covered grounds, was enough to appease the most peevish of dispositions. As she was taking her overnight bag from the boot, she saw her father walking across the lawn towards her with his usual purposeful stride, the pace of which had only slightly dwindled as he reached his eightieth year.

'Hello sweetheart,' he said, beaming. She hugged him warmly. 'Lovely day for it, eh? How was the drive? Your mother's here. I picked her up from the airport this morning.'

'Really? That was nice of you.'

He shrugged and took her bag out of her hand. 'No point her wasting money on a taxi. And I told her, you don't want to bother with those Uber things,' (he pronounced it 'Yuber'). 'A lot of the drivers are rapists, you know.' Marnie let forth a burst of shocked laughter.

'Well, that's very gallant of you,' she said, slipping her arm through his as they walked inside. 'Have you seen Guy yet?'

He nodded. 'He's around somewhere, seeing to some last-minute arrangements. Ah… here he is!'

Sure enough, there was her brother, striding towards them, grinning broadly, dashing in an impeccably tailored silver-grey suit, matching shirt and pale pink silk tie, his skin still tanned from a snowboarding trip a month before, his dark hair cut in a fashionable style (a little too young for him, Marnie thought, although she had to admit he looked marvellous).

He kissed her on the cheek, just as their father excused himself to go and get ready.

After the usual mutual greetings and inquiries into wellbeing were exchanged, Guy launched immediately into practical matters:

'Now, when you check in, say you're with the wedding party. The standard room price is £130 a night for a double room, but I've negotiated a £100 rate for wedding guests, so that works out at just fifty quid each for sharing. I've put you in with Mum.'

She nodded. 'Perfect.'

He went on. 'Dad's sharing with Vince. Obviously, Heidi's by herself –'

Marnie stared. 'What did you say?'

Guy was distracted, his hazel eyes scanning the crowd of people behind her. 'Hmm?'

'You put… Dad in the *same room as Vince*?'

He frowned. 'Yeah. So?

'Well… is Dad OK with that?' she spoke carefully, trying to keep her voice even.

40

''Course. Well, you know how he likes to watch the pennies.' His mobile beeped. Glancing at it, he said, 'That's the wedding planner. I'll see you in a bit, yeah?' and he disappeared.

Marnie clenched her fists and let out a long, controlled breath: her resolution not to let her feelings about her brother and his birth family's involvement spoil the proceedings had lasted all of five minutes. How could he fail to see the irony, the absurdity, the monumental insensitivity of putting his adoptive and biological fathers in the same room?

She went off in search of her father, who was sitting by the fireplace in the Blenheim Room in a high-backed chair upholstered in jade green velvet, reading the paper. Kneeling down on the floor beside him, she said:

'Listen… Guy's told me about the rooming arrangements. Are you sure you're OK with it?'

'Of course.'

'Are you sure? Because if it's a money thing, I'll pay for you to have a single room if you're not comfortable…'

He merely shrugged and said, 'I've shared rooms with stranger people.'

Oh, bless him! How she wanted to laugh and throw her arms around his knees and cling to him! She reflected, not for the first time, that the advantage of those who were slightly insensitive and tactless (as her father could occasionally be) was that they were often remarkably thick-skinned themselves, oblivious to potentially awkward or upsetting situations. Indeed, Martin Wade, like Guy, seemed so utterly impervious to the potential absurdity of the situation that for a moment, Marnie wondered if she was not being paranoid and over-sensitive.

At the reception desk she learned that her mother had already checked in and, taking her own key, let herself into the room where she found her sitting at the dressing table making the finishing touches to her make-up. She was wearing an elegant taupe-coloured silk shift dress with a primrose border. A wide-brimmed primrose hat was on one of the single beds. She rose to hug her daughter.

'Are you all right with this bed? I'd rather be nearest the bathroom, but if you'd rather…'

'No, it's fine,' said Marnie, slipping off her shoes and placing her bag on the bed. As she removed her sponge bag and wedding outfit – a turquoise and beige polka-dot wrap-dress – she looked up at her mother.

'Tell me something. Is it me, or is it completely bonkers that Guy put Dad and Vince in the same room?'

The hand applying mascara paused in mid-air for a second as Fay looked up and smiled wryly at her daughter in the mirror.

41

'It's *not* you.'

'Oh my God! *Thank you.*'

Fay put down the mascara, took a last look at her face in the mirror, and turned round to face Marnie.

'It is odd. But your father seems fine about it all. And as for Vince –'

'Who gives a toss what he thinks?' she said heatedly. And then, 'Sorry. But he's not our problem. And frankly, they're lucky to be here at all.'

Her mother remained characteristically unruffled and conciliatory, her voice even:

'Guy wants them here. And it's his day. And frankly, if your father can cope with this situation, you certainly should be able to. Now, why don't you go and get dressed then we'll have a quick sherry before the ceremony starts.'

Marnie, humbled by her mother's combination of good sense and forbearance, nodded obediently. When she emerged from the bathroom twenty minutes later having freshened up and slipped into her dress, she found her father had joined them. He was pouring Oloroso from a crystal decanter on the desk whilst her mother perched on the edge of her bed, glass in one hand, while the other slipped a primrose low-heeled pump onto her foot.

'Did you have a good drive down?' inquired her father, handing Marnie a glass of sherry.

'Pretty good. Made it in just over an hour.'

'Which way did you come? Down the M5?'

Marnie nodded, downed the sherry and held out her glass for a refill. As he poured her a second glass, he peered through the window. 'The guests seem to be making their way over.'

Marnie glanced at her watch. 'God, is it that time already?' she took a last gulp of sherry, put the half-full glass down on the bedside table and added the finishing touches to her outfit: nude ten-centimetre stiletto suede pumps and a nude fascinator.

Linking arms with her parents, she said: 'Let's go.'

It was a small party that assembled in the marquee behind the house: besides Marnie and her parents, there were just the bride's parents, her younger brother, Milo, his partner, Carmen, and, what Marnie privately referred to as the 'Biologicals:' Heidi, Vince, their daughter, Madison, her partner – a slightly portly, sunburned man in his forties in khakis and a lemon-yellow Ralph Laurent polo shirt, and their son, a rather unruly and noisy toddler.

Marnie had met Heidi once, many years ago, whilst she, Heidi, was staying with Guy before going off on a tour of the UK. She bore little resemblance to Guy: where he was tall and dark, she was short and fair-haired. She was also extravagantly thin. Quick mental arithmetic told Marnie she must be just over sixty now: but while her face showed every one of these years and more, from behind, with her girlish figure and style of dressing – she was wearing a close-fitting scarlet sleeveless dress showing off a fair amount of bare thigh, with twelve-centimetre scarlet platform wedge sandals – she passed for a much younger woman. Vince, on the other hand, she had never met; and if Guy did not favour his mother in appearance, the resemblance to his father was striking: the same tall frame, dark hair and hazel eyes. Indeed, one could easily imagine what Guy would look like in seventeen years – after several divorces and too much good living. For whilst Vince had managed to stay reasonably trim, the hazel eyes were rheumy and his nose and cheeks covered with broken veins. Based on his appearance, the way his eyes roved over her cleavage when they were introduced, and the few pieces of background information she had about him – essentially that he had been married and divorced three times, most recently to a woman half his age – Marnie quickly dismissed him as a superannuated Don Juan. Although at least, she conceded, taking in his well-tailored grey suit, he had made an effort to dress for the occasion, unlike his son-in-law.

They took their seats, Marnie in the front row as she was to do a reading, and the music struck up as Nova, resplendent in a froth of ivory tulle with an ivory satin laced bodice which complemented her olive complexion and jet hair to perfection, glided up the aisle on her father's arm.

The ceremony was brief: a few words from the registrar, after which the bride and groom exchanged the vows they had penned themselves, then the readings: one by Nova's brother, followed by a poem from Marnie (ugh, how she loathed E. E. Cummings!), and it was over. She thought fondly how young her brother looked – like a little boy – as he turned to face the guests, clasping his bride's hand, so obviously brimming with love and joy.

As the party filed out on to the lawn and waiters poured out of the house dispensing glasses of champagne and canapés, Marnie went to kiss and congratulate her new sister-in-law. With a sob of joy, Nova enfolded Marnie in her arms. Marnie then left the bride and groom to greet their other guests and went to join her parents, but saw they were deep in conversation with the registrar. She then thought of Nova's parents, a couple of amiable retired academics, but, judging by their tense expressions and body language, they appeared to be in the throes of some minor disagreement. Looking around her, she resigned herself to the fact that she would have to chat to the Biologicals at some point, and made her way over to Madison and her family.

The last time she had seen Guy's biological sister was around twenty years ago. Madison was a teenager at the time and her parents had sent her over to the UK for a fortnight to spend some time with her big brother, whom she had only met once when Guy had flown out to Arizona to meet his birth family for the first time. Marnie had quickly sized her up as a typical middle-class, suburban American teenager who had grown up in some material comfort but a certain degree of ignorance: a little spoiled, rather shallow, an habitué of shopping malls, shockingly oblivious to the geographical and socio-political reality outside the United States. But she was pleasant enough, and her girlish, gushing enthusiasm at the novelty of almost anything and everything English was endearing.

And now as Marnie walked across the lawn towards Madison, her thoughts drifted back to their previous encounter and she reflected – not without compunction – on that one particular evening when she had got her drunk at a party in Brighton. Marnie, Guy, their father and Madison had driven down there for the engagement party of an old friend of Guy's and somehow Marnie had been elected the designated driver – much to her disgruntlement. Upon arrival at the venue, she had sat at the bar with Madison and proceeded to ply her with Diamond White – an act which she later attributed to a combination of jealousy-induced spite and boredom (indeed, her status as driver meant that vicarious inebriation was the only safe, legal form of drunkenness she could indulge in). Her only concession to responsibility had been a half-hearted 'oh, you're used to drinking, aren't you?' before placing the bottles in front of her, at which point the girl had made an endearing attempt to sound sophisticated ('this is real good wine' – wine!).

After the inevitable intoxication that ensued, Marnie's feeble and rather disingenuous defence when faced with the admonishments of her brother and (to a lesser extent), their father, was that two ciders was nothing, and that she, Marnie, had been tricked by the girl's American precocity and apparent worldliness into forgetting her real age (this, although worthless as a defence, was partly true). She refrained from snapping at Guy that it was bad enough her being forced to be chauffeur for the evening, without being expected to act as babysitter for his 'sister' (oh, how she would have relished the air quotes!) as well, and merely contented herself with glowering throughout the drive back.

Madison must have been in her mid-thirties now, but she looked older. Her complexion was weather-beaten, aged and coarsened by years of sun exposure, and as she turned her gaze to Marnie, she saw that the Buchanan hazel eyes, heavily made-up for the occasion, seemed hardened, as if jaded by some disenchanting past experiences. The only vestige of her former appearance was the smudge of freckles across her slightly upturned nose (the same as Guy's). Her dark shoulder-length hair was tied back in a high ponytail, with a blunt-cut fringe that came down to her eyebrows. She was wearing a low-cut black cocktail dress that would have been more suitable for the evening but showed off her slim figure and tanned skin, and black strappy stiletto shoes.

Her greeting was cool. 'Oh, hi,' she said simply, with a bored half-smile.

Her partner was more congenial. He stepped forward with outstretched hand, grinning broadly. 'Brad. How are you? Good to meet you.'

'Marnie,' she said, shaking his hand. 'Guy's...er... other sister. Pleased to meet you.'

'Nice set-up here,' he nodded towards the house and gardens. 'What is that... Victorian?'

'A little earlier: Georgian, I think.' Not usually one for small talk, Marnie nevertheless felt obliged to fill the silence that ensued. 'I don't know if you noticed when you were driving down here but a lot of the buildings around here are made of that stone: it's typical of the Cotswolds.'

Brad's eyes widened in wonder. '*The Cotswolds*? This is the famous Cotswolds?' he said, as though it were Bora Bora or Patagonia. 'I didn't know that! Honey,' he turned to Madison. 'Did you know we were in the Cotswolds?'

His partner, who was apparently unable to summon any interest in English geography or architecture, merely said: 'I'm gonna see where Chester's got to,' and wandered off. Brad smiled sheepishly at Marnie and said, by way of explanation for his partner's rudeness, 'She's a real devoted mom.' Marnie, having nothing to reply to this, excused herself and went off in search of some refreshment. After helping herself to a glass of champagne and a plateful of mini arancini and prawn tempura with aioli, she wandered away from the crowd and stood in the cool shade of a cedar while she ate and drank.

The wedding breakfast passed off pleasantly enough. Had there been more guests, she would have been interested to see how Guy and Nova handled the seating plan: would Guy have put their parents *and* Heidi and Vince on top table? As it was, the need for such an awkward and potentially controversial decision was obviated as the thirteen (thirteen!) guests were easily accommodated around a single oblong table, with the bride and groom presiding. Marnie was sitting between her father and Nova's brother. They dined on goats' cheesecake with red onion jam, followed by roast guinea fowl with *boudin blanc*, black cabbage and chestnuts, then lavender lemon ice cream with Florentines. To drink there was New Zealand Sauvignon Blanc and Pauillac.

There was no dancing afterwards, and as the bride and groom retired to the honeymoon suite and the guests prepared to disperse, Vince, who seemed eager to prolong the festivities, asked if anyone fancied joining him for a nightcap in the bar.

One by one, the guests demurred: Heidi pleaded a headache, Martin and Fay were visibly tired; Milo and Carmen planned to go for a walk around the grounds and a smoke, and Nova's parents had to get up early the next morning to drive back to Barrow-in-Furness. Brad initially accepted his father-in-law's offer, but Madison intervened sharply, insisting they put Chester to bed.

Marnie looked across at Vince's dejected face and felt a stab of compassion.

'I wouldn't say no to a quick drink,' she volunteered.

His pleasure – or gratitude – was plain.

'Great! Shall we?'

They sat at the bar in the deserted, oak-panelled Sudely Bar and ordered brandy. For a while conversation covered the usual topics: their respective jobs (she learned that he ran his own software company specialising in human resource management systems), their personal circumstances. She pretended to know nothing about his three failed marriages, and in turn told him of her own divorce from Luc three years before.

After three-quarters-of-an-hour or so of small talk and two rounds of brandies, he suddenly said, 'So… Marnie.'

He seemed to savour those two syllables, using the rhotic pronunciation of the r. This was apparently the only sign, however, of his speech being influenced by his adopted country: his diphthongs were resolutely southern English. 'That's a great name.'

'Well, my Dad always loved his Hitchcock.'

'Yeah? Me too! He was the Master. Although, I preferred the stuff from his British period. *The Thirty-Nine Steps, Sabotage, The Lodger.'* He paused to take a sip of brandy. *'Young and Innocent.'*

Marnie felt herself beginning to warm to him: did the superannuated Don Juan have hidden depths?

'What about *Rebecca* though?' she challenged. 'It's a masterpiece! Even Daphne du Maurier approved. It was actually the only one of Hitchcock's adaptations of her books she didn't hate.'

He nodded thoughtfully, swilling his brandy around in the crystal balloon.

'Sure. But even in that he had to make compromises to satisfy the requirement of the Hays Code: having Maxim kill Rebecca accidentally, rather than murdering her like he does in the book.'

Marnie nodded her acquiescence. 'Yes. Then he had to change the end of *Suspicion* because RKO didn't want Cary Grant playing a baddie.'

'Exactly! Another one?'

Marnie nodded and Vince gestured to the barman.

'So,' he said again, turning in his stool to look at Marnie appraisingly. 'You know your Hitchcock, you can hold your drink. You're an interesting woman, Marnie.'

She laughed. 'I'm nothing special. You just haven't been back to the UK for a while. There are thousands of us; hundreds of thousands.'

He looked at her intently for a few seconds, before turning back to face the bar.

'That's true: I forgot how English girls could hold their drink. American women, now,' he took another sip of brandy. 'Two mimosas and they're anyone –' he stopped suddenly. 'Oh, I didn't mean... Hey, I would *never* take advantage of a woman who was... the worse for wear.'

'I'm sure you wouldn't,' she said, and, contemplating the expensive clothes, the good looks – albeit slightly faded and battle-scarred – and the glint of boyish charm in the hazel eyes, added: 'I'm sure you've never needed to.'

He drained the contents of his glass, his eyes never leaving hers, and, placing it on the bar, said softly: 'Would you like to get out of here?'

In the corridor outside the bar he turned to her and placed a hand on her waist. Together they half-leaned, half-fell against the wall, she with her back against it, facing him. With his other hand he gently brushed the curtain of mahogany hair from her face then, with the back of his fingers, stroked her cheek and moved downwards, tracing a line along her jaw and then down to her neck.

'Marnie, you are a very beautiful woman.'

She craned her neck up to kiss him: he briefly drew back, then smiled teasingly and kissed her gently, then more urgently. She put her arms around his neck and drew him against her, felt him press her against the wall. Suddenly, he broke away.

'Wait a minute... What I said just now, about not taking advantage of a woman who'd been drinking...'

'You're not! OK, I have been drinking pretty much constantly since about noon. (If you're interested, I've had a couple of sherries, two glasses of champagne, about half a bottle of red and those three brandies.) But, as you also just pointed out, we English girls can hold our drink.'

Temporarily reassured, Vince kissed her mouth and her neck, murmuring her name. Again, the dark head suddenly jerked back.

'Are you sure?'

'Oh, for Christ's sake! OK, fine. Ask me some Hitchcock trivia. Anything. I'll prove to you I am in complete possession of all my mental faculties and powers of judgement.'

For a moment he looked doubtful, then said: 'All right. Uh...name all the films he made with Cary Grant.'

She smiled seductively at him. *'Please.* Make me work a little harder than that.' Pulling gently on his silk tie, she said: 'In chronological order: *'Suspicion.'* She replaced the tie, smoothing it gently against his torso with her hand. *'Notorious.'* He was breathing heavily, and his heart, as she ran her hand over his chest, was thudding. *'To Catch a Thief.'* She brought her face within an inch of his. When she spoke, her voice was no more than a whisper: 'And last, but not least: *North...*.' She brought her lips even closer: *'by...'* and then, turning her head just before their lips brushed, she whispered in his ear: *'Northwest.'*

'OK,' he said quickly, 'you passed the test, you're not drunk.' He kissed her deeply, crushing her against the wall. She felt her body go limp with desire and arched her back away from the wall, pressing her pelvis into his groin. He moaned.

And then, suddenly, it was her turn to pull away.

'Wait. Where the hell are we going to go? We both have room-mates, remember?' She frowned as the realisation dawned: 'and they're... my *parents*. God, this is weird.'

Vince looked thoughtful. 'Good point.'

'Oh, fuck it,' she said, slipping out from between him and the wall and leading him along the corridor by the hand. 'Let's just find a cupboard somewhere, or we could go outside, into the grounds. It's a lovely night.' He stopped. She turned around: he looked appalled.

'Now, just wait a minute. We're not going to... *rut* in some broom cupboard or roll around under a bush like a couple of randy teenagers. I am not a young man anymore, and neither are...' he stopped himself, wisely. 'The point is, at my age, comfort is important, especially when I make love, and I am not without means, so, if you'll just wait here for a second, young lady...' As he wandered off in the direction of reception, Marnie began to laugh: at the absurdity of the situation, at his homily, with its endearing combination of gallantry and pomposity. Within minutes, he reappeared, a key in his hand.

'Shall we?'

Aside from one uneasy moment when he was removing her dress and she briefly allowed her mind and body to dissociate and observed that she was being undressed by her brother's father, the experience was more than satisfactory: Vince proved to be a dextrous and considerate lover, ever gentlemanly and solicitous for her comfort and pleasure.

Afterwards, as they lay side-by-side, his arm casually draped around her shoulder, he made a sweeping gesture around the room with his other hand and remarked: 'Isn't this better? Believe me, your brother was conceived on the backseat of a Ford Escort and I'm way too old for that sort of shenanigans.'

Propping herself up on her elbow, she looked at him bemusedly.

'What? What is it?'

'I'm just trying to decide what's more of a turn-off: your allusion to a past sexual experience, seconds after we've had sex, your mentioning my brother – again, right after we've had sex – or your use of the word "shenanigans."'

He looked sheepish. 'Ah. Showing my age, eh?'

'That's one of many things you're showing right now. No, it's fine. And honestly, I think you're being a little over-sensitive about your age. You must be about the same age as my ex-husband, you know.'

He looked surprised. 'Really? You were married to a guy my age?'

'Well, no, I mean, technically, he wasn't your age when we were married, but he is now.'

'Sure, but... I mean, you married a guy who was what, nearly twenty years older than you?'

Marnie laughed. 'OK, now you're being ridiculously flattering. Try fourteen years. And anyway, didn't you marry a younger woman after Heidi?'

He nodded. 'Well, sure, twice. I know why I marry younger women, I'm just always surprised that *they'd* want to marry someone my age.'

Both amused and touched by this self-deprecating admission, she went on: 'I don't know. For my part, I honestly never really thought about the age difference with Luc – my ex. It certainly had nothing to do with why we broke up.'

He listened attentively, nodding. Then suddenly, he reverted to gallantry: 'Are you OK? Can I get you anything? Something from the mini-bar perhaps?'

'Thanks, I am rather thirsty. Some sparkling water?' He nodded and, slipping out of the bed, took a bottle of San Pellegrino from the mini-fridge, poured it into a glass and brought it back to her. She drank half the glass thirstily and lay back down, settling in the crook of his arm.

'Anyway,' he continued, 'I guess I shouldn't be questioning your reasons for being attracted to a man old enough to be your father and just be grateful.'

'Again, you're not old enough to be my father. Come to think of it, you're barely old enough to be Guy's.'

'That's true.' And then he added, surprisingly: 'You know, I never wanted to give him up. I wanted to keep him. But Heidi convinced me: we couldn't have provided a decent life for him at the time. Like you said, we were still kids ourselves. But I often regretted it. Then when Heidi and I got back together and Madison was born, I thought about Guy and I wondered how on earth we'd been able to bear giving him up.'

For the second time that night, she found him touching, disarming.

49

'And then one day he showed up on my doorstep! Just like that. I mean, I knew he was coming; Heidi had told me he'd reached out to her, that he was coming to the States, that she'd given him my address. But seeing him there: I thought my heart was going to stop. I actually think it did, for a moment.'

The pleasant post-coital languor, the lingering thrill of her first sexual encounter in almost a year, the tenderness or empathy she had briefly felt for him at his moving confidences – all this was to evaporate within the next few seconds:

'He told me all about his life, his childhood, everything. Your parents sent you both to boarding school, huh? That was really tough on him.'

She felt as though he had thrown cold water over her.

'Well, yes, but it's a little more complicated than that. They didn't know about the bullying and all that, and as soon as they found out, they took him straight out of boarding school and he went to the local comprehensive and he was fine.'

Ignoring her, he shook his head gravely and went on. 'It's a typical English thing, isn't it? Boarding school, I mean. People don't do that in the States.'

Kicking off the sheets, Marnie picked up her dress and began putting it on. Vince, shaken out of his musings on the Brits' inhumane methods of parenting and education, turned to her in surprise.

'What's the matter?'

'I think it's time I went to bed,' she said tersely, retrieving her bra, pants and fascinator from the floor and stuffing them into her handbag.

'What? Did I say something wrong?'

She paused for a moment and looked at him. And then, after a deep breath:

'Vince, you seem like a nice bloke, really, and you have been – until about thirty seconds ago – very pleasant company this evening. But I'm afraid that… depositing sperm in a woman and subsequently abandoning the resulting unwanted offspring does not qualify you as a father and it certainly *does not* entitle you to slag off the people who actually took the trouble to raise and love that offspring!'

'No, I didn't mean –'

'Thank you for the drinks,' she snapped, 'and the…' she gestured vaguely to the rumpled bed that lay between them. 'Goodnight,' and with that, she scooped up her shoes and stalked out of the room.

As she closed the door behind her, it occurred to her that the very seed which she had just referred to and which had begotten her brother was at present working its way along her (albeit

50

decommissioned) Fallopian tubes. Chasing this rather disturbing thought from her mind, she hurried barefoot along the corridor and let herself quietly into her room, where she found her mother ostensibly reading in bed although she had clearly been waiting up for her.

'Oh, hello dear,' said Fay, making a feeble attempt to sound casual but unable to mask the relief in her voice.

'Oh, for Christ's sake, mother,' Marnie snapped, 'I'm forty-six! You don't have to wait up for me!'

Seeing her mother's crushed expression, Marnie immediately regretted her outburst. Depositing her shoes on the floor, she crossed the room and sat on her mother's bed.

'I'm sorry. It's been… an emotional day.'

'I know.'

'Listen, I'll put the kettle on, then I'm going to jump in the shower quickly and we'll have a cuppa and a chat. Unless you're too tired?'

Her mother shook her head and removed her reading glasses. 'I'll have a camomile tea if there is some.'

Five minutes later, having showered and put on the indigo silk pyjamas Luc had bought her from Rigby & Peller for her fortieth birthday, Marnie put a teabag in each of the two mugs, poured on the boiling water and carried them over. Having placed one on each bedside table, she suddenly blurted:

'Look, I have to tell you something. I need you just to listen until I'm finished, and I need you not ever to mention it again.'

Her mother, unperturbed, nodded.

And then she told her all about her tracing her birth mother nineteen years ago; about Deirdre contacting her, their correspondence, the rather abrupt ceasing thereof and her ensuing frustration and disillusionment. She spoke urgently, feverishly, scarcely stopping for breath.

'…and I regret doing it; I wish I'd never met her!' Hot, bitter tears began to run down her cheeks. 'And I'm sorry I never told you or Dad about it. Well, I'm not sorry, I stand by my decision: I didn't want to hurt you and it was just something I thought I had to do for me, it was nothing to do with you. But I'm sorry I did it in the first place. It didn't make me feel whole or fulfilled. There was no great… epiphany about who I really am. All it did is make me feel like crap and confirm what I had always known: that I didn't need it, I didn't *need* her or my birth father – whoever he is – and you and Dad are the only parents I ever needed or wanted, and that's it.'

Her mother, respecting Marnie's wishes to the letter, did not say a word and merely nodded sympathetically, reaching over and patting her daughter's hand.

'That's it,' Marnie said, sniffing and taking up her mug. 'Are you OK? I mean, you're not... upset?'

Fay smiled and shook her head. 'Not at all.'

Marnie nodded. 'Good. Is it OK if we talk about something else now?'

And thus they steered the conversation to safer, more comfortable ground: the ceremony, the food and wine, the guests' outfits. It was nearly two o'clock by the time Marnie kissed her mother, slipped into bed and switched off the beside lamp.

CHAPTER NINE

Sherborne, Dorset, 17 May 2019

'Excuse me, but would you, your fat arse and your mixed-race baby mind getting out of the way?'

The plump young woman with the tight, high ponytail – Portia had once told him this was known as a 'council house facelift,' which tickled him – pierced nose and a rather substantial belly spilling over jeans so low-rise they barely covered her pubic bone turned around and stared open-mouthed at Nigel as if he had shot her. Unfortunately, her speechlessness was short-lived and soon gave way to a deluge of profanity.

But Nigel Lovelace thrived on such provocation, and the foul-mouthed diatribe had about as much impact on him as had the sermon delivered every Sunday at St Bartholomew's, back in the days when his mother was alive and he forced himself to attend church to please her.

Having delivered her torrent of abuse, the outraged young woman spat on the floor and wheeled her equally over-nourished offspring through the doors of the Department for Work and Pensions.

The DWP (or DHSS, as Nigel still thought of it: God knows why they had changed the name, presumably because it was too reminiscent of orphans abandoned in Tesco bags outside churches), was, predictably, crammed with sponging single mothers and the sort of braindead wastrels who impregnated them. Not to mention the growing ranks of what he referred to as 'ragheads' – people hailing from the Indian sub-continent and the Middle East – who professed to despise the West and its decadent ways yet apparently had no qualms about living off state benefits.

Nigel's sincere, deep-rooted racism was, to his mind, perfectly justified by his experiences as a child growing up in Nigeria and, in particular, one isolated and particularly violent incident during which his house had been burgled and his family held at gunpoint by blacks. When his father had attempted to resist and raise the alarm, one of the assailants had pistol-whipped him.

He had recovered after a long spell in hospital but had permanently lost his sense of smell as a result.

Of course, such a thing would never happen these days. Nigel had a handful of old schoolfriends who were ex-pats in Africa and they all lived in gated communities, their houses fitted with state-of-the-art alarm systems and panic rooms and patrolled by armed security guards.

Be that as it may, nothing since that event – not the advent of political correctness, not the many, many vehement exchanges with his youngest, Dinah (who had somehow turned into a Leftist firebrand) – had caused him to question his beliefs or moderate his attitude and rhetoric.

He sighed and surveyed the roomful of parasites distastefully. As a rule, he made a point of avoiding such close encounters with the great unwashed but he had to sort out the Major's Attendance Allowance. The laughably called 'helpline' had been of no use whatsoever, thus forcing him to drive down to Dorset and deal with the matter in person.

His father was not a rich man: he had only his army pension, and that was not enough to pay for the kind of round-the-clock care he now required. As for selling Fawley House, the Georgian manor he had lived in since he and Nigel's mother first moved there as newlyweds, and putting him in a nursing home – as Nigel's younger brother, Rupert had suggested – that was simply out of the question. Rupert's own finances were scant: what little remained from his income after he had paid spousal maintenance to his ex-wife went into funding his current trophy wife and her vulgar and extravagant lifestyle. It therefore fell to Nigel to foot the bill for the Major's care, in the form of two extremely expensive yet efficient private nurses. Admittedly, he was hardly poor: in addition to the seven-figure golden handshake he had received from Bennet's and his substantial pension, there was also the annual £40,000 fee as non-executive director on the board of Bennet's, plus the £2,500 board meeting attendance fees a couple of times a year – although this last one barely covered Venetia's hairdresser bills, he acknowledged, though affectionately and entirely without rancour. Indeed, he was excessively proud of his wife's looks and gratified by the time, money and effort she put into maintaining and improving them for him. He also had the occasional, generously remunerated stint as an after-dinner speaker for Chambers of Commerce and the like – although, no doubt, not as many as his former arch-rival, Sir Philip Green.

Nigel twitched in irritation and disgust at the very thought of that odious man: after all these years, the knighthood still rankled. It was not just his vanity: it would also have been a source of inestimable pride to the Major to have a son knighted. As it was, the nearest thing his father would get to Royal favour would be a telegram from the Queen the following year – assuming he made it to his next birthday.

But really; how could they have bestowed such an honour on that *pleb*, and not him? But then, he reflected bitterly, that was the Jewish mafia for you.

In addition to his own, not insignificant sources of revenue, Venetia had a substantial private income of her own, inherited from her mother, which had been wisely invested over the years. Nevertheless, they had three daughters, the youngest of whom was still at university, and two homes – a townhouse in Eaton Square and Raddington Hall, a Palladian manor house near the Essex-Suffolk border – both of which inevitably required legions of staff to run. And as much as he despised the benefits culture and those who made a career out of exploiting it, his father was entitled to the Attendance Allowance. Why, the Alzheimer's alone qualified him; but even without this, Nigel reasoned, the Major was still technically entitled to the lower weekly rate of £59.70 a week due to his lost sense of smell: did not the government website clearly state that disability included sensory disability?

The reason for his presence at the DWP today was precisely to claim the higher rate of £89.15, which the Major's dementia certainly justified. True, it would barely make a dent in the cost of the nurses; but, dammit, eighty-nine pounds and fifteen pence was still eighty-nine pounds and fifteen pence. And surely a man such as his father – a decent, upstanding member of the community, who had served his country and paid his taxes, was a far more deserving beneficiary of the state's generosity than foreigners or the under-educated, under-skilled, over-sexed and over-fertile nonentities that peopled the council estates?

As he reluctantly joined the queue, he wondered, as he did each time he visited his father lately, ever since his condition had taken a marked turn for the worse, in what state he would find him today. The last time he had seen him, Major Lovelace had introduced Nigel to Gail, the daytime nurse, as his father, and had then proceeded to fret about being late for school. Yet, as is often the case with those afflicted by this condition, his ravings were interspersed with occasional moments of surprising perspicacity: only a month before, Nigel had visited with Harry Featherstonehaugh, an old army buddy of the Major's, and his second wife, a considerably younger woman named Lucy. After their departure the Major had murmured in Nigel's ear:

'She's been looking elsewhere, you mark my words.' Sure enough, the following week when Nigel bumped into Lt Col Featherstonehaugh in their local, he got extremely drunk and admitted that he had recently found out Lucy was cheating on him with a man from his lodge.

Nigel glanced at his watch impatiently. He wanted to get back to town by six: Venetia was having one of her dos, and Dinah was due home from Cambridge for the weekend sometime that evening, and he longed to see her. His Dinah. How odd, he reflected, not for the first time, that of his three daughters, it was his youngest who was his favourite. Dinah, with her eccentric and – to him – incomprehensible radical political views, her obsession with conservation and animal rights (there had been that rather awkward incident few months ago when they had gone to Raddington and she had started browbeating poor Anstruther, the master of hounds). And Lord knows her time at Cambridge would hardly go anywhere to curbing her knee-jerk liberal ways: the place had always been a notorious breeding ground for pinkos. As for her supposed Sapphic inclinations, he was in complete denial about these, dismissing them as a phase.

And yet, he adored her. True, she was not as good-looking nor as well-dressed as Portia, nor as charismatic as Cordelia – and, unfashionable a belief as it was these days – these were all important qualities in a young woman. But she was far cleverer than her older sisters; she had spirit. And she made him *laugh*, like no one else ever had – not even Venetia.

Portia was a fine young woman with many qualities; but she tried too hard. To be like him, to please him. Dinah, on the other hand, delighted him precisely because she quite clearly did not give two pins what anyone thought of her.

Cordelia was another kettle of fish. For she displayed what he recognised – all too painfully – as the classic symptoms of the Middle Child Syndrome: the pronounced streak of theatricality and exhibitionism, which she had since leveraged into a successful though not particularly lucrative career as a concert pianist, and which compensated for a profound innate shyness; the need to appease everyone.

In another parent, this recognition, this shared experience would have engendered some sort of empathy or fellow feeling. Not so with Nigel: it merely served as a bitter reminder of a handicap he had once had – and overcome. In his case, though, fate had eventually intervened when, in 1981, his older brother Marcus was killed in Northern Ireland, thereby changing his status within the family and breaking the curse of the middle child.

Of course, technically, Cordelia was not the middle child because Portia was not the eldest. But Miles didn't count: he was so much older than the girls, old enough to be their father, so they had not grown up together; and besides, his son had always refused to have anything to do with his step-mother or his half-sisters – poisoned, no doubt, by his mother. Nigel himself had not had any direct contact with Barbara or Miles in over twenty years. He had heard through mutual acquaintances that his son was some sort of journalist living in Italy, and, through his solicitor, that Barbara had remarried some time ago, thus mercifully releasing him from paying spousal support.

Three-quarters of an hour later, having successfully arranged for the Major's Attendance Allowance to be paid – at the higher rate – Nigel went to the florist's across the street then drove the Range Rover to the cemetery to pay his respects to his mother. After replacing the withered flowers with his new bouquet and contemplating the gravestone in silence for a few minutes, he headed to Fawley House, where Gail greeted him and informed him that, according to Natalie, the night nurse, Major Lovelace had had a fairly good night, but was 'a bit fuzzy' today. She added that he was in the conservatory, and here Nigel found him, clad in his ancient, moth-eaten maroon velvet smoking jacket over clean Marks & Spencer flannel pyjamas and tackling a Sudoku.

'Look who's here, Major!' chirped Gail with that appallingly forced joviality people of her profession seemed to insist on assuming.

The old man looked up at Nigel with dull, watery eyes.

'Who the devil are you?' he rasped.

CHAPTER TEN

A month had passed since the Brexit referendum and Marnie's resolution to obtain Irish nationality. It had taken her this long to steel herself to contact Deirdre again after fifteen years. How would she go about it? Would Deirdre want to speak to her again after what had passed between them? Was she even still alive?

She had briefly thought of confiding in Guy, but had promptly reconsidered. She was afraid: afraid of his overwhelming enthusiasm and approval at her decision – which he would invariably see as an attempt at a rapprochement with her birth mother – and of his inevitable disappointment and censure once he learned that the true purpose of the initiative was not to rekindle the mother-daughter relationship but merely to achieve Marnie's own cold-blooded, bureaucratic ends.

Brother and sister had quarrelled bitterly after she had told him of her decision to cut off contact with Deirdre all those years ago: to Marnie's incredulity and dismay, he had wholeheartedly taken Deirdre's side, saying Marnie had been unfair and oversensitive and should have given the other woman another chance. This had incensed Marnie (why the *fuck* was he defending some woman he didn't know from Adam over his own sister, whom said woman had hurt?)

No, the whole subject of Marnie and her birth mother was clearly too incendiary to be raised with Guy: his strong views and agenda on the matter, compounded by her defensiveness, meant that a rational, impartial discussion between them was quite out of the question.

In the end, after retrieving and metaphorically dusting off her original birth certificate, she had instead called Val, who, as expected, had been quietly encouraging and positive.

As she sat down at her desk to write the letter (assuming Deirdre was still alive, it was safe to suppose that her technophobia had only increased, not diminished, with the passing of the years, hence her use of the now outmoded means of communication), Marnie cursed herself –

not for the first time since the Brexit referendum – for not having simply applied for French nationality years ago, when she was still living in France and married to Luc.

Of course, she knew such regrets were futile: she knew that, then as now, nothing but a cataclysmic political, economic and ideological disaster such as this, nothing but the dystopian spectre of an isolated Great Britain would have induced her to apply for French nationality. Not because of any misplaced patriotism, but sheer obstinacy and outrage at the way French bureaucracy made one jump through hoops. For despite being married to a Frenchman for years and having a child with him, despite having spent almost two decades living and working and paying taxes in France, being a model citizen, she would nevertheless have had to go through a Kafkaesque process involving the production of unfeasible quantities of documents – including, incredibly, something called a *certificat de nationalité* Luc would have had to supply. For the mere fact of being French, being born in France of French parents and possessing a French ID card and passport was apparently not sufficient proof of Frenchness for the authorities: thus, Luc would have had to apply for a special document. In addition to providing this and countless other documents and certificates and being interviewed to ensure that she and Luc were a genuine couple, Marnie would have had to supply every single address she had resided at since her birth and been subjected to background checks – which the French authorities rather primly and anachronistically called an *enquête de mœurs*, an 'investigation of morals'– and the police were allowed to carry out random home visits, meaning they could bang on the door any morning, check the master bedroom, rifle through the bathroom, interrogate Rhiannon and ask her if Mummy and Daddy slept together. For these things had happened to friends and colleagues of Marnie's who had applied for nationality, and she had made up her mind not to be a part of it.

In light of the present situation, however – both the political one and her personal drama with Deirdre Kavanaugh – the expression 'cutting off the nose to spite the face' sprang to mind when she reflected on her boycott of French bureaucracy.

Taking a deep breath, she dashed off the letter.

Dear Deirdre,

I hope you are well. I imagine you will be surprised to hear from me after all this time. I will get straight to the point: my reason for contacting you is that, in the light of Brexit, I am applying for Irish nationality and require certain documents to prove my Irish origins.

I would therefore be grateful if you could please supply me with the following:

-Your original birth certificate

59

-A copy of your passport or driving licence.

To that end, I am enclosing a self-addressed stamped envelope.

I understand, however, if you are unwilling or unable to help me with this (she had originally put 'comply with these requests' but that seemed too cold and formal, even for this letter).

(How to sign off?) She had rejected 'love', 'best wishes' and 'kind regards' and settled for a more neutral:

'Yours,

Marnie Wade Barthélemy.

Putting both her maiden and married names obviated the need for any explanations: she did not wish to discuss her divorce or any other aspect of her personal circumstances with the woman. Before she could change her mind, she slipped the letter and SAE into an envelope, sealed, addressed and stamped it, and walked down to the end of the road to post it.

Just as it had been all those years ago, Deirdre's response was almost immediate. This time, however, it was by letter, not telephone: of course, Deirdre would not have any of Marnie's UK numbers.

It was substantially longer than Marnie's original missive:

Dear Marnie,

I confess I didn't think I would ever hear from you again.

I understand that some of the things I said – or rather, the things I didn't say – may have been upsetting or hurtful to you.

But sometimes life is hard. I know this better than most. Yet I have never complained nor blamed anyone for the things I have been through. We all have our problems. (Jesus, thought Marnie bitterly, why not say we all have our crosses to bear while you're at it?)

I am glad you wrote to me as I have something I have been meaning to tell you.

Two years ago, I was diagnosed with breast cancer. I underwent treatment and have been in remission for just under a year. But whilst I was sick, I began thinking about my family, my extended family, I mean: as you know, I had no other children and my parents and sister are all dead, so the only other family I have are my cousins in Ireland. We were never in contact – Daddy had broken off with them all when he emigrated back in the forties, and Mammy's people had more or less disowned her when she left the country.

Daddy had two brothers: David died in WWII, and Patrick, the youngest, passed away about twenty years ago, as I discovered a few years ago. My Uncle Patrick and Daddy had had some sort of feud – political, I believe. Anyway, they were estranged from the moment Daddy came to England until he died in 1981. But Patrick had three children – two daughters and a son. The son, John, died in the eighties, but I tracked down one of the daughters, my cousin Aiofe (so that would make her your first cousin once removed, I believe?)

I wrote to her to introduce myself and she got back in touch with me. Since then, we've maintained regular contact and I eventually went over to Dublin to see her and her sister Patricia. They are both married with children; Aiofe has four children and several grandchildren. She is a good person and a strong woman.

Anyway, the reason I am telling you all this is that I eventually told them about... well, you. The pregnancy, the adoption, and the fact that you and I had briefly been in touch.

I am well aware of your frustration at not knowing more about your real father. However, if you are ever interested in finding out about and perhaps contacting or even meeting members of your family on my side, you need not be afraid of making any potentially painful revelations or shaking 'skeletons in the cupboard', (which, incidentally, you would be doing should you persist in trying to trace your father, which is why I must urge you again not to pursue this course of action). (Bloody cheek!) *My cousins, however, know of your existence and would be happy to hear from you should you ever decide to contact them. To that end, I am enclosing my cousins Aiofe's and Patricia's details, to do with what you will and regardless of whether or not you and I resume contact.*

Regarding your Irish nationality application, I am enclosing the documents you asked for. I trust you have everything you need now. There is no rush to return my birth certificate.

I see you have moved back to the UK. I hope everything is working out as you hoped.

Best wishes,

Deirdre

PS If you have not already done so, you should get screened for breast cancer.

Marnie was astonished. She had expected many things, but not this. She immediately dashed off a brief reply, thanking Deirdre for her help in supplying the documents and saying she was sorry to hear about her previous medical worries and was pleased she had recovered. She made no mention of the members of her extended birth family or the prospect of making their acquaintance; she was not tempted to pursue this avenue. She had already opened Pandora's Box once and, having successfully closed it again, it would be utter madness to unleash its contents again.

CHAPTER ELEVEN

Dublin, 5 June 2019

Sitting slumped behind a table at his new local staring balefully into the beige scum of Guinness froth at the bottom of his glass, Dave wondered what could possibly make him feel more vanquished in spirit.

To recap: he was still barely closer to getting a divorce, things with Clare were awkward to say the least, although they tried to remain civil for Declan's sake. That crazy cow Tina, with whom he had had one drunken shag, had managed to get herself pregnant, and was not only determined to keep it but was adamant it was his – and there was no way he could prove the contrary without her consent. When he had expressed doubts about the veracity of her claims and suggested that perhaps she had not been as exclusive with her favours as she had said, she had called him a blackguard and sent one of her brothers after him. (It was fortunate for Dave that he kept himself in shape, played rugby and was a good head taller than Tina's brother.) He had then asked his mates to make a few discreet inquiries about Tina to find out about any other possible paramours – anything to throw suspicion on her claims – accusations, rather – of his paternity; but these investigations had yielded nothing.

Meanwhile, he was paying a small fortune renting a two-bedroom flat in St Stephen's Green. True, it was convenient for work; but what with that and the mortgage on the house in Killiney, he was barely keeping his head above water.

To cap it all, he could not even find solace and distraction in carnal pleasures: for the first time in his life, he was having difficulty seducing women. It was as though they could sense his despondency – despair, even – and it was a turn-off. So, apart from a few trysts with a client – the fifty-something Head of Purchasing of a well-known insurance group, classy, well-dressed and pretty tidy for her age – the only sexual encounter he had had in the past few months was that quickie with Clare a few weeks back – and that hardly counted.

As he contemplated the sorry, chaotic mess of his life and took alternate gulps of Guinness and sips of whiskey, his mobile rang.

'What?' he barked.

'Charming,' said Clare crisply. 'We need to talk, it's urgent.'

Dave sat bold upright. 'What's the matter? Is it Declan?'

'He's fine, I just need to talk to you about something. Can you come over?'

Dave sighed. 'Jesus, Clare, I'm really not having the best night…'

'Then I'll call each and every one of your mates and harass them until you do. I'm not joking, Dave; I need to see you.'

Swearing, Dave deposited some money on the table and rose. He was too far gone to drive, and by the time he had walked to Pearse Street Station, caught the next train to Glenageary and walked from the DART station to the house he used to live in, almost an hour had passed and Clare was fuming.

'What is it? He asked wearily. 'Do you need money?'

'Congratulations' she said tightly, 'you're going to be a Dad again.'

Fuck, he thought. *How the hell did she find out about –*

'I'm pregnant.'

Dave stared at her dumbly. '*You're* pregnant…?' Pulling himself together quickly, he adjusted the emphasis: 'I mean, you're *pregnant*? Are you sure?'

'Jesus, Dave. I've fallen twice before, I know how it feels, and I'm a nurse. Yes, I'm sure. And before you *dare* ask me, no, there hasn't been anyone else. It's yours.'

Of course it is, he thought bitterly. *I'm apparently responsible for siring every single fucking kid in the Republic.* He sighed. 'I need to sit down. Can I have a drink?'

'I think you've had enou –' she paused, and said more gently: 'Fine. You can crash in the spare room if you like.' She deposited a tumbler of whiskey before him and after a few seconds, took another glass from the dresser and poured herself two fingers.

'Are you sure you should?' asked Dave. 'In your… condition, I mean.'

'Jesus, Dave,' she sighed wearily, 'did you hear me? I'm pregnant: *we're going to have another baby.* God knows I need a drink, even if it is the last one I'll have for a while.'

Dave couldn't argue with her. They drank in silence for a few seconds. Then he spoke:

'I guess you've made your mind up then. To keep it, I mean.'

In response to her look of incredulity and disgust, he went on: 'Well, it *is* technically legal now. I'm just saying, there are, you know… options.'

Clare stared at her glass for a few seconds, then said:

'Yes. I want this baby. You know I always wanted more kids; then, after we lost the other one…' She took another gulp of whiskey. 'Look, things didn't work out for us, but whether we like it or not, this happened. I'm not saying I want us to make a go of things again. I'm not a fool. But I still want us to raise this kid. I don't know how we'll manage but we'll just have to work it out as we go along.'

Dave nodded slowly. 'Then, I suppose we'll have to,' he said quietly. He thought – but, wisely, did not say out loud: *well, at least Mam'll be happy.*

⋈⋈

Milan, 5 June 2019

'*Un marocchino con latte scremato e panna.*'

The barista did not bat an eyelid at Miles's rather eccentric order; they seldom did.

When Miles had first come to live in Italy all those years ago, it was one of Luca's first lessons on Italian etiquette: Coffee isn't a beverage in Italy, he had said. It's a way of life, and one we take very seriously. When you order, you have to be a prima donna. If you just ask for a simple, off-the-shelf espresso or cappuccino, they won't respect you.

At the time he had laughed, assuming Luca was joking, exaggerating. But he was right. He had once almost laughed out loud upon witnessing an extremely elegant woman in her late forties stride up to the bar in a café in Brera and request a *caffè macchiato freddo* – and adding, almost as an afterthought, that she would like the froth on her iced coffee to be hot as she was rather cold.

He thanked the barista as his own bespoke beverage was deposited before him. The decadent mixture of chocolate, hot milk and coffee was served – as it should be – in an Irish coffee glass; his little idiosyncrasy had consisted in requesting it be made with skimmed milk but with a dollop of cream on top.

Punctiliousness and eccentricity where coffee was concerned was just one of the ways in which Miles had embraced the mores of his adopted country. For in addition to his virtually flawless Italian, he prided himself on his chameleon-like acculturation to life in Italy. He now shared the locals' disdain of tourists who committed the typical mealtime solecisms, such as ordering cappuccino after lunch or dinner or – horror of horrors – as an accompaniment to any meal other than breakfast. Or requesting a spoon with which to eat their spaghetti, linguine or tagliatelle, or asking for parmesan to sprinkle on their *spaghetti alle vongole* or other fish- or seafood-based pasta dishes.

He had also become a devotee of the bidet. As a new arrival on Italian shores, he had been bemused by what he saw as Luca's extreme fastidiousness when he denounced the English and their primitive bathroom arrangements. And yet now, Miles considered the bidet as indispensable to personal hygiene as were soap, toilet paper and indoor plumbing.

Luca had been his one and only lover in Italy. Despite the other man's ethereal beauty and apparent skill, the experience had only served to strengthen Miles's conviction of his own asexuality, and he had remained resolutely celibate ever since. Fortunately, Luca had accepted his decision with good grace and the two had remained friends.

Despite their age difference – for Luca was fourteen years his junior – the two men had many things in common. In addition to their love of opera and art, they both had a taste for luxury: fine dining, five-star hotels and bespoke suits. Miles did not, however, share his friend's obsession with *calcio storico fiorentino*, that ancient, barbaric sport which was a mixture of football, rugby and gladiator flighting. Fortunately, Luca's fascination for the sport was purely as a spectator not as a participant and his interest derived chiefly, Miles suspected, from its undeniable homoerotic implications rather than its merits as a sport.

They were also both estranged from their fathers. Luca, the scion of one of the oldest and wealthiest families in Lombardy (reportedly descended from the House of Pallavicino, one of the Italian nobility's oldest dynasties), had been exiled due to his homosexuality and what they deemed his bohemian lifestyle (he ran a small art gallery in via Tortona). Exiled, but not cut off financially: he continued to receive a generous allowance, and it was this, and not the odd painting he sold, which funded his opulent lifestyle.

In Miles's case, it was he who had severed all ties with his father, even going as far as relinquishing his name and going by his mother's maiden name, Halliwell (although both Luca and Miles's Editor-in-Chief had told him that the more euphonious Lovelace would have looked better on his byline). Lovelace Senior had been a cold, distant father and a faithless husband, eventually abandoning Miles's mother for some socialite he was having an affair with. By then, Miles had already left home and was in his second year at LSE. After graduating he went to work for Reuters, first in London then in Milan. Three years later he had left to take a job doing the financial news slot on a local radio station but because of his language skills they had asked him to present the international press review. He had done some freelance journalism for a few years after that and had eventually landed his current job with *La Repubblica*, covering the business and economic news.

In addition to his negligence as a father and husband, his father was also an appalling reactionary, who would be horrified if he knew that his only son was not only an invert (albeit a sexually inactive one), but working as a hack for a left-leaning newspaper with the Eyeties, as he doubtless called them. Consequently, Miles had not spoken to him for nearly thirty years, although he occasionally read about him and his new family in the press. As a journalist he read both print and online media voraciously, and thus had, over the years, seen the odd article on his father in the *Financial Times, The Economist, Fortune* and trade publications such as *Retail Insights*, and the National Retail Federation website. As for his stepmother and the elder two of his half-sisters, they were frequently pictured in *Tatler Bystander* and *Hello*. Miles tried not to judge them solely on the basis of their media profile, not to dismiss them as silly, frothy, ornamental and empty-headed. After all, for all he knew, they might help out in soup kitchens and volunteer at food banks between point-to-points, gallery openings and fashion shows. It was not that he did not wish to think ill of his half-sisters in particular; he made it a general rule to be as forbearing and open-minded as possible with his fellow men, lest he turn into a seething mass of prejudices like his father. For Nigel Lovelace's worst qualities – his coldness, his snobbism, his blank intolerance – had been instilled in him by his own father, a bigot and a bully, ex-army, whom Nigel had always insisted on referring to as the Major. Miles shivered with distaste as he thought of his grandfather: he was a bona fide, hard-core Fascist. He remembered as a child once hearing him speaking approvingly – even admiringly – of the desecration of a Jewish cemetery by Neo-Nazis. According to Miles's mother, who had friends in Sherbourne, where her ex-father-in-law lived, the old man was miraculously – or rather, improbably – still alive: he must be nearly a hundred. How many men or women of his age – nearly fifty – Miles wondered incredulously, could claim to have living grandparents? But then, he reflected ruefully, a person's longevity was seldom directly proportional to their virtue: Robert Mugabe had lived to the ripe old age of ninety-five, while Leni Reifenstahl, Hitler's film-director of choice and a fervent Nazi sympathiser, had successfully eluded Nazi-hunters and war crime trials until she was a hundred and one.

Like Luca, Miles also received a private income – though considerably smaller than his friend's – from his mother, and was thus able to keep up, to a certain extent at least, with the younger man's jet-setting, high-flying lifestyle.

Right on cue, Luca walked into the bar, wearing a beige linen suit with a lavender silk scarf around his neck. His blond hair was still damp and curly from the shower. He glided up to the bar, requested a *caffè corretto*, and kissed Miles on both cheeks.

'Am I late?' he asked airily in English, and, without waiting for an answer, proceeded to give an explanation for his tardiness: 'I picked up a boy in Il Gattopardo last night and I couldn't get rid of him this morning.' He paused to take a sip of his grappa-laced coffee. 'He was beautiful, but disgustingly common.'

Miles winced inwardly at this last remark. Luca was the most dreadful snob. He was also lazy, potty-mouthed, sexually promiscuous and an alcoholic, with a propensity for frivolity and gossip.

But he was also intelligent and cultured – although, in Miles's opinion, he was wasting his gifts in that excuse of an art gallery; he was often amusing, and had always been a good and loyal friend to him.

'Why are we speaking English?' Miles wanted to know.

'I have decided only to sleep with non-Italian men from now on,' Luca declared, and drained his cup. 'So, I need to brush up on my English.' Signalling to the barista for a refill, he offered Miles another coffee.

Miles shook his head. 'I've got to get to work.'

Luca rolled his eyes melodramatically. 'You are so bourgeois sometimes,' then making a shooing gesture with his hands, said: 'Off you go then.'

Miles waved goodbye and just as he was walking up to where he had parked his moped, his phone beeped. It was an acquaintance of his, the Sales Director of a big tech firm:

I have a scoop for you. When can we meet?

CHAPTER TWELVE

Bristol, 7 June 2019

Somehow, Guy found out about Marnie's ill-advised one-night stand with Vince at the wedding.

Of course he did. She had never been able to keep anything from him, not since they were children, nor had she been able to lie to him when he confronted her – as he did this time, calling her after he and Nova returned from their three-week honeymoon in Costa Rica.

It was typical of their arguments: a heated exchange that flared up and would be quickly forgotten. Although, in this instance, the anger was mostly on her side: Guy contented himself with being censorious, primly deeming her tryst with his father 'inappropriate.' She did not bother asking how he had found out: she knew better than that after all these years.

'What's the big deal?' she asked, somewhat disingenuously. 'We're both single – and if it's the age difference that's bothering you, he's barely older than Luc.' *As I pointed out to him,* she would have loved to say, *right after I shagged his brains out.*

The conversation may have taken a rather different turn had Guy not said what he did next. The truth was, Marnie was painfully aware of the colossal lapse in judgement sleeping with Vince had been: she could barely look back on that night without cringing. But Guy's sanctimony only made her defiant and (outwardly, at least), unrepentant.

'The age difference is neither here nor there,' he retorted. 'It's inappropriate because of…'

And there it was: he used the F-word: '…because of the *family* link.'

It was at this point that Marnie lost her temper.

'Look, you brought these people into our lives. You foisted them upon us, crowbarred them into what should have been a family event…'

'They *are* fa –' he began.

'Don't say it!' she interjected shrilly. 'Don't you dare say it, so, help me *God*! The point is, you wanted us to like them, wanted us all to get along like some fucked up, blended family…'

'Get on, yes! As in, make small talk, not go and shag my father!'

'Fuck off, Guy,' she snarled, hanging up. Just as she did so, another call came through: it was Rhiannon.

'You're welcome!' she snapped.

'What? Mum? What are you talking about?'

'I mean you should thank your father and me *every day of your life* for not inflicting a sibling on you!'

'OK… Did you forget to take your HRT or something?'

'Don't be impertinent!' She took a deep breath, then said, more calmly: 'I'm sorry. Guy's just getting on my wick. Anyway, how are you? How's college?'

'Pretty good, thanks. Listen, I need to talk to you about something.'

'I assumed as much. You don't usually just call for a chat, and no, I'm not having a go. So, what's up, Pussycat?'

'I'm afraid I won't be coming home this weekend after all. There's been a change of plans. I'm sorry.'

'Oh, OK. Is everything all right?'

'Yes, everything's fine, only… well, something came up.'

'Well, it would have been nice to see you, but it's no big deal. We can do it another time.'

'Absolutely! How about next weekend?'

Marnie looked at the kitchen calendar. 'Yep, sounds good.' She shook the kettle, filled it from the tap and switched it on. 'So, what are you doing this weekend? Anything special?'

There was a few seconds' silence on the other end, and then:

'Actually, I've met someone and we're going away for the weekend.'

Marnie held her breath, and, trying to keep the excitement and curiosity from her voice:

'Oh, yes? Well, that's nice. So, tell me about him!'

Another hesitation. 'He's… very smart. Brilliant, in fact.'

'Great, good for you. What does he do?'

'He's… in academia,' she began evasively, then suddenly let forth a flustered sigh. 'Look, he's a lecturer here, OK? He's my Cognitive Science professor.'

'He's one of your *lecturers*?'

'Yes, look, Mum, don't make a big thing out of it…'

'So, let me get this straight: you called me to say you're not coming home this weekend because you're going on a dirty weekend with one of your lecturers?'

'Well, if you must put it like that.'

'Is he…' Marnie steeled herself for further shocking revelations: 'Is he married?'

'Divorced. Three children…well, they're all grown-up now.'

Marnie's knuckles went white as she clutched the kettle handle.

'How *old* is he?'

Another pause. 'Fifty-three.'

Boiling water splashed onto the teabag, filled the mug and overflowed. Carefully, she replaced the kettle and sat down at the island.

'Mum? Are you there?'

'Yes, I'm still here.'

'Look, you did ask. Would you rather I'd lied?'

'Frankly, yes! I mean, *fifty-three*.'

'So what?!'

'Well, it's a big age difference…What is it? Father issues?'

'Hmm,' Rhiannon observed tartly. 'Talk about the pot calling the kettle gerontophile.'

Marnie gasped softly. 'That's… I'm not…' she stuttered, then, pulling herself together: 'Your father's fourteen years older than me; this guy is nearly *three times* your age…'

'Whatever, Mum. Look, I realise this is a shock for you, but…'

'Fine, forget the age thing for a minute.' She sighed. 'What's his name?'

'Dr Scutt. Gulliver.'

'Gulliver Scutt? What the bloody hell kind of name is *that*?'

'Really, Mum? Taking the piss out of his *name*? Very mature.' She paused. 'Look, we obviously can't talk about this rationally now. I'll call you in a few days, OK? Goodbye.' She hung up.

Marnie put her phone down and sat staring into space. She took a swig of scalding tea, burning her tongue: the pain shook her out of her stupor.

She got down from the stool and wiped up the spilled water from the countertop. As she put the milk back in the fridge and closed the fridge door, her eyes fell upon a magnet bearing the slogan *Bristolians Do It Better*: Rhiannon had bought it for her last year when they were wandering around St Nicholas Market one Saturday afternoon. Marnie felt a sudden pang of nostalgia for those days of easy companionship and uncomplicated shared pleasures: exhibitions at the Arnolfini; fish and chips or falafels on Wapping Wharf; walks (and, very briefly, until the novelty wore off for Rhiannon, runs) around Brandon Hill or across the Downs. There had also been very occasional shopping trips together, although Rhiannon generally eschewed the bland high street brands and rampant consumerism of Cabot Circus in favour of vintage shops along Gloucester Road.

Scolding herself for her sentimentalism, she grabbed an ice-cube from the freezer and, after wrapping it in a sheet of kitchen paper, placed it on her scalded tongue and went into the living room where she picked up her laptop and settled into an armchair. With one hand holding the ice against her tongue, she used the other to visit the website of the University of Warwick. On the home page, she clicked the 'Schools and Faculties' tab, then 'School of Psychological Science,' 'Staff', and typed 'Gulliver Scutt' in the search engine.

The profile photo of Dr Gulliver Scutt (BA Cantab, MA Cantab, PhD), showed a thin face with a beaky nose, high forehead and beady brown eyes. Other than the shrewd-looking eyes and angular features, he showed none of the stereotypical characteristics of a middle-aged male scholar: instead of a shock of unkempt white hair, he sported a closely shorn military cut and wore no spectacles.

She heard the click of the cat flap and seconds later, Roger wandered in. Marnie reached down distractedly and rubbed her head with one hand whilst the other hovered over the touchpad. After a few minutes, the cat, sensing that Marnie's attention was engaged elsewhere, stalked back out of the room, taking a half-hearted swipe at the dozing Tim with her paw on the way.

As she skimmed through Gulliver Scutt's biography tab, she replayed the recent phone conversation in her head. Rhiannon's jibe, in response to her mother's comment about older men and father issues, had stung (God, that girl could be sharp: where on earth did she get it from?)

Setting her laptop aside a few minutes later, Marnie was forced to admit that, her daughter's impudence aside, the remark had also smarted because it carried a hint of veracity. For Marnie *had* always been drawn to older men, and – pop psychology and clichés aside – she could not dismiss the possibility that her ignorance of her biological father's identity had something to do with it.

There was another reason – unbeknownst to Rhiannon – why her revelation had touched a nerve with her mother. For during her second year at Exeter, Marnie had had a crush on her French theatre lecturer, Dr Putnam, one which had intensified when Marnie auditioned for and got the part in a production of Ionesco's *La Cantatrice Chauve* which Putnam was directing. Yet despite the obvious mutual attraction, neither had acted upon it – beyond a vague, clumsy pass he had made at her one evening during a French Department wine and cheese party, and which she had rebuffed. She had often regretted not succumbing to his advances, wishing she

71

had been bolder, more reckless and uninhibited. She felt a flush of shame at being jealous of her daughter.

Two nights later, she was standing at the stove sipping from a glass of Petit Chablis and carefully stirring a pan of asparagus and mushroom risotto when her phone beeped. It was a text from Rhiannon:

Hi. Hope you've had time to recover from the other night's bombshell. Anyway, just saw this and thought it might interest you x

Clicking on the link below the message, Marnie saw the page of a news site open with the arresting headline:

I was found as a baby wrapped in my mum's coat – but who am I?

Switching off the hob, she took her wine glass over to the island and sat down to read the article.

A septuagenarian retired joiner from Waltham Abbey, she read, had been abandoned as a baby at the bandstand in St. James's Park in 1943. He was subsequently taken to the local police station, and after no one came forward to claim him, was named James Parker (according to the article, it was common practice at the time to name unclaimed foundlings after the place they were found). After being fostered for nearly two years, he was adopted and subsequently rechristened by a childless couple from Bermondsey and grew up to be a contented, healthy and cherished little boy – his happiness marred only by his total ignorance of his origins and parentage. Marnie skipped impatiently over the dewy-eyed evocations of Parker's idyllic childhood with his adoptive parents, and resumed her interest when the article began to recount his search for his birth parents. He joined a Facebook group for foundlings (at this, Marnie rolled her eyes, muttering, 'Jesus wept',) and via this improbable medium came into contact with someone calling herself a 'DNA detective' – a genetic genealogist. This woman, named Ruth Culpepper, apparently made a rather successful living employing her combined skills in genetic science and genealogy to help people trace their parents via DNA samples. After months of scouring archives to no avail, Culpepper had sent a DNA sample of Parker's to a privately owned company that offered DNA matching with other clients on their database: Marnie was both horrified and fascinated that such entities even existed.

She did not finish the article to read about Parker's discovery of his ancestors and (no doubt) subsequent tearful reunion with his long-lost cousins. Finishing her wine, she opened another web page and typed in Ruth Culpepper. The first search came up with the name and

72

the subheading 'Cracks cold cases.' Her heart pounding, she clicked on the link, and after briefly scouring Culpepper's credentials and success stories, clicked on 'contact me' in the menu bar and, in the window that opened, began typing feverishly.

❄

Dublin, 30 June 2019

As usual on a Sunday morning, Dave awoke with a hangover. More surprisingly, though, he woke up alone. For although he had recovered his confidence of late and with that, apparently, his attractiveness to the opposite sex, the whole double pregnancy business had driven him practically to abstinence: he was terrified of spilling so much as a drop of semen within a half-mile radius of any female between puberty and menopause lest she become with child. He was still occasionally seeing the Head of Purchasing, of course, but she was safe, being well past childbearing age. Anyway, she was married and could never stay overnight with him – which suited Dave just fine.

It was not just fear of impregnating yet another woman, though: it was worse than that. For between them, Clare and Tina had driven him to the brink of misogyny. Impending motherhood had unfortunately done nothing to improve either of their characters: it had made Clare more shrewish and sarcastic and Tina even madder – if that were possible.

Yawning and rolling over onto his stomach, he reflected on the last twenty-four hours. He had spent a fairly pleasant Saturday: after picking up Declan from Clare's in the morning as he did every other Saturday, he had taken him to Phoenix Park and the zoo and then round to his Mam's in Broadstone for lunch. Afterwards he had a rugby game, and Declan and his Mam had watched him play. He took Declan back to his flat for tea, played with him, and Clare had rolled up at six o'clock sharp to pick the boy up. For even though it was his weekend with Declan, she had asked if, just this once, she could have him on the Sunday as her Dad was coming into town and wanted to take his grandson out for the day.

Dave had never cared much for Rob McElhatton: he'd been a shitty father to Clare, abandoning her and her mam and sisters when she was three, and was a pretty poor grandfather to Declan, showing only a sporadic and half-hearted interest in the boy. Yet he was trying to be as conciliatory as possible with his ex, 'choose your battles' being his mantra since their separation.

After Clare had taken Declan, he had changed and met Andy and Chris and the boys for drinks. He rubbed his head and wondered what had possessed them to go on a pub-crawl in Temple Bar, of all places. And then he remembered: Ben and Lisa had just broken up, and it had been decided that the best way to cheer him up was to get him laid. And what was the easiest, most reliable way of achieving that objective on a Saturday night in Dublin? Why, trawling Temple Bar, where all the pubs were positively heaving with drunken, loose-moraled tourists. Hen-nights, mainly: hundreds of easy English girls who would drop their knickers for a few overpriced pints and the proverbial accent. It was ridiculously easy. That said, Ben himself had not had any success in the shag-a-Sassenach campaign, although Dave had received the rather persistent attentions of a peroxide blond from Liverpool in her early thirties. Her best friend – the future bride – who was dressed in the standard issue hen-night uniform of mini-veil with devil horns, stockings and garter, spent the evening rather good-naturedly performing a series of tasks set by her coven of revellers, ranging from the merely pointless and frivolous to the downright degrading.

Although Dave's admirer was passably desirable in a brassy, vulgar way and had the sort of medieval serving-wench demeanour that suggested she would – as Andy put it up – 'be up for anything', Dave had no desire to avail himself of her favours and politely tried to steer her in Ben's direction. But much to Ben's dismay, as attractive and amiable as he was, he was frankly no match for a six-foot, raven-haired fly-half with ice-blue eyes. Incidentally, he rather regretted talking about rugby to the woman as she was a fan and claimed to have a particular penchant for outside halves (she was probably working her way through all the positions, he reflected cynically, and had got to number ten).

'Has anyone ever told you you look like Cillian Murphy?' she asked.

For fuck's sake.

'No, never,' he lied. 'We have very different hair.'

'You've got lovely hair,' she cooed. She pronounced it 'er', to rhyme with 'her'. Another point against her, he reflected: he could never perform to the Scouse accent. If they did ever find themselves in that situation – which they wouldn't – he would have to gag her, and he really wasn't into that shit. After his polite, subtle attempts at repelling her advances failed, he decided to reveal his circumstances to her: surely saying he was legally separated with a kid and one – possibly two more – on the way would put her off?

And yet she was undeterred. She merely shrugged, drained her Slippery Nipple, observing that everyone 'had their baggage' and winked lasciviously at him.

Uh-oh, thought Dave: definitely time to move on. He excused himself and went over to Chris and Andy to suggest they try a different hunting ground. However, his friends seemed to think Ben was making progress with a French student and that they should stay for another round. Dave relented and got another round in – seeing as it was for a good cause.

Everything after that point was a Bacchanalian blur: he could remember one of the hens getting into a fight with some other woman, which rather conveniently resulted in their being ejected from the pub. But the woman who had been chatting Dave up must have given him her number at one point because he later found a scrap of paper in his pocket with a UK mobile number scribbled on it. They must have moved on to at least one more establishment, but he had no idea of timeframes. He didn't remember walking home and getting into his flat. He must have passed out on the sofa at some point, for he awoke there sometime in the early hours, head throbbing and mouth dry. He then arose, undressed, washed some ibuprofen down with a pint of water and staggered into his bedroom where he slept until around eleven.

Later, feeling half-human again after a shower, a bacon sambo and two espressi from the machine one of Clare's sisters had given them as a wedding present and for which he had obtained custody – but only because the smell of coffee made Clare nauseous since her pregnancy – his mobile rang. When he saw 'Loony Mooney' displayed, he heaved a sigh and answered.

'What's up, Tina? Are you OK?'

'I been thinking,' she said.

Wonders never fucking cease, he thought, but merely said: 'Oh, yeah?'

'Look, I know you have doubts about the kid being yours, so I've decided I want us to have a paternity test.'

He was stunned. 'Don't you have to wait till after the birth to do that?'

'No, they can do it before it's born. They stick a needle in my belly and take some fluid out and take it to a laboratory and do tests and they tell you who the father is.'

Dave tried to digest this information. 'Well... Are you sure you want to do this?'

'It's the only way we can settle this. When I prove it's yours, then you can't object to paying for its upkeep and all.'

Dave suddenly felt like an utter blackguard. 'Well, no, I'm sure that won't be necessary. I mean, surely it can at least wait until after the birth. Won't it be less... invasive, doing it then?'

But she was insistent. 'I want to get it all sorted before it's born, so it can come to the world without any doubts hanging over it.'

'Well... All right, if it's what you want.'

'Defo. There is just one thing...You'll have to pay for it. It could cost a bit.'

'Like how much?'

'I dunno, couple o' hundred euro. Maybe more.'

'All right, listen, I'll look into it and get back to you and we'll set up an appointment, OK?'

Tina seemed satisfied with this course of action and hung up.

Putting his coffee cup in the dishwasher, Dave opened his laptop and spent the next half an hour searching the Internet. He learned that there were a number of outfits in town that provided prenatal DNA testing. He went onto the website of one such establishment and read the spiel. The cynic in him could not help but be amused at their attempts to be tactful about the services they offered – which, given that they were targeting women of dubious morals who'd been ridden by so many different blokes they had no idea who'd knocked them up – was no mean feat. They spoke of providing 'peace of mind.' *Yeah, right*, he thought.

According to the site, there were two ways of establishing paternity, and, despite what Tina thought, needles were not unavoidable: she could opt for a Non-Invasive Prenatal Paternity test (NIPP), which would involve just a blood sample from Tina and a cheek swab from him. The more invasive procedures to which she had vaguely alluded were amniocentesis or Chorionic villus sampling (CVS). Dave had some experience of amnio as Clare had had one with Declan when they thought there was a risk of Down's: it wasn't a particularly pleasant experience, from what Clare said. According to the website, the NIPP was not only non-invasive but less risky and more accurate than the other options. It seemed like a no-brainer. He winced, however, when he saw the price: just over a thousand euros!

Fuck, he thought, this is all I need: on top of rent and solicitor's fees and Clare's and his new baby on the way, and now this?

On the other hand, he reasoned, if it proved that, by some stroke of luck, he was not the kid's dad, Tina would be out of his life for good and it would be worth every penny. Without a moment's further hesitation, he clicked 'Order Now.'

CHAPTER THIRTEEN

Monza, 2 July 2019

Amedeo arose early on the day of the funeral and ate his customary solitary breakfast. But on this day, more than ever, he was thankful for these moments of silence and seclusion before he faced a crowd of colleagues and total strangers.

As he carefully loaded the dishwasher with his breakfast things and went into to the bathroom to brush his teeth, he recalled the last time he had seen Gabriele, on the day of his death. They had passed each other in the stairwell: Amedeo sometimes thought they must have been the only two of DigInnova Italia S.p.A's 357 employees to eschew the lift consistently. They had exchanged their usual greeting before Amedeo had continued his downward trajectory to a meeting he was due to chair on the third floor, whilst Gabriele had proceeded to the rooftop terrace from which, just a few minutes later, he was to throw himself.

He walked down to the garage (for he never used the lift at home either), and began to back out the brand-new Toyota Corolla Hybrid. At least now Marnie could no longer accuse him of being a half-hearted ecologist: for before he had exchanged the BMW for this more environmentally friendly vehicle, she had often pointed out to him the inconsistency of his insistence on maintaining the temperature in his flat at a punishing 17°, even in the depths of winter, whilst polluting the planet with his daily commute.

As he greeted Siri and commanded it to navigate to the funeral venue, it occurred to him that his first and last conversation of almost every day was with a virtual companion. Yet it was utterly without self-pity that he made this observation: on the contrary, it reminded him of that old joke about talking to oneself not being a sign of madness but simply the only way of guaranteeing intelligent conversation.

Marnie, who seemed to have an opinion on most aspects of his life, often told him she didn't believe in his hermit act: she thought his misanthropy was a mere pose, like those self-styled 'Nihilists' she had known at school.

As he drove through the still semi-slumbering town centre and turned off the roundabout for the motorway, he reflected how, just weeks ago, the dead man's hands had touched the very steering wheel he now held, when he took delivery of the new car. For as Facilities Manager, part of Gabriele's job had been looking after the company car fleet. That, and managing the office leases, overseeing building security and maintenance and supervising the cleaning staff and other external service providers – which had once prompted Santevecchi to joke scornfully that Gabriele's job title should have been 'Head of Air-Conditioning and Toilet Rolls.'

Not that Santevecchi could talk, Amedeo thought: for even back in the days when he was a mere Sales Director, before he had embarked on a campaign of betrayal and vengeance of Aeschylean proportions that had finally culminated in his appointment as CEO, he had pompously insisted on being referred to as 'Chief Commercial Officer.' Marnie often derided the Italians' fondness for titles: *Ingegnere, Dottore.* How desperately insecure and vain they must be, she remarked, to insist on such labels of status.

Santevecchi. How he loathed him! He was nothing but a playground bully, a street hoodlum with an expense account. He had the sartorial taste of a pimp and the business ethics of a white slaver. For years Amedeo had also privately suspected his involvement in some very shady dealings – money-laundering, possibly through shell companies – but he had never, alas, been able to gather enough proof.

Marnie had laughed at him when he had referred to Santevecchi and his henchmen as his archenemies. No one had enemies in the corporate world, she had teased. Rivals, yes, detractors, certainly. But not enemies. He was exaggerating, melodramatic, paranoid. It was so Italian of him, she would say. She didn't understand; she had no idea what it was like.

Traffic was light and within less than half an hour he had reached the outskirts of Milan. When Siri announced that he had reached his destination, however, he thought there must have been a mistake: the putative funeral venue looked more like an elementary school or a gym than a place of worship. But, sure enough, a sign said: *Chiesa di Gesú Cristo dei Santi degli Ultimi Giorni.*

Of course! He remembered now someone mentioning that it was a Mormon church. Gabriele was a Mormon? Did that mean he had a string of wives and didn't celebrate birthdays? Or was that the Jehovah's Witnesses? And which were the ones that refused medical treatment? His ignorance of cults aside, Amedeo realised, not for the first time since Gabriele's death, how little he had known of the man's life in general, despite their working for the same company for seven years.

Then as he parked the Corolla, it suddenly occurred to him that perhaps Gabriele had not been a practising member of the Church of the Latter-Day Saints after all: as he had ended his own life, the Catholic Church would have refused to bury him and thus his relatives had been forced to resort to a more forgiving creed. The Mormons were their back-up faith, not their first choice.

God. That somehow struck Amedeo as the most depressing thing of all: it wasn't just that a middle-aged man had been driven to leaping to his death from the roof of his place of work, but that he had been posthumously snubbed by his religion and forced to make do with some half-baked sect. Also, although Amedeo had long since turned his back on his Catholic upbringing, it struck him, inexplicably, that there was something fundamentally – he searched for the word – *un-Italian* about Mormonism.

Still, who was he to knock a colleague's choice of obsequies? Locking the car, he buttoned the jacket of his suit and walked towards a group of people bearing a flower-festooned casket into the church. For a moment, he wondered for the second time that morning if he had come to the right place, for he did not recognise a single face amid the mourners. But as he had never socialised with Gabriele nor met any of his family or friends, this was perhaps not so surprising.

But it was indeed Gabriele's funeral, for there, ostensibly offering condolences to a woman who could have been Gabriele's widow or sister, whilst looking down the front of her blouse, was Amedeo's Nemesis.

He was as impeccably and gaudily turned out as ever, a preening peacock in a black bespoke three-piece suit and pink silk shirt, with his customary silk handkerchief – also pink today – in the breast pocket, his raven hair artfully sculpted and lavishly gelled. But before Amedeo could avoid him, Santevecchi had spotted him and was now striding over, beaming, a manicured hand outstretched, enveloping him in a cloud of *Eau Sauvage* and self-importance.

'*Ciao*, Amedeo!'

He nodded and reluctantly clasped the other man's hand. 'Matteo.'

'This is a bit weird, isn't it? Can you believe I had to cancel a meeting with –' (he mentioned the name of Italy's leading energy provider – one of DigInnova's biggest clients) 'to come to this? Still, it wouldn't look good to the troops if I didn't turn up. Besides, Lele's family would expect it.'

Amedeo privately doubted that either the departed's family or his former colleagues cared whether his boss turned up, but said nothing and merely nodded.

But what struck him more than this example of Santevecchi's pathological self-absorption – this, alas, had ceased to shock him after years working for him – was the CEO's use of the

79

diminutive form of the dead man's name. He had not supposed him to be on such familiar terms with Gabriele, or even to acknowledge his lowly existence, as to call him 'Lele.'

Together they followed the other mourners into the church. Just inside the entrance stood a roll-up banner – the sort typically used at trade fairs, seminars and other customer and corporate events – with a blown-up photo of Gabriele. It was odd, inappropriate. Amedeo actually found himself wondering if whoever had had the banner made had thought to use DigInnova's usual suppliers: they could surely have done it for free, under the circumstances.

Strange as the banner was, the rest of the proceedings were even kitscher and more bizarre: after the (priest? Pastor? Chief Executive Brainwasher?) welcomed the congregation, there was a eulogy from a portly, grey-haired man who turned out to be Gabriele's older brother, in which he spoke fondly of their idyllic childhood in Sardinia, their weekly poker games, the deceased's passion for cosplay, and then the church began to fill with the familiar strains of *Bohemian Rhapsody*. For, as his brother explained, in addition to gambling and dressing up, 'Lele' had also been an avid Queen fan, even forming his own tribute band with three friends (oh God in heaven, please, don't let them play now!)

Mercifully, they were to be spared this particular ordeal: the congregation was already filing out of the church to Freddie Mercury's rich, haunting vocal accompaniment.

Amedeo sighed: he had done his duty, paid his respects, said goodbye to that poor man, a man whom he had barely known in life and would therefore forever associate him with that one, final, desperate, violent act.

For violent it was: after all, had not Dante condemned suicides to the Seventh Circle of Hell, that of Violence? A few verses of Canto XIII of *Inferno* suddenly came to him:

Quivi le brutte Arpie lor nidi fanno,
che cacciar de le Strofade i Troiani
con tristo annunzio di futuro danno.

All of a sudden, he felt hot and slightly dizzy. He pulled off his jacket, undid the top buttons of his shirt. As he walked back to the car, a blur of pink and black in his peripheral vision told him that Santevecchi was still lurking, circling the few remaining mourners like a vulture. Gritting his teeth, he got into the Corolla, and drove home fast with the air-conditioning on full blast and at 18°.

Immediately he got home he kicked off his shoes, stumbled upstairs and fell face-forward onto the bed and into a deep, troubled sleep.

He dreamt he was walking barefoot through a dark forest with trees from whose trunks black blood oozed: it was the Wood of the Suicides. He heard a sickening cry as one of the souls imprisoned in a tree was tormented by the Harpies (one of whom, incidentally, looked uncannily like Marina Del Prà, the HR Director). Somehow, he knew the soul was Gabriele. And yet, as he approached the tree, the Harpies voraciously and mercilessly devouring the leaves, he saw that it was not Gabriele's face peering out of the gnarled bark, but his own. He ran screaming from his tree-self and the Harpies and presently came to a bright clearing, where a group of black-clad mourners gathered.

It was Santevecchi's funeral.

Suddenly, he was in a frenzy of jubilation. He danced on Santevecchi's grave, raped his widow, ripping open her black silk blouse, pouring champagne over her naked breasts and licking it off greedily – and all before the horrified gaze of her brood of semi-orphans...

When he awoke it was dark. He was panting, drenched in sweat – and fully erect. Ashamed and horrified by the lurid fancies of his subconscious – and even more so by his arousal – he stripped off his shirt, trousers and underpants and padded into the bathroom where he threw his soiled clothes into the laundry basket and stepped into the shower.

He remained under the icy jets of water until his fever had abated and his erection subsided. Afterwards, he went downstairs with a towel around his waist, drank a glass of tap water and sat on the sofa. He switched on the TV. It was a wildlife documentary; he liked them, they soothed him (except the ones showing footage of predators stalking and devouring their prey).

Perhaps he would call his *notaio* in the morning: it was time he made plans for his own send-off. For when he thought of the people in his life now, he shuddered to think what his funeral would be like if things were left to them. At least, he reflected grimly, he had no widow for some other man to defile, no offspring to be scandalised.

After helping himself to more water, he picked up his iPhone and plugged it into the charger. Then, picking it up again, he said:

'Siri: plan my funeral.'

Within seconds, the jovial, disembodied voice rang out:

'Would you like me to find a funeral parlour?'

'No, Siri. I just... *God*, I don't really want to die, but I know we all have to, but when I do go, I don't want a bunch of people who didn't even give a shit about me turning up at my funeral and taking the piss out of my taste in music and speculating about my private life, and my *mother* – oh, she'll be there, trust me: she'll bury us all – saying it was all my own fault for going vegan and how could I do this to her? But most of all, I don't want that bastard

81

Santevecchi there, sententiously saying what a dedicated, valued member of his team I was, when he's essentially spent the past ten years pillaging my brain, stealing my ideas, exploiting me and taking the credit for my work. But I don't actually even care about that! He can have the glory and the limelight: I don't mind being his ghost writer, I have no ego. I just want to *work*, to build something, see my vision through. What I can't bear is the way he's running the company into the ground, and in the process, he and Sartori and his other cronies are gang-raping my ideals and values and beliefs, shitting on everything I stand for: integrity, equality, hard work…'

'I'm not sure I understand.'

He sighed. 'No, I don't suppose you do. *I* don't understand it myself. I mean, is there even any point in *being* here at all, when there's just… nothingness. We come from nothing, and we go to *nothing*.'

Silence, then:

'Would you like me to order *Being and Nothingness* by Jean-Paul Sartre?'

He laughed. 'Goodnight, Siri.'

CHAPTER FOURTEEN

June 2017 was the month in which Donald Trump announced the US's withdrawal from the Paris Climate Summit and suicide bombers attacked the Iranian parliament in Tehran and the mausoleum of Ayatollah Khomeini, killing 12.

Rafael Nadal won the French Open for the tenth time and Leo Varadkar made history in Ireland when he became both the youngest and the first openly gay Taoiseach.

Closer to home, eight people were killed and 48 injured in the Borough Market attacks in London; Theresa May and the Conservative Party lost their majority; and a horrendous fire in the Grenfell Tower block killed 79 and injured 37.

For Marnie Wade, this period was also marked by two significant events in her personal life. One such event – albeit one of only symbolic significance – was her obtaining, just under a year after sending off her application, an Irish passport. The other was the appearance of Dave Mullan in her life.

Since receiving, a year before, the letter from Deirdre informing her of her illness, recovery and subsequent contacting of her Irish family, Marnie had maintained her decision not to reach out to her second cousins, or first cousins once removed or whatever they were, and distance herself from the whole birth family business in general.

But Fate – or, as it turned out, social media – had other plans. For one morning at work, when she was in the midst of grappling with a particularly lengthy and indigestible document on IT security for the CISO, she received a notification via the Linkedin app on her phone. Grateful for any distractions, she consulted it and saw that a certain Dave Mullan, Senior Account Manager at Valerian in Dublin, (531 connections), had sent her a connection request. Neither the name nor the company rang a bell, so she proceeded to read the accompanying message – which was not the standard, automatically-generated connection request.

He explained that his mother, Aiofe Mullan, (*née* Kavanaugh), had told him of an estranged cousin of hers who had got in touch with her and her sister, Patricia – his Auntie Tish – a while ago, that the women had become acquainted and were regularly in touch.

Upon reading this, and anticipating what was inevitably to follow, Marnie felt a chill seep through her body, despite the stuffy atmosphere in the pen (for the air conditioning was off as one of the interns – who, incidentally, was dressed in a short skirt and camisole – coughed and pleaded imminent pneumonia each time Marnie attempted to switch it on).

And there it was: Deirdre had told her cousins of her secret illegitimate child, had said they had been briefly in touch, but had not, he stressed, divulged Marnie's name nor her contact details. He then admitted to having found Marnie's name by doing 'a bit of sleuthing' and eventually tracked her down via Linkedin. He realised this was perhaps not the most appropriate platform for such a personal matter as this but that it was the only way as Marnie 'didn't seem to be on FB or Insta or any other socials,' something which no doubt astounded him as much as it did Rhiannon and probably anyone under the age of forty who didn't belong to a cult or monastic order. (For a cursory look at Dave Mullan's CV showed her that he had graduated in 2004, making him in his mid-thirties now.)

He went on to apologise for the intrusion, hoping it wasn't 'too weird' for Marnie, assuring her that he was not 'stalking her or anything,' but that if she 'felt like reaching out sometime,' he would be glad to make her acquaintance, but if she did not wish to take this step, it was 'totally cool.'

How *forbearing* they're all being, Marnie rather sardonically reflected, with their discreet, tentative offers of friendship and magnanimous acceptance of her possible rejection thereof.

She felt suddenly and unaccountably outraged at the Irishman's presumptuousness and indiscretion, and with this, a wave of heat suffused her body. Standing up abruptly, sending her swivel chair skidding several metres across the floor, she strode over to the air conditioning control box and switched it on, and as she did so, saw in the corner of her eye Zara, the intern, open her mouth in protest. But before the intern could vocalise her objection, Marnie silenced her with a gesture of her right hand.

'Not a word, Zara. Are you cold? Yeah, well, boo-bloody-hoo: I'm having a hot flush and it's age before beauty, or rather, menopause trumps foolhardy youth who come to work dressed in their *fucking underwear*!'

With that she returned to her desk and resumed her translation, typing frenziedly, her cheeks burning.

A few evenings later however, during her weekly Skype with Val and with a glass of Cloudy Bay in her hand, Marnie related the incident. True to form, Val was quietly sympathetic, uncritical, circumspect.

'Yes, I can see how strange and shocking that must have been for you.'

'I haven't replied to him.'

'Well, don't if you don't want to.'

'Hmm...' Marnie took another swig of wine. 'I don't know... I suppose I am a bit curious. I mean, I'm not looking to build a parallel family or anything, but I suppose I'd like to find out about that side of the family. I am officially Irish now, after all.'

Val nodded. 'And you don't have the same... emotional connection as you do with Deirdre. They're just cousins, after all: they didn't... give you up or reject you. They didn't even know you existed until a short while ago. The stakes aren't the same. So, you know, if you *did* decide to get in touch with Dave and his mum, then perhaps it wouldn't feel as...' Val searched for the word... 'emotionally charged or complicated as it was for you with Deirdre. There wouldn't be any resentment or frustration for you: you'd just be tracking down some long-lost, distant relatives.'

Marnie paused to reflect on this. Val continued: 'But obviously, that only makes sense if you feel up to it. You don't owe any of these people anything: it's about what you want.'

Twenty minutes later, Marnie had signed off, finished the bottle of Cloudy Bay and replied to Dave via Linkedin:

Hello Dave,

Good to meet you. It was rather odd and unexpected hearing from you, but I'm strangely glad you did reach out. Below are my email and mobile: let's have a chat sometime.

The next day she had received a cheerful, enthusiastic message from him via WhatsApp, and they had proceeded to exchange a few lengthy emails, in the course of which they had discovered, among other things, a mutual love of rugby. Then, in early September he had announced he was due to go over to the UK on business for a sales seminar at his company's head office in Swindon the following week and how would she feel about meeting up IRL? He was happy to jump on a train to Bristol, it wasn't far. Before she knew it, she had given him the name of a coffee bar at the Harbourside and arranged to meet on the Thursday afternoon after his seminar was over.

And so it was that, on a sunny September afternoon in 2017, Marnie left the co-working space in a building near the Corn Exchange where she worked a couple of days a week to relieve the monotony and solitude of her home office, and, leaving her car where she had parked it that morning in the multi-storey on Rupert Street, walked along to the harbour to meet Dave.

She arrived at the café five minutes early, ordered a flat white, and five minutes after the appointed hour, Dave walked in.

On seeing him in the flesh for the first time, she actually gasped. For his Linkedin profile picture (in which he was wearing sunglasses, rather inappropriately for a professional social network, Marnie thought), failed to do him justice. Indeed, her first thought was that it was somehow unseemly to be even remotely related to such a beautiful and seductive member of the opposite sex: for before her stood a taller, burlier version of Cillian Murphy, although without that haunted, poetic look the actor had in his eyes. For the gaze Dave Mullan fixed upon her, although of the same improbable, other-worldly blue, was that of a man unburdened by existential torment, yearnings, questionings: it was almost indecently carefree and edged with laughter lines.

One evening several years later, after many gins (Marnie) and Jameson (Dave), they shared their mutual first impressions. Upon hearing hers, Dave laughed good-naturedly yet without a hint of false modesty or self-deprecation – any attempt to pretend he was anything but an Adonis would have indeed been absurdly disingenuous – and reciprocated by revealing his initial thoughts on seeing Marnie. It was a far more concise appraisal, a mere acronym, in fact: MILF.

Yet that was to be much later. For their first meeting, Marnie began by asking how on earth he had discovered her identity, at which Dave had shrugged and said that the abundance of information on the Internet combined with the increasing amount of practical advice and tips on how to use the available resources to trace one's ancestors, look up records and birth and death registers and so forth, ('family trees and shit, it's all the rage now,') had made the process surprisingly easy. It was then that Marnie learned, thanks to Dave's newly acquired genealogical knowledge, that they were indeed second cousins.

Coffee was followed by a glass of wine each (there was no draft Guinness at the café), and then a bottle was ordered – but only after various logistical arrangements and adjustments had been decided and made; namely, that Marnie would leave her car in Rupert Street for the night, Dave would push his flight back until the following day, they would both get a cab back to Marnie's later where he could sleep in the spare room, and the next day they would get a cab to Temple Meads together so that Dave could catch a train to Paddington and thence take the Heathrow Express. This suited Marnie as, the next day being Friday, she had to get the train to London for her weekly team-brief at head office. At that time, she and Rhiannon were still living out in the suburbs: after Rhiannon went up to university in October 2018, Marnie had sold up and got a smaller place nearer the centre of Bristol.

After the wine was finished, they walked up to an Indian restaurant in Park Street, where, over Goan-style mussels, fish Amritsari, chicken Lababdar, Hydrabadi lamb, tarka daal and mushroom rice – washed down with more wine for Marnie and Cobra for Dave – Dave related the colourful Kavanaugh family history.

'In her letter, Deirdre mentioned something about a feud between brothers: that is, my grandfather and his brother, your grandfather? Is that right?' Marnie wanted to know.

Dave, it turned out, was quite the storyteller. He nodded, tore off a piece of nan bread the size of his hand, and, having used it to mop up the last of the daal, requested another dish from a passing waiter (God, but the man could eat!)

'We need to go back a generation first,' he said. 'To their father – our great-grandfather, Fearghus Kavanaugh. His wife Aislinn had a brother, bloke called Rory Quinn, who was a member of the IRA, involved in the Easter Rising in 1913.' He paused, leaning forward across the table. 'How's your Irish history? Irish War of Independence? 1919 to 1921, and Fearghus and Aislinn's kids were born during and just after it, just to give you an idea of timelines.'

Marnie nodded acknowledgement. 'Anyway, Rory got beaten to death by the Black and Tans during the Irish War of Independence.'

'Ah, yes,' nodded Marnie, with mock earnestness. 'A dark chapter in British history. Sorry about all that.'

Dave made an airily dismissive gesture with his hand. 'Shit happens. Anyway, Fearghus and Aislinn had Fenian sympathies. But their kids were divided on the subject: the youngest, Patrick – so, my granddad – sided with his folks and embraced the Republican cause; the elder two, however – so, *your* granddad, Michael, and my namesake, David – were pro-British, even to the extent that David Kavanaugh defied not only his parents' beliefs but Irish neutrality –' Another pause. 'You know about Irish neutrality, right?'

'Vaguely; isn't it –'

Another dismissive wave. 'Google it later. So, David went to fight for the British Army in WW2 and got killed in the Normandy landings in '44. Before then, he'd of course alienated his entire family and was branded a traitor to his country.'

'Well, if it's any consolation whatsoever, I'm sure I speak for the entire British nation when I say we're most grateful for his sacrifice.'

'Thanks,' he replied drily, 'I'm sure that'll warm the cockles of the mouldy, dried-out cavity where his heart used to be. Now, yer man Michael wasn't quite so pro-British – at least, he didn't fancy dying for them.'

'Fair enough.'

'But as soon as the war was over he emigrated to Britain with his wife, and had your mam – I mean, Deirdre – and Oona, and as far as I know, he cut himself off from the rest of the Kavanaugh clan for good.'

'Blimey,' said Marnie, trying to digest these revelations. 'So, let me recap: I'm the illegitimate granddaughter of a traitor. An abomination in the eyes of staunch Irish Catholic Republicans.'

Dave nodded. 'Believe me, I can hardly fuckin' bear to look at you.'

Marnie burst out laughing. After requesting the bill, which Dave insisted on paying ('I'll expense it'), Marnie suggested they move on to a bar at the bottom of Whiteladies Road, where, after a few rounds of shots and exchanging some childhood memories, they staggered out and caught a cab back to Marnie's house in Easton-in-Gordano.

Ever since, they had chatted regularly and met again twice – once in the UK after another work function of Dave's, and then in Dublin to see England-Ireland during the VI Nations.

Another happy by-product of Dave's initial contact with Marnie was that neither Zara nor anyone else in the office ever dared mention the air-conditioning again.

CHAPTER FIFTEEN

Dublin, 8 July 2019

It is not 2019. We are in 2000, the summer I turned 17. I am surfing in Strandhill with the lads. A gang of us – Andy, Ben, John, Mickey, Emmet, the two Chrises, Damian, and Cillian – whatever happened to him? took the bus to the west coast with our tents, torn wetsuits and boards. It took nearly seven hours. We then spent two weeks camping in the dunes. Best summer I ever had.

Of course, we still go to Strandhill. But nowadays we go in our company cars, stay in our summer houses and drink pints of Guinness in the Strand Bar while regaling all the young lads with tales about twenty-foot waves we once caught at three in the morning in our underwear, drunk as monkeys.

It cannot be here and now. I cannot be thirty-six, separated, with one kid and one – possibly two – more kids on the way. This cannot be happening. This cannot be my life.

So, I'm sitting in my car on the god-awful estate Tina and her clan live on in Inchicore. We're due to get the results of the paternity test any day now, but I can't wait. I have to see her first.

See, something's been bothering me about this whole CVS business. It doesn't add up. I want to get it straight once and for all before we get the results.

I get out of the car – fuck, I hope someone doesn't nick it – and make my way past two kids in hoodies blowing up snails with firecrackers, up the stairs and along the walkway to the Mooney residence. A dark-haired, pre-pubescent girl answers: a younger, unsullied version of Tina. A pretty face, but puppy fat is spilling out of the gap between her unforgiving crop-top and skinny jeans. Some bloke in a viscose jumper, shell-suit bottoms and a St Christopher is sitting on the sofa in front of the telly. Ma Mooney waddles out from the kitchen and mumbles something to her younger daughter, who then scuttles off. I hear Tina's voice in the background. Ma Mooney eyes me up and down and calls Tina.

God, she looks terrible, the putative mother of my child. Pale, drawn. Great purple swathes of anxiety and insomnia under her eyes. She is naturally surprised to see me.

We need to talk, I say – casting a meaningful glance at Shell-suit and hoping he'll get the hint. He scowls then gets up and pushes past me out of the flat, lighting up a smoke, muttering 'fuck youse.' Ma Mooney goes upstairs.

I need to know why, I blurt out: why this sudden change of heart about the paternity test? She looks blankly at me – which is pretty much her default expression.

Further clarification is needed.

I mean, I say, why did you suddenly go from flatly refusing to admit even to the possibility of the kid not being mine, from being offended like some fucking Victorian virgin at the very suggestion that there may have been other blokes, to suddenly asking to have an invasive procedure that carries a risk – albeit a one in a hundred risk – yes, I've done my research – of miscarriage? And especially when there's a perfectly safe, non-invasive alternative? Can you explain to me why one minute there was no one else but me in the running, and the next, not only are you not sure about who fathered it, but you'd rather go through this than have a simple blood sample taken?

She flinches, turns away, her lank black locks swinging. She won't look me in the eye.

I force myself to calm down, come across a little less threatening, less desperate.

Look, I say more quietly, if you've been seeing other guys, it's no big deal: God knows I'm the last person to judge you on that score. But… I need to know what was so important that you had to do the test this way. OK, the NIPP would have been more expensive, but that's my problem, not yours.

Tell me, for the love of God, tell me!

She suddenly looks up warily at me and says in a strangled voice: not here.

She pushes me out of the flat and hurries along the walkway and down the staircase. I follow.

Tina, I say, what the fuck –

And then she starts screaming like a wounded animal, like something not quite human. People are looking. I take her by the arms, try to calm her down, but she's hysterical, it's like something out of a fucking Greek tragedy.

Then she starts babbling: He said it was all right… we couldn't make a baby like that… not in that position, I couldn't fall. It was safe.

Who are you talking about? Who said that?

Uncle Vinny! she sobs.

I feel as though the concrete is about to swallow me up. There is a dull thudding in my ears.

Your uncle? He... oh, no. Agonising Christ, Tina don't tell me he...

She's on her knees now. He said it would be all right, that I couldn't have a baby that way, that's why I thought it must be yours, there hasn't been anyone else you see, I swear. But then... I was talking to Janine about it the other day, and she said that's not true, that you can *get pregnant like that, it's just a... what's it called? An old wives' tale says you can't. And then I got worried; you hear all those stories about babies born from people who are... from the same family, and they always have something wrong with them, don't they? They're Mongoloid or deaf or have two heads, and, well, if it was like that, if it was* his *and had something wrong with it, I wouldn't want to keep it, I'd give it up. It's too late to get rid of it now. So that's why I wanted the...the thing with the needle in my belly, so I could find out if it was his and if something's wrong with it, because if something* is *wrong with it, then at least I can... prepare myself for giving it up. Not get too attached to it, like.*

She rubs her belly as she says this, still on her knees.

Not knowing what to say, I pull her to her feet as gently as I can and walk her to the car (thank fuck, it's still there). I put her in the passenger seat and put my jacket around her: she's shivering, although it's quite warm. Neither of us says a word as I start up the engine and drive away, past the kids in hoodies blowing up snails with firecrackers.

CHAPTER SIXTEEN

Monza, 16 July 2019

His enemies had finally closed in on him, as he had known they one day would. It was with this sense of fatalistic resignation, and not with self-pity, that Amedeo reflected on the events of the last seventy-two hours.

It had begun with his being summoned unexpectedly by HR on the Friday afternoon. It was true that his relationship with Santevecchi had deteriorated considerably over the past few months, with Amedeo openly challenging his boss on matters of strategy, business and ethics. But that it should come to this?

That harridan Del Prà had done her best to contain her glee – for she must have relished this moment, she had always despised him – behind an expression of stony impassiveness. There had been no preamble: she had simply informed him of his immediate suspension, and, in response to his incredulous protestations, had proceeded to list his transgressions – a risible collection of trumped-up charges and hearsay: allegedly he had lost the firm an important client, he was unprofessional, uncooperative and even obstructive with his colleagues. It was absurd, Kafkaesque! He wondered that they had not added accusations of sexual harassment. But then, he reflected sardonically, such was the systemic misogyny and prevalent machismo at DigInnova Italia that citing sexually inappropriate behaviour as grounds for dismissal would be as unthinkable as the Ku Klux Klan banishing one of their members for using racially offensive epithets.

He had demanded to see Santevecchi. The boss was in a meeting off-site, she had replied curtly. She then told him to collect his things and vacate the premises.

But, he spluttered, he had a meeting with a customer in half an hour! That, Del Prà retorted coldly, was no longer his problem.

Some men in his position would have felt an urge to grab her by her peroxide hair and thrust her head through the glass wall. But he had never experienced the slightest violent impulse – least of all against a woman; the very idea was repellent to him. Nevertheless, after a while he could no longer bear to look at her face: the shocking pink mouth distorted with contempt, the glint of triumph in her hard brown eyes. He fixed his gaze instead on the contents of her pencil cup, the row of Post-it notes dangling from the bottom of her computer monitor. His eyes then fell to the floor. She was wearing sandals today and under the desk he caught a glimpse of a bony, bunioned foot, the toenails painted a fluorescent lime green. He was unpleasantly reminded of the Dantean nightmare he had had after Gabriele's funeral in which she had appeared as a Harpy, and her green toenails suddenly seemed as threatening and repellent as that mythical creature's claws.

Fighting back a wave of nausea, he rose and, as if in a daze, walked out of the office, along the corridor to the lift and hit the button for the carpark. Seated at the wheel of his car, he dialled the number of the Union Rep. He was marginally more sympathetic than Del Prà, but seemed largely embarrassed. He informed Amedeo of the procedure: that he had seventy-two hours in which to respond and appeal – but, this being Italy, it was not three *working* days but three *calendar* days. The *bastards*, he thought: they had purposely done this on a Friday so he would have to spend the weekend building his case.

The Union Rep then asked him if he had a lawyer (Amedeo did not), and recommended one. And thus Amedeo made his second fatal error – the first being to consult and trust the company's Union Rep in the first place: he took down the lawyer's details, assuming that he would have Amedeo's best interests at heart.

The lawyer, a harried-looking man in his late fifties in a crumpled, ill-fitting suit, had presented the rather unappealing options: either he sue for unlawful dismissal, but this could take years, would cost a lot of money, and the result was uncertain. Alternatively, he could go quietly and accept a settlement.

Feeling confused and utterly defeated, Amedeo had chosen the latter; and thus, at three o'clock on the Tuesday afternoon, he walked out of a drab office on a bleak-looking industrial estate in the company of his lawyer with a cheque for a year's salary.

That was it: after thirteen years of service, a year's salary. And he would not even be eligible for unemployment benefit.

He drove home in a trance, made himself a ginger and lemon *tisana* and sat on the living room sofa. Scrolling through his WhatsApp messages, he saw one from Marnie asking how the meeting had gone. His reply was bluntly economical: *They fired me.*

She was suitably shocked and horrified, offered to call and talk it through, but he demurred, saying he needed time to process it all first.

He did not imagine then that just a few weeks later he would think back on this humiliating ordeal and feel a wave relief and gratitude.

⋈⋈

Voidokilia Beach, Greece, 6 August 2019

Marnie stretched languorously on a sun lounger, having turned it slightly so that just her head was in the shade of the parasol whilst her body remained exposed to the sun, and picked up George Eliot's *Scenes of Clerical Life*. She had just slathered more sun cream on – SPF thirty on her legs, arms and torso, and fifty on her decolletage. Generally attentive to her appearance and worried about the ravages of age, she had a particular horror of that delicate skin becoming battered by the elements into a rough, red hide, as was the case with so many women of her age.

On the sunbed beside her, entirely in the shade, reclined Val with a chic-lit novel. Jolyon was swimming in the sea with Medora; Josh was snorkelling a little further away.

It was the fourth day of her two-week holiday in Greece with the Appelbaums. Finding Athens unbearably hot, they had immediately fled to Delphi and thence to the Peloponnese, where they planned to spend the rest of the holiday. The day before they had visited Olympia, and were now spending a few days at the various beaches on the west coast and camping. For the second week they were renting a house up in the hills near Kalo Nero.

They had just enjoyed a delicious, protracted lunch at a beachfront restaurant, sharing dishes of *taramasalata, tzatziki*, courgette fritters, octopus salad, grilled feta cheese with chilli peppers and stuffed vine leaves – homemade, Marnie had noted approvingly, not the tinned variety so many places served – accompanied by the inevitable chilled bottle of Retsina: she could still taste the slightly acrid, aromatic, piney tang of the wine.

For Marnie, this voluptuous, post-prandial idyll was soon to be disrupted by the sound of Dean Martin singing 'but in old Napoli, that's amore' – announcing a WhatsApp message from Amedeo. Setting her book down and picking up her phone, she saw there was just a link to an article in one of Italy's leading newspapers. The title read:

Scandalo finanziario a Milano: fatture false per 16 milioni.

The byline caught her eye, mainly because it was an English-sounding name: Miles Halliwell. As she scanned the article, a more familiar proper name stood out: DigInnova Italia S.p.A.

Other words leapt out at her: *frode fiscale e riciclaggio*. Tax fraud and... recycling? That couldn't be right. On consulting an online dictionary, Marnie realised it was money laundering.

Of course. Amedeo had said he suspected something dodgy was going on. Sure enough, his boss's name also featured in the article: Matteo Santevecchi.

'Oh my God,' she said softly.

'What's up?' said Val, looking up from her book.

'Amedeo sent me an article that's come out about my company's Italian office. Apparently, there's some big financial scandal the top brass has been involved in.'

'God. Will that affect the rest of you?'

Marnie shook her head, scrolling down through the article. 'I've no idea... I'm just trying to figure out what exactly happened. There are a few words I don't know but I can get the gist of it...'

'Why don't you Google Translate it?' suggested Val.

Putting down her phone, Marnie looked up at her friend and frowned.

'Asking a professional translator to use Google Translate,' she said rather pompously, 'is like telling a GP with stomach pains to carry out an Internet self-diagnosis, or... consult a witch doctor.' She resumed her reading of the article. 'I prefer to use a more... organic approach: rely on my existing language skills with a little help from online dictionaries – as opposed to automatic translation software – for the odd word or expression I don't know.'

'If you say so,' said Val, amused.

Marnie replied to Amedeo, expressing suitable shock at the revelation. A thought then suddenly occurred to her: was *he* the whistle-blower? – the "inside source" the article mentioned, this "former member of the senior management team?"'

This he denied emphatically, pointing out that he was not the only disgruntled ex-employee of DigInnova Italia and Santevecchi had made plenty of other enemies.

'It's unbelievable,' she said out loud to Val. 'It looks like they were running a huge scam, going back six years, worth sixteen million euros. Through fake invoices and shell companies and all sorts. You know, Amedeo once told me his boss had *three* PAs, one of whom was purely in charge of his personal errands – shopping, dry-cleaning, contacting the various high-class prossies and mistresses he apparently has on tap.' She shook her head in incredulity. 'God!

And when I think back to when I was organising that Marketing and Comms seminar in the spring: I suggested we have it at the Milan office this time instead of at head office, and the Italian team agreed, but said they didn't have any budget for it – it all had to come out of our pocket. While all this time, that bastard Santevecchi was stealing money to keep his hookers in Prada and Gucci! Ugh!'

'Well, all I can say is your company sounds a lot more glamourous and racy than mine,' observed Val. 'The most ethically questionable thing engineers do is occasionally nick fluorescent marker pens from the stationery cupboard for their kids and expense their dry-cleaning.'

Just then Jolyon ambled over to them. 'The water's amazing,' he said, picking up a towel and rubbing his face and hair. 'So, what are you girls talking about?'

'We were discussing corporate ethics and how they vary from one industry sector and country to another,' summed up Val.

'Corporate ethics,' repeated Jolyon, pulling his sun lounger out of the sun, and then, misquoting Gandhi, said: 'I think that would be a very good idea.' He threw himself down on the sun lounger. 'Now, what are we doing for dinner?

CHAPTER SEVENTEEN

The National Gallery, London, 26 September 2019

'"You're dead to me."'

Marnie stared at her incredulously.

'He actually said that to you? God, what a drama queen.'

Nisha shrugged. 'Good riddance. To be honest, he was only ever half-alive to me. For the past few weeks, he's been in a coma to me at best. Including when we were shagging.' She frowned reflectively, appeared to reconsider. 'Especially when we were shagging.'

Marnie laughed. 'Well, let's hope this takes your mind off things a bit.'

Marnie had first met Nisha Anwar at a sales seminar in Marbella five years ago. At the time, Nisha, the daughter of an electrician and a housewife who had come to Basildon from Islamabad in the seventies, was DigInnova UK's youngest ever Senior Account Manager. A brilliant saleswoman, she consistently topped the rankings and had won countless incentive trips. She had once said her name meant 'courage' in Urdu, and Marnie thought how aptly she had been named: for it surely took a great deal of grit and determination to survive – and thrive – in DigInnova UK's essentially white, middle-class, male-dominated sales team. But it was not just her gender, ethnic origin and Estuary-accented English that made Nisha stand out from her peers: she was refreshingly down-to-earth and refused to take herself too seriously, unlike the drove of strutting Alpha males and divas who lorded it over the other departments lest they forget for one minute that they, the sales force, were the lifeblood of the company.

Nisha had also earned Marnie's eternal gratitude and respect as, on that first night in Marbella, she had come to the older woman's rescue. Marnie's flight from Paris had been delayed by almost two hours and when she finally checked into the resort – a vast, sprawling luxury complex consisting of two swimming pools, three restaurants, four conference centres, a spa, and, by way of accommodation, hundreds of individual bungalows to which newly checked-in guests were escorted by staff from Reception in golf carts – it was almost ten o'clock at night and she was exhausted, frazzled and ravenously hungry. After a quick shower and change, she had just left her bungalow and was wandering around the complex in search of a place to have a bite to eat after which she intended to retire immediately to bed, when she was ambushed by a group of her Marketing colleagues from France who insisted she accompany them for a 'quick drink' in one of the bars. The quick drink had turned into half a dozen, and at one point the UK's Marketing Director had introduced her to some of the Sales team, including Nisha. Marnie remembered a petite, slender and rather mouthy girl in her mid-twenties with olive skin, jet bobbed hair and hazel eyes. The two women had immediately hit it off and before Marnie knew it, it was past two in the morning and the combination of alcohol, fatigue and an empty stomach had somewhat impaired her faculties: she realised with a jab of panic that she was incapable of remembering the location of her lodgings, let alone negotiating the labyrinth of bungalows and alleyways to reach it. Fortunately for her, Nisha, despite her diminutive frame, could hold her liquor, thanks to years of wining and dining clients and celebrating deals in pubs with her male colleagues, and, with admirable presence of mind, had accompanied Marnie to Reception where she had inquired which bungalow the señora was booked into, and subsequently escorted her to her door.

Since moving back to the UK, Marnie made a point of meeting Nisha for lunch or coffee when she came to head office for her weekly team briefing.

Now, after shedding their coats and leaving them in the cloakroom, they agreed to meet in the coffee shop three-quarters of an hour later: Nisha had expressed an interest in looking at the English painters whilst Marnie intended to make a beeline for the three Caravaggios, (possibly followed by Joseph Wright of Derby's *Experiment on a Bird in the Air Pump*, whose use of chiaroscuro was, according to an art historian whose work she had recently read, clearly influenced by the Italian artist). After mounting the staircase and turning right, they parted ways as Nisha went off to Constable and Gainsborough and Marnie pursued her own single-minded quest.

It had all started after her work trip to Naples a month ago: her Caravaggio obsession. After snatching a few hours after the annual seminar to see an exhibition of his Naples period at the Museo Capodimonte, she had done some desultory Internet searches on the painter and been sufficiently intrigued to purchase and read a biography of him. Admittedly, her initial enthusiasm had stemmed more from a prurient fascination for his rock 'n' roll lifestyle – the legions of whores and catamites, the feuding, the bar-room brawls and his inevitably violent and untimely demise – than from an interest in art history. However, upon reading the book, her thirst for the former had soon led to a genuine curiosity for the latter, and she had subsequently purchased an enormous, extremely heavy coffee table book featuring his complete works, over which she would pore for hours whilst reading the biography, all the better to study the paintings in all their gloriously magnified detail. Suddenly a still life was no longer merely a collection of flowers, fruit and other victuals for her to admire superficially, but a myriad of symbolism. For there in the figs and grapes and jasmine was sex and death and resurrection!

And thus, armed with her newfound knowledge, Marnie had resolved to see and re-see as many Caravaggios as possible all over the world – at least those in Europe. Hence, after her weekly team briefing was finished, she had decided to bunk off early and walk from the office on Victoria Street through St James's Park to Trafalgar Square for a more enlightened examination of the *Supper at Emmaus, Boy Bitten by a Lizard* and *Salome Receives the Head of John the Baptist*. Fortuitously, Nisha's recent, acrimonious breakup with Doug from Financial Control had meant that she was both instantly available and disposed to escape from the office with her.

Just as she was gazing at *Emmaus* and trying to remember what the art historian had said about the difference between this Jesus and its counterpart in the Pinacoteca di Brera version (something to do with his facial hair?), a museum guide drew up just next to her, in front of the *Boy Bitten by a Lizard*, followed by a small group of sexagenarian women. Gratified at the prospect of gleaning further insights into the masterpiece and its author, she cocked her head towards the group, ready to listen, whilst ostensibly continuing to look at *Emmaus*. She tuned out while the guide, a bearded, slightly-built man in his late thirties, gave his introductory spiel about Caravaggio's background – and then prepared to be enlightened.

Monumental disappointment ensued. Marnie, with the true arrogance of the neophyte, was exasperated by the man's apparently sketchy and superficial knowledge of Caravaggio's work – or, for that matter, art in general. Indeed, she was unsure whether his reluctance to use any remotely artistic terminology was a deliberate ploy to vulgarise his subject for the benefit of his audience or simply evidence of his shaky grasp of the subject. His apparent ignorance was compounded by his tedious and puerile insistence on referring to Caravaggio's much-documented penchant for young men. Why did everyone make such a big deal about that? And in any case, for every boy he seduced, he almost certainly bedded at least one prostitute, including his models – the lovely Fillide and the bewitching Lena. It was preposterous to label him gay: he was clearly bisexual. As she thought this, she could almost hear Rhiannon's voice tutting in her head from over a hundred miles away – for she would surely have reproved her mother's binarism. Fine. Caravaggio was *pansexual*. Whatever.

At one point the guide actually said:

'As you can see, the gestures the boy makes with his hands as he recoils from the lizard are a bit effeminate,' which raised a scatter of polite sniggers from the group.

For fuck's sake.

Taking a deep breath, she turned to her right, away from the guide, and attempted to concentrate on *Salome*.

'Now, people often ask what this picture means…'

Ah! Her interest was piqued again. She turned back to him: *Go on,* she thought. *This is your time to shine.* Or at least redeem yourself after that last, cretinous remark.

'…But, you know, sometimes a painting doesn't really mean anything. It's just an image that's captured, that's just meant to be appreciated at face value. There isn't always a "hidden meaning…"' (actual air quotes at this!)

She stared at him in astonishment, and then at his audience, at their reaction. A few were nodding sagely. Marnie was further incensed. They were content with *that*? That was all they came for? All they deserved?

Unable to contain herself any longer, she blurted: 'Vanitas!'

The group all turned to stare at her.

'I beg your pardon?' asked the guide.

'The… symbolism.' She cleared her throat. 'In the still life.'

A blank look from the group; embarrassment and a flash of annoyance in the guide's eyes.

'Sorry…You just said the painting doesn't mean anything. But it's full of symbols!'

'Well, I don't think…' the guide began awkwardly.

Ignoring him, she turned to the group. 'Er… in this type of painting, the fruit and flowers have a symbolic significance. In this case, the cherries and apples represent temptation – there's a… um… sexual subtext: if you succumb to temptation – well, you get your finger bitten! Not literally, of course: the bitten finger here is possibly a symbol for the… the phallus, the lizard's mouth is the vulva, so, the punishment for sins of the flesh is venereal dis –' She trailed off under the baffled and in some cases, scandalised stares of the ladies. *Know your audience!* she scolded herself.

'I mean…' she went on, 'Well, the point is, there's a moral message. It's called a vanitas painting.'

The sexagenarians stared back at her in silence.

Then, a woman in a pink North Face jacket and hiking boots ventured tentatively:

'Do you mean, like when they have skulls in paintings? As a…*memento mori*?'

'Yes!' Marnie whooped, beaming with relief and gratitude. 'Exactly!'

She would have loved to illustrate the point further by referencing other similar works by Caravaggio – *Bacchus, the Basket of Fruit* – waxing lyrical about the Eucharistic symbolism of the grapes, showing off her recently acquired knowledge on the hierarchy of genres, explaining how Caravaggio, in his quest for a high-profile patron in the upper echelons of the Catholic Church, when faced with an ostensibly mundane commission – a still life – had astutely managed to shoehorn a few symbols in, thus transcending the lowly subject matter and showcasing both his erudition and his religious sensibility.

Alas, it was not to be. Her enthralled audience (well, perhaps not enthralled, but she had definitely got their attention), was not to benefit from her insights, as she was soon to be rather unceremoniously ejected from the premises. For the weasel of a guide, clearly feeling castrated by Marnie's unsolicited intervention, had called security, claiming she was 'impersonating a guide-lecturer,' (*Please*, she thought, *you're not a bloody policeman or even a cab driver, just a nonentity with a degree from some sub-standard provincial art school and a lanyard)*, and disrupting the tour.

The security guard, to his credit, looked suitably sheepish as he approached her and seemed relieved at her willingness to comply, thus obviating the need to manhandle her. For Marnie, who always knew when she was beaten, went meekly, texting Nisha on her way downstairs with instructions to meet her outside and promises of imminent explanations.

Having substituted lattes in the Gallery's Espresso Bar with Pineapple Daquiris at All Bar One in Leicester Square, the friends discussed their respective museum experiences.

'What a *twat*!' said Nisha of the officious guide-lecturer, as a second round of cocktails arrived. And then, devouring a maraschino cherry and leaning across the table with a sudden look of concern: 'God, you're not barred for life, are you?'

Marnie shook her head. 'They just escorted me out. But honestly, it was worth it. It felt amazing, stepping in like that. I mean, you know me, I *never* usually–'

'Er…Can I help you?' Nisha inquired sharply of someone behind Marnie.

'Well, well, well….' said an ominously familiar voice. She turned around to behold the aforementioned Nonentity with Lanyard. 'If it isn't our resident Caravaggio connoisseur.' He all but spat out these last two words, his mouth distorting with disdain and sarcasm as it ejected the plosives.

'Oh…' said Marnie, flushing crimson. 'Hi.'

Then, fortified by alcohol and a reassuring wink from Nisha, she screwed up her courage.

'Look, I'm sorry about earlier, it's just that I felt you weren't really doing justice to the painting.' Ignoring his guffaw, she battled on: 'I just thought your… interpretation was a little limited. I mean, going on and on about irrelevant details such as Caravaggio's sexual preferences, whilst completely overlooking the symbolism –'

'Ah, yes, the *symbolism*!' he cried, raising arms skyward in a mock-histrionic gesture. 'Aren't we pleased with ourselves about *that*?' He bent down, his face inches from hers. 'Half an hour cramming on Wiki-fucking-*pedia* and you think you can do *my job*?'

'No, of course not, I... As a matter of fact, it wasn't Wikipedia...'

'Do you think I'm going to let some menopausal, pseudo-art buff make me look like –'

'Right, that's enough,' Nisha said sharply, on her feet now and ready for combat. 'Why don't you fuck off, mate.'

Other patrons were starting to turn and stare now, the scent of blood proving more potent and intoxicating than the alcohol in their happy hour drinks.

'Yeah,' said Marnie, standing up. In her ten-centimetre heels, she towered over him. 'Before *I* call security and accuse *you* of impersonating an art lover and expert when you're clearly just an insecure, misogynist, homophobic jobsworth, and have *you* chucked out!'

Lanyard said no more and, shaking his head contemptuously at the two women, shuffled off.

'Go on, call me a Paki, I *dare* you,' Nisha said under her breath as she glared at his departing back, 'gimme a real excuse to kick you in the bollocks.'

'And another thing!' Marnie shouted after him. 'For your information, I am *not* menopausal yet! In point of fact, I'm *perimenopausal*.'

'OK, Marn...Quit while you're ahead, eh?' Nisha muttered with a nervous laugh, signalling to the waitress for another round.

'I don't get that insult,' said Marnie, sitting down and shaking her head. 'It's some bizarre sub-category of misogyny. I mean, if it's just a synonym for old, fair enough. But if it's a dig based on the fact that we're no longer menstruating, how does that work? I mean, he's probably the sort that thinks women are slaves to their cycles – a seething mass of hormones – so surely he'd be grateful when we stop bleeding?'

Nisha shrugged. 'Fuck knows.' She raised her glass. 'Cheers.'

'Oh no...' said Marnie, looking at her phone in dismay.

'What's up?'

'Just got an email from Kate. Our whole department's been summoned by HR next Tuesday.'

'Ah.... Well, that don't necessarily mean anything bad.'

'Come on, Neesh. You don't believe that. Ever since that scandal in Italy broke out, it's been going from bad to worse: we're haemorrhaging clients all over Europe – you know that – and they're desperately trying to make cuts wherever they can. It's different for you lot in Sales, you're safe – for now – but they've started a major cull everywhere else: IT, HR, Marketing… I guess it's our turn now.'

'But they'll never give you the boot! Without you they'll have to Google bloody Translate all their press releases! Look, try not to think the worst, yeah? Drink up.'

Marnie obliged. By the time she got to Paddington Station an hour later – just in time for the 17:05 back to Bristol – she was half-cut and in a decidedly morose and pessimistic frame of mind.

CHAPTER EIGHTEEN

Royal Leamington Spa, September 2019

'What's this fad with tracing ancestors about?' asked Rhiannon.

It was a grey Saturday afternoon and she and Gulliver were lying in bed in his house in Rugby Road sharing a post-coital bottle of Argentinian Cabernet Sauvignon.

Seeing his puzzled look, she briefly apprised him of the article she had sent her mother about the man's search for his birth parents and Marnie's own attempts at tracking down her biological father.

'I didn't know your mother was adopted.'

She frowned at him. 'Why *would* you? Anyway, I just don't *get* this craze with genealogy. You would not believe the number of websites, Facebook groups, forums, TV programmes, all dedicated to family trees… I mean – why?'

'Well, Lacan would say –'

'Bugger Lacan,' she said dismissively. 'What's *your* take on it?'

He turned onto his side, propping himself up on his elbow.

'Well, first of all, there's nothing remotely modern or fad-like about it. It's not a product of the modern era: digital technology has merely facilitated genealogical research. But the need to maintain a link with one's forebears has always existed, everywhere. It's actually one of the few things that all civilisations from all ages have in common. Ancestor worship is a fundamental part of religions across the globe and throughout the ages: in Taoism, Hinduism with the Sraddha ritual, the Day of the Dead in Mexico…'

She nodded thoughtfully, then interjected suddenly: 'Got any chocolate?'

He looked at her quizzically.

'You know – sweet stuff, made from a bean native to the Amazon basin. The Aztecs worshipped it – or something – tastes good, releases endorphins…'

'Ah, *that* chocolate. I should have a box of Belgian chocolates knocking around somewhere. They were a present from a colleague in the Maths department but I haven't opened them yet.'

Her eyes widened. 'Now, you're talking! Can we?'

'Be my guest. They should be on my desk in the study.'

'Brill!' she leapt to her feet and jumped down naked from the bed. 'Chocolate and red wine is an *orgasmic* pairing, you know. In fact, chocolate and anything red: red berries, for example.'

'There's a raspberry bush in the garden; should be ready for harvesting now.'

She spun round and cried: 'My cup runneth over! Let's have a chocolate and red food picnic – right here, right now!'

'Why not?' he said, amused and endeared by her childlike delight and gluttony.

'Where in the garden, exactly?' she called out from the landing.

'In the bottom left corner, by the hydrangeas.'

'The hy-what?'

He laughed. 'I see horticulture is not among your considerable panoply of talents.'

She came back and stood in the bedroom doorway.

'Come on, Gull, I spent most of my life in a flat in Paris. Don't be a dick.'

He smiled. 'The bush with the big mauve flowers.' He nodded towards his bathrobe hanging on the back of the door. 'You might want to cover up first. My next-door neighbour's a dirty old man.'

'Takes one to know one,' she muttered, slipping on the robe and padding back out of the bedroom.

Five minutes later, just as he had shifted onto his stomach, his head towards the foot of the bed facing the door, she returned with an open Tupperware container full of freshly picked raspberries in one hand and the box of chocolates in the other. After placing both on the bed beside him, she shed the robe and joined him.

'So,' she said, her mouth full of raspberry and ganache, 'Where were we? Oh yeah... family trees. '"Who do you think you are?"' She snorted. 'People feeling special because their great-grandmother was knobbed by a member of some obscure branch of the nobility, or their great-great-great-uncle was hanged as a highwayman. It's pathetic. Self-indulgent, narcissistic and bourgeois. I tell you, if people spent half as much time looking outside their little lives and trying to solve real problems – climate change, social injustice – as they do navel-gazing, the world wouldn't be in quite such a dismal state.'

He reached out and stroked the curve of her hip with the back of his forefinger.

105

'I think you're being a little harsh. After all, it's a perfectly reasonable and natural desire to know where we come from. You've always known who your birth parents are, you take it for granted. You don't know what it's like not to know.'

She shook her head vehemently. 'It's nothing to do with that. Even if I had been adopted, I wouldn't care. That's the point: I see identity from a purely psychological perspective. It's not about blood; that doesn't define us. We're defined by our experiences – good and bad – and how we deal with them, how they affect us. By our choices, our acts.' She paused to scoop up a handful of raspberries with one hand whilst extending her wine glass to him for a refill with the other. 'The existentialists were spot-on. You know, Sartre used the example of a paper knife to illustrate –'

'Thank you, I am familiar with the paper knife analogy,' he said mildly.

She shrugged and helped herself to a curl of chocolate-covered candied orange peel and washed it down with a swig of wine. 'I'm a firm believer in free will. Determinism is a total cop-out. Hmmm...' she moaned, 'fuck me, that's good.'

'You know,' he said, his hand travelling lazily across her stomach and up towards her breasts, 'I really don't see how you expect us to conduct a serious philosophical discussion on existentialism versus determinism if you persist in trying to arouse me again.'

Ignoring this, she said, 'It's like JPS said: "*L'existence précède l'essence.*"'

'Hmm...' said Gulliver reflectively. 'I find myself torn between reprimanding you for showing off by quoting Sartre in the original, and encouraging it because it's preposterously sexy.'

She eyed him mischievously. 'Really? Well, I wish I'd known that before...' Licking chocolate off her fingertips, she stood on all fours over him, her back arching down towards him teasingly, and said: "'*SNCF. À nous de vous faire préférer le train.*"'

'My French is a bit rusty but I'm fairly sure that's not Sartre anymore.'

She shook her head. 'It's an advert for the national railways.'

Grasping her hips with both hands, he pulled her down onto him: 'Fine. That works too.'

Laughing, she pulled away and scrambled off him, and, gathering two raspberries, lay on her back beside him and placed a berry on each nipple.

'*Allons, enfants de la patrie...*' she sang, as he bent his head to her breasts.

⋈⫶⋈

It was a crisp, cool, dry Saturday afternoon and Marnie had taken herself out for a walk on Brandon Hill to clear her head.

She had never lost a job before. Never; not during the series of menial tasks she had performed during her youth and student years; not in her many years as a translator, first doing hackwork for agencies – ID and admin documents – before landing her first corporate gig as an inhouse translator and website content editor for a small comms agency, then her second, better-paid position with DigInnova at their HQ in the suburbs of Paris, where she had specialised in IT and digital and had worked for eleven years before transferring to their UK office after she split with Luc and moved back. They had admittedly been most accommodating about this, even acquiescing to her wish to be based in Bristol, travelling to the office in London once a week and working from home the rest of the time – on the understanding that she would remain available for the annual executive seminar and the occasional event at the Paris HQ.

It is of course often cited as one of the chief causes of stress in life – losing one's job – along with divorce, moving house and bereavement. As far as the comparison with divorce went, Marnie's being made redundant had been a far more brutal and shocking experience than her relatively civilised and mutually desired separation from Luc three years before.

But her own, uncommonly amicable divorce aside, the more she replayed that humiliating interview with HR, the more disturbing and absurd parallels she began to see between a romantic breakup and parting ways with one's employer. Thus, when her Line Manager, Kate, and Felix the HR Director, after telling her she had done a great job for the past fourteen years but times were hard so they had to part ways, went on to say that they would always need a good translator and how would she feel about continuing to work with them on a freelance basis, it was rather like a husband saying to his wife after years of marriage that he no longer loved her, but a man had his needs and she was good in bed, so how about a quickie every now and then, no strings attached? (Oh, but you can't stay for breakfast.)

Extending the analogy further, she thought of those colleagues who had been fobbed off with vague promises of positions opening up elsewhere in the organisation, and who, after a series of humiliating and soul-destroying enquiries and interviews in various other departments were either offered poorly paid roles that were way beneath their abilities and qualifications, or simply informed that all recruitments were frozen due to budget cuts. This ordeal was akin to a husband informing his wife he was walking out on her after over a decade of connubial bliss, but that there might be a bloke in his office who'd give her one.

Bastards, she thought bitterly as she gazed up at Cabot Tower. She thought of the absurd, inhuman language employed by HR in such situations, the grotesque euphemisms: *we're letting you go; we have to terminate you* – as though she were an unwanted foetus.

By some Herculean feat of poise and restraint, she had fought back the tears and anger throughout her termination interview, had barely even spoken at all, other than monosyllables to convey her acknowledgement and understanding. It was part shock, part prudence: some instinct, subsequently corroborated by advice from various friends and colleagues she had consulted, had told her to remain dispassionate and non-committal throughout the proceedings. Having accomplished this, she had risen, looked Felix and then Kate in the eyes and shaken their hands, before retreating without a word. After sobbing briefly in the Ladies', she had splashed cold water on her face and followed Kate's advice to take the rest of the afternoon off. As her train back to Bristol was not until 17:32, she called Nisha, who had promptly taken her out to drown her sorrows at a pub behind the office. She had also texted Val, who called her back an hour later when she came out of her meeting – by which time Marnie and Nisha were just starting on their second bottle of Pinot Grigio.

'Where are you?' Val had asked.

'Having a drink with Nisha from Sales.'

Val, who had never met Nisha but privately believed her to be a nefarious and corrupting influence on her friend, said: 'What, the Essex girl? That lush who's shagging the bloke from Accounts?'

Before Marnie could protest that the young man in question was from Financial Control and that they were no longer an item, Val, with her usual calm pragmatism, instructed her friend to get herself to West Hampstead, forget her train home and stay the night with her and Jolyon and the kids. Marnie, still too stunned – and slightly tipsy – to argue, had obeyed, getting the Victoria line to Green Park, then switching to the Jubilee line and arriving at Val and Jolyon's end-of-terrace Victorian house in Solent Road just before six.

From the moment she stepped over the threshold, she had been enveloped in a wave of overwhelming kindness, solicitude and efficiency that brought forth a fresh wave of tears. After husband and wife both hugged her warmly, they ushered her into the comfortable drawing room and sat her down on the sofa, then Val went off to make tea whilst Jolyon began dispensing legal advice. Had she been in touch with a lawyer yet?

'Of course not, Joly,' Val called out from the kitchen. 'She's only just found out; she's barely had time to register it, let alone consider her options.'

Jolyon immediately began scrolling through his phone contacts. 'This woman's formidable,' he said. 'Specialises in employment law.'

'Oh, right…' said Marnie. 'Well, I don't yet know if I'm going to go down that road –' But he was already calling the formidable employment lawyer: 'Beattie. Jolyon Appelbaum from Latimer & Thorpe. How are you? Yes, it has… Listen…' she didn't hear the rest as he stepped out into the hall. He occasionally popped his head around the door to ask Marnie various questions – how long she had worked for the company, what kind of contract she had – information which he subsequently passed onto Beattie. Ten minutes later, when Marnie was sipping her tea, he returned.

'She thinks you have a solid case based on what I've told her. You'll have an even better one if you can persuade some of your colleagues who also got the b –' he caught Val's stern look and checked himself, '– who were also made redundant to come on board. Anyway, if you do decide to go that way – and, for what it's worth, I think you should – call her. I'll text you her details.'

Marnie had merely nodded dumbly as Jolyon gently took the mug of tea out of her hands, placed it on the coffee table and said softly: 'now, let's get you a real drink.'

Two weeks had now passed since that day. She began climbing the spiral staircase to the top of Cabot Tower, hoping that the view of her beloved city would soothe her.

And for a moment it did. When she had decided to move back here after twenty years in France, it was not just the typical picture-postcard images that had lured her back – Christmas Steps; the Suspension Bridge; Brandon Hill; the brightly-coloured Victorian houses in Clifton Wood; the many elegant Georgian terraces typically associated with nearby Bath but which also abounded in certain areas of Bristol. For despite the undeniable charm of these sights, it was the memory of her very first impressions of the city all those years ago that had drawn her. When she was sixteen, her mother had been offered a job with a consultancy firm in Bristol and moved there from rural Hampshire, where the Wades had lived until Fay and Martin divorced. Marnie's father still lived in that county, although now in the suburbs of Southampton, whilst Guy and Nova had purchased two acres of land in the New Forest with an eighteenth-century water mill they were currently renovating. When her parents had decided to have Marnie sit her A-levels in a more academically challenging environment than that offered by St. Ursula's, she had opted to follow her mother to Bristol and attend a day school there. With hindsight, Marnie acknowledged this decision as the first important one of her life, the first steps she had taken to shaping her own destiny. It had not occurred to her at the time to ask either of her parents' opinion on the matter: for the first time, she had an opportunity to control the course of her life, and she intended to seize it. It was for this reason that she and Luc had given Rhiannon the same choice when they had split: stay in Paris, live with her father and do her baccalaureate at a local school, or move to the UK with her, attend an English school and sit her A-levels. Despite her devotion to her father and her attachment to her friends, the nearly sixteen-year-old Rhiannon had decided that she needed a radical change of scenery, and opted to join Marnie in Bristol.

As for Marnie's own defection as a teenager, her father had warned her of the perils and temptations of city life: compared with the sheltered, bucolic existence she had hitherto led, first in the village in Northern Hampshire, a stone's throw away from Jane Austen's house, then at boarding school in the Sussex Downs, Martin Wade saw Bristol as a seething nest of juvenile delinquency, drugs, violence, poverty and racial unrest (the St Paul's riots in 1980 had made the headlines eight years before).

But for Marnie, it was intoxicating: the racial and social diversity – conspicuously absent in rural Hampshire – the shops, the arthouse cinemas, the student population. And the music scene: for it was the era of the Bristol Sound: Massive Attack and Portishead and Tricky. Not that Marnie was at the beating heart of this vibrant urban scene: she and her mother lived in a suburb called Fishponds, in a semi-detached house not unlike the one Marnie was to purchase and live in with Rhiannon almost thirty years later. But the city centre, with its promise of excitement and adventure and culture, was just a short bus ride away.

As she stood now at the top of the tower named for the famous Venetian navigator Giovanni Caboto – better known by the anglicised version of his name – Marnie thought of the other illustrious people, past and present, whose names were associated with the city: Edward Colston. Isambard Kingdom Brunel. Cary Grant. Banksy. A myriad of other things came to her mind when she thought of Bristol: Art and music. Seafaring and maritime prowess. Cider and slave-trading.

She descended the tower and left the park via Upper Byron Place, then, remembering she was out of milk, went around the Triangle to Sainsbury's. Walking back down Jacobs Wells Road she went past Queen Elizabeth's Hospital and, gazing up at the dramatic, imposing edifice, which looked like a cross between a Scottish castle and a Victorian asylum or prison, she remembered the one and only time she had set foot inside it thirty years before. The Upper Sixth classes of her school had been invited to a ball at QEH – then only a boys' school. Marnie had met a pretty, sullen-looking blond boy whose name she could no longer remember, and after a brief conversation, followed him upstairs to the games room where they had indulged in half an hour of heavy petting on the pool table.

The following Monday at school, she discovered that she had been inexplicably ostracised overnight. After a morning of being subjected to accusatory glares in the corridors and pointing and whispering in the library, she made some inquiries among her friends, and was informed that the boy she had dallied with was the ex-boyfriend of Katharine Palmer – the Head Girl and most popular girl in the school. Remembering the many other such incidents she and her peers had been subjected to at Clifton High School for Girls – the vicious rumours, the snide comments, the slut-shaming, the anonymous letter someone had once sent to Marnie's mother saying Marnie and her best friend at the time were lesbians – something which Fay Wade had laughed off – Marnie reflected now that there were fewer species more narrow-minded, pettier or more intolerant than the provincial, middle-class, sexually-frustrated adolescent English female: the product of a parochial, middle-brow education by *Daily Telegraph-* and *Daily Mail-* reading, net curtain-twitching parents in some backwater Tory stronghold.

Turning her back on QEH and the unpleasant memories it had conjured up, she crossed the street onto Lower Clifton Hill and fifteen minutes later arrived at Dowry Square. After Rhiannon had gone up to university the previous year, Marnie had sold the three-bedroom semi in Easton-in-Gordano they had shared for the past two years and for the same price had purchased a two-bed basement flat in a Grade II Georgian building in Hotwells. It was near the harbour, and near enough leafy Clifton, with its university buildings and handsome Victorian and Georgian terraces – but without the extortionate Clifton prices. Although Luc had never seen her flat, she felt sure he would have approved of the elegant building, for he had a horror of red brick, which is why he was so dismissive of much of the architecture of the British Isles: he admired what he had seen of Bristol precisely because of its abundance of handsome stone architecture. He would have been less enthusiastic, however, about the lower ground floor location: like many French people, he deplored the idea of living underground, found it dark, dingy and oppressive. But even he would surely have admitted that the refurbishments the previous owner had undertaken, with the huge lightwells everywhere, made it a more than tolerable living space. There was a tiny yard for the cats to run around in, with barely enough room for a small wrought iron table and two chairs, but she had access to the communal garden in the middle of the square.

As she was putting the milk in the fridge, she received a What's App from Dave:

You never told me you were a social media phenomenon! I can't believe I've only just seen this!

Baffled, she replied with a series of question marks. Seconds later, a YouTube link came through: the title of the video was *Heckler hijacks Caravaggio tour at National Gallery*.

Feeling the blood drain from her face, Marnie clicked on the video. The amateur footage showed the group of elderly ladies, the rodent-faced guide, pink with indignation, and Marnie, in a black trouser suit saying: 'the fruit and flowers have a symbolic significance. In this case, the cherries and apples represent temptation – there's a… um… sexual subtext…'

One of the ladies in the tour must have been filming the guided tour and had inevitably immortalised Marnie's performance. Gasping, she hit 'pause,' and her eye drifted – unwisely – to the list of comments below. These ranged from encouraging – even adulatory (*'You go, girl!'; 'This woman is brilliant!'*) to the inevitable lambasting from trolls: *'What a smug bitch'; 'Karen goes to the museum. LOL,'* etc.

She messaged back to Dave: *Am mortified. Can't believe someone filmed that.*

He replied: *Rubbish. No such thing as bad publicity. Enjoy.* Then: *PS: I thought you were fucking spectacular. Possible new vocation?*

The exchange was interrupted by her phone ringing. It was Beattie, her lawyer. She sounded elated, triumphant.

'I've got good news. They agreed to everything! They did *not* see this coming.'

'What?'

'I'll talk you through the details later but, long story short, you'll be getting a bloody big cheque soon.'

CHAPTER NINETEEN

Dave had driven straight from work to pick up his sister Marie and her husband, and thence on to Auntie Tish's house in Prosperous. During the drive from Dublin, his brother-in-law interjected at regular intervals with his usual barbed little comments that passed for attempts at conversation: ('I see ye're still keeping the X5 going, so?') How the fuck was he supposed to respond to that? And, as Dave parked the offending vehicle in front of Auntie Tish's house:

'Clare not joining us?'

Marie, in the passenger seat, seeing her brother's fingers tightening on the steering wheel, lay a placating hand on his arm and shot a warning glance back at her husband, who merely shrugged and gazed morosely out of the window.

'Who's waked from home these days, anyway?' said Dave moodily as they walked up the garden path. 'Jesus Christ, it's 2019.'

'More's the pity,' said Paul sententiously. 'Yet another beautiful Irish tradition that's being obliterated.'

'Yeah, well so was the Potato Famine, but we've managed without that for the past hundred and seventy years,' muttered Dave.

Marie chuckled but was silenced by her husband's stony, disapproving glare.

'I didn't even know they were that devout,' Dave went on. 'I tell you, if they start fuckin' *keenin'*, I'm out of there.' Marie dissolved into giggles, grabbing her brother's arm for support.

Paul stopped dead and turned his censorious, glowering glare upon them.

'For Christ's sake, will ye show some respect!' he hissed.

'Sorry,' said Marie, 'nervous laughter. The emotion, you know.'

'Well, get it out of yer system before we go in.'

With their heads hanging in a show of mock penitence, they followed him up to the house like scolded children.

Auntie Tish greeted them at the door dressed in a dark grey wool dress under a moth-eaten black cardigan. Her watery blue eyes were puffy and grief stained. She kissed her niece and nephew without a word and ushered them into the house. A few feet behind her in the dark over-heated hall hovered her sister Aiofe – Dave's mother – and Tish's daughter, Méabh.

Méabh's was the first vulva Dave had ever seen. It was in the summer of 1991 and they were spending their holidays in the Aran islands, as they did every year for about ten years. She had caught him and her brother Fionn having a pissing contest in a cave on the beach and later that day, Dave – already bold at the age of eight – cornered her as she was going into the bathroom and declared that it was only fair that he get to see *her* thing now after everything she had witnessed. She had stared at him defiantly, and, without a word, lifted up her cotton sundress and pulled down her pants.

She was now, at forty-one, a successful speech therapist with her own thriving practice, married to a hedge fund manager and living in a huge, gated property in Sandycove next door to the bassist from a famous Irish rock band. There was an Aston Martin Vanquish and a Jaguar E-type in the garage and a Bacon triptych in the study. She was tall and handsome in an angular, slightly androgynous way, with high cheekbones, a long nose and dark brown hair cut in a sleek pageboy. This evening she was wearing a well-cut black trouser suit that looked like a name and high-heeled black patent court shoes. She looked out of place in this poky terraced house, with her impeccable designer suit and that stiff, imperious way she held herself, her back ramrod straight. Her grief was more contained than her mother's.

'Hello Dave,' she said, 'thank you for coming.' Dave hovered awkwardly in front of her and then kissed her swiftly on the cheek. 'I'm sorry about your dad.'

'Thank you. He's in the front room if you want to go and see him. Then go through to the kitchen and help yourself to a drink. The others have congregated in there.'

She motioned behind her. Dave nodded and proceeded dutifully into the front room. The room had remained the same for as long as he could remember: there was the same threadbare maroon carpet, the hulking Welsh dresser that seemed to take up half the room, the pair of hideous china Pekinese dogs that sat on each side of the clock on the mantelpiece, the ducks on the wall.

Except that this time, instead of sitting in his favourite armchair by the fireplace reading the racing results in the paper and chain-smoking, Uncle Oscar was lying in a coffin. As he beheld the dead man's waxy white face, Dave was briefly reminded of his own father's wake five years ago, at the funeral parlour. He and Clare were still happy at the time. Declan was a baby and had recently been baptised – an occurrence that had been the subject of prolonged

114

debate and controversy. Both Dave and Clare were agnostic but had decided to capitulate in the face of family pressure for the sake of Dave's then dying father.

'He can always get de-baptised when he's older,' Dave had observed. In response to Clare's quizzical and rather sceptical glance, he had continued:

'No, really. It's a thing. You can download a form off the Internet. It basically says you wish to give up a religion you don't believe in and had thrust upon you before you were old enough to decide for yourself.'

'Does it include a clause about embracing Satan again?' a bemused Clare had asked.

She had been dressed in a simple black shift dress that was perfectly chaste with its turtleneck and knee-length hem but showed off her firm round rump to perfection. Clare had a lovely arse. Dave remembered feeling guilty about feeling horny at his father's wake. Oscar, naturally, had been at his brother-in-law's wake.

'He was a fine man, Dave,' he had said, clasping Dave's shoulder.

Dave had always had the rather uneasy impression that Oscar preferred him, his nephew, to his own son, Fionn; he had practically admitted as much once after a few Jameson too many. Fionn had always been sensitive and rather bookish: not what Oscar deemed a 'man's man.' As a child he had been sickly and wheezing, always preferring his train sets or model aeroplanes to rugby or hurling. Dave, on the other hand, had always been a natural athlete and had grown up to drink like a fish, pursue women relentlessly and become captain of his rugby team.

As for Fionn, after graduating from Trinity he had successfully co-run a management consultancy firm for a number of years until his partner did a moonlight flit. The business had gone into receivership, Fionn had had a breakdown and briefly moved back in with his parents. He now bought and sold tin soldiers on the Internet.

'Loada bollocks,' his father had said at the time. 'If you can make a living doing that, then I'm the fuckin' bishop o' Cork.'

There Fionn was, in the kitchen doorway; tall and lanky, he had the sort of colouring that gave the impression of being watered down: pale green eyes, almost translucent milky complexion, insipid yellow-orange hair. He looked up and nodded to his cousin.

'Dave,' he said simply. Dave expressed condolences, shook his hand, then after a few minutes' small talk offered to fetch them both drinks. Fionn declined, slightly raising the bottle of lager he had dangling from the end of his fingers. In the kitchen, having helped himself to a can of Guinness, Dave leaned awkwardly with his back to the kitchen sink and began to sip.

'Do you fancy a real drink?' said a deep, husky voice.

115

He looked up to see Méabh.

'I'm driving.'

'Yes, well, I'm not going anywhere tonight,' she muttered, and brushed past him on her way to the larder.

The scent she exuded was one of luxury and affluence: Chanel *Coco* (*eau de parfum*, not *toilette*), expensive wrinkle cream – the kind that is made from exotic, barbaric, toxic-sounding ingredients such as snake venom and iguana foetuses – and the leather upholstery of her Jaguar E-Type. She returned with a bottle of Redbreast 15 Year.

'Where are you staying tonight?'

'With Marie and Paul.'

'In Newbridge?'

'That's right.'

She turned around to take a tumbler from the draining board and poured whiskey into it. While her back was turned, she asked: 'So, how have you been?'

Dave laughed humourlessly. 'I'm sure you've heard about my… circumstances.'

Méabh turned slowly round and nodded. 'Mammy told me. I'm sorry. I always liked Clare.'

'Really?'

She took a sip of whiskey. 'Yes. You seemed to suit one another. When's the baby due?'

'March.'

'Do you know what it is?'

A fucking mistake is what it is, Dave thought. 'The sex, you mean? No. Clare wants it to be a surprise and… well, I'm not really bothered either way.'

'Long as it's healthy, eh?'

Dave nodded. He found the platitude curiously comforting; it certainly made a change from the torrent of censure and sermonising he was surely to expect from certain other members of his family. As if on cue, he heard Ciaran out in the hallway. His elder brother appeared in the kitchen door and greeted Méabh. He was wearing stone-coloured chinos with perfect creases and a white shirt buttoned up to the top. At forty-four, Ciaran was to most observers – as harsh as it sounded – a second-rate version of Dave: he had the same ice-blue eyes and jet-black hair – albeit in rapidly diminishing quantities – and was just as tall but flabby where Dave was taut and muscular. His chin was a little weak and he had broken his nose one too many times from his rugby days, whereas Dave's features had remained flawless and intact.

The brothers shook hands stiffly and exchanged pleasantries about their respective business affairs. As by far the most pious of the Mullan children, Ciaran had seemed destined for the priesthood. Yet instead of entering the seminary, he had trained as a Licenced Conveyancer. He was a bachelor and, as far as Dave knew, had never been in a relationship with a woman. Before long conversation inevitably turned to what Ciaran saw as Dave's callous desertion of his expectant wife.

'You're not reconsidering your position, so?' he ventured.

Dave sighed. 'It's not as simple as that, is it? Even if I wanted to go back – which I don't – Clare wouldn't have me.'

'Then you should beg for her forgiveness.'

He resented his brother's obvious assumption that he, Dave, was the guilty party. Admittedly, he had bedded (although not, as it turned out, impregnated) another woman, but Ciaran didn't know that.

'Yeah, right. Listen, if I ever need to sell my flat, I'll come to you for advice but I'm sure you won't take offence if I don't seek your counsel where marriage or relationships are concerned.'

His brother was about to respond when Clodagh, the eldest and Dave's favourite sibling, intervened.

'Jesus, are you two at it already? Ciaran, you're not giving him the third degree again, are you?' Before he could respond she kissed both brothers on the cheek. Dave hugged her warmly back. She was wearing an ankle-length black belted cardigan over a creased grey linen shirt dress. A dozen bangles jingled on her fleshy forearms and a silver pendant lay against her ample bosom. She wore her shoulder-length dark hair, already liberally streaked with grey, pinned back in an untidy bun and her face was unadorned by make-up.

'Mam's looking for you,' she said to Ciaran. After he sloped off, muttering something under his breath, Clodagh turned back to Dave and rolled her eyes.

'God love him, but I thought you could do with a break!'

'What's his fuckin' problem?' Dave muttered. 'I didn't ask for his opinion.'

Clodagh shrugged. 'He's just unhappy. Poor man hasn't had a shag since the Divorce Referendum.'

She linked her arm through his and said, 'I'm going out the back for a ciggie; keep me company?'

Outside on the tiny patio, they sat on plastic garden chairs, Dave sipping his ale and Clodagh lighting a cigarette. After briefly reminiscing about childhood holidays spent with Oscar and Patricia and Méabh and Fionn, and discussing the latest on Clare's pregnancy and

117

birthing plan (as a fellow nurse, Clodagh had a professional interest in such matters), they fell into a comfortable, companionable silence for a few minutes.

Almost three months had passed since Dave had got the results of Tina's paternity test. The child – a girl, as the CVS had also revealed – was not Dave's, so presumably her Uncle Vinny's, yet despite this and Tina's fears about the perils of consanguinity, was perfectly healthy.

He had never imagined that he would experience anything but overwhelming relief upon learning that the child was not his. And yet, when it was confirmed that he was not to be saddled with the burden of fatherhood to the child of a woman he had never loved nor even liked, he had found himself incapable of jubilation. Instead he was engulfed with a mixture of overpowering pity for Tina and shame at having taken advantage of that poor, simple, ill-used girl. His rather limited, and essentially testosterone-fuelled antenna had failed to detect the loneliness and self-loathing behind her flirtatiousness, the vulnerability masked by her brazenness. He had not looked beyond his male ego being flattered.

He had seen her only once since the day they had received the results. He had called her a week after the results had come to ask after her and they had arranged to meet at Christ Church (her choice of venue). They had gone down to the crypt, and by the mummified cat and rat, Dave, in a momentary and uncharacteristic surge of guilt-fuelled altruism, had thought of offering her money, or even to beat up her satyr of an uncle – anything to assuage his feeling of helplessness and worthlessness.

And yet something held him back: cowardice? Selfishness? Or merely a realistic, pragmatic sense of self-preservation, a need to distance himself from the squalid mess that was her life. He could not fix Tina. She had been broken long before he briefly drifted into her life. He had clasped her arm and said goodbye softly.

Clodagh and Dave re-joined the others inside. People were standing around with cups of tea, glasses of whiskey and plates laden with ham sandwiches, frozen sausage rolls and mini-quiches, pickled onions and crisps. New additions to the gathering included Oscar's sister and her children and Tish and Oscar's next-door neighbour, John. John was something called a horticultural therapist, which, as far as Dave could make out, involved teaching recovering smackheads how to plant azaleas. Walking out of the kitchen into the hallway, Dave saw Tish sobbing quietly in her sister's arms in the dining room. For a moment Dave's eyes met those of his mother's over Tish's heaving, crumpled form and his mother smiled sadly at him. Fionn was sitting at the bottom of the stairs talking to Michael, one of his cousins from Oscar's side of the family. Michael was inquiring about the profitability of selling toy soldiers on the

Internet and Fionn was explaining that his business model consisted in buying up whole regiments for a bargain price and selling them off individually – and at considerable profit – to various collectors.

Dave suddenly experienced an acute need for a strong drink. Finding Marie in the front room talking to an elderly woman with a blue rinse, he asked her how many drinks she had had.

'Just a sherry. Why?'

Pushing the keys to the X5 into her hands, Dave said, 'Best switch to orange juice.'

Before she could protest – which, given her saint-like disposition, was highly unlikely – he kissed her on the cheek and threaded through the throng of mourners to the kitchen where Méabh's bottle of Redbreast was standing on the worktop. After pouring a few fingers into the only clean receptacle he could find – a chipped mug with the face of Pope John Paul II on it – he made his way to the downstairs lavatory, and, finding it occupied, decided to use the upstairs bathroom. Just as he was heading for the stairs, his phone beeped. Taking it out of his pocket, he saw 'Family Secret' on the screen: it was Marnie, reiterating her condolences and assuring him of her moral support.

As he made his way up the stairs and felt the comforting sweet burning of the whiskey coursing through him, he found himself musing about Marnie and her unexpected eruption in his life two years ago. He had reached out to her at a complicated time in his life (was there any other kind?): Clare had just had a miscarriage and this event and the ways they had each dealt with it had thrown the flaws in their marriage, which until then they had succeeded in ignoring, into stark and ugly relief. It was like shining a blacklight torch on ostensibly spotless hotel bed linen and suddenly seeing countless traces of bodily effluvia. In addition to this personal setback, he had lost his job with HVL two months before after they were taken over by an American group. Luckily, Valerian had headhunted him soon afterwards, but the brief period of stress and uncertainty had done little to ease the tension at home.

Marnie, for her part, was also at a turning point in her life: she had recently divorced and moved back to the UK with her daughter after nearly two decades in France, only to witness the collective lunacy of the Brexit referendum. Amid their respective personal crises, a strange sort of bond had grown between them. As a man used to categorising and compartmentalising almost every aspect of his life and the people in it, he found himself incapable of qualifying their rather peculiar relationship: it was unlike any that he had with any of his other cousins – or for that matter, with his siblings. He could almost call it friendship, only Dave didn't have female friends. Indeed, he was endowed with sufficient self-awareness to realise that he wasn't suited to platonic relationships with people of the opposite sex. He had never actively sought the company of women other than for the sole purpose of satisfying his primal biological urges, and the only other women in his entourage weren't friends: they were either just women he had not got around to bedding yet, or his friends' wives' or girlfriends – so, off limits anyway.

As he reached the top of the stairs, he saw Méabh swaying on the landing, a tumbler of whiskey between the manicured fingers of one hand whilst the other gripped the banister in an attempt to steady herself. She had removed the jacket of her trouser suit, revealing a sleeveless cream silk blouse. She sat down on the top stair and patted the carpet beside her. Dave obliged and joined her.

'How are you doing?' he asked gently.

She stared straight ahead of her and raised the glass to her lips.

'Is that a general inquiry into my physical and metaphysical wellbeing, or a particular question about how I am coping with my father's death?' she deadpanned.

'Both.'

'Well, as for Daddy, I'm as well as can be expected. As for the rest…' she made a vague sweeping gesture with her hand, causing the amber liquid to slosh perilously close to the brim of the glass, 'well, my husband doesn't fuck me anymore, but apart from that, I'm grand.' She brought the glass to her lips slowly and drank.

Dave almost flinched at the combination of intimate revelation and uncharacteristic profanity from this usually cool, reserved woman. He said nothing.

'And I really need to be *fucked* right now,' she went on in a dull, toneless voice, 'not for the …gratification or tenderness or intimacy – although God knows I could do with all of that – but just so I can *feel* something…feel something else, something other than this bottomless pit of …' And then she began sobbing, drawing up her knees and burying her face in them, her bony, milk-white shoulders heaving.

Still reeling from her unsolicited disclosure and further mortified by this equally unexpected effusion of emotion, Dave tentatively drew his arm around her. She stiffened and resisted but gradually yielded and leaned into his embrace. After a few moments, her shoulders became still and he felt her relax. She then took a deep breath and drew away from him, wiping her eyes with a paper napkin.

'Right,' she said, clearing her throat and composing herself, 'I'd better get downstairs and relieve Mammy. She's been sitting with Daddy for hours.'

'I can stay if you like,' he offered as she stood up. 'You know, all night. So you and your mam can get some rest.'

Altruism was a novel experience for Dave. It was rather like trying on a three-piece tweed suit in a shop: a momentary whim, a glimpse of what he could be. But ultimately it was not his style and he had no intention of buying it.

She shook her head. She was once again the old Méabh – cool, self-possessed, impeccably mannered. 'Fionn and Michael are helping, and John from next door, but thank you.'

He followed her downstairs, and as she went into the front room, he looked at the clock on the wall in the hallway: it showed a quarter past four. The clocks had been stopped, as a traditional mark of respect. Taking his dad's old fob watch out of his trouser pocket, he saw that it was nearly midnight.

A few minutes later, when the final respects had been paid and he was slumped in the back of the X5 while Marie started up the engine, he thought of poor Méabh: grieving, forsaken and untouched by her husband, childless, whose life was a bleak, loveless void. Suddenly he ached for the warm physical presence of another human being: he longed to hold his son in his arms, thought wistfully of burying his face in a woman's full, soft breasts and drifting to sleep, lulled by the gentle throb of her heartbeat beneath him. God, he couldn't remember the last time he had fallen asleep in a woman's arms, as opposed to withdrawing and then either jumping up and pulling his trousers back on or retreating to the other side of the bed with his back turned, waiting for her to leave. He suddenly yearned for that sense of peace and completeness and wondered if he would ever experience it again.

CHAPTER TWENTY

Bristol, November 2019

'Who's Amedeo, again?'

During their weekly chat on the phone, Marnie had told Val that Amedeo had recently called to say he was due to go to Paris in the new year to meet some potential investors in his start-up. As they had not seen each other in almost a year – nor would they be likely to again, at least in a professional context – and as Marnie had some time on her hands, not to mention her severance cheque burning a hole in her pocket, they had arranged that she would come out to Paris and join him for dinner during his stay.

But little did Val know when she made her ostensibly innocuous inquiry what a conundrum it raised: *Who was Amedeo?*

Who, indeed.

Quite apart from the complexity of the answer, the question itself was of course far from simple. It was a two-fold one: on the one hand, it meant, who was Amedeo, in terms of his identity, origins, his personality.

But, far more complicated, Marnie reflected, was the other question, namely: who, or what, is Amedeo to me? How could she define their relationship?

Strictly speaking, they were colleagues; at least, that was how they had started, over a decade ago, although referring to him as such seemed terribly reductive.

Work friend? Again, too simple, too limited, too superficial. The One That Got Away? No, that was far too melodramatic. And inaccurate. Something between the two? Was there such a thing? Straight Gay Best Friend?

The truth was, Marnie had long ago given up trying to label both the man and their relationship, having concluded that both defied categorisation. If absolutely pushed, however, she would have termed it a 'romantic friendship.' She rather liked this expression, and, when looking it up one day, had learned that it referred to: *"a very close but non-sexual relationship between friends, often involving a degree of physical closeness beyond that common in modern*

Western societies, for example holding hands, cuddling, sharing a bed, as well as open expressions of love for one another."

That was, she agreed, a fairly accurate description of their relationship.

As for Amedeo... He was just Amedeo. There was no one else like him, and certainly no one who filled the role in her life that he did.

While she was married, she had never allowed herself to think of him as anything but a friend and colleague, but even now that she was divorced, she found herself unable to look upon him as a potential lover. There was undoubtedly a bond between them, an intellectual affinity, a great deal of affection. But it was not sexual. And even if it were, there were a thousand reasons – geographical and professional, to name two – why they could not be together.

She remembered their first meeting back in April 2006, at the company's annual executive seminar in Morocco. Officially, it was a corporate event designed to inform the key stakeholders of the company strategy, strengthen team spirit and foster inter-departmental communication and networking; but it was essentially a huge, extravagant, alcohol-fuelled tax write-off jolly. The seventy-odd delegates, including the CEO, the top-tier managers from the thirteen countries DigInnova operated in, including Amedeo, who at the time was head of R&D for the Italian branch, and some support staff from marketing and comms, were put up in a five-star hotel near the Medina in Fez. Marnie, as was usual at such events, was there partly in her capacity as translator, partly to provide general support to her marketing colleagues for the general event organisation (and, she suspected wryly, for sheer ornamental value).

It was the first day of the seminar, and Marnie's then boss, the Comms & Marketing Director, Ghislaine Dessuant, had taken her aside whilst they were queuing at passport control at Rabat airport and told her in hushed tones that DigInnova was in the process of buying out its main competitor and they were preparing a press release. Consequently, later that day, whilst the other delegates were being taken on a guided tour of the company's call centre, Marnie spent the afternoon sitting outside the call centre under a palm tree – not in a palm grove or an oasis, but on an industrial estate just outside Rabat – translating the urgent and highly confidential press release. Ghislaine, meanwhile, stood a few feet away, speaking alternately on her mobile to the CEO and the company's PR agency. During these exchanges, numerous amendments and rewrites were made to the press release, which Ghislaine subsequently communicated orally to Marnie, who then adjusted the English version accordingly in real time.

The press release finally completed in both languages and issued, Marnie and Ghislaine, hot, dusty and exhausted, were driven to the hotel in Fez later in the afternoon. After checking in, Marnie had just enough time to dash up to her room, shower, change and go back downstairs to join the other delegates for cocktails in the bar.

It was there that she and Amedeo were introduced by a man called Santevecchi, who at the time was, at thirty-two, Italy's youngest ever Sales Director, but had since then clawed his way to the top of the Italian pecking order and was now Amedeo's boss. Marnie would despise Santevecchi if he weren't so absurd, if he did not conform so perfectly to the textbook, clichéd image of an Italian male. First, his physique: the tall, lean frame, deep olive skin, jet-black hair, full lips and piercing, liquid black eyes – which to Marnie looked as dead, soulless and predatory as a shark's – left her utterly cold, yet were deemed by an alarming majority of Marnie's female colleagues as handsome, even sexy. Then there was his ostentatious, flamboyant dress sense: he wore flashy tailored suits for business whilst the smart casual uniform he sported at such events as these was that of an arrested teenager (albeit one who had made a lot of money dealing crystal meth): skin-tight designer jeans, snowy-white designer trainers, silk shirts in pastel shades and tailored jackets with a silk handkerchief in the breast pocket. And then there was his gait: the confident strut of the Alpha male. The first time Marnie had met him, two years before, she had privately summed him up as a Gucci-upholstered walking penis.

He was invariably surrounded by a coterie of fawning cronies, some of whom worshipped and admired him, but most merely appeared terrified of him. He was, by all accounts, a born salesman, a gifted orator and charismatic leader, although Marnie was constantly astounded at how heavily the Italian Comms team relied on this charisma for their internal and external communications. Website, press releases, newsletters, social media posts: everything smacked of the cult of the personality, to a degree that would have made even Stalin blush.

Insignificant and unpleasant as he was, it is important to give such a detailed portrayal of Matteo Santevecchi to provide the context for Marnie's first impressions of Amedeo. For Amedeo was the anti-Santevecchi. To such an extent that the first time Marnie met him, she thought he was gay – not because he had any effeminate mannerisms. It was simply that Amedeo displayed none of his fellow Italian colleagues' brash sexism, with their relentless and unapologetic ogling: he never looked at her breasts when talking to her, never flirted with her.

In her defence, Marnie was not the kind of woman who assumed that any man who was not obviously attracted to her was a homosexual. But after several years working for a French company, years of attending these testosterone-fuelled corporate events, of casual sexual harassment, her values and judgement had been somewhat warped and blunted by the rampant, systemic sexism as personified by Santevecchi and so many others.

The objective truth was that Amedeo Di Meglio was cosmopolitan, urbane (she noted on that first evening that, when ordering drinks, he called a rum and coke 'Cuba Libre'), mild-mannered, somewhat reserved, and with that old-school gallantry she had rarely witnessed in men of his generation: later that night, for example, after dinner and drinks at a local restaurant, Marnie, Amedeo and two Dutch colleagues had shared a cab back to the hotel and Amedeo had leapt out to open the cab door for her. No one had ever done that for her.

On the last night of the seminar there was a sumptuous dinner at a restaurant in the Medina, after which half of the delegates had migrated to the hotel bar. After a gin and tonic, Marnie fancied a late-night swim in the hotel pool and asked if anyone else was up for it. There were no takers, but Amedeo offered to come and keep her company. So, after Marnie had finished her laps whilst Amedeo sat patiently by the pool, they sat on sun-loungers, talking and staring up at the stars. She only realised how late it was when the beguiling tones of the Isha rang out. They retired to their respective rooms and by the time Marnie went down to breakfast the next day she heard the Italian delegates had left for the airport on an early shuttle.

She felt a small surge of disappointment, thinking wistfully of the night before – the stars, the call to prayer, their quiet, easy companionship – when she heard an email notification on her phone and saw it was from Amedeo. The brief message, expressing his pleasure at meeting her and his regret at not having said goodbye, was the first of many emails, texts and WhatsApps they were to exchange over the years; and once or twice a year, they met at similar company events.

Later, his heterosexuality clearly established (he had been engaged once and had a string of other relationships with women), she saw subtle indications that he may have romantic feelings for her and wondered why he had never made a move on her. Knowing him, his strict principles had probably prevented him from doing so whilst she was still married to Luc. But when he still had not done so years after her divorce, she suspected it was shyness or fear of rejection. Then, over the years, in the course of their exchanged confidences of the more intimate kind, he told her of various conquests of his youth and she began to see a pattern form: he appeared to have been seduced by a number of extremely enterprising young women. Indeed, some of the stories seemed to Marnie to bear a suspicious resemblance to the scenarios of low-budget soft porn films: a hotel maid during a business trip to Vienna who had one day stripped before him and mounted him on his bed; a sensuous brunette he had encountered during a camping trip with a group of friends in his teens, who, one night during a sing-along around a campfire, had lured him into her tent under the pretext of needing help to locate a lost earring; the older woman (some sort of relative, she had gathered) who had taken his virginity.

It was then that Marnie realised that he was simply used to women taking the initiative, and perhaps this had made him somewhat passive and timorous.

Or, she reflected, she was reading the signs wrongly and he just didn't fancy her. Either way, it was just as well: she was glad nothing had disrupted the harmony and balance of their relationship.

In answer to Val's question, she began to give her a brief summary of her acquaintance with Amedeo.

'Oh, right,' said Val, recollection dawning. 'Of course, I see who you mean now. The gay guy?'

'Well, actually, he's not –' Marnie paused, laughed to herself, then said: 'Yeah, that's the one.'

⋈⫶⋈

Sandycove, Co. Dublin, 5 November 2019

As Méabh O'Neill Taylor stood in her beautiful, spacious, spotless kitchen – impeccably designed, superbly equipped (not that she herself would actually know what to do with the Thermomix, the La Cornue Flamberge Rôtisserie, or even the Le Creuset casserole dish – that was Imelda's domain), she tried to trace the timeline of the demise of her marriage.

She supposed it had begun with Sheridan's promotion a year ago. For once he had become Vice President, Private Equity Fund of Funds, he spent even less time at home – ostensibly working fourteen-hour days at the office, although God knows what he was doing half the time. When he did make an appearance at home, he was stressed, irritable and, quite often, drunk.

The next worrying development was the gradual dwindling then complete cessation of any form of sexual activity between them. For he had not been near her since July, when he had favoured her with two minutes of half-drunken intercourse in their four-poster bed at Galloways – the preposterous, sprawling country estate in Waterford he had felt the need to purchase in the wake of his promotion. She had lately given up attempting to lure him back to her bed: aside from the humiliation of rejection, she could no longer summon up the enthusiasm herself.

Then there were her frequent suspicions of his infidelity, his increasing coldness and occasional cruelty towards her – though this had never taken a physical form. The final straw was when, after not even bothering to attend her father's wake, he had turned up late for the funeral.

She no longer even wondered whether things would have been any different had she been able to fall pregnant. Nothing seemed to matter anymore but extricating herself from their sham of a marriage.

And now, after months of denial and procrastination, she had decided to confront him. Tonight.

Opening the door of the Miele Integrated Bottom Mount Fridge, she selected a bottle of Condrieu, opened it, and poured herself a large glass. She then carried the glass into the drawing room and sat on the sofa – an antique Victorian fainting couch upholstered in emerald velvet that Sheridan had bought her for their fifth wedding anniversary – and waited for him.

At half-past nine she heard the wheels of the Aston Martin crunching on the gravel. Then came the series of other familiar, and this time, ominous sounds announcing his arrival: the footfalls up to the front door; the key turning in the lock; the clanging of his car keys as he tossed them into the cut-glass Lalique dish on the hallway table. The heels of his handmade shoes clicking across the chequered marble floor towards the drawing room. The door opening.

Taking a deep breath, Méabh drained her glass and attempted to compose herself for the ensuing battle.

'Evening,' he said mildly, striding over to the drinks cabinet. Whilst pouring two fingers of Talisker from a Waterford crystal decanter into a matching tumbler he asked – with his back to her – if he could get her anything.

Boldly, Méabh said yes, she'd have a divorce, please.

The hand holding the stopper froze for a nanosecond – and then descended slowly back onto the decanter. He took a swig from his glass and finally turned to face her.

'A divorce?'

She nodded silently.

He frowned. 'How's that going to work, exactly? You. On your own?'

She said nothing. He walked over to the couch and bent down over her, his face inches from hers, enveloping her in a waft of sour whiskey breath: he had clearly started drinking hours ago.

'Without me, my sweet,' he said softly, 'you're just a…' his cold green eyes swept over her contemptuously as he searched for suitable epithets, 'an undernourished, overgroomed, *barren'* – he relished seeing her flinch ever so slightly at this – 'suburban nonentity.' He laughed harshly. 'Why don't you use that for your Tinder profile.'

Méabh swallowed and maintained her icy silence.

'And then there's the moolah. Do you really think you'll be able to keep yourself in Louboutins and Botox teaching backwards kids not to lisp?' he laughed scornfully.

She sighed wearily. She knew by now it was useless reminding him yet again that the practice – her practice – was doing better than ever, that her patient list included the offspring of some of Dublin's most illustrious denizens: she was currently treating the Irish Minister of Defence's son for his dysphasia and had done wonders for the daughter of the rock star from next door and her stutter. As for trying to defend her chosen profession to Sheridan, convincing him of the worth and relevance of her work – even getting him to have just the vaguest grasp of what it entailed – she had more hope of persuading Boko Haram to donate to the National Organization for Women.

He went on: 'I mean, you may think freedom has no price now, but I tell you, in a few months, when it's pissing down in Dublin and your tan needs topping up, you'll be longing for that mini-break in Dubai.'

Méabh sprang to her feet. It was one thing to insult her, to mock her childlessness and denigrate her vocation. But this was not to be borne.

'Dubai!' she crowed. 'I *never* wanted to go to flaming Dubai! It was always your idea! It's a desert, in every sense of the word: cultural, environmental, ideological – not to mention human rights. Who in their right mind would choose *Dubai* as their ideal destination? Nothing but a brainless, soulless, morally-bankrupt, materialistic shell of a human being – like you and your cronies and their trophy wives.' She paused and added, her mouth twisting with scorn: 'and footballers and WAGs.' She laughed mirthlessly. 'Dubai! It's Dante's Ninth Circle of Hell.'

Sheridan shrugged, apparently unperturbed by her diatribe.

'Whatever. I'll just take someone who appreciates it next time, and *you*' – he pointed to her with one hand as he helped himself to more whiskey with the other – 'can go to a caravan park in Dingle with your mam.'

'That's a hardship I'm willing to bear,' said Méabh drily. 'And now,' she stood up, smoothing down the skirt of her Diane von Furstenberg wrap dress, 'I'm going to bed. You can sleep in one of the guest rooms tonight. But tomorrow I want you out of the house.'

He stared at her coldly. For a moment she thought he might lash out, shout, strike her, even. But in the end, he did not even protest.

'Fine,' he said stiffly, 'I'll go to the flat in town – for now.' Turning on his heel, he walked over to the door, placing the tumbler down on the windowsill as he did.

Just as she heard his footsteps clicking back across the hall floor, she was suddenly engulfed by an overwhelming sense of indignance, of injustice. She felt cheated somehow by Sheridan's cold-blooded acceptance of her decision, his apparent complete indifference to the fate of their marriage. For as anxious as she was to be free of him, she could not help feeling hurt that he had not protested for a second. He had merely questioned *her* ability to exist without *him* – but had not once expressed any objection to living without her.

Running out into the hall after him, she called out his name. He turned around, looking mildly exasperated. 'What?'

'I want you to know that I... I kept *trying*. For a long time. I never wanted it to come to this. You seem to have given up on us months, years ago but I...' she sighed, defeated by his resolutely, mercilessly impassive face. 'I kept trying, hoping. You were always in my thoughts.'

'In your *thoughts*,' he repeated, nodding thoughtfully. 'Well,' he deadpanned, 'that would explain why I've been so unbelievably bored all these years.' He walked slowly up to her, reached out and, tapping his forefinger against her temple, whispered:

'There's not much going on in there.'

Fighting back the tears that burned her eyes, she grabbed his wrist and flung it from her.

'Get out!' she hissed, shoving him back towards the front door. He obeyed. And as he began backing the Aston Martin out of the drive, she shouted after him:

'Forget Dubai! This marriage was Dante's Ninth Circle of Hell!'

CHAPTER TWENTY-ONE

Dublin, 24 December 2019

The infant Moses's mother placed him in a reed basket and sent him to float down the Nile; yet despite this inauspicious beginning, he grew up to orchestrate an uprising against his oppressors and lead his people across the Red Sea to freedom. Oedipus, after being left for dead on Mount Cithaeron by his paranoid – yet, as it turned out, prescient – parents, went on not only to survive but to become King of Thebes. However, his past eventually caught up with him, resulting in tragedy and mayhem.

Who could know what fate would one day befall Olivia Keira Whitney Mooney as she navigated the treacherous waters of childhood and adolescence towards womanhood, after she too had been forsaken by her progenitor at the tender age of two weeks?

Of course, in her case, it was not in a reed basket on the Nile nor on a barren mountain top in Greece that she was so unceremoniously deposited, but in a Mothercare baby car seat, retrieved from a skip by one of the more resourceful of her mother's manifold siblings, and on the doorstep of a ground-floor apartment in an elegant Georgian square in one of the most select areas of Dublin. And on Christmas Eve.

Dave Mullan was spending Christmas with his son as Clare was on call over the holidays. Although it was nearly ten o'clock, he had only just got Declan to bed. After a dinner of take-away pizza and mini-Magnums, they had spent an hour playing Lego Jurassic World on Dave's 75-inch flat screen TV – although, if Clare asked, he would say they had read Beatrix Potter books. Clare was a bit of a Nazi about screen-time, but Dave had read an article somewhere that video games stimulated reflexes and hand-to-eye coordination in under-sixes. Anyway, it was Christmas.

The doorbell rang just as he was coming out of Declan's room. He did not immediately recognise the plump, slovenly-looking, fifty-something woman on the doorstep carrying a baby car seat.

'Can I help you?'

When she spoke, the coarse Northside tones refreshed his memory unpleasantly:

'You've got to take the baby.'

Ma Mooney. Tina's mother.

He stared. 'What's that now?'

'Our Tina. She's not… copin,' like. I always said she wasn't ready for a baby. She's a bit, simple, like…' she tapped her forehead, the universal sign language denoting mental deficiency. 'Anyway, I've raised six kids of me own, I can't be doin' wit' it. So, you'll have to step up.'

'What the fuck…' Dave protested. But she had put the car seat down and was already turning to leave.

'Wait a minute! You can't just… Hey! I'm not even…' He glanced around nervously, although none of his neighbours were out in the street, and lowered his voice. 'It's not even mine!'

Ma Mooney appeared not to hear – although it suddenly occurred to Dave that Tina had most likely hidden the identity of the baby's father from the rest of the clan.

He hurried after her. 'Does Tina even know you took her kid?'

Ma Mooney laughed. 'Believe me, she was glad to get shot of it.' She climbed into the passenger seat of a battered transit van parked across the square. Dave recognised the driver: it was one of Tina's brothers, the one he knew as Shell-suit. He was glaring contemptuously at Dave.

'Look, you can't just dump her kid on me…'

But Shell-suit had started up the engine, and with one hand on the wheel and the other held out of the open window with his middle finger extended, drove off.

Dave ran back to his doorstep and looked down in horror at the car seat. It contained an infant with a mop of black hair wearing a pink Babygro. She was fast asleep.

'Fuck…fuck… *fuck*!'

Shutting the front door softly, he pulled his mobile out of his pocket and dialled Tina's number. It rang for a long time. When she finally picked up, she was slurring slightly. There was hip-hop – of the insipid, mass market-targeted, excessively autotuned variety – playing in the background.

'Dave! What's the craic?'

'Listen,' he blurted, 'It's OK. Olivia's with me, she's fine. Your mam brought her over here, fuck knows why. Anyway, you're going to have to come over and fetch her asap, 'cause I'm on my own with Declan and I can't…'

'I know where she is,' trilled Tina in that singsong, little girl voice she sometimes used.

'What? You mean you told your mam to…'

'No, but she knew Olivia'd be better off with my baby Daddy.'

'I'm not your fuckin' baby D' – Jesus, who even talked like that? The girl watched too much American shite on TV – 'I'm not the father!' he hissed. 'Remember?'

Any protests on Dave's part, however, were in vain, for Tina was at that moment at home with her new boyfriend, Brendan, watching one of the aforementioned American series on Netflix, drinking Tesco Chardonnay and eating Nando's chicken wings.

'I know you'll do the right thing,' she said dreamily, and hung up.

Swearing softly, he dialled Clodagh's number. Clodagh would know what to do: she was a nurse, and a mother. You could always count on Clodagh.

She picked up after two rings.

'Emergency!' he said. 'I need you. Can you come over right away?'

She was there astonishingly quickly – within five minutes. Equally surprisingly, she was with their cousin, Méabh. What were *they* doing together?

'What is it?' asked Clodagh breathlessly.

Then her eye fell on the car seat.

'What's that? Surely Clare's not due for another couple of months?'

Dave explained, as concisely as possible, that a friend had given up her baby and said infant had somehow found its way to his doorstep.

'Is it yours?' Clodagh inquired sharply.

'Of course not!' said Dave, in an exaggerated display of outrage.

'Well then, why the hell…' Clodagh shrugged, and began rummaging in her capacious shoulder bag. 'Whatever. It doesn't make any difference. We're calling the police *right now*. Let Tusla and them handle it.' Dave wearily nodded his assent.

'No, don't do that.' Méabh stepped out from behind Clodagh. She was as immaculately turned out as usual, in a beautifully cut ankle-length black wool coat and black patent stilettoes, her bob freshly honed by the hairdresser. Clodagh spun round.

'What are you talking about? We have to call them. Now.'

In her deep, refined voice, Méabh calmly explained:

'This girl – the mother. She might not know what she's doing. She just gave birth, she's probably exhausted, overwhelmed. She may even be suffering from post-partum depression.' At this point, she turned to Clodagh imploringly, as if seeking confirmation – presumably due to Clodagh's profession.

132

Yet any support she was expecting from her cousin was not forthcoming. Putting her hands on her ample hips, Clodagh stood firm. 'That's not our problem. It's for Tusla to decide.'

'Look,' persisted Méabh in the same civilised, composed tone, 'all I'm saying is, maybe this poor girl just needs a few days to rest and get some perspective. If you contact Tusla or the police, the baby will be taken away, and when they find out her mother abandoned her, she probably won't get her back…'

'I should bloody well hope not!' interrupted Clodagh reprovingly.

Ignoring this remark, Méabh continued evenly: 'The child will go from foster home to foster home, and her mother may spend the rest of her life regretting some snap decision she made when she was half-crazed from sleep deprivation and God knows what else.' She paused and took a few steps closer to the car seat, peering down at the infant who slept on, oblivious to the chaos she had unwittingly caused.

'I'm not saying don't call them – of course we should eventually, Clodagh's quite right. Just not for a few days.'

'Who the hell's going to look after it in the meantime?' asked Clodagh.

'I can't!' protested Dave. 'I've got Declan for Christmas, for Christ's sake, we're going round to my mam's for lunch tomorrow. How am I going to explain having a fuckin' baby in tow? And it'll eventually get back to Clare and she'll just assume the worst and then…'

'I'll take her.'

Dave and Clodagh stared at their cousin.

'You?'

Méabh turned from the baby to face them. 'Why not? The practice is closed for the holidays, I've got plenty of room, and Imelda can give me a hand.'

Dave privately wondered what this Imelda – presumably some domestic employee of his cousin's – would think of her mistress suddenly and inexplicably producing a new-born. But he said nothing. A solution had been found, and at minimal inconvenience to him: that was all that mattered.

Clodagh flung up her hands in incredulous exasperation.

'Fine. But I wash my hands of this whole thing. Although –' she turned sharply to Méabh. 'If you don't call the authorities by Boxing Day, I will.'

She nodded solemnly. 'You have my word.'

Shaking her head, Clodagh turned on her heel and stalked off down the street while Méabh picked up the car seat, gazing tenderly at its contents.

Dave watched the two women place the baby seat in Méabh's Jaguar, parked just across the square from his place, and drive off, then, shivering, he hurried back up the steps to his front door and let himself in.

Inside, he gasped suddenly as he turned around to see his son standing in the doorway of his bedroom.

'What's up, wee man?'

'Who was at the door, Daddy? Is it Father Christmas?'

'No, no… you know he only comes down the chimney. That was just… carol singers.'

Scooping up his son in his arms, he kissed him and carried him back to bed.

CHAPTER TWENTY-TWO

Altea, Spain, 24 December 2019

It was aperitif time on the Costa Blanca and as Marnie stood on the terrace of her mother's villa drinking chilled Tio Pepe while Fay Wade bustled about dispensing *pan con tomate* and little ceramic bowls containing waver-thin slivers of *jamon iberico*, marinated olives and toasted almonds with chili, she reflected that in her forty-seven years on earth, she could not remember having spent a more bizarre Christmas.

That it was never going to be a traditional, conventional family get-together, she had expected: back in early November, her mother had informed her of her intention not to come over to the UK for Christmas this year, but saying that she and Rhiannon were more than welcome to join her in Spain. As Guy and Nova had longstanding plans to spend the holidays in Barrow-in-Furness with Nova's people – an invitation which had been extended to include Martin – Marnie saw no particular reason to stay in the UK.

Besides, the forecast on the Costa Blanca was seventeen degrees and sunny, compared to freezing fog in the West Country, and ever since she had been made redundant, Marnie had been feeling uncharacteristically spontaneous and adventurous. Having consulted her daughter and received a suitably enthusiastic response, she had made up her mind and booked the flights to Alicante – although Rhiannon's was a single ticket as she was flying to Paris on Boxing Day to see Luc before getting the Eurostar back to the UK in time to spend New Year's Eve with friends.

So far, so good. Things, however, began to take a turn for the distinctly unusual and, as far as Marnie was concerned, uncomfortable, just a week before Christmas. She and Rhiannon were wrapping presents at Marnie's flat when Rhiannon suddenly slipped out of the room to take a phone call and returned fifteen minutes later looking flushed with excitement and nerves.

'That was Gull,' she said.

'Oh, yes?' said Marnie, a sense of foreboding creeping upon her.

'He's just had a bit of bad news, actually…' Rhiannon proceeded to explain how her lover's Christmas plans with his family had fallen through. His elder two were going to their mother's in Croydon, whilst the youngest, Samantha, and her boyfriend Mark were to come to Gulliver's in Leamington Spa. However, the boyfriend's eighty-three-year-old grandmother had apparently just suffered a stroke – her second – and was at death's door, hence their decision to rush to her bedside and spend Christmas with Mark's parents instead.

'So poor Gull's going to be on his tod for Christmas.'

Marnie nodded fatalistically. 'Oh, I see. You're not coming to Spain.'

'Oh no! I mean, yes! I mean… I still want to come…' She looked downwards, apparently concentrating on gently kicking a stray bauble from the tree across the parquet floor towards Tim, who promptly pounced upon it. 'I was just wondering if –'

Marnie set aside the wrapping paper and the half-wrapped Bluetooth speaker she had purchased for her mother. 'No. You can't be serious, Ree.'

'Why not?'

Marnie threw up her hands in incredulity and exasperation. 'You want to bring your lover – your much older, lecturer lover – to your grandmother's for a family Christmas? It's out of the question. You must see that.'

'I want you to meet him, and this is just as good an occasion as any. Please, Mum.'

She crossed the room to where her mother was sitting on the floor by the sofa, surrounded by wrapping paper, ribbons and sundry assorted items, and knelt beside her.

'If Mamy's OK with it,' she said softly, 'can I bring Gull? It'll only be for a couple of days, we'll both be leaving on Boxing Day, he's going back to see his kids and I'm going to see Papa. *Please*,' she clasped her mother's forearm with this last plea.

Marnie sighed. 'Is this an 'either-we-both-come-or-neither-of-us-come'-type of scenario, because I warn you, the way I feel right now, you won't come out well from this.'

Rhiannon smiled and lay her head on her mother's shoulder. 'Now, really. You know I'm above resorting to emotional blackmail or ultimata.'

'Hmm,' grumbled Marnie. 'Not above being a cheeky cow, though.'

Kissing her on the cheek, Rhiannon jumped up, announcing she was going to call her grandmother.

Unfortunately, the awkwardness and malaise that was to pervade the festivities was not due solely to the presence of Dr Gulliver Scutt. For a few days afterwards, the day before their departure, Fay called to discuss last-minute travel arrangements.

'Don't worry about picking us up from the airport,' assured Marnie. 'We'll grab a cab or an Uber or whatever.' Fay still owned a car and a driving license but, at seventy-six, was increasingly reluctant to drive beyond a five-kilometre radius of her home.

'No, that won't be necessary,' said Fay. 'Javi will come and fetch you.'

'Javi?'

She heard her mother take a deep breath.

'He's... a friend. He's *my* friend. We've been... seeing each other for about six months.'

'Oh. I see.' That her mother had not retired to a convent since her divorce from Martin thirty years before did not surprise Marnie; yet, in that time, Fay had never introduced her to or even spoken of any suitors. This one must be serious, she thought.

And so it was that when Marnie and Rhiannon came through the arrivals gate at Alicante Airport on 23 December, they saw a handwritten sign bearing their names, borne aloft by a short, dapper, silver-haired man with an abundant yet neatly trimmed moustache, wearing a beige linen jacket over immaculately pressed (by her mother? Marnie wondered idly) jeans, and a pink polo shirt.

'Meet your new stepdad,' murmured Rhiannon mischievously in her mother's ear as they approached him.

Beaming, he lowered the sign and extended a hand.

'I am Javier Garcia De Blas. Welcome.' He spoke with a thick accent.

Marnie and Rhiannon shook his hand in turn.

'Pleased to meet you,' said Marnie formally. 'Thank you for picking us up.'

He made a self-deprecating gesture with his hand and took their suitcases. They followed him out to the carpark where he loaded the luggage into the boot of a dusty, mud-spattered Suzuki Jeep.

After a forty-five-minute journey, during which Marnie, in the passenger seat, made polite comments and inquiries about the weather and scenery – pointedly avoiding any personal questions – they parked in the driveway of Fay's house, a small, detached, white-washed villa, identical to the others on the little estate: neat and well-appointed but devoid of any real architectural or aesthetic merit, but with two large terraces commanding spectacular views of the Mediterranean.

Fay stood in the front doorway, arms outstretched, and kissed and hugged her daughter then her granddaughter. Javier she favoured with a brief affectionate smile as her hand brushed his arm. She looked marvellous, thought Marnie: her short silver hair looked freshly set and the jade-green knee-length shift dress showed off her still shapely calves and ankles.

137

To Marnie's surprise, minutes after depositing her and Rhiannon, Javier took his leave.

'Oh, aren't you? I mean, you don't…'

Fay smiled, and explained: 'Javi doesn't live here,' (an unspoken 'yet' hung in the air), Marnie thought. 'He has his own place in the old town.'

Javier nodded and said, with a slight bow: 'I will see you tomorrow, ladies.'

After the Jeep drove off, Fay linked arms with Marnie and Rhiannon and led them into the kitchen. 'Tea? Or something stronger?'

Both opted for the latter, and after a glass of Cava, were shown to their respective rooms: Marnie noted with silent resentment that, as the only single guest, she was relegated to the tiny third bedroom downstairs with the single bed whilst Rhiannon was shown into the spacious upstairs bedroom with en suite bathroom – the room she, Marnie, usually occupied during her stays there.

Her mild dissatisfaction with the accommodation notwithstanding, the first evening passed pleasantly and without incident, with a dinner of grilled sea bass and salad, followed by a few games of Scrabble.

But now, twenty-four hours later, the dynamic had shifted considerably. That morning, Gulliver had flown in from Birmingham and Fay had lent Rhiannon her battered VW Golf to go and fetch him from the airport. Fay was immediately charmed – as was no doubt intended: Gulliver arrived gushing compliments – on the house, the location, the view – and laden with gifts: two bottles of Duty Free Veuve Clicquot and a Marks & Spencer luxury Christmas pudding for his hostess, and a box of sugared almonds for Marnie.

Shaking hands and thanking him, she wondered wryly whether he himself had asked Rhiannon what Marnie's favourite confectionery was or if her daughter had volunteered the information.

Her scepticism aside, she acknowledged that Gulliver Scutt had an interesting, intelligent face, without being conventionally handsome, and a lean, athletic frame. And after his (in her opinion) over-enthusiastic initial overtures, he appeared to scale back the charm offensive for the rest of the day, showing himself to be merely amiable, polite and mild-mannered, an attentive listener and generally a gracious guest. Moreover, she was immeasurably grateful that he and Rhiannon had the good taste to refrain from any displays of affection in front of her and Fay: indeed, they barely touched one another and did not use any terms of endearment, so that Marnie could occasionally almost forget that this man, who was six years her senior, was sleeping with her daughter

The same could not, however, be said of her mother and Javier, who joined the party just in time for cocktail hour. It was not that they were excessively demonstrative; but the tender smiles they constantly exchanged, the frequent caresses of the other's arm or patting of the hand suggested an obvious intimacy which provoked simultaneously in Marnie a stab of envy and a pang of sorrow as she realised she had never seen her mother favour her father with those adoring glances and kittenish smiles.

Gulliver introduced himself to Javier and said a few words in what sounded like fairly proficient Spanish – much to Rhiannon's apparent surprise and admiration. As Fay filled Javier's glass with sherry, he apologised softly to her for his lateness, saying something about having to examine the neighbour's dog.

'I am…I *was* a veterinary,' he explained, turning to the other guests. He pronounced it 'beterinary.' 'I retired last year.'

Only last year, thought Marnie. He certainly only looked in his mid-sixties at most. So, what was he doing with someone her mother's age? Aloud, she said some platitude about how gratifying it must be to work with animals, adding: 'My sister-in-law's a horse osteopath.'

His eyes widened with interest. 'Really?' He turned to Fay. '*Querida*, you never told me.'

Fay shrugged and helped herself to more fino.

'And you, Marnie,' said Javier, turning back to her. 'What do you do for a living?'

She was slightly taken aback: rightly or wrongly, she had somehow assumed her mother would have apprised him of her circumstances. After glancing briefly at Fay, whose face was a model of impassiveness, she gave Javier a brief account of her career as a translator and her recent redundancy.

'Since then I've been doing a bit of freelancing,' she concluded, 'but I'm actually thinking of starting a business – something completely different.'

'Really?' said Fay. 'What sort of business?'

'It's really interesting,' encouraged Rhiannon. 'Tell them, Mum.'

Suddenly self-conscious and wary of the sea of expectant faces around her, Marnie finished her sherry and placed the glass on the coffee table – at which point Javier shot forward with the bottle and refilled it.

'I'm thinking of setting up a sort of travel agency that specialises in organising custom art-themed trips. So, for example, fans of Caravaggio can go on a trip to Italy to see his main masterpieces in Rome and Florence – but not just his works: I also arrange tours of his birthplace and other places he lived and worked at key points in his life – in Milan, Rome, Naples, Sicily and Malta. And between museum visits and cultural activities there will be

139

wining and dining at great restaurants – and possibly vineyard tours too, I'm just looking into that. It's a sort of art and gastronomy experience – hence the name: Bacchus & Minerva.'

'Wine and war?' said Gulliver.

Marnie frowned. 'No – Minerva was also the goddess of the arts. Damn – I was worried people would think that.'

'Ah, yes, of course,' said Gulliver, adding apologetically, 'it's been a while since I read Robert Graves.' He paused. 'You could also have called it Athena & Dionysus.'

Rhiannon, whose sensitive antenna had detected her mother's growing sense of unease, turned around sharply and fixed her lover with an exasperated look. 'Well, she didn't. She used the Roman version of the names.' She turned back to Marnie. 'Go on, Mum.'

Marnie staggered on: 'Well, I sort out the accommodation and general logistics. The whole package.' Murmurs of encouragement and admiration ensued. 'For the moment I'll be focusing on tours in Italy – Caravaggio, Titian, Da Vinci – and France.'

'The Impressionists?' ventured Javier.

'They would be the obvious choice, yes. The Americans and Japanese love them. So, I'll organise guided tours of the Musée d'Orsay and the Orangerie in Paris – followed by dinner somewhere nice, then up to Giverny to visit Monet's house and gardens.'

'Cool idea, isn't it, Mamy?' Rhiannon enthused to Fay. 'Don't you think Mum'd be brilliant in that sort of role?'

'I do,' Fay agreed, turning to Marnie. 'I always thought you were cruelly underutilised translating users' guides and press releases.'

Marnie was astonished. 'Did you?'

'Absolutely. You're so cultured. I never understood why you gave up on the idea of literary translation and wasted your talent all those years doing hackwork for a big, soulless corporation…'

'OK, Mum,' Marnie muttered, frankly embarrassed by now.

Gulliver came to the rescue. 'How did you come up with the idea?'

She told him of the various online self-assessment tools she had availed herself of following her dismissal, the personality tests and aptitude tests, and of her desire to do something more intellectually fulfilling, something in the field of culture. She omitted the incident at the National Gallery, her run-in with the disgruntled tour guide and her ensuing occupational epiphany, for fear that any of them had seen that cursed video.

'Good for you,' Gulliver said warmly. 'It takes guts and imagination to change career paths after…' he said tactfully, 'after doing the same thing for a number of years.'

Moved and slightly embarrassed by the attention and kindness, Marnie stood up suddenly, drained her glass and offered to give her mother a hand serving up.

After the tapas, there was *arroz negra* followed by roast lamb, then Javier brought in a selection of traditional Spanish festive sweetmeats: *turrón de Alicante* and *pestiños*, delicious honey-glazed, aniseed-flavoured pastries. Fay opened one of Gulliver's bottles of champagne for dessert, followed by the second one.

After clearing the table, Javier, Rhiannon and Gulliver stood chatting on the terrace whilst Marnie helped her mother load the dishwasher.

'Javi seems nice,' Marnie ventured.

Fay smiled lightly. 'But…?'

'But nothing.' She toyed with her half-full champagne flute. 'It's just… Well, he didn't know what Nova or I do for a living.'

'And?'

'Well, I just thought that in, what – six months – you've been going out with him, the subject of your kids would have come up occasionally.'

'Of course it does, dear,' Fay replied evenly, wiping down the worktop with a cloth. 'I assure you, you and your brother are all we ever talk about. Even when we're in bed.'

Marnie stared at her, shocked. 'Christ, mother!'

Fay abandoned the cloth and looked at her daughter. 'What bothers you the most, Marnie?' she asked, her voice still calm and measured, a model of equanimity. 'That you two aren't the centre of my universe anymore, or that I'm still having sex at my age?'

Dumbfounded, Marnie said nothing.

'I've met a delightful man and am happy and… fulfilled for the first time in a decade. But instead of being happy for me, you're having a hissy fit because it's not enough about you.'

Marnie was not often speechless. She wanted to burst out, like a child: *why are you being so mean to me?* but refrained. Her mother continued:

'Were we negligent parents? Really? Is that why you both went looking for the other ones?'

Marnie gasped. 'I can't believe you're throwing that in my face!' she spluttered. 'If you had any idea how hard it was for me to tell you about it – and how hard it was to keep it from you. I didn't want to hurt you and Dad. Guy and I argued horribly about it: he thought I should have told you from the start. Christ!' Fighting back hot angry tears, she strode out of the kitchen and to her monastic cell of a room, closing the door behind her.

Pulling herself together, she almost laughed out loud as the sheer absurdity of the situation dawned upon her: for here she was, in her late forties, actually sulking in her bedroom like a teenager after arguing with her mother! As she was reflecting on the regressive effect family gatherings could have on adult children, there was a knock at the door and her mother entered.

Without a word, she sat beside Marnie on the bed. 'I'm sorry,' she said quietly. 'That was rather unforgiveable.'

Marnie shrugged. 'Not unforgiveable,' she mumbled, wiping her eyes with the back of her hand. 'Several bloody meters below the belt, though.'

Fay shook her head. 'I don't know what came over me. I just…Well, I may be acting a bit blasé about Javi but the truth is, I've been awfully nervous about your meeting him. And Christmas is always an emotional time. And then there's Rhiannon and her new chap – now, what to make of that!'

'It bothers you, too? God, *thank* you. I thought I was being funny!'

'Well, of course, dear! A man that age… He is very attractive, mind.'

Marnie shrugged. 'I hadn't noticed.'

'Really? You do surprise me. I would have thought he was just your type: the wiry, laconic, intellectual sort.' Marnie said nothing.

'Of course,' her mother went on, 'one doesn't dare say anything. She's not a child anymore and she wouldn't listen to us anyway. We'd just push her away. And then I worry about you.'

'Me?'

'Well, losing your job like that. Oh, I know you're clever and you'll rally, but when I think about how those dreadful people treated you, after all these years. It's shameful. And I worry that you get lonely, that you won't meet someone else.'

It was almost more than Marnie could bear. 'You don't need to worry about me,' she muttered, patting Fay's hand awkwardly.

'And if I haven't talked much about you and Guy to Javi, it's not because you're not important to me – how can you even *think* that?'

Marnie nodded, her cheeks burning with shame.

'It's just that I… compartmentalise. We both do. We don't feel the need to drag every aspect of our lives into our relationship, and vice versa.' She looked at Marnie intently. 'All right?'

Marnie nodded. 'I get it. I'm sorry too for being such a drama queen. As you say, it's been a funny few months, but I'll get there.'

'Of course, you will.'

'And as for being defensive about Javier,' she went on, standing up and inspecting her tear-smudged face in the mirror. 'There's absolutely no need. Really, it's no odds to me if you're getting a good seeing to by some Spanish gigolo.'

'Impertinent brat! I knew your father and I should have arranged for a private adoption through respected breeders, instead of settling for some insolent urchin of doubtful provenance.'

There was a knock at the door.

'Come in,' Marnie called.

It was Rhiannon. 'What are you doing? Listen, Gull's had a brilliant idea: let's go clubbing in Benidorm! Tonight.'

Gulliver, behind her, popped his head gingerly around the door. He had changed into jeans and a close-fitting crisp white shirt that showed off his lean torso. 'I thought it might be interesting,' he said. 'Well, if nothing else, from a purely sociological – even anthropological – standpoint.' Rhiannon giggled.

Marnie thought she would rather run upstairs and hurl herself off the terrace, impaling herself on one of the cacti below, that an evening spent watching her mother and Javier rutting like street dogs would seem a less excruciating alternative.

But she sat back down on the bed and, after exchanging a brief, mischievous grin of connivance with Fay, said:

'Thank you for the invitation. But you know, one of the few pleasures of getting old is that you know what you want and don't want, and can be utterly unapologetic about just pleasing yourself. Which is why we shall decline your tempting offer, but off you go, conduct your research, and we expect a detailed report of your findings at breakfast.'

Nodding, Fay said: 'Yes! You young pe –' after a glance at Gulliver, she corrected herself – 'you *people*, go off and have fun.'

As the bedroom door, and soon after that, the front door closed, Marnie and her mother dissolved into giggles. 'Nightcap?' suggested Fay.

CHAPTER TWENTY-THREE

Drumcondra, Dublin, 26 December 2019

It was Boxing Day and Aiofe Mullan had a full house.

In addition to her own four children, her son-in-law Paul, and her four grand-children – Clodagh's India, Marie and Paul's two boys Aidan and Ross, and Dave's little Declan – she had also invited her sister Tish and her two children, Fionn and Méabh.

Her niece's presence at this event was something of a deviation from customary practice: throughout her married life, Méabh and her husband, Sheridan – who by all accounts was a snob and had always shunned his in-laws – had gone to his people for Boxing Day. But since their recent separation, Méabh had begun spending more time with her extended family. It was, moreover, her mother's first Christmas as a widow, and Méabh had resolved to spend as much of the holiday with her as possible.

Unknown to almost all the people attending this gathering, however, there was soon to be another addition to the family.

Fionn had driven his mother to Aiofe's, arriving just after noon. His sister, he explained, would be arriving separately. As Clodagh helped her mother arrange leftover turkey and stuffing onto a plate and prepare various salads, she thought back to Christmas Eve and the phone call which – had either of them but known it then – had potentially radically altered the course of Méabh's life forever.

The rapprochement between the two cousins had begun about a month after Uncle Oscar's funeral, when Clodagh had been somewhat surprised to receive a phone call from Méabh. They had been close enough as kids; Clodagh had been like a big sister to her. But since entering adulthood, and particularly since Méabh had married that prick Sheridan, moved to Sandycove and started moving in more exalted spheres, a gulf had opened up between them. Consequently, Clodagh had privately dismissed her as a stuck-up cow and had virtually nothing to do with her aside from the inevitable meetings at weddings and funerals.

During that phone conversation back in November, Méabh had explained that she was in the process of separating from her husband and, as Clodagh had been through a similar experience, would she care to meet for a drink and a chat sometime? Clodagh, surprised to hear that her cousin's apparently perfect existence was anything but and equally astonished that she had chosen to turn to her for succour, was sympathetic to her plight and disarmed by her humility.

'I did think of Dave, of course,' explained Méabh as they sat down in a wine bar in the Docklands. 'But I didn't want to bother him, you know, with him being right in the middle of his own divorce, and then Clare and the baby…' She put down the menu and looked at Clodagh. 'And besides, you and I… used to be close.'

And so it was that, over a glass of Chardonnay (Méabh) and a half of Guinness (Clodagh), the two women had raked over the ashes of their failed marriages: Sheridan's callous indifference, Jordi's immaturity and womanising.

'I suppose it was to be expected,' Clodagh said, with a rueful laugh. 'I mean, you don't grow old with some charming Dutch guy you fall for in art school.'

'God, that's right!' exclaimed Méabh. 'I totally forgot about your stint at NCAD! I remember Mammy calling you the Bohemian.'

'Yes, well, after one term I realised I had no talent, dropped out and did my nursing training. It took me a bit longer to realise Jordi and I weren't soul-mates; but by that time I'd fallen pregnant with India and…well, there was no going back. So, we got married. Big mistake, but what else could we have done?'

After that first evening out, they had occasionally spoken on the phone, and on the morning of Christmas Eve, it was Clodagh who had called Méabh to ask her out for a drink. India had come back to Dublin to spend Christmas with the family but had plans to go out with her friends that evening. Méabh had accepted enthusiastically but had insisted they go somewhere grand, and on treating her cousin.

And thus it had come to pass that they were sipping cocktails at the Shelbourne Bar – just around the corner from Dave's flat – when he had called Clodagh with his cry for help. It was typical of her brother's self-absorption, Clodagh reflected later, that he had not once questioned their arriving within minutes of his summons.

After they had taken baby Olivia off Dave's hands, Méabh had dropped Clodagh home in Drumcondra and then driven back to Sandycove.

And now, it was Boxing Day, and, as close as they were, Clodagh had every intention of making good on her threat to confront her cousin about contacting Tusla and arranging for Olivia to be taken away.

At twenty past twelve, just as Clodagh was mixing a bowl of Marie-Rose sauce to pour over the defrosted prawns, Méabh's Jaguar drew up in the driveway. After greeting her family and presenting her aunt with a bottle of champagne and a cake – a rather elaborately decorated iced affair from one of Dublin's most exclusive pastry shops – and dispensing gifts to the children, Méabh finally met Clodagh's meaningful, expectant gaze across the room and nodded towards the conservatory. As Clodagh followed her out of the room, Méabh murmured into her ear: 'and ask Dave to join us, could you?'

Puzzled, Clodagh complied and fetched her equally intrigued brother.

'What's going on?' he asked.

Once the three of them were alone in the conservatory, Clodagh began:

'What's happening? Did you call Tusla?'

Méabh took a deep breath. 'Not exactly, not yet…'

Clodagh threw up her arms in exasperation. 'Christ, Méabh…'

'Please, just hear me out.'

Clodagh shrugged and sat down on a wicker chair and listened as her cousin explained. She had evidently spent the better part of the past thirty-six hours, between feeding, bathing and caring for Olivia, completing her online research – something she had apparently already begun weeks ago, before her path had crossed with baby Olivia's – into the lengthy, complex and extremely frustrating process of adoption. In addition to the reams of forms to complete, there was a protracted assessment process, consisting of home visits from a social worker, Garda vetting, a medical examination, financial checks, referees who would eventually be asked about the prospective adopter's suitability as a parent. As she spoke, she produced a sheaf of papers from her Céline handbag and placed it on the wicker table. Peering at the documents, Clodagh saw they were printouts from the Adoption Authority of Ireland's website.

'Well, don't get your hopes up,' she said baldly. 'A colleague of mine tried to adopt. It's tough.'

Méabh nodded. 'I know; and domestic adoptions are virtually non-existent in Ireland. I'd have a much better chance if I were Angelina flaming Jolie, collecting orphans from overseas!' She cleared her throat nervously after her attempt at humour. 'Anyway, to cut a long story short, it could take years. But there are ways to… expedite the process.'

Clodagh said nothing, merely raised a censorious eyebrow.

146

'Oh, it's nothing illegal,' her cousin assured her. 'Basically, there are four types of domestic adoption: by a step-parent, by a relative or member of the extended family, domestic infant adoption and long-term foster care to adoption. With adoption by a relative, the birth mother can place the child with a relative who wants to adopt it, either directly or through the State childcare system.'

Clodagh nodded. 'OK. So?'

'*So…* that might be a way for me to adopt Olivia!'

Clodagh frowned. 'How does that work? I mean, you're not –' a thought suddenly occurred to her. 'Where *is* the baby now, by the way?'

'I left her with Imelda for a couple of hours.'

Clodagh continued: 'You're not related to… what's her name again, the mother?'

'Tina,' said Dave dully, already bored by the discussion.

'Not to Tina, no,' said Méabh, and taking a deep breath: 'But I am related to the baby's father.'

She fixed her eyes on Dave.

'What?' he exclaimed. 'Jesus… I told you the other night; I'm not the kid's father! I've got a DNA test to prove it. The real Dad's Tina's uncle; he was abusing her. Don't fuckin' ask…'

Méabh shook her head gently and said patiently: 'I know; I believe you. But even if you're not the biological father, it doesn't matter. You just have to say you are: to Tusla, I mean. Just to establish that you – and by extension, me – are related to Olivia, thus making me eligible for an adoption by a relative!' Her smile of triumph contrasted sharply with her cousins' expressions of bewilderment and dismay.

'But…' protested Dave, 'that's nuts. Won't they check?'

She shook her head firmly. 'No! I checked. Their offices are closed at the moment, but, well, I know some people… Anyway, unless there's reason to doubt a child's paternity – in other words, if someone questions it – proof of paternity won't be required. Your consent won't even be required as, even if you were the real father, you and Tina aren't married and you're not the child's legal guardian. All we need is Tina's consent – ' at this point, Méabh appeared to remember something, causing her face to fall – 'assuming, of course, that she hasn't changed her mind about giving Olivia up. And, of course, we need you to say you're the father – or at least, for Tina to say so, and for you not to deny it if you're asked.'

Dave was outraged: for one of the many contradictions of his character was that, in spite of the deceit he practised on a regular basis, both as a salesman with his clients and, previously, as an adulterous husband to Clare, he prided himself on his integrity and moral rectitude in certain areas. He said, not without a certain dignity:

'I'm not going to perjure myself to Tusla!'

Clodagh rolled her eyes. 'It's not the bloody Supreme Court, you eejit.'

It was a wonder Méabh managed to say what she said next without a trace of amusement or irony, but somehow, she succeeded:

'Of course you're not, Dave, and I respect that. I don't want to put you in a difficult position or make you do anything that goes against your principles. But like I said, it won't come to that. I just need you to let them believe you're the father for the purposes of my adoption application, but that's it: you won't ever be accountable as the father in any way – especially once Tina gives her consent for the adoption order. As long as everyone agrees and no one is opposing Olivia's adoption, there's absolutely no reason for any official legal proceedings.'

Dave shook his head doubtfully. 'I dunno… I mean, OK, let's say I do say I'm the father and Tusla has you vetted and whatever and it all goes well; are you sure this is what you want? *Tina's kid?'*

'Of course,' said Méabh evenly. 'Why not? That little girl needs a home and I'd like to give her one.' Shaking his head again, Dave snatched up one of the printouts and started reading aloud from it:

'"You must be over the age of twenty-five" – check – *"have a spare bedroom"* – yeah, about ten in your case – *'"you need a full driving licence, must have flexibility in your working arrangements."* Well, how the fuck are you going to swing that?'

Unfazed by his belligerent tone, Méabh continued calmly:

'I can make adjustments. I'll talk to my partner, explain the situation, say I plan to scale back and offload some of my patients to her and one of the new –'

Ignoring her, Dave read from another page:

'"The social worker will discuss such areas as previous and/or current relationships, motives for adopting…"'

'Dave,' said Clodagh sharply.

'Yes, my motives,' said Méabh with a sad laugh. 'I'm sure they'll grill me about that. I realise my marital status won't help. They'll probably assume I just want a baby to fill the void left by my husband.'

'Well?' said Dave defiantly. 'Don't you?'

'For Christ's sake,' hissed Clodagh, 'leave the woman alone!'

Méabh raised a conciliatory hand. 'It's all right,' she said to Clodagh. 'It's a fair question and one I'm going to have to get used to answering a lot over the next few months.'

As it turns out, she was prevented from doing so. *'"Motives for adopting,"'* Dave continued, *' "expectations of the child and the ability to help a child to develop his/her knowledge and understanding of his/her natural background."'* He gave a bark of cynical laughter. *'"Her natural background!"* Brilliant! So, in this case, you'll have to help Olivia understand that she comes from generations of in-bred alcoholics, smackheads and kiddy-fiddlers. The Mooneys: Inchicore's finest. Their gene pool's a fuckin' puddle, a cesspit. And Olivia's got a double dose of Mooney, as her mam and dad are related! Jesus...' He tossed the printout back onto the table. He looked at Méabh; she was still perfectly composed. He sighed and said, more calmly: 'Look, adopt a kid, why not. Just not *this* kid. The odds are she'll have the IQ of a fuckin' jam donut and be sniffing marker pens before she can walk.'

Méabh flinched ever so slightly, but said nothing.

'I'm just sayin',' he went on. '*Caveat emptor.*' Then, seeing his sister's raised eyebrows: 'Don't look so fuckin' surprised, I'm not a complete ignoramus: I do remember some of the Latin I learned with the brothers. I quite liked it, actually. Brother Tristan – the Latin master – he was all right. Well, he was the only one who didn't beat the crap out of us.'

'Well,' said Méabh, ignoring Dave's digression on the benefits of a Classical education. 'I don't believe that: I don't think you should just write someone off based on their biological heritage. If Olivia lives with me, she'll have the best of everything, the best education, the best care, all my love and affection.'

Dave replied, calmly but mercilessly:

'If you think Montessori, private school and dressing her in Burberry Kids will overcome generations of bad breeding, then you're either incredibly arrogant or just plain deluded.'

She seemed slightly dismayed at his lack of understanding, but otherwise, not remotely offended:

'With all due respect, Dave, you don't know me. It's not about the money. And this isn't some sociological experiment: I just want to give a home to a little girl.' A few seconds' awkward silence followed, then she said briskly. 'Look, I think we'd better get back to the others. I can't stay long anyway: I promised I'd relieve Imelda at two.' Clodagh nodded and mumbled something about joining her in a moment.

Méabh turned to Dave. 'Will you please just think about it?'

He shrugged and nodded. As soon as the conservatory door closed behind Méabh, Clodagh turned on her brother.

'Dave, God knows I love you and you've always been my favourite, but Jesus, you can be an arrogant, insensitive prick.'

He shrugged. 'I just don't think she knows what she's letting herself in for.'

'Why is that *your* problem? She wants a kid! You've no idea what it's like to want a child and not be able to have one. It's easy for you, spreading your seed left, right and centre.'

'What the fuck?' Dave threw up his arms towards the ceiling. '*Excuse* me, but I've only ever got a woman pregnant three times – that I know of. And it was the same woman!'

'Whatever. I'll say it again: I love you, but I'll tell you this: if I believed in biological determinism as much as you apparently do – and, if we lived in a more progressive country where such a thing was easy – I'd have told Clare to have an abortion.' As she stepped through the door, she turned back and added savagely:

'All three times.'

CHAPTER TWENTY-FOUR

Paris, 10 January 2020

It is a truism that the places one has lived or spent time in as a child seem smaller when revisited many years later as an adult.

To Marnie visiting Paris for the first time in three years – for she did not count two brief work trips during which she had gone directly from the airport to the office in the suburbs and back – the city seemed at once smaller, dirtier, and more gentrified.

Since booking her trip and arranging to have dinner with Amedeo, Marnie had been moving forward with her plan to set up Bacchus & Minerva; consequently, she had decided to take advantage of being in the French capital to meet with some potential future partners, and had managed to secure meetings the following day with the Louvre and the Musée de l'Orangerie (though no one from the Musée d'Orsay had been available to see her), as well as arranging to visit two hotels, including an enchanting boutique hotel tucked away in a leafy corner of Montmartre, with a view to putting clients up there as part of her Impressionist tour and, time permitting, a quick coffee with Luc near the Gare du Nord before catching the train home.

Marnie's old friend Cécile had invited her to stay in her flat whilst she was in town, although Cécile herself was away in Normandy nursing her elderly mother at the time. After the fifteen-minute journey from the Gare du Nord, Marnie emerged from the metro and walked the short distance to Cécile's building, an unsightly Brutalist tower block in the twentieth *arrondissement*, a stone's throw away from where Edith Piaf had been born in well-documented – and somewhat romanticised – squalor. Looking around her, and narrowly avoiding being run over by a cyclist (God, the city seemed to be covered in cycle lanes now), she noted with satisfaction that the area continued to defy categorisation and stereotypification. The eclectic assortment of shops on and around the Boulevard de Belleville testified both to its Afro-Caribbean and Asian immigrant roots and the inevitable incipient gentrification: Caribbean greengrocers selling yams, Habanero peppers and coconut oil stood alongside vast

Chinese supermarkets, organic grocers, tiny artisan cheese shops run by hipsters or burned-out former dotcom executives and North African bakeries with their multicoloured array of glistening pastries stuffed with pistachios, dates and marzipan and drenched in orange flower water and honey.

After calling on the concierge on the ground floor to retrieve the keys, Marnie went up to the flat, a comfortably disorderly place on the tenth floor with views of the Sacre Coeur and the Eiffel Tower. After washing her hands, drinking a glass of tap water and depositing her bag in the guest bedroom, she set off out again.

It was a cold, sunny, dry day, and Marnie went for a long walk across the city, heading south towards the Seine then crossing over the Pont Neuf to the Left Bank and down to Eugène Delacroix' house, one of her favourite small museums. After wandering around the artist's former studio and resting for a while on a bench in the little walled garden, she walked up to the Boulevard St Germain where she caught the number 96 bus back.

Back in the flat, exhausted after the early start and her walk, she lay down on the bed with Jack London's *Cruise of the Snark* and was asleep after two pages. When she awoke almost two hours later it was dark. After showering she dressed in a knee-length black leather pencil skirt, cream polo-neck jumper, black tights and black high-heeled ankle boots, and left the flat to meet Amedeo for dinner.

The choice of venue for their meeting had given Marnie considerable trouble. For, despite Amedeo's protestations, she had insisted they go to a vegan restaurant. When she first came to live in Paris in the mid-nineties, there was simply no such thing: the concept of veganism itself was something the French had difficulty grasping. Even vegetarianism was an enigma at the time: many restaurateurs had some vague notion it involved eating fish but not meat, whilst others genuinely thought a sprinkling of *lardons* on a salad did not constitute eating meat. Things had of course changed considerably since then, but it was still a long way from becoming the capital of vegan gastronomy. A handful of restaurants, however, had received good reviews from diners and critics alike, although Marnie herself had never been to one during her many years in the city (after all, why would she?)

But her apprehension about the evening was not exclusively catering related. She also had some slight misgivings about their relationship: after all this time, would they fall easily back into their former intimacy? Now they were no longer colleagues, would they discover that they had little of substance in common? And there was that lingering, niggling feeling that there was something unresolved between them. Ever since they had arranged this reunion, Val's question had been looming in the back of her mind: *Who is Amedeo?*

152

The place she had eventually booked a table at was in the Marais, a historic district in the centre which, over the centuries had undergone a number of startling transformations: swamp, fiefdom of the aristocracy, ghetto for the Ashkenazi Jewish community, artisans' neighbourhood, rat-infested slum, Mecca of the gay scene, home to the *bourgeois bohémien* set. It had now been gentrified to within an inch of its life: more and more former residential buildings were being taken over by rapacious retail moguls and filled with designer boutiques. But it still retained much of its original charm: the narrow streets, the achingly beautiful baroque townhouses, most of which had since been vacated by their patrician tenants and turned into museums and picture galleries.

He arrived precisely on time, five minutes after her, dressed in jeans and a grey cashmere sweater under a black wool coat. He was clean-shaven and his dark hair had grown to his collar since their last meeting; it suited him, she thought.

Marnie had already ordered a gin and tonic to steady her nerves and was already feeling buoyed after two hefty gulps. Smiling, she rose to greet him, almost withdrawing after the second kiss (she forgot he always kissed four times).

After menus had been consulted and orders placed, he asked how her genealogical research was progressing. She told him about the newspaper article Rhiannon had sent her and her attempts to contact Ruth Culpeper, the self-styled DNA detective.

'But she never got back to me. I gather she's very much in demand. Been on TV and stuff. Anyway, after chasing her up a few times, I decided to do my own research.'

She went on to explain how, about a month before, she had come across a website offering free support and practical advice on researching birth parents and decided to sign up. But as she was filling out the contact form, after the usual requests for name and date of birth, she was asked to tick a box next to the declaration: 'I am a member of The Church of Jesus Christ of Latter-day Saints. Use my record information to help me get started,' and a request for something called a church record number.

Marnie recalled her yelp of terror at this discovery, how she had physically recoiled, her fingers jerking away from the keyboard as if she had received an electric shock. She had hastily closed the web page and – somewhat irrationally, she now laughingly admitted – proceeded to erase her browsing history, as if she had stumbled upon a paedophile site or a forum for white supremacists or jihadis.

Amedeo, nodding approvingly as he sampled a forkful of roast sweet potato with olive tapenade, rocket and hazelnut pesto, was equally surprised. *'Mormons?'*

She nodded. 'Didn't you have a colleague who was one of them? The guy who killed himself?'

He nodded and topped up her wine. 'Gabriele. Well, presumably. He was buried as one, at any rate. I never knew anything about his faith while he was alive.'

'Well, it turns out they're really into their genealogy. In fact, they're behind most of the online resources on the subject – the main ones, anyway, which intrigued me, so I looked into it. Apparently, it's because it helps get you into heaven. They believe families are together in the afterlife, so it's important to strengthen family ties in this one. They have something called a sacred sealing ceremony.' In response to his quizzical look, she shrugged. 'Christ knows – literally. Anyway, the point is, I eventually found a website that has no apparent affiliation to any cults, and sent off for a home DNA testing kit. It arrived a few days later, I took a couple of cheek swabs and sent them off for a paternity test.'

'I see. And if they do find anything in their databases, if they identify your birth father, what do you hope to get from that? Surely it won't change anything; you've always said that the only parents that mattered were the ones who raised you.'

She nodded emphatically. 'I stand by that. But I just… want to know. If I don't even try to find out, I know I'll feel frustrated.'

He nodded. 'I see that. Speaking of parents, how was Christmas with your Mum?'

'It was… interesting. Lots of food and drink; a little bit of drama.' She told him about Javier, Gulliver, her emotional exchange with her mother.

'I mean,' she said, 'I would expect – or hope – that, at my age, my daughter is more sexually active and fulfilled than I, but to learn that my septuagenarian mother is, was, I admit, quite a shock. What's even crazier,' she added, draining her wine glass, 'is that both the men in question are closer to my age than Rhiannon's or my mother's.' She gave what sounded – even to her – like a slightly forced laugh.

Amedeo was eyeing her thoughtfully.

'Were you… attracted to either of them?'

She stared at him blankly. 'Of course not! That's ridiculous! What makes you say that?'

'Nothing, it just sounded as though maybe you thought… you would be a more suitable match for Javier or Gulliver.'

Marnie flushed crimson. '*That*…is twisted.'

Damn, he thought: I forgot how touchy she could be.

'Hey… I'm sorry, *tesoro*…' he said hurriedly, patting her hand. 'I didn't mean to offend you.'

'Jesus…what must you think of me?'

With a sad laugh, he said quietly: 'I think you know by now what I think of you.'

An awkward silence fell upon them, mercifully interrupted by the arrival of the next course: some sort of stuffed buckwheat pancake for him and for her, something called *cassoulet de la mer*, which turned out to be neither *cassoulet* nor anything fishy but pink lentils with smoked tofu.

As she poked warily at the cassoulet with her fork, she broached a new topic:

'Listen, I've been meaning to pick your brains about something. You know my art tourism business idea?' He nodded. 'Well, I was wondering if you had any contacts – clients past and present, partners – in the tourism or culture industry in Italy. Museums, hospitality, even city or regional councils.'

He nodded thoughtfully. 'I know someone who works for the Lombardy Tourist Board.'

'That would be great if you could put us in touch.'

She suddenly felt the need to steer the conversation towards him. Indeed, she was often worried that his modesty, self-deprecation and eagerness to listen turned her into a self-indulgent egomaniac who monopolised the conversation. And so, she invited him to tell her about the potential investors he was meeting with the next day, how his project was progressing in general. Eventually, inevitably, conversation drifted back to DigInnova and the injustice they had both suffered at its hands. At one point, she surprised him by apologising:

'I thought you were being paranoid when you talked about Santevecchi and your enemies conspiring. And you were right about everything all along. I'm sorry I didn't take you more seriously.'

He smiled. 'Let's just be thankful all that's behind us now.'

She nodded. 'How's the food?'

'Good. And you?'

She frowned. 'Surprising. I honestly couldn't identify what's in it if I hadn't read the menu. It actually does taste like smoked fish or seafood. It's quite remarkable.'

'Ah… Could you finally be coming round to our cause?'

She laughed. 'Vegan? Hardly. And, as memorable and interesting a culinary experience this has been, I don't think I'll be bringing my future clients here. Gastronomic tourists come to France for the whole *foie gras, steak-frites, cassoulet* experience – oh, and the cheese, of course. I simply can't inflict veganism on them – no offence.'

When their dishes had been cleared away, Marnie took a sip of Crozes Hermitage and Amedeo mildly pointed out that she had drunk from his glass.

'Oh...' she said, 'well, don't worry, I don't have the plague.' She gazed at him intently, a glint of mischief in her eye. 'And besides,' she went on, leaning across the table, 'What are you complaining about? This may be the closest you and I will ever get to exchanging bodily fluids.'

She loved to provoke and shock him. And yet, for someone with so many principles – or, as she saw it sometimes – restrictions and inhibitions – he seemed impervious to all her attempts to outrage him: at this last comment of hers he merely laughed, affectionately telling her she was terrible. He was either a model of serenity and self-possession, she thought – or deeply jaded. She had not yet quite made up her mind which.

After dinner, they walked across the Seine to the Ile Saint Louis and stopped at a café for a glass of Armagnac. Marnie had fleetingly contemplated asking him back to the flat for a nightcap, but decided against it. The sensible, pragmatic rationale behind this decision was that both of them had an early start and a hectic schedule the next day: he had his meeting, whilst she had her appointments at the museums and hotels.

But there was another reason behind her reluctance: somehow it seemed both too soon and too late for anything like that between them. Not for the first time, she felt that she and he had missed their very brief window of opportunity – without being able to pinpoint exactly when that window had presented itself.

For all that, she was happy to see him, as ever. She loved the way he saw her: the goodness and potential he seemed to see in her. And for the time they spent together and a few hours, sometimes days afterwards, she could let herself believe she was everything he thought she was.

CHAPTER TWENTY-FIVE

In Loving Memory

Please join us for a memorial service honouring

EU Britain

1973-2020

31st January from 7pm GMT (8pm Brussels time)

Chez Appelbaum

39, Solent Road, NW6

Dress code: black, or the traditional costume of your European country of choice

When Marnie had received the invitation a week before, printed on thick cream vellum, she had laughed out loud. How very *Val*, she thought.

The invitation had been particularly serendipitous as she was still reeling from what was possibly one of the most anti-climactic experiences of her adult life: the results of her DNA test had come through from MyRoots. She had enthusiastically clicked on the link in the email, which opened up her personal space on the MyRoots website. Clicking on the 'DNA' tab, she saw at the top of the list of DNA matches:

'Deirdre Kavanaugh – estimated relationship: mother. Shared DNA: 49.7%.'

She was surprised to see Deirdre's name; not, of course, to see confirmation of their relationship, but the fact that it was on the website: that could only mean Deirdre had signed up to MyRoots, which was interesting. Had Marnie's reaching out to her all those years ago sparked curiosity in the other woman as to her own family history? Or were the two unrelated?

The other DNA data – largely incomprehensible (*what the devil was a cM?*) and probably irrelevant – Marnie ignored. The next match on the list was the only other name she recognised:

Aiofe Mullan – Dave's mother – estimated relationship: first cousin once removed or second cousin, with a DNA match of 3.8% – and after that, the percentage was increasingly lower.

That was it. Nothing about her father. As she scrolled quickly through the hundreds – thousands – of people with whom she apparently shared an extremely tenuous biological link, she scolded herself for her foolishness and naivety for having harboured such high expectations of this procedure. As if a few cheek swabs could instantly unlock the secret to her true self, could make her feel whole!

On the evening of the party, she was standing in the Appelbaums' kitchen while Val finished preparing the buffet – a pan-European feast featuring specialities from various member states: there was *tortilla, pan con tomate*, pickled herrings, Swedish meatballs, *insalata tricolore*, a selection of French cheeses and saucisson – and a plate of frankfurter sausages covered in a spicy-smelling sauce.

'Currywurst,' explained Val, making a face. 'Josh fell in love with it on his exchange trip to Cologne last term. He made the sauce himself.'

Jolyon, meanwhile, was in the drawing room concocting a special cocktail of his own design; the kids were in their respective rooms.

Val's outfit for the occasion was simple and to the point: she had simply wrapped herself in a European flag over a black leotard and tights. Her ash-blond hair was styled in a neat chignon and Medora had painted a circle of twelve gold stars on her face. Marnie, meanwhile, having briefly toyed with the idea of wearing a St Patrick's Day costume to reflect her Irish nationality, had decided to pay homage to her former homeland instead and put on a Breton top, black capri pants and a beret, with a fake string of onions around her neck, and blue, white and red vertical stripes on her cheeks.

'So,' said Val, planting a miniature Spanish flag in the middle of the omelette, 'I want to hear all about it: Christmas with your Mum's toyboy and Rhiannon's sugar daddy, and Paris with the guy who's not gay.'

Marnie shrugged and nodded. 'That's pretty much it in a nutshell: Amedeo's still not gay, but still not my soul-mate; my mother's a cougar and my daughter's a gerontophile. But at least they're getting some. I, on the other hand…'

She broke off as Jolyon entered the kitchen in a matador costume and bearing a cocktail shaker.

'I need your opinion on this,' he said, setting the shaker down on the island. He took three highball glasses from the cupboard, filled them with a greenish liquid from the shaker and handed them out.

'I'm calling it a Maastricht Massacre: there's absinthe from France, Sambuca from Italy, London gin and Sicilian lemon juice. Cheers.'

Whilst Marnie and Jolyon swore, winced and grimaced at their first swig, Val's face remained impassive yet thoughtful. She took another mouthful, rolling the liquid around her mouth before swallowing and finally announced her verdict:

'Obviously, it needs sweetening...' She opened one of the cupboards behind her, opened a tin of apricots and poured some of the syrup into the shaker. 'And try some bitters.' She turned to her husband. 'We do have bitters, don't we?'

Jolyon nodded and withdrew to the drawing room to perfect his cocktail.

'Wow,' observed Marnie, looking after him. 'There aren't many blokes who can get away with matador pants...'

'And he's no exception,' agreed Val. 'Bless him. You were saying?'

'My moribund sex life. Yes, there has been no activity in that department since I shagged my brother's father at a wedding over six months ago. Oh, and just in case that weren't embarrassing enough, I...' she lowered her voice. 'I found Rhiannon's bloke quite attractive. Go, on say it.'

'What? That you're carving a niche for yourself in highly inappropriate relationships?'

Marnie shrugged and speared a piece of currywurst with a cocktail stick. 'Hardly relationships: a one-night stand in the one case, and a vague crush in the other – hmm, that's actually quite nice; it's like chip shop curry sauce. The point is, there's not the remotest romantic or sexual prospect on my horizon.'

Val gave an enigmatic smile. 'Well, it's funny you should say that,' she said, drizzling olive oil over tomatoes, mozzarella and basil. 'Joly's invited a friend of his tonight; I thought you two might hit it off.'

Marnie reached for another chunk of currywurst and flashed a wary glance at her.

'No offense, but given your track record in matchmaking, I'm not about to rush out to John Lewis and register for a wedding list.'

Val frowned. 'What? Oh, you mean that weird mate of Matt Tierney's who had a pet rat? Please, that was thirty years ago; I've got better at it. This guy's nice, clever, funny, got a good job. Divorced, no kids. And I've always found him quite sexy: tallish, quite fit, mixed-race – his Dad's Indian. A bit younger than you, but maybe it's time you broke that mould.'

'How young are we talking?' inquired Marnie dubiously.

159

'Oh, about our age, give or take.' She placed a mini Italian flag on the plate of salad and wiped her hands on a tea towel. 'More like take. Joly?' she called, opening the kitchen door. 'How old's Ben?'

'Forty-four, forty-five. You know, you were right – as usual: the apricot syrup and bitters did the trick.'

Marnie and Val began gathering up platters of food and carrying them through. After laying the buffet out on the dining table, they allowed Jolyon to serve them a Maastricht Massacre V2. He then stepped out into the hall and called the kids.

Josh made an appearance first. At fourteen, he was already the tallest member of the family, standing at six feet one. A mop of curly dark hair fell over purple-framed glasses through which peered shrewd dark blue eyes. In addition to his height, a number of things stood him apart – and possibly alienated him – from his peers: his superior and precocious intellect, his occasionally outmoded speech, his eccentric sartorial style: today he was wearing a brown corduroy three-piece suit over a white T-shirt and threadbare Dunlop Green Flash trainers. Marnie was about to ask what his costume was supposed to be, then thought better of it. He mumbled a greeting to her.

'Hi, Josh. Where's your sister?'

'Adding the finishing touches to her Nazi slut outfit,' he drawled.

Marnie shot an inquiring glance at Val, who rolled her eyes and mouthed: 'Don't ask.'

The doorbell rang and Jolyon went to answer, returning with two couples in late middle age bearing bottles of wine, dishes and Tupperware boxes whom he subsequently introduced as their neighbours. Just as Val was gratefully accepting the offerings from the new arrivals and taking their drinks orders, Medora walked into the room.

Marnie eyed her friend's daughter: with her preposterously long, (what was it with young girls today? Did they think they were mermaids?), impossibly straight, glossy hair, which she no doubt spent hours taming with straightening irons each morning, her penchant for flashy designer labels and her tireless self-promotion – or 'branding' as Marnie believed they called it – on social media, Medora Appelbaum was as conventional, conformist, popular and academically mediocre as her younger brother was eccentric, overachieving and virtually ostracised. In the merciless world of the secondary-school pecking order, Marnie reflected, not for the first time, Medora was surely at the top of the food chain and her brother at the bottom. Marnie had personally always had a soft spot for Josh. His sister was a nice enough kid, but she could identify far more easily with the quirky underdog than the vapid Queen Bee.

Beholding Medora's outfit, Marnie suppressed a snort of laughter as she thought of Josh's comment: for the girl was indeed wearing a dirndl, complete with a laced bodice that emphasised her stalk-like waist, low-cut white blouse, and a skirt and apron that only reached about a third of the way down her thigh. Her bare colt-like legs looked endless in the black ten-centimetre stiletto pumps; her face was heavily made-up.

'You know,' observed Josh, 'if you were going for full-on ironic – or controversial – you should have just come as Eva Braun.'

Marnie sensed she would have liked to spit out some withering riposte to her brother but good manners prevented her from doing so in front of guests. She contented herself with glaring venomously at him.

There followed an awkward silence, broken by one of the neighbours, a plump, sandy-haired woman named Nancy who was dressed like the protagonist of Vermeer's *Milkmaid*:

'Well, you've certainly got the legs for it, dear.'

Medora smiled sweetly at the compliment and requested a Maastricht Massacre from her father. He consented to serve her a half-glass, but declined Josh's request for a beer.

'These look good,' said Val, inspecting the contents of the container Nancy and her partner had brought. 'What are they? Some sort of pancakes?'

'Potato *lefse*,' said Nancy, sitting down heavily on the sofa and slipping off her clogs. 'You don't mind, do you? These things are killing me.'

'What's that, a Dutch speciality?'

Nancy shook her head, accepting a glass of Chardonnay from Jolyon. 'The Netherlands isn't much of a culinary hotspot, so I thought I'd bring a Norwegian dish instead.'

Marnie, Jolyon and Val exchanged amused looks but said nothing.

'Norway isn't in the EU,' said Josh flatly.

Nancy stared at him over the brim of her wine glass for a few seconds, and then said:

'Are you sure, dear?'

'We could call Ursula von der Leyen and check,' deadpanned Josh, 'but I'm thinking she's got other things on her mind this evening.'

'All right, Joshy,' said Val briskly. 'Come and give me a hand in the kitchen.'

Fortunately, what Nancy lacked in knowledge of the European member states, she more than made up for in good humour. She shrugged, and, looking at her watch, said, with a little laugh, 'Oh well, neither will we be in just over four hours.'

The other guests began to arrive: more neighbours, some engineer colleagues of Val's, and a friend of Josh's – a lanky red-headed youth with severe acne dressed in jeans and a Che Guevara T-shirt.

Jolyon's Maastricht Massacre proved something of an acquired taste, with few takers: apart from Jolyon himself, only Marnie and Val continued to drink it throughout the evening – the former out of loyalty to her host, the latter reasoning that any further drink mixes would result in a cataclysmic hangover and she must go on as she had started. Medora would also have liked a second glass, purely because it was the strongest drink available, but her parents had put their foot down.

Food was eaten, more drink drunk; various guests recalled their reactions at learning the referendum results – was it really nearly four years ago? At around ten-thirty, by which time Marnie was rather bored and restless and had consequently drunk too many Maastricht Massacres, two late-comers arrived: Jolyon's friend Rob, who arrived with a bottle of Nuit Saint Georges and a large rectangular box, and a trim man in his forties with an olive-gold complexion, dark brown eyes and short raven-black hair with fashionable stubble on his chin and upper lip. He was wearing slim-fit jeans and a Barbour.

'I thought we could play a game,' said Rob, removing his coat to reveal a black mourning armband on his left arm and placing the box on the coffee table: it was a special European Union Edition of Monopoly. 'My old man got it as a Christmas present years ago. Thought it would be appropriate for tonight. It's a bit of a museum piece – came out in '92, when there were only twelve member states. Still, we could give it a whirl.'

A group of people, including Val, Josh and Che Guevara, Nancy and partner and Val's colleague Sander, accepted Rob's invitation and began setting up the game and choosing tokens, which were miniature European monuments. Marnie, who detested Monopoly and was a wretched loser, wisely demurred and wandered into the hallway where the slim dark-haired guest was removing his Barbour and hanging it on the coat-stand. He looked up at Marnie and she saw a flicker of recognition followed by what seemed like faint amusement in his dark eyes. He looked away.

'Ben! There you are.' Val came hurriedly out of the drawing room and grabbed the man by the arm. He beamed at her and kissed her cheek.

'Val. How are you, darling? Sorry I'm late.' His voice was rich and smooth, with just the hint of a Northern accent.

Val turned to Marnie and beckoned her. 'Ben, I don't believe you've met Marnie Wade, one of my oldest friends; Marn, this is Ben Balakrishnan.'

162

Here we go, thought Marnie, shaking hands unenthusiastically with the guest.

'Hello,' she mumbled.

Ben looked at her intently as he shook her hand; again, that knowing, vaguely mocking smile.

'No, I haven't met Marnie,' he said, his eyes still on her, 'although I am familiar with her work.'

She frowned at him in puzzlement. 'Sorry?'

'Mum!' Josh's voice called out from the drawing room. 'It's your turn.' Val excused herself, and, with a mischievous smile at Marnie, withdrew.

'The video,' Ben explained. 'At the National Gallery? You telling that guide –'

'Yes, yes,' she said irritably. 'I know what I… I *was* there.'

'You know,' he went on, the same playful smile on his lips, 'I seem to remember Joly saying you were a bit Amish when it came to social media, and yet, here you are: the star of a viral video…' He trailed off, noting Marnie's evident growing discomfort. His smile faded, and he said quickly, as if trying to console her: 'I only heard about it because a friend of mine is Exhibitions Curator there – at the National Gallery. He thought you were great. I told him he should hire you.'

'Really?' Marnie retorted curtly. 'And what do you do for a living?' She looked him up and down: 'and why aren't you in fancy dress? Unless of course you're representing the Republic of Piss-Taking.'

He smiled wryly. 'I believe they were denied EU membership. As to your other question, I'm afraid I don't do anything as highbrow as working in a picture gallery. I work for a charity.'

'Oh, come off it, Ben,' laughed Jolyon, who had just emerged from the kitchen carrying a bottle of wine. 'It's not like you work behind the till at the local Age UK Shop.' He turned to Marnie: 'He's being ridiculously modest. He's actually Head of Fundraising for the Heathcliff Foundation.'

'The Heathcliff Foundation?' asked Marnie, holding out her glass to Jolyon for a refill. 'What's that when it's at home?'

'It's an adoption charity,' said Ben. 'We provide information and support for adoptive parents.'

'Well, there's something you guys could talk about!' said Jolyon enthusiastically. 'Marnie was adopted,' he explained to Ben.

'Really?' Ben turned to her with interest.

'Yes, but… sorry, I don't really feel like talking about it,' she said hurriedly, glaring at Jolyon, who smiled sheepishly and retreated. She turned back to Ben:

'So…Heathcliff?'

He nodded. 'The founder wanted to name it after a famous orphan from literature.'

'And he or she chose what is arguably the most unattractive male protagonist in the history of English literature.'

'Not a Heathcliff fan, then?'

Marnie rolled her eyes. 'Are you joking? I mean, when I first read *Wuthering Heights* at school I thought he was dashing and romantic, but I read it again a couple of years ago and revised my opinion. What a *tosser*.'

The amused look had returned, only this time Marnie didn't sense any ridicule in it. 'Who would you have chosen?'

She shrugged and took a swig of wine. 'I don't know. I'm a Dickens lover so probably one of his orphans – God knows there are enough of them. Maybe Estella Havisham? Or Hephzibah.' Seeing the blank look that had descended on Ben's handsome features, she explained: 'That was Eppie's full name. In *Silas Marner*.'

'Oh, was it? I never read that one. The Hephzibah Foundation,' he said thoughtfully. 'It does have quite a ring to it.'

A momentary silence fell, then Marnie said: 'Well, it was nice to meet you. I need to discuss some…er, legal stuff with Jolyon.' And with that, she wandered off in search of the host, whom she found sitting on the stairs talking on his mobile. After a few moments, he hung up.

'Damn,' he said softly.

'Bad news?'

'I was supposed to go to an important meeting in Milan next week – a company we're representing. It's been called off: the client's in hospital. Some virus he picked up when he was in China. Looks like it's that SARS-type thing they've been talking about on the news.'

'Oh, that thing? It'll blow over, just die out after a couple of months like SARS did.'

He nodded. 'Let's hope so. So… what do you think of Ben?'

'I don't know. He seems OK. A bit cocky. How do you know him?'

'We met through work. I do some pro-bono consulting for the Foundation.'

She frowned. 'What does an adoption charity need with an environmental lawyer?'

'Oh, it's not for environmental law specifically. I basically act as their Legal Counsel.' He was prevented from giving further explanations by a shriek from the drawing room:

'Cheat!'

Intrigued, they both got up and went to investigate.

'You only moved forward four places!' protested Josh. 'You threw a five. That makes you land on Schiphol Airport – which is mine, so you owe me rent.' Snatching up his mother's Sagrada Familia token, he placed it on the appropriate space, shaking his head and muttering, 'Unbelievable. Every time.'

Val pleaded honest mistake, but he ignored her protestations, holding his hand out, palm upturned:

'Whatever. Come on, Val, pay up.'

'Hey, it's nearly midnight,' announced Rob, putting down the Parthenon token and picking up his glass of Burgundy. 'What shall we drink to?'

'Let's be awfully original and go with "the end of an era,"' suggested Jolyon.

Glasses were raised. 'The end of an era.'

CHAPTER TWENTY-SIX

Bristol, 8 February 2020

'So, you're not a believer in the "when in Rome" thing then?' observed Marnie as Dave deposited a pint of Guinness and one of Thatcher's on the table. She nodded towards the Guinness. 'You're in Bristol, mate. You *have* to have cider.'

'Clare was always saying I needed to broaden my horizons,' he said, before raising his glass to her and dipping his upper lip in the froth. 'Although, she also used to say I should stop sleeping with other women: she didn't have much luck in that department either.'

Three days before, Marnie had been sitting at the dining room table in Dowry Square simultaneously rereading the biography of Caravaggio (as research for the Caravaggio tour she was putting together) and glancing at the revised mock-ups of her website Anaïs, her web designer, had just sent when she had received a text from Dave: how did she feel about an impromptu visit from her favourite second cousin that weekend? Twenty minutes later, after she had emailed her thoughts on the website to Anaïs, she called him.

'Hey! What's up?'

He explained that his current circumstances – both professional and personal – were particularly propitious for a brief sojourn away from Dublin.

'Let me guess,' said Marnie. 'Is it the bailiffs? Or has some woman's husband – or father – put out a contract on your head?'

'Nothing so dramatic,' he replied. 'Just having a shite week: just lost a major account at work and I had another barny with Clare about money and custody and birthing plans. My current lady friend is out of town with her old man this weekend, it's Clare's turn with Declan, I've got nearly enough airmiles on my account for a return to Bristol and – most importantly – in a month the new baby'll be here and I won't get another opportunity to go anywhere for God knows how long.'

Marnie had to admit he had made a compelling argument. She herself had nothing particular planned for the weekend – although, ever since she had lost her job and particularly ever since she had started working on the new business, weekdays had had a habit of merging seamlessly and indistinguishably into weekends. In any event, Dave was always a tonic for her. She told him to book his flights.

She had fetched him from the airport on Friday night and they had had a quiet dinner and a bottle of wine at home. The next day was mild and sunny so she decided to take him on a long walking tour of the city. After a leisurely breakfast of eggs benedict, freshly-squeezed orange juice and coffee, they had started out from Marnie's flat and walked up the hill towards Clifton, skirting the Village and continuing to the university, through the Royal Fort Gardens, then down St Michael's Hill, Colston Street and down Christmas Steps. They had then continued along Christmas Street and Broad Street to St Nicholas Market where Dave, after purchasing a bottle of Psycho Juice from the Hot Sauce Emporium, had declared a raging thirst, so they stopped at the Crown for a drink.

'Seriously,' Marnie persisted as Dave finished his Guinness. 'You can't be here and not try some proper cider.'

He shook his head. 'Nah, you're all right. I've never really been a fan.'

Marnie threw up her hands in despair. 'That's because you've never had the decent stuff. You're used to that chemical shite like Magners. Come on,' she said, standing up. 'I'm going to give you the proper Bristol experience.'

Dave relented and allowed himself to be taken to a barge moored on the quayside a few minutes' walk away. Ordering him to sit at one of the tables on the quayside, Marnie boarded the barge and emerged a few minutes later with a couple of pints of a cloudy-looking substance.

'I've got you some Old Bristolian,' she said; 'the house brew. Go easy on it, mind: it's 8.4%.'

Dave took a swig and immediately pulled a face, setting the glass down.

'It's flat!'

Marnie laughed. 'It's supposed to be! Come on, have another try: let your palate acclimatise.'

He obeyed. It was dry and tangy, yet not sour.

It soon became evident that a young woman two tables away was trying to catch his eye.

'Am I cramping your style?' asked Marnie, nodding towards his admirer. 'Make sure she's on the Pill, mind.'

'Ha fuckin' ha.'

'Oh, come on. Surely I'm allowed to make at least one joke about your plans to repopulate the Republic?'

167

'You are not, and may I remind you, Tina's *wasn't mine!*'

'You should put that on your gravestone. Or just your social media. #TinasWasntMine.'

'Yeah, maybe I should. And anyway,' he said, lowering his voice and jerking his head towards the girl eyeing him up, 'I wouldn't take *that* one lampin'.'

'Ah, still as gallant as ever.'

He shrugged. 'Well, I'll grant you she's pretty tidy, but she's got that mad look about her. Reminds me of a girl I was seeing at college. Stalked me for weeks. I met her in a bar one night, had a bit of a snog but was too drunk for anything else and to be honest, I didn't really fancy her that much, so we went home separately. Next day she was waiting for me outside the lecture theatre: was all over me, acting like she was my girlfriend, like, and I could see it: that manic glint in her eye. So, I kicked her into touch.'

'"Kicked her into touch,"' marvelled Marnie. 'Excellent. I love how you use rugby metaphors to refer to affairs of the heart.'

'Absolutely,' he said, taking another appreciative draught of Old Bristolian (she was right: it was growing on him). 'In fact, I'm all for introducing more rugby expressions into everyday parlance, to replace some of your more clichéd sports metaphors.'

'Hmm…' said Marnie thoughtfully. 'So, instead of saying, "that was a bit below the belt," for example, people could say "that was a bit above the shoulder," or "that was a really high tackle."'

He raised his glass in approval. 'There you go. I'm counting on you to help me make this a thing. Start using it in conversation.'

Their cider finished, they continued around the Harbourside, crossing Queen's Square to the Arnolfini Arts Centre and across the bridge. Dave was peckish (like a baby, he needed feeding every four hours), so they stopped for fish and chips then carried on past the SS Great Britain and Marnie showed him Banksy's *Girl with a Pierced Eardrum*. Thirsty after the fish and chips – no doubt from the copious amounts of salt and vinegar – they stopped at the Nova Scotia where, over pints of Thatcher's, he told her about his cousin's plans to adopt baby Olivia, and his rather vociferous expression of his opinion on the matter.

Declining to weigh in on the nature-nurture debate, Marnie simply said, 'Well, I hope everything works out for everyone. And who knows? Méabh adopting Olivia might be right for them both.'

He shrugged. 'Maybe. Anyway, I agreed to say Olivia was mine so Méabh could apply to adopt her as a relative. She's got the ball rolling, and in the meantime Tusla are letting her foster her. The rest is up to her now.'

168

'Good for you,' Marnie said approvingly.' Then, looking pensively into her glass of cider, she went on: 'I remember years ago watching an episode of *Inspector Morse* – did you ever watch that?' Seeing his blank expression, she rolled her eyes. 'Oh, God, you're probably too young, you bastard. Anyway, the storyline of this particular episode was about a girl who was adopted and years later, when she grows up, she tracks down her birth mother and stabs her to death. The back story was that her adoptive parents had got divorced at some point and she'd gone into care.' She took a hefty swig of cider. 'Supposedly, the trauma of being rejected twice – once by her birth mother, then by her adoptive parents – pushed her over the edge. Now, speaking as someone who was adopted by a couple who ended up divorcing, I remember being outraged and offended. I wanted to *kill* the morons who wrote that. I mean, I don't know what's more preposterous: the idea that adoptive parents divorcing is an aberration, that they shouldn't be as likely – or have as much right – to fall out of love as a couple that had their own kids. Or that, once they'd divorced, they'd just give the kid back. Or the idea that an adopted kid should seek out their birth mother and bump her off!'

'So,' said Dave a few minutes later when she returned with another round. 'You've never wanted to take a knife to Deirdre for giving you up?'

She laughed. 'Honestly, no. I can totally see I was much better off where I ended up.'

He nodded. 'Yeah, you do seem pretty cool with all that.'

She raised her eyes at him over the rim of her glass.

'Well, I wouldn't say that exactly… I mean, for years I thought I was totally fine with it, that it had had no effect on me. But years ago, I decided to see a therapist for a while – not about that specifically, just stuff in general, relationships. Anyway, she made me realise, over the course of our sessions, that, despite what I thought, being adopted – or, rather, knowing I had been given up for adoption – had a profound influence on most of the relationships and friendships in my life.' She stopped and studied him for a few seconds: was she boring him? Embarrassing him with her confidences? But his handsome face bore an expression of genuine curiosity. She continued.

'In my teens and early twenties I got… caught up in a few very intense, exclusive, stifling friendships with girls. One in the sixth form then in my first year in Paris – a girl I shared a flat with for a while. It wasn't sexual, but very… symbiotic. They were very clingy and possessive. It began to drive me crazy but it always took me ages to extricate myself. A mixture of cowardice… and well, good manners, I suppose.'

His eyes widened in bemusement.

169

She laughed. 'No, really: I was paralysed by my upbringing: it's rude to break someone's heart; it's unseemly to make a scene. So, I endured it for far too long. Then it all seemed so obvious when the therapist pointed out what this pattern was all about. You know, if I'm with a woman who loves me that much – who loves me more than I love her – then, I can be sure–'

'That she'll never abandon you like your mam did,' Dave said, nodding.

After a few moments' silence, Marnie stood up, swaying slightly. 'Right, I don't know about you but I'm definitely going to need a little lie down before dinner.'

Fortunately, it was only a five-minute walk from the pub back to Marnie's, where they collapsed on their respective beds. Dave was snoring loudly within minutes, and after three pages of Caravaggio, Marnie too succumbed and sank into a deep sleep.

She had The Dream. As usual, she was wandering around a vast house, exploring the seemingly infinite numbers of bedrooms, connected by a bewildering array of corridors and staircases. Staircases, indeed, featured heavily in the Dream House, often of the more elaborate, complex variety: double-spiral, Penrose. Years ago, during a session, her therapist had provided an interesting – and, with hindsight, fairly obvious – interpretation of the dream: it was the sub-conscious manifestation of Marnie's doubts, uncertainties and anxiety about her origins, her adoption, the mystery surrounding her birth father.

It was just after six when she awoke. She had a shower and was in the kitchen making a cup of tea when Dave too rose and disappeared into the bathroom, emerging fifteen minutes later in a cloud of steam and Paco Rabanne One Million.

'Right,' he said. 'Where to next?'

It was a twenty-minute uphill walk to the Clifton Triangle where Marnie had booked a table at a Sri Lankan place. As their table wasn't quite ready, they stood at the bar sipping cocktails: in keeping with the spirit of gustatory intrepidity, Dave had let Marnie persuade him to try a heady concoction of Ceylon Arrack, turmeric-infused Cointreau and ginger beer.

Ten minutes later, after the waitress had taken their orders, Dave asked:

'I was just thinking about what you were saying earlier about how adoption affected your relationships with women. What about men?'

She nodded, smiling. 'There was a pattern there too. You see, I've never got the whole 'bad boy' thing: sure, I've had the odd one-night stand or fling in the past with guys like that. But when looking for a mate for life, I've always gone for *nice* guys – decent, honest, trustworthy, constant, faithful types. Ones that wouldn't run off and leave me and their kids, like my birth father did. Good men, like my actual dad – my adoptive father, I mean.'

'Didn't your folks split up?'

'They left each other, but they didn't abandon Guy and me. There was no infidelity on either side, I'm sure of that. None of them went off with other people, and they shared custody of us.'

He nodded. 'Was your ex-husband like that? One of the good guys, I mean?'

'Absolutely.'

'So, you would never have ended up with someone like me then?' he said with a wry smile.

'Christ, no! No offence.'

'None taken. Clare's dad was a bit of a lad. I guess she has a type too. Although, I'd never abandon my bairns like he did.'

Conversation took a turn for the more light-hearted once the food arrived – half a dozen little dishes of colourful, pungent-smelling delicacies. As they feasted on goat curry, black pork belly, *hoppas* – coconut milk pancakes – fiery curried chicken on the bone, pumpkin cooked in coconut milk and devilled prawns, and ordered another round of Drunken Sri Lankans, Marnie reflected contentedly on their mutual penchant for such gleeful epicurean abandon. For they both loved to eat and drink as though there were no tomorrow – although, in Marnie's case, after such indulgence, tomorrow would inevitably involve going for a run, doing an hour of yoga and ingesting nothing but cabbage soup and detox tea.

However, she was soon to be jerked out of her blissful haze of repletion and insouciance. As they walked unsteadily back home from the restaurant, her phone rang: the ring tone was the chorus of Fleetwood Mac's *Rhiannon*.

'Hey! What's up, Pussycat?'

Silence on the other end.

'Rhiannon?'

Nothing – and then a sort of muffled squeak.

'Mum… It's over. Gulliver…' was all she managed before dissolving into floods of tears.

CHAPTER TWENTY-SEVEN

Bassett, Southampton, 22 February 2020

'The *Pocket Guide to Yugoslavia*?' Marnie exclaimed. 'God, that's got to be a collector's item. No… wait: what's this? The *Pocket Guide to the Federal Republic of Germany*! Honestly, Dad, why do you keep these relics?'

They were in the living room of Martin Wade's house. Marnie had come down to Hampshire for the weekend: it was her father's eightieth birthday and Guy and Nova had arranged a small celebration. They had originally intended to throw a rather spectacular surprise party at some grand local venue, but Martin had made it quite clear some weeks before that he had no intention of celebrating his birthday and that if he got so much as the slightest inkling that any such plans were afoot, he would simply boycott the event and contrive to be away on the day in question. Consequently, Guy, Nova and Marnie had been forced to rethink their original plan, although they refused to cancel the event altogether. It had therefore been decided to host a small luncheon party at Martin's favourite French restaurant with a dozen guests: in addition to the four of them, there would be Auntie Eileen – Martin's widowed sister – her son, daughter-in-law, and their two teenaged children, his oldest friend from his schooldays, Arthur, and a quartet of golfing pals. Rhiannon, still nursing her broken heart and grateful for an excuse to escape from Warwick, was also in attendance. Against Marnie's advice, Guy and Nova had insisted on maintaining the element of surprise: officially, they were having a quiet family lunch out with just the five of them: when they reached the restaurant, the other guests would be lying in wait.

On the morning of the day in question, Marnie, as part of her research for devising art-themed tours for her new business venture, was perusing her father's collection of Berlitz travel guides in search of inspiration.

In response to his daughter's comments, Martin Wade shrugged, his hands thrust deep into the pockets of his mustard-coloured corduroy trousers. 'Well, they may be a bit out of date, but you never know: they might come in handy again one day.'

'*A bit out of date?*' she exclaimed. 'No! I mean, OK, they are completely out of touch with the current geopolitical landscape. But I'm sure there are some great addresses of cafés in Dubrovnik and Munich. Now, what else do you have in your astonishing repertoire of irrelevant and anachronistic guides to non-existent countries? A *Guide to the Upper Volta*, perchance? What about the Ottoman Empire? Surely you have a Baedeker on that tucked away somewhere?'

Martin chuckled and shrugged off his daughter's teasing good-naturedly.

'Ignore her, Grandad,' said Rhiannon, rising from the sofa. 'Now, why don't we have a little glass of something before Guy and Nova get here?'

Glancing at his watch, Martin said: 'Well, it is nearly twelve… Go on then: I'll have a brandy and ginger.'

'Straight onto spirits,' said Rhiannon admiringly, 'Rock 'n' roll! Mum?'

'Whatever you're having,' Marnie muttered distractedly, examining the back cover of a Crete Pocket Guide from the mid-eighties. 'Actually, no: I'll have a sherry. Whatever Grandad's got.'

By the time Rhiannon had prepared their drinks and was distributing them, there was a knock on the living room window and seconds later, Guy and Nova let themselves in the front door.

Marnie had not seen her brother and sister-in-law since their wedding nine months ago. Both were looking tired and flustered: Marnie suspected they had been overseeing work on their house right up until they had had to leave to drive here. After hugging them both, she asked how work on the site was progressing.

'Slowly,' said Guy curtly, kissing Rhiannon on the cheek. 'Spent the morning doing the guttering on the garage. It's a nightmare.'

'Have a drink,' said Rhiannon. After receiving Nova's assurance that she would drive, Guy gratefully accepted a gin and tonic.

'Cheers, Pops,' he said, raising his glass to Martin. 'Happy birthday!'

It was soon time to leave for the restaurant, a ten-minute walk away.

Marnie's fears about her father's reaction to being ambushed with a birthday party turned out to be entirely unfounded: after his initial shock, he graciously resigned himself to being the centre of attention for the next two hours, and even appeared to enjoy himself.

Marnie had been seated next to her cousin Gordon. He asked how her project was progressing; she described the development of the website and her imminent field trip to Italy to scout venues, meet partners and test-drive her prototype tour – the Caravaggio Experience.

When Gordon remarked that it sounded very glamourous, she pointed out it wasn't all free meals in restaurants and tours of picture galleries: there were also the scores of daily phone calls and email exchanges with potential partners in Italy and France and the endless red tape. After all her years living in France she had thought she had seen the worst of bureaucracy but Italy was in another league altogether. She suddenly had a newfound respect for Amedeo: his patience and forbearance must be truly saintlike.

After the main course dishes had been cleared away, Marnie, on Nova's advice, invited some of the guests to switch tables for dessert to encourage more mingling.

She herself ended up next to Guy when the dark chocolate tart with cappuccino ice-cream and orange sesame brittle was served. He was curious about their mother and Javier.

'Do you think he's after her money?' he inquired bluntly.

'What money? She isn't exactly rolling in it. And he's hardly on the breadline. He was a vet, had his own practice. She pointed out his house when we were in town one night and it's a lot bigger than her place.'

Guy frowned. 'Hmm. Still sounds dodgy though. I mean –' they were interrupted by a trilling sound which Marnie now recognised as the notification from the motion detection app he and Nova had installed on their phones as part of the surveillance system for their property.

'Bollocks,' he muttered, picking up his phone. 'Sorry, it's probably nothing but I have to check…Nope, nothing, just another spider on the CCTV cameras.' He put his phone back on the table and refilled both their glasses with Saint-Amour.

'Rhiannon's looking well,' he observed, winking at her across the table. She raised her glass and smiled in return.

'Well, she's not really.' She proceeded to recount the dismal tale of Gulliver Scutt's betrayal: how he had lied about his original plans for Christmas – he had in fact been intending to spend it with his ex-wife, with whom he was evidently in the midst of a reconciliation. Only the ex-wife had somehow found out he was seeing Rhiannon on the side and had sent him packing and banned him from her Christmas celebrations – hence his fabrication about the sick in-laws so he could insinuate himself into their family Christmas at Fay's.

'Cheeky fuck,' muttered Guy. 'Want me to sort him out?'

Marnie stared at him with a mixture of disbelief and horror. 'You're not serious?'

'Of course. I know some blokes in Birmingham who could –' His phone trilled again. 'Fuck's sake…' He snatched it up again, shaking his head. 'Nova!' he barked. His wife, who was chatting animatedly with Martin at the other table, looked up.

He brandished his phone at her. 'We need to sort this. Bloody spiders keep triggering the alarm.'

Nova blinked. 'What do you want me to do about it now, darling?' she inquired evenly. Marnie never failed to marvel at the woman's ability to remain unruffled in the face of her brother's querulousness and impossibly exacting standards.

Surprisingly, Guy backed down. 'Well, I just hope this Spanish bloke Mum's shacked up with is kosher,' he said. 'I'd hate to have to beat the crap out of Dr Cradlesnatcher *and* Señor Gigolo in the same week.'

Laughing, and reflecting that he was the only person in her life who showed his undeniable loyalty to the family by offering to commit ABH on its perceived enemies, she rubbed his arm affectionately. 'So, what's happening tonight? You said something about a surprise?'

He nodded. 'Yeah, but this one's not for Pops. Nova and I were thinking it might be fun to camp in the Mill tonight. Just the four of us, I mean.'

'Camping? Won't we freeze our arses off?'

Guy shook his head. 'It's going to be about ten degrees tonight – are you going to finish that?' Scooping up the remains of her chocolate tart, he went on: 'We've got loads of blankets and duvets and a couple of airbeds; it should be pretty cosy.' Glancing sideways at his sister, he saw her brow contort with scepticism and nudged her in the ribs. 'Go *on*. When was the last time you and I did something like this together? It'll be fun. We've got plenty of torches, we'll crack open a bottle of wine or three.'

A few hours later, having bid the guests goodbye and walked Martin back to his house where they left him to enjoy some peace, solitude and rest after the emotional and physical rigours of entertaining, Marnie, Rhiannon, Guy and Nova set off to Lymbrook, arriving three-quarters of an hour later.

Lymbrook-on-Sea is one of those idyllic, chocolate-box New Forest villages, complete with thatched cottages, a flint Norman church and a village green. Yet, unlike so many English villages, its high street has not yet been overrun with designer boutiques and achingly hip cocktail bars, to the detriment of the traditional local shops and businesses. True, there is a craft gin pub and an Asian-fusion restaurant; but there are also two grocers, a butcher's, a fish and chip shop, two antique shops, three pubs, a beautician's, a charity shop, a haberdasher's and a tea-room.

Hipsterdom, however, is not the only aspect of modern life that has bypassed the village: for Lymbrook, like the New Forest in general, is also conspicuous by its monoculturalism. Indeed, when Marnie had first visited the village, whilst acknowledging that it was no doubt a pleasant place to live (if you liked that sort of thing), after years living in Paris and Bristol, she found the almost complete lack of racial diversity strange and anachronistic.

The eighteenth-century disused watermill they were planning to camp in that night was one of three ruins on the two acres of land Guy and Nova had purchased and were in the process of rebuilding. Before they could even start on the long, tiring and stressful enterprise of building their dream home, they had devoted eighteen gruelling months to the planning application – a process which was made all the more complicated by that fact that all three of the houses they planned to renovate were listed buildings, and the land was a flood risk area covered in woodland. Thus, in addition to the inevitable paperwork and spending many hours – and tens of thousands of pounds – on architects, conservation consultants, tree experts and drainage experts, it had also required tireless lobbying: endless coffee mornings, open days and distributing flyers in an attempt to convince the villagers of the aesthetic, architectural and environmental merits of their venture: that they were not soulless property developers looking to make a quick buck by covering the property with eyesores before selling up and moving on. Their Herculean efforts had finally paid off and the project had been approved unanimously by the planning committee.

Whilst building progressed, Guy and Nova had made a makeshift home in the smaller of the buildings, a tiny derelict miller's cottage, which they had made just about habitable, although the lack of central heating would make winter particularly arduous, the only source of heat being a wood burner in the living room.

After Guy took Marnie and Rhiannon on a tour of the estate, they all clambered up the ladder to the top floor of the mill – evidently freshly swept by Guy or Nova – and began setting up camp. The two double airbeds were inflated and covered with sleeping bags, duvets and pillows, and a sheet was hung from the beam in the middle of the room as a makeshift partition between the two sleeping quarters. Music was provided via Guy's Bluetooth speaker, candles were lit, and gin and tonics poured. After drinks, Rhiannon and Nova walked into the village to fetch fish and chips. Whilst Guy walked off to adjust the tarpaulin on the roof of one of the other buildings, Marnie took advantage of the few moments of solitude to check her phone; there was a text from Val and a voicemail from an unfamiliar number. She read Val's message first:

Remember Ben from the Brexit party? Hope you don't mind but I gave him your number. x.

Rolling her eyes and laughing, she called her voicemail and heard that deep, slightly Northern-accented voice:

'Marnie, this is Ben Balakrishnan. We met at Val and Jolyon's a couple of weeks ago? Hope you're well. Listen, I've been given a couple of tickets to a private guided tour of the Tate Modern next Thursday evening and, if you're in town, I was wondering if you'd like to come with me and heckle the guide?' A nervous laugh. 'Well, the heckling is strictly optional. I'd like you to come either way. So… give me a call. Thanks. Bye.'

'Cheeky fuck,' she muttered under her breath and promptly sent a brief text thanking him for the invitation and informing him that work would be keeping her in Bristol for the next few weeks.

Her daughter and sister-in-law arrived with the fish and chips, which they ate sitting crossed-legged on the floor with a couple of bottles of Sauvignon Blanc. After dinner they played a few rounds of cards until around midnight when, armed with torches, they climbed downstairs and crossed the courtyard to the cottage where they brushed their teeth in the tiny bathroom before returning to the mill to retire for the night.

Just as Marnie was climbing into bed, she saw Rhiannon grinning at her phone as she messaged someone.

'Not *him*, I take it?' she ventured.

Rhiannon raised an eyebrow at her mother. 'Give me some credit. No, it's just India.'

'The country? I didn't realise you two were on such intimate terms.'

'India Veenstra.'

'Who on earth is India Veenstra? Presuming that's someone's actual name.'

Rhiannon placed her phone down by the bed and gave her mother a vaguely impatient look.

'Clodagh's daughter. Dave's niece.'

'Dave…?'

'Mother, why are you being so obtuse? Dave Mullan. Your biological second cousin?'

Marnie sat up in bed. 'You're in touch with those people? The Kavanaughs?'

'Did you think you had the monopoly on them?' she replied tartly. 'I'm in touch with India. You and Dave are quite buddy and I was curious about them. I found his niece India on Facebook, then started following her on Insta. She's twenty-three, works as a graphic designer and illustrator, lives in Berlin. She's really talented, her stuff is amazing.'

Marnie lay down on her side facing her daughter, propped up by her elbow.

'You've been stalking your – what would that make her – your third cousin, on social media? "Preeing," I believe it's called.'

The use of this term – so entirely unexpected from her mother's mouth – elicited a wary look from her daughter.

'It's hardly that. I reached out to her, introduced myself, told her we were vaguely related, and we've been in touch ever since.' She studied her mother's expression carefully. 'Is this going to be a problem? I mean, is it weird for you?'

Marnie assured her it was not.

'Good, because she's really cool. You have to check out her Insta.'

'I think that highly improbable, my love: you know I'm not in the habit of checking out people's Instas. But I'm glad you've become friends. I had no idea.'

Rhiannon shrugged. 'It's no big deal. It's just… well, you know: I'm an only child, I don't have any cousins, nor am I ever likely to, as Dad's an only child and' – she nodded towards the cottage where Guy and Nova were still performing their ablutions – '*they're* not likely to produce an heir.' She was perfectly matter-of-fact, without a trace of self-pity. 'I admit, at first I didn't get why you were getting into all this family tracing stuff. But with you getting in touch with your birth mum and now Dave, I realised it opened up new… possibilities. And like I said, India's cool.' She stretched out under the covers and yawned. 'Speaking of birth family, did you hear about Heidi?'

'Guy's birth mother?' Marnie's curiosity was piqued. 'What about her?'

'Nova was just telling me when we went to get supper. A few months ago, Guy persuaded Heidi to trace her birth parents – did you know she was adopted too?'

Marnie nodded. 'He did mention it, although I didn't know she'd done anything about tracing her biologicals.'

Rhiannon shook her head in astonishment. 'God, imagine being adopted, then having a kid yourself and putting it up for adoption! In family tree terms, you've got neither branches nor roots: you're just suspended in mid-air.' After gazing wistfully into the distance for a few seconds, she shook herself out of her whimsical musings. 'Anyway, a few weeks ago Heidi found her birth mum and reached out to her! Her name's Gracie, apparently, and she's in her early eighties. Lives in Newcastle. And guess what? Guy's been up there to meet her! His grandmother! How weird is that?'

'For fuck's sake,' muttered Marnie under her breath, rolling onto her back.

'What?' Rhiannon asked irritably. 'Why does that bother you?'

Marnie signed. 'It doesn't matter why. I'm sure he's very excited about it all and I don't want to ruin it with my cynicism. Let's talk about something else… You for example? How have you been doing since….' she hesitated.

'Since I found out that bastard was still shagging his ex and lying to us both? All right.' She turned to Marnie. 'No, really, I'm OK. Although, I do need to talk to you about something.'

They were interrupted by the sound of footfalls on the gravel outside, then the mill door opening and the ladder creaking as Guy and Nova mounted.

Rhiannon looked at her mother. 'We'll talk in the morning,' she said lowering her voice. 'I'll tell you everything then.'

'Right!' announced Guy as his head appeared at the top of the ladder. 'Let's take it in turns to tell ghost stories.'

CHAPTER TWENTY-EIGHT

Paris, 23 February 2020

Luc was sitting contentedly on his tiny balcony reading a biography of Napoleon III and enjoying the rays of wintry sun that had appeared that afternoon. His solitude and tranquillity were soon however to be violently interrupted by a hysterical phone call from his ex-wife. Was he aware that 'his daughter' was in the process of sabotaging her future?

He sighed; she always had been incapable of perspective. Yet his suggestion that this was a situation in which cooler heads should prevail was met with vehemence.

'*Christ*. Have you just met me?' she snapped. 'I don't *have* a cooler bloody head. This is my head, and its default temperature is hot!'

Silently he scolded himself: experience should have taught him that interrupting or suggesting Marnie calm down would only serve to antagonise her further. It was best to let her vent her spleen. So, putting his mobile on speakerphone, he went back inside to fetch his stash. By the time he had finished rolling, she had finished her tirade. After a brief pause, she added: 'You don't sound surprised, so I'm assuming you already knew about this?'

He confirmed that Rhiannon had spoken to him of her unhappiness, her disillusion not only with respect to her affair with Gulliver but with her life at university in general. She had mentioned her plans to leave Warwick and take a sort of sabbatical, during which she planned to travel round the world, do some sort of volunteer work with an NGO.

'And you didn't think to talk her out of it? Or tell me?' she snorted. 'No, I suppose you encouraged her. This is the kind of thing you'd approve of: chucking in her studies and becoming a professional activist.'

'Give me some credit,' he said irritably. 'Do you honestly think this is what I'd want for her? Just because I dropped out of school and went on a few marches and handed out some tracts.' He was, as they both knew, somewhat downplaying his career as a political activist with the French Communist Party and then the *Ligue Communiste Revolutionnaire*: for if Marnie was the High Priestess of Hyperbole, Luc was a Master of Litotes. That said, even after his most violent episode, involving a home-made petrol bomb at an anti-fascist march, there had been no casualties and – as he had been a minor at the time, no criminal record.

'You can't compare her to me when I was young,' he went on. 'It was a completely different time, and my parents were nothing like us. You know I wanted her to have all the opportunities I didn't; do I need to remind you I've been paying half her tuition fees and rent?'

'No,' she muttered. 'Of course not. I'm sorry. This business has really thrown me. I suppose I'm just worried that she'll end up…well, like us.'

'Meaning?'

'Oh, come on. You know what I mean. Doomed to being underutilised and unfulfilled professionally: wasting her abilities.'

Indeed, one of the many things she and Luc had in common was that neither of them had ever fulfilled their potential in their respective careers. After obtaining her Masters, Marnie had soon abandoned her ambitions to be a literary translator, specialising in introducing exciting new French writers to the English-speaking market, and had settled for a comfortable yet unexciting and largely unchallenging career doing commercial and corporate work. Luc, for his part, could have gone to university and chosen any number of professions – journalism, architecture, the law – but instead had dropped out of school the year before he was due to sit his baccalaureate and had spent six months dabbling in political activism and lurking on the fringes of juvenile delinquency before his father, in a rare display of paternal concern, had given him a job. At that time, Barthélemy *père* had recently divorced from Wife Number Two and returned from the Côte d'Azur to Paris where he had co-founded an estate agency. Luc had thus spent nearly forty years doing a job he mostly despised before taking early retirement, opening the bookshop and finally finding a gratifying occupation.

If Marnie and Luc shared this shortcoming, their reasons for failing to live up to their potential, however, were quite different. For in Luc's case, it was due to a combination of a complete lack of parental involvement in his education and the typical inability of a large, understaffed and underfunded state school to cater to pupils who were either gifted or experiencing learning difficulties. Thus, Luc's exceptionally high IQ and his dyslexia had both gone undetected. How different it was from nowadays, Marnie had often thought when reflecting on how the school system had failed her ex-husband: today it seemed that any middle-class parent whose children were underperforming academically immediately assumed that they were either a genius or on the spectrum.

As a working single mother, Luc's mother had been too busy and too tired to follow her son's academic progress; as for concerns about his future career prospects, unemployment in the mid-seventies in France was virtually non-existent.

Marnie, on the other hand, had benefited from a good education and the support of encouraging, exacting parents. Yet despite a solid academic record, she had never reached dizzying heights, suffering as she did from a chronic lack of self-confidence and a crippling fear of failure, resulting in a lifelong pattern of underachievement, beginning with her decision to apply to red-brick universities in spite of several teachers' insistence that she was Oxbridge material.

'Let's face it,' she went on, 'Rhiannon's DNA is that of above-averagely intelligent underachievers.' She sighed. 'What are we going to do about this? We clearly failed her as parents.'

'Speak for yourself,' he replied archly. He was smarting slightly from her underachiever comment, accurate as it was.

'Ha, ha.'

'So, what else did she tell you? You may have some info I don't.'

'She plans to go to Asia then Australia. Her first stop is Cambodia, where she'll be volunteering for this non-profit, teaching English and Community Management.'

He blew out smoke and coughed. 'Yes, it's a French outfit, I believe? I've never heard of them.'

'I have,' Marnie replied. 'Funnily enough, DigInnova had a partnership with them, a corporate volunteering programme – you know the sort of thing: they encourage employees to go off and teach coding or PowerPoint to disadvantaged kids from rural areas of south-east Asia to show they're not a bunch of heartless, bloodsucking capitalists. I actually did a bit of pro bono translating for them, although, oddly enough, Rhiannon didn't hear about them through me: her friend India who's a graphic designer did a gig with them teaching InDesign and Photoshop and recommended it to her. Anyway, they're a legit outfit. Google them: they're called Passeport numérique.'

'*Attends,*' said Luc. '*Et voilà:* "Passeport numérique: bridging the digital divide. Offering underprivileged young people in Cambodia and the Philippines education in the digital and IT sector so they can improve their skills and employability and escape from poverty…" Bla bla bla…' he scrolled down the page of their website. Then she heard him whistle softly.

'What?'

'I'm just looking at their staff page. Their founder, Comms Director and head of fundraising are all heavyweights: top business schools followed by high-flying careers in the private sector before they grew a social conscience.'

'Yes, I know the Comms Director, Océane. She was the one I dealt with for the pro bono work I did. But about Rhiannon: did you understand how she's financing her trip?'

'Well, as I understand it, the NGO pays for her ticket to Cambodia and her living expenses.'

'Yes,' said Marnie impatiently, 'but the rest of it, I mean. That's just two weeks; she's planning on travelling for at least six months.'

'She said she's going to be a travel blogger. Did you know she was already quite a successful Instagram influencer?'

'Oh please, stop pretending you know about all that stuff.' She gave a snort of derision. 'Travel blogger, Instagram influencer. For God's sake, how is that a thing?'

'Well, like it or not, and as alien as it is to our generation, it is a thing – and potentially quite a lucrative thing. I've been looking into it. An influencer can make between €50 and €200 per post. Rhiannon's already got over 7,500 followers, and if she does sponsored campaigns with tourist boards and airlines and the like, which she's planning to do, she could make really good money.'

This information had the merit of silencing Marnie for five whole seconds.

'Oh,' she finally said. 'I see. I didn't know that. OK, so she won't starve, but what about her education?'

'As I understand it, she's planning to reapply next year. Surely she mentioned that?'

'Well, she might have been going to,' Marnie admitted sheepishly. 'I'm afraid our conversation was interrupted by my having to storm out of the room and have a stroke. You know she chose to drop this bomb on me in the middle of a family gathering? It was Dad's eightieth and we came down for the weekend. She knew I wouldn't make a major scene in front of Guy and Nova.'

'Or maybe,' he ventured, 'she thought it would be better to use the opportunity to tell you about an important decision she had made in person instead of over the phone.'

She said nothing.

'Are you both still at your dad's now?' he wanted to know.

'No, I'm on my way back to Bristol and Rhiannon's heading back to Warwick. She was going to stay on for another few weeks or so – her rent's paid up for this term, after all. But as I'm going to Italy next weekend for my work thing, I suggested she pack up her stuff then come back to Bristol and cat-sit while I'm away, then she can stay there until she flies to Phnom Penh on 20 March. And anyway, even if she does plan to go back to college next year, how will that work? Surely it's too late to apply for next year's intake? UCAS applications closed at the end of January.'

'I gather she was able to make a late application. There were… extenuating circumstances. She said she had a sort of breakdown or burnout – a slight exaggeration of the truth, perhaps, but she got her ex-boyfriend to write to the Head of Department or the Vice Chancellor or whoever, and make her case. Being a Psychology professor, he was able to provide testimonies as to her mental and psychological state; and under the circumstances he was…willing to help her.'

Another brief silence on the end of the line; then:

'Are you saying…she *blackmailed* her ex-lover into helping her get back in?'

'I'm not sure that's exactly how it happened. Possibly he offered to help her out of guilt. What can I say: she's always been very resourceful. Speaking of which, you should know I made it very clear to her that, if and when she goes back to further education in September, she can use the proceeds from her new career as a social media guru to pay for it – her first year, at least – because we won't be.'

'Absolutely. I don't see why we should fund her whims.'

'I'm so glad you agree,' he said lightly.

'Anyway, thanks for filling in the gaps. You seem infinitely better informed of our daughter's plans than I.'

He ignored this remark, with its obvious implication of collusion between father and daughter. She was fishing, and he saw no reason to pander to her jealousy and paranoia.

'You know what, it doesn't matter,' she went on. 'I just feel so bad that she was so wretched and felt she couldn't talk to us about it. Not just the thing with Gulliver – she cried on my shoulder about that, but the rest of it: her plans to chuck it all in and go off around the world.'

'Probably because she knew we'd worry, and try and talk her out if it,' he said gently. 'You know what, I would tell you she'll be OK, that you're a good mother, but I know how you thrive on guilt so I might just let you wallow in it for a bit.'

'Fuck off,' she said, half-heartedly.

He laughed and then said:

'Marnie. It is going to be OK. She's going to be fine. Look, it might not be exactly what we wanted for her, but she's taking control of her life. Is it really the end of the world if she takes a few months off to see the world, help people, make some money? And surely taking a few pictures and doing some… hashtags or whatever, is better than being a lap-dancer or a drug mule?'

'I suppose so. Look, I'll call her later to make sure she got back OK and tell her… well, that we're not thrilled about this but we're here for her. Oh, *bollocks!*'

'What? What have I done now?'

'Nothing, there's been an accident on the M4, I'm going to be stuck here for hours. Listen, I'd better go. Thanks.'

'Take care and have a good trip to Italy.'

'Yeah, thanks. I'm sure it'll be pretty dull. Work, work, work.'

CHAPTER TWENTY-NINE

Marnie walked into the pub and ordered a half of Strongbow from the bar – wine from pubs was too hit-and-miss. Taking it over to a corner table, she glanced at her watch. She was early; her guest – someone of whose existence she had not been aware until four days ago – was not yet late.

It had been a fairly ordinary Tuesday afternoon. She had just got back from the pool and was sitting at the dining table trawling through her emails. There was one from the freelance graphic designer she was working with showing her the revised version of a logo he had designed for Bacchus & Minerva; half a dozen from Italian and French museums – Capodimonte, Uffizi, Galleria Borghese, Palazzo Barberini, Doria Pamphilj Gallery and the Musée d'Orsay – a quote from a restaurant in Rome, and a reply to her inquiry about a hotel in Malta: all these she immediately filed away in her Bacchus & Minerva folder. There was also a message from someone she had met at a networking evening at the Bristol Chamber of Commerce a month ago, one from British Airways notifying her that her flight to Rome on Sunday was now leaving twenty minutes later than originally scheduled, and a request for a quote for a translation from her erstwhile employers: DigInnova's new head of Corporate Social Responsibility had 'heard good things about her from his predecessor,' and wondered if she would be interested in translating the Whistleblowing Charter they had just drafted. Marnie wanted to laugh out loud at this last one – talk about closing the stable door after the horse has bolted! In his defence, she reflected, this person was new to the company and may not have been aware that she, along with hundreds of others, had been made redundant in the wake of the Italian fiasco. In any event, she was tempted to reply to him that she would sooner pimp out her daughter than work for them ever again.

There was also an email from Vince in which he made half-hearted overtures to her, as he had done a few times since their tryst at Guy's wedding, a notification from Google Photos informing her that Guy Wade had shared an album with her, and a notification from MyRoots informing her some new DNA matches were available. These last three she ignored and turned her attention to the work-related messages. Then at a quarter-past-six, just as she was pouring herself a glass of Viré Clessé, she received a video call from Rhiannon.

Her daughter looked and sounded better than she had for a while; the colour was restored to her cheeks and there was once again a glint of enthusiasm in her eyes. Marnie was soon to discover the reason for this renewed appetite for life: Rhiannon informed her (very wisely, after the fact) that she had just returned from spending four days in an HS2 protest camp in some woods somewhere in Buckinghamshire with a twenty-two-year-old climate activist named Jared whose acquaintance she had made just days before. As she spoke fervently of the camaraderie, the shared sense of purpose and community, she sent her mother a series of photos from the trip, which Marnie perused with alternate wonder and dismay: the camp appeared to be relatively well-organised, with a series of treetop habitations that seemed to provide adequate shelter. One picture depicting a large flayed carcass suspended from a tree immediately put her in mind of a painting in the Louvre – was it by Goya? Or maybe one of the Dutch masters. She shuddered as Rhiannon explained it was the remains of a recently run-over deer they had found in the road and subsequently skinned, roasted and consumed. The conversation ended, Marnie exhaled slowly, trying to digest the information that her daughter had run off to some sylvan Utopia to build barriers and eat roadkill with some tree-hugger she had met on Tinder (who, apparently, resided in a squat). After her initial alarm, however, she reflected that she should be proud to have a child with a social conscience, something she willingly acknowledged was entirely down to Luc. Why, Rhiannon had gone on her first march at the age of fourteen, whilst at that age, Marnie's main concern, she recalled ruefully, was where her next tube of Boots' Bahama Blue mascara was coming from.

She finished her wine and browsed through the photos Guy had sent. The album, entitled *Newcastle with Gracie*, featured her brother in an unfamiliar urban landscape in the company of an equally unfamiliar elderly lady.

And then she remembered. Rhiannon had mentioned that Gracie was the birth mother of Guy's own birth mother: he had recently helped Heidi track her down. Marnie began messaging her brother, all the while despising her petty disingenuousness, knowing it was beneath her, yet unable to control herself: *Nice pics. Who's your new friend?'*

He replied immediately: *Gracie. My grandmother!*

'For fuck's sake,' she muttered aloud. *She's not your grandmother!* she wanted to scream at him. *She's just the woman who abandoned the woman who abandoned you!*

But she refrained, texting back instead some suitably amiable platitude. For every acrimonious argument she had with Guy invariably left her feeling drained, diminished – almost sullied somehow.

Finally, she logged onto MyRoots to view the latest DNA matches. Based on previous experiences, she had been expecting yet another stream of 0.7% matches, (estimated relationship: third-fifth cousin). She was therefore surprised to see a double-digit match – her only one other than Deirdre.

'Dinah De La Pole Lovelace' – what a name! To Marnie the lover of Victorian literature, it sounded like a heroine of Trollope or Wilkie Collins – 25% match.

25%. Marnie's mouth went dry as she read the estimated relationship: half-sibling.

Deirdre had had no other children, therefore it had to be on her father's side. Could it be the child her father already had with his wife when Deirdre and he had their affair?

No, it couldn't be: Marnie seemed to remember Deirdre saying the man had a son, not a daughter; besides, reading on, she saw that the age group indicated for Dinah De La Pole Lovelace was '20s'. So, it must have been a child he had subsequently had with another woman, nearly thirty years after she, Marnie, was born.

Her heart thudding almost audibly, it seemed to her, she took the bottle of wine out of the fridge and poured herself another glass. This was the closest she had ever come to tracking down her father. She was tempted to contact the young woman immediately.

But what could she say? In all probability, Dinah De La Pole was unaware of Marnie's existence. Just because she had signed up to MyRoots, it did not mean she was ready for revelations about her father's past indiscretions. There was no help for it: she had to leave it. Perhaps Deirdre had been right after all.

Taking a fortifying gulp of wine, she closed her laptop and forced herself to attend to other matters: ironing, packing, consulting her checklist of things to do before her trip.

Then, two days later, just as she was settling in front of the television after dinner with a cup of herbal tea, she saw on her phone that she had received another email from MyRoots: this time it was a message – from Dinah.

She started, almost spilling ginger tea in her lap, and clicked on the link to read the message.

'Hello Marnie. I imagine you were as surprised as I was to discover we are apparently half-sisters!' Possibly not quite as surprised as you, thought Marnie. *'Assuming this isn't some sort of mistake or hoax, I'd like to speak to you. I have so many questions. Could you please call me?'* A mobile number followed.

Her heart racing, she had dialled the number. The voice that answered had a distinctly Sloaney accent – not merely educated, middle-class like Marnie's. After thanking Marnie effusively for calling, she launched into a series of questions: how exactly were they half-sisters? Where was Marnie from, what did she do? Marnie was initially cautious, urging Dinah to speak to her father first. But the other woman was insistent: perfectly courteous, but insistent.

Marnie relented. 'I was adopted at birth,' she began, 'my birth mother's name is Deirdre Kavanaugh and it would appear that my birth father – is your father.'

A silence on the other end of the line.

'I'm sorry to be the one to tell you all this,' she went on. 'I know what a shock it must be.'

'No… It's…' and then suddenly: 'Can we meet?'

Marnie was taken aback.

'I… Yes, if you like. Where are you based? I'm in Bristol.'

Dinah had explained that she was in Cambridge, and that perhaps London would be a good midway point to meet.

'Do you ever come up to town?' Dinah inquired.

Marnie smiled in amusement at this expression, so redolent – like the girl's name – of nineteenth-century literature. She was half-tempted to reply: 'Only for the season,' but instead explained that she was due to fly from Heathrow to Rome for business that Sunday, and staying with friends in London the night before: why didn't they meet up for a drink or coffee on the Saturday afternoon or early evening? Marnie had to be back at the Appelbaums' by seven at the latest as Val and Jolyon – who were nothing if not persistent – had invited Ben Balakrishnan over for dinner. They had therefore agreed to meet in a pub in Baker Street.

At five o'clock sharp, a woman walked into the pub. She was short – several inches shorter than Marnie's five feet nine – and slightly plump. She was not conventionally beautiful but had a pleasant, intelligent face framed by long, dark chestnut hair. She was wearing a battered biker jacker over a knee-length blue floral tea dress, black tights and scuffed Doc Martin boots. She surveyed the room and as she approached hesitantly, Marnie found herself looking into a pair of absinthe-coloured eyes – the same as her own.

She stood up. 'Dinah.' There was no interrogative inflection at the end, for Marnie was sure it was she.

The green eyes widened.

'Marnie? Wow. You're very attractive,' she blurted.

Marnie blushed slightly at what was to be the first of many examples of the other woman's startling candour and made a self-deprecating gesture.

'No, truly. You've got amazing skin and legs I'd kill for. I hope I look half as good as you when I'm your –' She screwed her eyes up ruefully and stamped her foot lightly.

'Sorry, I can be a twat sometimes.'

Marnie laughed. 'Believe me, when you get to my age, you're grateful even for backhanded complements about your looks.' She waved to the seat opposite her. 'Please. What can I get you?' Dinah insisted on getting it herself and returned moments later with a glass of red wine.

Sitting down and raising her glass to Marnie, she said:

'Sorry again for what I said. You're a good sport, I can see that. But, really, you are lovely-looking – for any age. Do you see we have the same eyes?' Marnie nodded. 'They're Pa's eyes' – this she said without a trace of sentimentality – 'Cordelia has them too; Portia has brown eyes like Ma. Portia doesn't like the Lovelace eyes – she says they're like snakes' eyes.'

'They're your sisters?'

'Oh, yes! Sorry. My sisters and your other half-sisters. I'm the youngest. Portia's twenty-eight and does something in PR; Cordelia's twenty-five and a musician. I'm twenty, studying Classics at King's College.'

Marnie almost choked on her cider. 'God! I have a daughter your age!'

'Really?' the green eyes lit up. 'What does she do?'

What, indeed? thought Marnie. She gave the simpler, edited version of the truth: 'She's reading Psychology at Warwick.'

Dinah nodded and then said: 'So… where do we start?'

Marnie sipped her cider thoughtfully. 'Well… we've established that you knew nothing about me. And again, I'm so sorry to have dropped this bombshell on you.'

Dinah shook her head vigorously. 'Please don't be.'

Marnie continued. 'But I didn't see any other close matches on MyRoots: so I'm thinking neither your sisters nor your father' – she could not bring herself to use the first person plural possessive determiner when referring to him – 'are in their database.' She paused. 'May I ask why you are on there? I mean, were you also researching your family history?'

Dinah laughed. 'God, no. The De La Pole's – that's Ma's people – are in the bloody Domesday Book, we know all about that side of the family for the past ten centuries. And what I've seen of Pa's family has not exactly induced me to dig any further there.'

Marnie noted how the girl pronounced her mother's maiden name – 'Dellapool' – and felt grateful (whilst despising herself for caring about such things) that she had heard it before she herself had attempted to say it, thereby committing a solecism that would inevitably reveal her as non-U.

Dinah sipped her wine and continued. 'No, I heard about MyRoots through a friend from college. He was tracing his ancestry and when he showed me the results, I saw they do a sort of ethnic breakdown of your DNA?' Marnie nodded confirmation. 'Well, I suddenly thought: I wonder if there's anything remotely... *exotic* in my background. If I could prove I had even one percent of anything not entirely Anglo-Saxon in my genetic make-up, Pa would be incandescent! That would shut him up. So, I just did the DNA test for a giggle.' Seeing Marnie's puzzled expression, she explained:

'Pa's an awful Fascist, you see. And believe me, unlike most people my age, I don't use that word lightly – it's not like when I was a disgruntled fifteen-year-old and he wouldn't let me go to an all-night party. No, he's genuinely, passionately, irretrievably racist, elitist and homophobic.' She paused and her hitherto animated, jocular expression became more sombre and subdued. She continued, more quietly:

'I'm his favourite. He doesn't realise I despise him deep down. Although, politics and sexual orientation aside, we are alike in many ways – everyone says so: Ma, my sisters. We're both strong, ambitious.' She brightened again, smiling. 'Tell me more about your daughter – my niece! What's she like?'

'Smart, feisty, politically aware. Sensitive. A bit confused right now.' Marnie briefly summarised Rhiannon's current circumstances; Dinah listened attentively and sympathetically.

After Marnie had bought another round, she said:

'What else can you tell me about... him. What's his name? What does he do?'

'Oh, didn't I say? He's called Nigel Lovelace. He used to own a few shops. He's retired now.'

The name was vaguely familiar to Marnie, and if he was indeed the Nigel Lovelace she had occasionally read about in the business section of newspapers and periodicals, 'owns a few shops' was like saying Mark Zuckerberg had a moderately successful start-up: for Lovelace was a captain of British industry, a retail magnate with a vast portfolio of high street brands.

Having digested this last piece of information, Marnie said:

'This will sound incredibly trite, but as a kid I always wanted a sister. My brother and I – my adopted brother – we fought like cat and dog as kids.'

'Really? Well, I have two sisters, and I dislike them both intensely. One's a cringing sycophant and the other's a self-involved diva. And they're so shallow it makes me want to be physically sick.'

Marnie noticed how, in the midst of this diatribe, the girl's voice remained even, the intelligent face impassive: no distasteful curling of the mouth, twitching of the small upturned nose or narrowing of the eyes.

Then Dinah laughed. 'This is also trite, but no one's ever content with their lot: you had a brother and wanted a sister, whereas I've spent most of my life cursing Portia and Cordelia but would have loved to have met Miles.'

'Miles…?' Marnie inquired.

'Pa's first-born by his first wife. Alas, he doesn't want to know us – any of us – which I can understand.' She took another sip of Merlot. 'Pa never talks about him. I don't think he misses him or minds not having him in his life.' She put down her glass and looked intently at Marnie. 'Like I said, our father is a pig. I mean, we knew Ma was originally his mistress and that he walked out on his first wife and son for her. But that he had already cheated on his first wife with another woman – your mother – and just abandoned her, while she was carrying his child? It's despicable.'

'Well, for what it's worth, I didn't have a horrible childhood. I was adopted by some decent, loving, fairly normal people.'

'Really? Well, that's something, I suppose.'

'What about your mother?' Marnie ventured. 'Are you close?'

Dinah shrugged. 'Inasmuch as one can be close to someone who is devoid of intelligence or morals.' At Marnie's raised eyebrows, she said simply: 'She was shagging Pa while he was married to Miles's mother! Because of her, a boy grew up without a father, and one that he grew to hate. No, she's just as bad as Pa.'

Marnie's usual response when faced with someone expressing such a naively Manichaean outlook on human relationships would be to say that no one truly knew what went on in other people's marriages, that perhaps Nigel and his first wife were terribly ill-suited and unhappy; that these things happened. But in this case, she felt no desire to defend her birth father's actions, nor indeed those of any of the women who had thrown in their lot with him – Deirdre included. She simply said:

'I'm sorry you're not close to your family.'

Dinah shrugged. 'As soon as I come into my money, I'll be gone.' She must have noticed the brief glint of surprise and disapproval in Marnie's eyes, for she added, 'Oh, I'll give most of it away; half will be used to support various struggling artists – I have some friends who want to set up a theatre company and another who's a terribly talented sculptor in need of a patron – and the rest will go to the SWP. I don't need it.' She added airily: 'I'll have graduated by then and I'll be able to walk into any job I want.'

Ah, the confidence of youth! Marnie marvelled. In this case, it was bolstered by a background of unimaginable privilege and wealth: a mixture of old and new money, an exclusive independent school, no doubt, then Oxbridge. But after Dinah's rather cavalier reference to her inheritance, a thought suddenly occurred to Marnie.

'Listen,' she said, 'I've been trying to find out about my father because I'm curious: I'm not… after his money. I mean, until a few minutes ago, I didn't even know he *had* any. I'm not looking to cheat you and your sisters –'

She cut her off with a dismissive wave of a pale, plump hand, the short nails painted a glossy black. 'Of course not. Although,' she added, 'If it were up to me, you'd have your share of Pa's loot.'

Uncomfortable, Marnie changed the subject.

'Have you spoken to your parents and sisters about any of this since we spoke the other day?'

Dinah shook her head. 'I wanted to meet you first, before Pa had a chance to deny it, or try and poison me against you.' Seeing Marnie flinch slightly at this last remark, she said: 'I'm sorry, I just –'

Marnie raised her hand. 'No, it's fine. I wasn't expecting much from him as it is, and after what you've said…'

'But… we can stay in touch, can't we?' The green eyes were full of hope.

Marnie smiled warmly. She rather liked this strange, endearing, forthright girl.

'I would very much like that.'

Smiling, Dinah stood up and shook her hand.

'Well, goodbye then, Marnie. Thanks again for meeting me.'

'My pleasure. And good luck with… well, everything.' She then added, 'Oh, I meant to say, I like your dress. May I ask where you got it?'

Dinah looked down at the skirt of her dress. 'Oh. Thanks! A thrift shop in Norwich.' She added, with a wry smile: 'Don't worry: it's not some tat from one of Pa's shops made by kids in Indonesia or immigrants paid five quid an hour in some sweatshop in Leicester.'

Marnie had a last sudden thought. 'By the way, did you find anything 'exotic', as you put it, in your ethnicity estimate on MyRoots?'

'Kind of: apparently, I'm 0.8% Indigenous Amazonian. Not much, but still enough to taunt the old man with.'

And with a wink, she walked out of the pub.

$$\bowtie\!\Box\!\bowtie$$

A few hours after Marnie's meeting with Dinah, Nigel Lovelace closed the door of his study, poured himself two fingers of Aberlour 16 Year Old and sat down heavily in his favourite chair, a nineteenth-century Gothic Revival button-backed leather library chair Venetia's parents had given them as a wedding present.

Venetia didn't like him drinking spirits but it had been an extremely trying day. The Major had taken a turn for the worse of late: he was becoming increasingly confused and occasionally aggressive, and that very afternoon Nigel had received a rather disturbing telephone call from the nursing agency in charge of his father's care informing him that he had insulted one of his nurses. Natalie the night nurse was off sick, and his father had apparently refused to be attended by the replacement the agency had sent, a woman of Afro-Caribbean extraction. When she had attempted to help him to bed, he had started screaming, calling her a 'bloody nig-nog' and ordering her to 'get her filthy claws off him.' When the day nurse had relieved her the following morning, she had promptly informed the agency that she would not be returning to care for Major Lovelace.

And then there had been that extremely unpleasant confrontation with Dinah. First, she had turned up unexpectedly that morning, saying she had decided to come home for the weekend, but had been rather cool and distant with him. Then she had disappeared somewhere that evening and come back a couple of hours later with a bee in her bonnet, storming into his study and interrogating him about Deirdre Kavanaugh's by-blow, of all things! Evidently, she had just met the woman who had no doubt given her some sob-story about her sad childhood. Dinah was predictably outraged by what she saw as his inhumane treatment of Deirdre and was further scandalised when he had made no apology for his 'behaviour,' nor expressed the slightest interest in meeting the accidental fruit of their union.

Deirdre. He had not thought about her in years; as for the child, he had no more thought of it or wondered about its fate than he would have had Deirdre followed his advice and procured an abortion. In fact, he had long since blocked out that entire unfortunate episode of his life: he had been briefly happy with Barbara during the first year of their marriage, but pregnancy had instilled in her a desire to return to her hometown – like a salmon returning to its river of origin to spawn – and he had reluctantly agreed to move up North. This ill-advised decision was to trigger a series of events which would prove detrimental to Nigel's personal and professional life. Living so near Barbara's parents and working as a salesman for Reginald Halliwell's printing business was a disaster: he and his father-in-law had fought constantly.

Even fatherhood had failed to fulfil Nigel: as far as he was concerned, Miles was just an added complication, another responsibility; more disturbingly, Barbara was slavishly, obsessively devoted to the child, to the exclusion of everything and everyone else. It was no wonder he had strayed: if only she had not neglected her marital duties, been a proper wife to him, he would probably have never been attracted to a girl like Deirdre, the daughter of a friend and fellow-Rotarian of his father-in-law's. She was pretty enough with a fine shape on her, but nothing out of the ordinary, and there was something fundamentally... *parochial* about her. But after Barbara's recent coolness and neglect, Deirdre's wide-eyed adoration had flattered his male ego, disarmed him, and he had succumbed.

They used to meet about once a fortnight; finding a venue for their trysts was a constant problem. In those days, you couldn't just go to an hotel with someone you weren't married to – at least, not in a small town like theirs where everyone knew each other. So, apart from one extremely risky (and therefore, for Nigel, highly erotic) afternoon at his parents-in-law's house whilst they were holidaying in the Lake District, they usually drove out to the country, through the pretty villages on the edge of the Pennines, then park in a remote spot and make love in the car.

The 'affair' had lasted a few months; then she had got herself pregnant. He had offered to pay for a termination, but the woman would not hear of it, thanks to the Papist principles hammered into her by her Paddy parents. Nigel shuddered as he briefly contemplated some parallel universe in which he had married Deirdre: God knows he hadn't been fond of Barbara's parents, but they had been infinitely preferable to Deirdre's people who, for all old Kavanaugh was a solicitor and a Rotarian – a pillar of the community – were still ignorant, rosary-fumbling, off-the-boat immigrants.

So, Deirdre and he had parted ways; she had told him she planned to go away and have the kid adopted. He had never heard from her again, and a few months later he had resigned from his father-in-law's firm and taken Barbara and Miles back down South.

What on earth did Dinah think would induce him to acknowledge, let alone form any sort of bond with the child Deirdre had spawned? It was grotesque!

He was disappointed in his favourite child. For all her academic prowess – the scholarship, the excellent A-levels, then winning a place at one of the world's greatest seats of learning – she understood so little of life. (Like many people who have succeeded in spite of a poor academic record, Nigel – who had left school at sixteen with one O-Level in geography – had an inferiority complex about his lack of formal education and qualifications – a chip on his shoulder, as Dinah herself, the cheeky wench, had once put it.)

For, as clever as she was, she did not understand that it was not possible – nor even desirable – to give everything of oneself to all the people in one's life. In Venetia he had a beautiful, accomplished and adoring wife; but she was also an extremely demanding and possessive one who had always required his full and undivided attention, even after the girls were born. Consequently, they had all been sent to boarding school so he could devote all his time and energy to the business and her.

Not that the girls had anything to complain about, mind: a childhood of comfort and luxury and a first-rate education, albeit at separate establishments – Portia had been to Roedean, Cordelia Wycombe Abbey, and Dinah Bedales – for they would have murdered each other otherwise. As adults, they continued to benefit from his largesse, as well as his reputation and contacts, and of course, their mother's excellent pedigree.

Miles, on the other hand, he had never understood, but had nevertheless provided for him for eighteen years. That they had been estranged since his marriage to Venetia was no great tragedy for either of them: he, Nigel, was no longer lumbered with a judgemental, resentful son who had been brainwashed by a vindictive, embittered, jilted woman, and surely Miles was better off without a parent who could neither love nor understand him.

Miles. Deirdre's bastard. Dinah. Sloshing more whiskey into his glass, he thought bitterly of his offspring: whining, ungrateful, mutinous wretches that they were.

For whilst having a legion of children with a harem of women was undeniably a testament to his virility, the truth was children were a bind, a drain on one's time, resources and energy, who, in his case, had grown up either to hate him or disappoint him, with the exception, until very recently, of Dinah – his precious ewe-lamb – and even she was turning against him now.

The ungrateful hussy! Deirdre's pregnancy had been an unqualified mistake, an accident; but, if he was honest with himself, he had never really actively wanted any of his children. Miles had just happened; after that, Barbara had had some mysterious gynaecological issue which prevented her from having any more children – which suited Nigel admirably, and he had happily resigned himself to never procreating again.

But then he had met Venetia when he was in his forties. She was younger than he and had made her ambitions for motherhood abundantly clear to him, and he had never been able to refuse her anything. (Nigel was famous for his uxoriousness: indeed, his former Finance Director had once – unbeknownst to Nigel – called it his only redeeming feature.)

Venetia, incidentally, he reflected, was another excellent reason not to acknowledge this *foundling*, even if he wanted to. For his wife was – to his immense gratification – as jealous as a tigress. As it was, she was relieved that Miles, and by extension, Barbara, were no longer in his life, so she would be unlikely to welcome any other evidence of her husband's sexual past.

Sexual jealousy aside, she was also paranoid about the money: she was convinced that, as soon as he, Nigel, shook off his mortal coil, Miles would reappear and somehow rob the girls of their birthright. So any other children of his would invariably be seen as ruthless gold-diggers looking to stake a claim on his estate.

No, it was best he kept this whole matter to himself. Dinah, strangely enough, had assured him she would not disclose anything about her recent discoveries to her mother or her sisters, remarking rather primly that it 'wasn't her place.' He had half a mind to disinherit the little minx, only he was half-afraid she might blackmail him over this business, threaten to tell her mother and God knows who else, even go to the tabloids, despite her assurances to the contrary.

He sighed and took another gulp of whiskey: until a few minutes ago, it would never have occurred to him that his Dinah was capable of such devious, treacherous behaviour.

Shaking his head in dismay, he quoted out loud:

'"How sharper than a serpent's tooth it is to have a thankless child."'

CHAPTER THIRTY

Naples, 6 March 2020

As Marnie hurried across Piazza Plebiscito, pulling up the collar of her mac against the rain, she glanced up at the stately façade of the Palazzo Reale and briefly recalled, with a shudder, her first visit to Naples in 2015. At the time, the palace walls had been covered with a gallery of photos of Camorra victims: she could still remember the haunting spectre of their magnified faces staring down at her.

Arriving at Caffè Gambrinus, she decided against the terrace and strode directly into the coffee house where she sat at one of the tables with a sigh of relief. For in the elegant, plush gilt and marble interior, with its snowy linen tablecloths and ornate chandeliers, she felt sheltered from both the elements and the brutal, sordid reality of organised crime warfare.

A waiter immediately stepped forward and she decided to have an espresso while waiting for Amedeo, for she needed fortifying before drinks and dinner.

Almost a week had passed since Marnie's meeting with Dinah Lovelace. Afterwards she had got the Tube back to Val and Jolyon's house, feeling slightly lightheaded after the encounter and Dinah's revelations about the man who had impregnated Deirdre. As soon as she had walked through the door, Val, who was sitting at the kitchen table with Jolyon, had taken one look at her friend and shot a meaningful glance at her husband, who had promptly stood up, muttering something about having some emails to catch up on.

Marnie had then proceeded, over the mug of strong sweet tea Val had placed in front of her, to recount the events of her encounter with her half-sister. Val listened, occasionally asking questions. Marnie then Googled Nigel Lovelace and looked at the many photos that came up, studying the jowly face, the long, narrow nose, the cold, green eyes (were they objectively cold, she would later wonder? Or had Dinah's unflattering portrait of him led her to impute certain qualities to his physical features?)

She had been thus occupied when the doorbell rang.

'That'll be Ben,' said Val. 'Are you up for socialising?'

'Sure, as long as we avoid the subject of adoption, parents, families and DNA testing.'

Val had patted her friend's hand and got up to open the door.

Ben was still sporting fashionable stubble but had evidently had a haircut since the last time Marnie had seen him. Under his Barbour he was dressed in jeans and a salmon-pink shirt.

Dinner was enjoyable; Val's succulent *osso buco* with polenta followed by Jolyon's grapefruit meringue pie, accompanied by a couple of fairly good bottles of burgundy (Ben's contribution), and the easy dinnertime conversation provided just the kind of pleasant distraction Marnie needed.

After dinner, whilst Val and Jolyon were in the kitchen cleaning up – having categorically refused any assistance from their guests – Ben and Marnie sat in the drawing room. He asked about her upcoming trip to Italy and listened attentively as she told him about her plans for Bacchus & Minerva.

'Sounds great. It's a good idea. Are you just doing tours in Italy and France or have you thought about the UK?'

'Not really. I mean, I did briefly consider doing a Constable Country tour in Suffolk, but I'm sure that's been done to death.'

He nodded thoughtfully, then said: 'You live in Bristol, right?' She nodded. 'Well, why not do something there? After all, presumably you know it like the back of your hand and...' he paused. 'They do have museums there, don't they?'

'Oh, yes,' she said earnestly. 'Let's see: there's the tractor museum that's open two days a week from 3pm to 4:15, and the Museum of Inbreeding and Cider. Of course they have bloody museums! The Bristol Museum and Art Gallery is a world-class museum with extensive collections, then there's the Arnolfini, a contemporary arts centre. God, Londoners!'

He smiled sheepishly. 'Right. Of course. Sorry.' He frowned. 'Isn't Banksy from Bristol?'

She glanced up at him. 'Yes. There are a dozen or so of his works around the city... That's actually not a bad idea: I could take people on a walk around the city, taking in the main sights and the street art, plus the museums and there are loads of great restaurants and bars.' She looked at him appreciatively. 'Thanks.'

'You're welcome. And listen, about that video of you at the National Gallery –' She rolled her eyes. 'I know, but, listen. Whatever you think of it, it'll be a great advertisement for your business. Especially for the Caravaggio Tour.'

Marnie had excused herself and retired for the night shortly afterwards, pleading an early start the next day. Sleep, however, had eluded her: as she lay in the guest bedroom, her thoughts inevitably drifted back to the meeting with Dinah as she attempted to understand how this new information advanced her in what, since reading a biography of Thomas Cromwell, Val had begun referring to as 'Marnie's Great Matter.' Marnie had approved of this choice of epithet: partly for reasons of convenience – a codename is simple and concise – and partly because it appealed to her sense of the dramatic, although even she realised that her search for information on her birth father was not quite comparable to Henry VIII's annulment of his marriage to Katherine of Aragon and the political and theological crisis it precipitated.

She wondered – not for the first time since she had embarked on her Great Matter – whether it was curiosity or simply masochism that led her to pursue it. For how could knowing her biological father was such a man as Nigel Lovelace make her feel more fulfilled, more complete? Would he get in touch with Marnie after Dinah confronted him? Somehow, she knew he would not.

She eventually managed to snatch a few hours of fitful sleep before the alarm went at 6:30. She left for Heathrow, resolving to throw herself into work as soon as she arrived in Italy.

And she had done just that. It had been an exhausting and intense six days, but also productive and gratifying. Rome had been a whirlwind of meetings and visits, during which she had walked an average of fifteen kilometres a day, partly because the weather had been cool but fine and dry and Marnie had no desire to inter herself in the Metro, but also for practical reasons: much of the Roman leg of her planned Caravaggio tour was to take place on foot and she needed to try out her planned itinerary and thus verify the feasibility in terms of timings and, where necessary, adjust it accordingly. She had met with the directors, curators and guides of half a dozen museums, been to the church of San Luigi dei Francesi, which housed Caravaggio's three Saint Matthew paintings, the Basilica di Sant'Agostino to see the hauntingly beautiful *Madonna di Loreto*, and the Cerasi Chapel at Santa Maria del Popolo for the *Crucifixion of Saint Peter* and *Conversion of Saint Paul on the Way to Damascus*.

She had then taken the train to Naples, where Amedeo had joined her from Milan. Marnie was staying in a well-kept Bed & Breakfast which he had recommended to her, up on the hill in Vomero, a haven of green spaces and elegant villas with breathtaking views over the bay of Naples, whilst he himself had gone to his mother's house in Rione Sanità.

On the previous morning Marnie had set out from the B&B after breakfast and walked the short distance to Castel Sant'Elmo. After visiting the castle and admiring the view of the bay from the battlements, she had taken a bus up to the Museo Capodimonte to admire the *Flagellation* and have a brief word with the curator of an exhibition on Caravaggio's Naples period which the museum had put on the previous year and whom Marnie had contacted a few weeks previously. She had then walked the two or three kilometres down to the church of Pio

Monte della Misericordia – deciding it was possibly too far to take her clients on foot – where Caravaggio's *Seven Acts of Mercy* altarpiece was displayed, and thence taken the more manageable fifteen-minute walk to the next leg of the Naples pilgrimage, the Locanda del Cerriglio. Tucked away in a tiny alleyway in Borgo Orefici, the labyrinthine Jewellery district, Locanda del Cerriglio was now a restaurant but in the seventeenth century was both a popular tavern frequented by artists and poets, and a brothel catering to a wide range of sexual tastes. It was outside this establishment one evening in October 1609 that Caravaggio, having availed himself of the services it offered, was ambushed by a group of his enemies and viciously assaulted, an attack which had brought about a decline in his health and artistic abilities and ultimately, his untimely death nine months later.

In the spirit of killing two birds with one stone – essential given the number of places and people to see in such a brief timeframe – Marnie had arranged to meet a local guide for lunch there. The aim was both to sample the restaurant's fare with a view to including it on her tour, and to meet in person a guide she had been in touch with, a sprightly sexagenarian and retired history teacher named Giacomo, to assess his suitability for doing her Caravaggio in Naples tour. The idea was that he would accompany the groups around the main points of interest and entertain and inform them with just the right combination of historical and cultural information, anecdotes and gossip. Giacomo had exceeded her expectations: in addition to his perfect command of English, he was lively, amusing and capable of speaking about his city and its history with both encyclopaedic knowledge and obvious affection. When he pointed out to Marnie that, although an authority on the history of Naples with extensive knowledge of Caravaggio's time in the city, he was by no means an expert on art history, she assured him that a specialist museum guide would take visitors around the Museo Capodimonte.

All in all, then, Marnie was satisfied with her reconnaissance trip: aside from the hotel she had stayed at on her first night in Rome which turned out to be rather grimy, and one of the guides she had met at the Galleria Borghese whose English was too halting, she was impressed with the venues and partners she had chosen, and confident that, with a little tweaking here and there, the Caravaggio Experience would be a success with the particular demographic she was targeting, namely, discerning, educated, urbane, middle-class, late-middle-aged, professional *bon vivants*.

Indeed, this last criterion was essential: for the past week had also been an orgy of gluttonous delight: in Rome she had sampled some superb *pappardelle* with a wild boar sauce at an *osteria* in the Centro Storico, while the next day she had traced Caravaggio's footsteps from Vicolo del Divino Amore, where he had lived in 1604, to Campana, Rome's oldest *trattoria* which the artist himself had frequented. Here Marnie had supped on typical Roman specialities: *carciofi alla romana,* followed by lamb sweetbreads.

But it was here in Naples that Marnie's culinary experience had begun to transcend merely sensuous enjoyment and approach the divine: it had all been sublime, from the simple yet truly perfect pizza in a restaurant Amedeo had taken her to in Vomero near her B&B on the first evening, to the *spaghetti alle vongole* and *fritto misto* she had had by the sea in Borgo Marinaro, and the plate of *salsicce e friarielli* – succulent sausages with some leafy greens which, bewilderingly, only seemed to thrive in the Campania region – served by a toothless crone in a tiny backstreet dive in the heart of the Quartiere Spagnolo, the kind of establishment where there is no actual menu and credit cards are not accepted. And then there were the pastries: *sfogliatella* and *pastiera napolitana,* depraved concoctions of almond paste, ricotta and candied citrus peel.

And the wines! When Marnie closed her eyes, she could almost taste the liquorice and blackcurrants in the bottle of Aglianico she and Amedeo had shared the night before, or the chilled white Greco di Tufo, with its earthy, peachy flavour.

She was bewitched by the plethora of flavours, subjugated. In her more whimsical – and slightly pretentious – moments, Marnie reflected on the name of her company: Bacchus and Minerva. Art and excess. Uplifting the soul and indulging the senses. Indeed, what else makes us feel truly alive, she wondered?

Each time she had gone to a restaurant with Amedeo, he invariably went through his routine of asking the waiter – always with his trademark infinite patience and courtesy – what, if anything, they had to offer that would not violate his ethics. Often, he ended up with just a plate of plain risotto or some fried potatoes and beans; but he never complained in the slightest.

Their Epicurean gratification was, however, marred somewhat by the ever-present shadow of the pandemic: the mask-wearing – not yet universal or mandatory, but fairly widespread – the almost obsessive-compulsive rituals of applying hand sanitiser every few minutes (Marnie felt as though her hands had aged fifty years in a week, so dry, red and chapped were they from constant disinfecting); the gloved and masked barmen and waiters who wiped down door handles after each entrance and exit and gingerly placed straws in their spritzes with tweezers.

Yet all this, Amedeo had explained, was nothing compared to the situation in the north, and particularly in Lombardy, which was a *zona rossa,* a red zone, with its checkpoints, patrolling Carabinieri and prevailing paranoia. In another lurid flight of fancy, Marnie thought of the extracts from Manzoni's *I Promessi Sposi* her Italian teacher had got her to read and pictured Milan as it was during the bubonic plague of the seventeenth century, with the *untori*, the plague-spreaders, roaming the streets of the city and propagating the evil miasma.

Just then, she looked up and saw Amedeo arrive and waved. He smiled and ambled over to the table.

He looked different in his native town, she remarked as the waiter arrived with the two spritzes accompanied by a lavish array of savoury *aperitivo* canapés. She had never before seen him in his natural habitat: he seemed empowered, energised. That said, she knew Amedeo had something of a love-hate relationship with the city in which he had been born and spent the first twenty years of his life. He identified intensely with it, and yet felt curiously alienated from it; he was both proud and ashamed of it. She vividly remembered a conversation they had had, years ago, when they first met: she had asked about his origins and he had embarked on an impassioned condemnation of the decline of the Kingdom of Naples over the centuries, from the invasion by Giuseppe Garibaldi to the Camorra signing lucrative partnerships with corporations from Northern Italy to dump their toxic waste on the outskirts of the city.

'Naples,' he had said, 'is like a woman who was once noble, beautiful, highly respected and admired, but has since been used and abused by scores of men and is now sullied, repudiated, ruined and broken. And yet, in her eyes, there are still traces of that former glory and faded beauty. I cannot cast her completely aside: she is part of me and I of her. I am Naples. *Io sono Napoli.'*

'So, where are you taking me for dinner tonight?' she asked with a small thrill of anticipation, hoping the rain would hold off the following morning so she could go for her daily run along the *lungomare* to burn off the calories.

He took a sip of spritz. 'A place in Marechiaro, overlooking the sea. I think you'll like it. I've booked a table for eight.'

'Sounds lovely.' She glanced at her watch. 'We'd better drink up then.'

Had they had any inkling of how things would change in the next few days, perhaps that evening they would have savoured and cherished those simple pleasures – a sea view, a meal in a restaurant, a moonlit walk – pleasures which, along with robust health and the basic freedom and security they had come to take for granted, would soon be denied them for months.

'If you ask me, that Modigliani guy is overrated.'

Marnie stiffened and cringed at the Brummie tourist's comment – not least because of the way her nasal West Midland drone mangled the artist's name, vocalising the silent g ('Modee-glee-ahni').

Who in their right fucking mind would ask you anything? she wanted to scream – and then immediately chastised herself for her censoriousness. She was here to enjoy the art, not judge other people's perception of it. In fact, she resolved there and then to try and isolate herself from the other visitors and imagine she was entirely alone with the paintings.

She soon realised that this was quite impossible. If nothing else, she found she could not ignore her companion – the recently maligned Modigliani's namesake – and his sensibilities. For as breathlessly enchanted as she was by the masterpieces on display, as the inevitable and omnipresent *Madonna col bambino* gradually gave way to still lifes and bucolic domestic scenes, she could not but wonder, for example, how a committed vegan and confirmed pacifist such as Amedeo (and one with a particular horror of violence) could stomach the wanton cruelty and gore on display. She could only imagine his squeamishness at the images of limp, lifeless game strewn over marble tables, the glistening piles of fish, the silver dishes of vermillion crustaceans, and that grotesque, impish peasant boy in *The Poultry Seller* who, the carcass of some unidentifiable furry beast draped around his shoulders, stared defiantly at the beholder as he wrung a goose's neck.

Yet this callous disregard for animal rights was nothing compared to the barbarity depicted in the Biblical paintings: the countless crucifixions, the legions of marble-white, arrow-punctured Saint Sebastians, not to mention a particularly gruesome *Head of Saint John the Baptist*, in which Maineri illustrated, with astounding and disturbing anatomical precision, the severed trachea, oesophagus, cervical vertebra and spinal cord. Surely this represented everything that was abhorrent to him – not only from an aesthetic point of view but from an ethical and ideological one? For, in addition to being a pacifist, Amedeo was also a fervent atheist – neither of which, she imagined, could sit comfortably with his family's traditional Italian values and military background.

She was suddenly enveloped by a wave of guilt: after convincing him to pose as her associate and sit in on her meeting with the Pinacoteca's General Director to help with translation – for the director's English was very approximate, and Marnie's Italian wasn't strong enough to understand certain nuances of the Italian language and the bureaucracy of cultural institutions – she had insisted they visit the museum's collections and see, among other masterpieces, Caravaggio's other *Emmaus*. She bit her lip in shame: she had been high-handed and insensitive, inflicting upon him endless images that must surely be repulsive to him – and all this when they were both tired after the early-morning flight from Naples.

Yet, the occasional furtive glances she stole of him showed that his countenance betrayed nothing of the emotions she attributed to him: his face, with its aquiline nose and olive skin remained as impassive as ever, his deep brown eyes still unfathomable.

They moved on. More chubby, genetically ill-favoured country folk purveying their wares: *The Fruit Seller, The Fishmongers*. This last one at least, unlike many of the genre, demonstrated a passable degree of realism where the aquatic subjects were concerned. For as both an habitué of art galleries, with a particular fondness for still lifes and rustic tableaux, and a bon vivant with a penchant for seafood, Marnie noted with approval that the shelled and scaly creatures in the painting would not have looked out of place on a stall in Billingsgate. The same could not, however, be said of Franz Snyders' *Fish Market:* she remembered the first time she had seen it at the Louvre during a sixth-form art history excursion and how she had marvelled at the artistic (or rather, zoological? Piscatorial? What was the correct term?) licence the artist had taken in painting such a bewildering array of fauna, many of which were neither fish nor even edible (was that an otter or a sea lion lurking beneath the stall?), and some of which looked positively mythological: indeed, a kraken would scarcely have looked out of place.

Glancing now at the Campi canvas, her eyes wandered to the wailing toddler with the vicious prawn gnawing at his pudgy finger and she thought wistfully of the *linguine ai gamberi e zucchine* she had devoured (albeit rather guiltily, as she invariably did when eating meat or fish in Amedeo's presence) at the restaurant in Naples the night before.

Why did picture galleries always make her hungry? Glancing at her watch, she decided that right after viewing Emmaus they would go and get some lunch, and made a mental note to avoid making such outings on an empty stomach in future.

⋈⬚⋈

Why did picture galleries always make him think of sex?

Perhaps because most places and situations did.

Or perhaps it was being surrounded by beauty and death that did it. He also had a vague notion that there was something about the church-like atmosphere of such places, the reverence and silence they inevitably commanded, that awoke in his iconoclastic soul an irresistible desire to transgress. Certainly it was not that the female protagonists of the paintings and sculptures themselves were particularly alluring – with the notable exception of Caravaggio's *Mary Magdalene in Ecstasy*, arguably the most erotic work of art he had ever beheld, and a postcard of which had, in the pre-Internet-days of his youth, been for many months his masturbatory aid of choice.

He looked over at Marnie, her cat-like, peridot gaze apparently riveted by a couple of satyrs leering over Venus. Was it his imagination or was there something studied and self-conscious about the way she was looking at the painting? The way she held herself, shifted the weight from one leg to another, gently tugged at the chain of her necklace, as if she were aware of his eyes on her? As gratifying as this thought was, he quickly dismissed it as, with a sudden, chastening pang of self-awareness, he remembered what John Berger had said about women being conditioned by a patriarchal society to watch themselves constantly.

And yet at the same time, he was also reminded of a trip to the Louvre with Viola over thirty years before. At the time he was living in London, busking on the Tube by day and alternating between various squats and friends' sofas at night. His father, alarmed by the increasingly sporadic and evasive nature of his son's communications, assumed he must by now be reduced to eking out a living as a rent boy (the English were, after all, notorious pederasts), and wired him some money – almost all of which Amedeo had decided to blow on a weekend in Paris with his paramour.

He remembered strolling languidly around the museum with her, hand-in-hand, both far more absorbed by one another than by any of the paintings. As they wandered through the Flemish and Dutch painters in the Richelieu Wing, he could see that Viola was relishing the sensation of being observed while observing. With a surge of desire, he watched as she posed prettily in front of moustached burgomasters and their austere, white-collared wives, affectedly tilting her head, feigning contemplation, or when she took a step back from tableaux of corpulent, ruddy peasants grinning inanely, hands on her narrow, angular hips. At one point she would run her fingers through her hair and turn slightly to give him the benefit of her three-quarter view. As they continued on to the next room, where the walls were covered with pasty, bleeding Christs, he positioned himself so that she could just see him looking at her from the corner of her eye, and watched her respond accordingly: this time she stretched and arched her back, causing her cropped crocheted top to rise, revealing her concave, alabaster belly.

And as he gazed at her, he reflected with a swell of pride that it was her frail, slender frame, her diaphanous skin and long, curly tresses, the colour of which the French call *blond vénitien* – that shade so popular in Botticelli's works and which, according to a tour guide at the Uffizi during a childhood trip to Florence, the models in Botticelli's time obtained by bleaching their hair with horse urine – that all the other men in the museum would be admiring. Not the mottled thighs of Rembrandt's Bathsheba, nor the moon-like forehead and plump, rosy cheeks of Vermeer's *Lacemaker,* nor even Gabrielle d'Estrées' pert naked breasts.

Afterwards they had returned to their grotty hotel room near Place de Clichy and made love vigorously for the rest of the afternoon, finally emerging at dusk from a coitus-induced slumber to stumble half-dazed to their local bistro where they had feasted on wild boar terrine, *lapin aux pruneaux* (for this was back in the Dark Ages, long before his ethical and nutritional epiphany, when he still partook of animal flesh), *crème brulée* and two bottles of Gigondas.

How his tastes had changed since Viola! He would no more lust after such a coltish, flat-chested slip of a girl now than he would – well, eat rabbit or wild boar or egg- and cream-based desserts.

Thus aroused and nostalgic for other distant conquests, he now reflected how one of Vincenzo Campi's peasant wenches put him in mind of the girl who had taken his virginity the summer he turned sixteen. Indeed, Bianca, who was his grandfather's stepdaughter (his step-aunt?), was also plump and calf-eyed but with a sumptuous bosom, creamy skin and – most importantly, for him – shapely ankles. (He had never been able to abide women with 'tree-trunk legs': the absence of a clearly defined Achilles' tendon was as unappealing in his eyes as cellulite, abundant pubic hair or a flat chest were to other men.) They were at his grandfather's house in Teggiano: he, his brothers, parents, grandfather, his grand-father's new bride, and her daughter from a previous marriage, Bianca.

She was twenty – a woman! They had exchanged few words, but one evening, she had been staring at him throughout dinner, her bovine gaze baldly lascivious, and whilst helping him to her mother's *carciofi alla giudia* (passable, though not a patch on his own mother's), she had pushed her décolleté forward and let her leg rest gently against his beneath the table.

Later that evening, whilst he was lying on his bed reading *Gli indifferenti*, she came into the room, her arms laden with freshly laundered tablecloths, and silently went over to the huge walnut dresser where, turning her back to him, she began putting linen in the drawers with what seemed deliberate, calculated slowness. Putting down his book, he sat on the edge of the bed and, leaning forward, reached out and caressed her calf with the back of his fingers. She said nothing, didn't turn around, but continued with her linen, albeit even more slowly.

Emboldened, he allowed his fingers to travel upwards, beneath her skirt, stroking her inner thigh now. After placing the last tablecloth in the drawer, she closed it and laid her hands on the edge of the dresser, while he continued to stroke her. She leaned forward slightly, gradually edging her feet apart. He heard her breathing quicken as his hands went higher still, and as they encountered the warm moistness, she gasped and her hands gripped the edge of the dresser. He was unsure what to do with his fingers but her cries of pleasure, what seemed like only seconds later, were encouraging. His subsequent sexual experiences in the years that followed would teach him that very few women were pleasured so quickly and easily.

Breathless and still unspeaking, she finally turned to face him, pushed him back on the bed, and in one swift movement, knelt over him, unzipped his flies and pulled him inside her. He could still remember the faint odour of clean laundry on the plump, soft hand she clapped over his mouth to stifle his cries as he reached his own equally swift climax.

To this day, the crisp, clean scent that emanated from newly ironed linen always brought a rush of blood to his loins.

ⅩⅪ

Just before eight the next morning Marnie awoke in the guest room of Amedeo's duplex. In her rather limited experience, for which she compensated with a mixture of imagination and stereotypes, bachelors lived either in abject squalor – filthy bathrooms, kitchens in which vast ecosystems of bacteria thrived, the bedroom and living areas strewn with soiled underwear, pornography and half-empty takeaway food containers – or clinical cleanliness and quasi-monastic austerity.

Her friend clearly belonged to the latter category: for the place was spotlessly clean, the décor tasteful and minimalistic yet rather impersonal: there were few books, and no ornaments, pictures or photographs adorned the walls or shelves aside from a single framed snapshot on the desk of his home office area on the landing of the upper floor. It depicted a seven- or eight-year-old Amedeo with two other boys, presumably his brothers. The youngest boy, who looked about three or four, sat on the lap of a middle-aged man who was certainly Di Meglio Senior. Whilst the two brothers flashed unselfconscious, semi-toothless grins, Amedeo stared unsmiling at the camera, his dark eyes already intense and full of a worldly wisdom – if not quite world-weariness – beyond his years.

Kicking off the duvet, Marnie wandered into the en suite bathroom to splash cold water on her face. The bathroom, like everywhere else, was immaculately clean and featured a walk-in shower – equipped with new, unopened bottles of shower gel and shampoo – and a bidet, something Marnie had hitherto only seen in hotels, but almost never in private homes.

She slipped on her kimono and wandered downstairs, expecting Amedeo, a creature of routine and self-discipline, to have been up for hours, having already completed his early-morning yoga session, breakfasted, showered and dressed ready for the day.

Yet there was no sign of him in the kitchen or living and dining area, and his bedroom door, she had noticed as she passed it on the way to the stairs, remained closed. Perhaps he had gone out for a run, or to carry out some errand?

But there was no note on the kitchen or dining tables. Marnie set about making herself a coffee then, realising with dismay that there was no coffee machine of any description – not even a moka pot! What sort of Italian was he? – decided on tea, then, remembering that there was no milk in the house, settled for a cup of ginger herbal tea, which she took out onto the vast balcony.

Fifteen minutes later, she returned upstairs and just as she was stepping into the shower, heard her phone beep. It was a message from Amedeo saying he was feeling under the weather: he had had a bad night and woke with a terrible headache and was going to sleep it off. There followed detailed instructions on how to get to the local station on foot, a link to the Monza-Milan train timetable, and another to a map of the metro. She crossed the landing, knocked on his bedroom door and, without entering, asked if he was all right and would he like her to pick up any groceries or medication for him. In a feeble voice he thanked her but assured her he just needed to sleep it off.

Just over an hour later, Marnie alighted from the train at Milano Centrale. Having originally planned to go to the Pinacoteca Ambrosiana to see Caravaggio's *Basket of Fruit*, she had changed her mind and decided, for the first time since she had arrived in Italy a week before, to treat herself to a purely personal, recreational cultural outing, entirely unrelated to Caravaggio or Bacchus & Minerva. She was thus looking forward to seeing Da Vinci's *Last Supper*, and, as it was a fine, bright day, set out on foot to the Cenacolo Vinciano.

She arrived there three-quarters of an hour later to find the main entrance closed and a notice fixed to the gate:

Avviso: con l'entrata in vigore del DPCM 8 marzo 2020 da oggi fino al 3 aprile 2020 sono chiusi TUTTI i musei, istituti e luoghi della cultura sull'intero territorio nazionale.

Other than the unfamiliar acronym, the message was clear: all museums and cultural establishments were closed, effective immediately. She swore out loud.

Thank God she had managed to fit in all her other museum visits in time! But how long would they remain closed? And what to do with the rest of her day? With the picture galleries closed and the prospect of shopping failing to excite her, the possibilities seemed considerably limited. There was always the *duomo* – assuming churches did not come under the cultural institution umbrella. Yes: the cathedral, followed by a coffee somewhere, then back to the station and home to check on Amedeo. She keyed her destination into Google Maps and set off.

It was just before noon when she emerged from the cathedral and crossed the square to a cafe where she sat at a table and ordered a double espresso. The place was empty but for a young woman in front of a laptop and a tall, elegantly dressed man of about her age standing at the bar holding a glass mug of some sort of creamy, frothy beverage and talking on the phone. After speaking for a few minutes in Italian – too quickly for Marnie to catch more than the odd word – the man suddenly switched to English. And not just any English: the man was evidently a native speaker, and spoke with a public-school drawl.

'What on earth for?' he said, laughing. 'I thought the whole point of practising your English was to help you seduce Anglophone men; and now that you're stuck in bed with a deadly virus and practically under house arrest, surely your chances of copulating with anything of any nationality in the foreseeable future are virtually non-existent?'

Marnie looked quickly away, pretending to be absorbed by the crowds of tourists and workers on their lunchtime break crossing the square, embarrassed at having overheard and understood the conversation. Should she cough? Pretend to receive a phone-call of her own and thus reveal her native language to the stranger at the bar?

Then, silently laughing at the absurd scenario she had briefly contemplated, at her crippling English upbringing, she finished her coffee, paid, and left.

Tired after her long walks around town, she took the metro to the station and caught the next train back to Monza. When she let herself into Amedeo's flat twenty minutes later, the place was silent. She went straight upstairs and tapped on his bedroom door, softly calling his name.

His voice was feeble, barely above a croak. 'Don't come in!'

'Why? God, what's wrong?'

'I have a fever, I feel terrible.'

'Oh, poor you. Shall I call a doctor?'

'No, it feels like flu, I just need to rest. But don't come in, please – ' he paused to cough. 'I don't want you to catch it.'

Marnie acquiesced, and, after fetching a jug of water and a glass and placing them just inside his door, went downstairs and settled on the sofa where she reached for her phone and checked in for her flight back to Bristol the following afternoon – a flight, which, did she but know it then, she would not be on.

CHAPTER THIRTY-ONE

Milan, 12 March 2020

After filing his copy – another bleak report on the cataclysmic state of the Milan stock market since Conte had announced the national lockdown three days before – Miles went off to the kitchen in search of a glass of wine before settling down to his usual nightly ritual of going on Twitter. He made a point of restricting his social media activity to a half-hour daily time slot in order to avoid becoming embroiled in endless, pointless discussions or side-tracked by trivia and gossip.

He was about to pour out the remains of the cheap bottle of Valpolicella he had opened two days before, when, on an impulse – and in the spirit of foolhardy, *carpe diem*, end-of-the-world hedonism that had occasionally seized him of late – reached instead for the bottle of Sassicaia 2015 that Luca had given him a few months back, and which he had been saving for a special occasion.

As he swirled the blood-red liquid around the glass, it occurred to him that this must be how Luca lived all the time: for he did not wait for a global, potentially lethal pandemic or indeed any other disaster to strike to indulge his every whim, satisfy his every urge, without a thought for the future consequences. To use the expression Miles had once heard somewhere, Luca lived every day like a sailor on shore leave.

It was highly likely that this very recklessness, combined with his usual promiscuity and general cavalier attitude to his health, had led Luca to contract the virus, and which, had he been born a few decades earlier, would have probably resulted in his death from AIDS – or, a century earlier than that, syphilis.

Of course, that he was suffering from *The* virus was purely an assumption: for all anyone knew, it might have just been the flu. Testing capabilities were still extremely limited, and hospitals in Italy were already overrun: the instructions given to potential patients was to stay at home, isolated from loved ones, rest, and only come to hospital if symptoms worsened and if the patient started having breathing difficulties.

In any event, whatever was ailing Luca, his mother, upon hearing of his condition, had persuaded her husband to bring back his estranged son from exile so she could care for him at home. Consequently, Luca had for the last ten days been languishing at the family pile in Lodi province, no doubt sequestered in some draughty turret with a dour uniformed retainer bringing his meals on a tray. (Miles, never having been invited to Luca's family seat, imagined it as a cross between the Castle of Otranto – Walpole's romanticised version of it – and Thornfield Hall.)

Poor Luca, he reflected. Although, during their FaceTime session the night before he had looked a little better, and certainly seemed back to his usual self, even complaining that Paola, (the dour uniformed retainer, Miles presumed), had overcooked the risotto.

Taking a long, appreciative draft of the wine, savouring the explosion of cedar, red berries and – chocolate, possibly? – on his palate, he returned to his laptop and scrolled through his Twitter feeds, starting with his official account.

As usual, Patrizio Pirola had something to say. Today his post was about the mafia – when did he ever talk about anything else? Miles wondered. Accompanying his post was a link to an article he had published on a well-known news site in which he described how organised crime was taking advantage of the health crisis and the resulting economic slump to line its pockets, by pouncing upon struggling businesses and offering their money-lending and racketeering services.

Privately, Miles thought his fellow journalist overrated. Judging by the many interviews he had given since the publication four years ago of *Caos*, his best-selling exposé of the Camorra's activities and the subsequent fatwa issued against him by that organisation, he was, for a journalist, disappointingly inarticulate and rather vulgar. And as much as he admired his courage in pursuing his anti-mafia crusade, at the cost of his personal safety and freedom, Miles could not help but think he was milking it somewhat: the omnipresent police escort, the whining about not being able to go back to his beloved native Napoli to enjoy simple pleasures such as walking down the street with an ice cream, or eating a *fritto misto* at O Tabaccaro. Well, what did the man expect? he thought irritably. One couldn't have everything. And then there were the constant, inevitable comparisons with Salman Rushdie. Don't kid yourself, thought Miles: *Caos* was an admirable effort but it was no *Satanic Verses*. No; as far as he was concerned, their similarities ended with the police escort and looming death threat.

Miles's personal and professional misgivings about Pirola notwithstanding, his unwavering commitment to freedom of the press and freedom of expression forced him on principle to defend to the death the man's right to say whatever he wanted. Indeed, he had leapt to his defence on social media a year or so ago when Matteo Salvini, during his tenure as Deputy Prime Minister and Minister of the Interior, had, as a spiteful response to Pirola's savage and very public criticism of Salvini's handling of the immigration crisis, threatened on Facebook to withdraw the journalist's police escort – thereby effectively condemning him to death. His journalistic integrity aside, it was not difficult for Miles to defend anyone against a man such as Salvini: he was a brute and a bigot, and his political convictions made him loathe him with every fibre of his being.

Abandoning Pirola and resolving, not for the first time, to unfollow him one day, he turned his attention to a rather sanctimonious tweet by Taddeo Sartori, Miles's source for the article on the DigInnova financial scandal.

As DigInnova Italia's Sales Director for years, Sartori had been the lieutenant of the company's former CEO – a thoroughly shady character named Matteo Santevecchi. In addition to being greedy and utterly unprincipled, Santevecchi had also evidently been a tyrannical and paranoid leader, and during the few months before the fraud story had broken, had begun summarily dismissing the members of his inner circle, including his Sales Director and Chief Strategy Officer. Whilst the latter had apparently gone meekly, Sartori had decided to wreak vengeance on his former boss by disclosing the financial and fiscal indiscretions that had taken place over the past six years to Miles, whom he had been introduced to by a mutual acquaintance the previous year at an event organised by the City of Milan. The fallout from the exposure of the scandal had been considerable and far-reaching, involving the *Guardia di Finanza* descending upon DigInnova's Italian headquarters, the arrests of Santevecchi, his Chief Financial Officer, and a dozen other company heads who were involved in the money laundering and false billing scam with DigInnova, the confiscation of various ill-gotten assets including a yacht and a fleet of luxury sports cars, not to mention irreparable damage to the reputation and financial health of the group as a whole. Indeed, there had evidently been mass redundancies, not only in Italy but at the company's parent company in France and across its various European subsidiaries.

Since blowing the whistle on his former employers, Sartori had set himself up as some sort of consultant and a poster boy for business ethics: case in point, he was currently plugging some thinktank he had set up on greater transparency in the financial sector.

Miles gave a snort of derision at the tweet. For as grateful to Sartori as he was for providing him with one of his biggest stories of 2019 – it was certainly much sexier than his usual market reports and mergers and acquisitions – he did not trust the man one iota and had no doubt whatsoever that his denouncing DigInnova's illicit activities had sprung purely from spite and resentment towards his former boss and mentor, not from any sense of moral outrage. He was a cynical opportunist, nothing more. Deciding it was time to distance himself from the man, Miles clicked on the 'following' button next to Sartori's name and began writing a post.

Today's tweet was about abusive fines the police had been dishing out to people allegedly flouting lockdown rules, and included a link to an article from a local news site in Piedmont. Apparently, a man out on his bike was stopped by the *carabinieri* who had checked his backpack, finding three bottles of wine and a packet of pasta, and fined him €102.50, saying that wine did not qualify as an essential item (that, reflected Miles laconically as he took another appreciative sip of Sassicaia, was entirely a matter of opinion). The police had also said that he was committing a double offence: by cycling with bottles of wine in his backpack, they averred, he was likely to cause a road accident, thus placing an additional burden on already over-stretched hospital staff.

He then switched to his alter-profile, the one for which he used the handle @MiloAmorpizzo. Today he was commenting on an article he had read about researchers at Oxford who claimed to have an explanation for the astronomical and continually rising number of fatal cases of the virus in Italy: apart from demographics (one in four Italians was over sixty-five), it was, they claimed, because Italian society was so family-oriented, with lots of inter-generational cohabitation. Plus, everyone knew how tactile the Italians were. Miles posted the link to the article, tweeting that only the cold, phlegmatic Brits could find a way to attribute mass deaths to people hugging too much and spending too much time with their families.

Just as he finished posting, his phone beeped. Picking it up, he saw a headline from one of the British tabloids he subscribed to had popped up on his screen. His pulse quickened as he saw an unpleasantly familiar name:

NIGEL LOVELACE'S SECRET LOVE-CHILD

Reaching numbly for the bottle of Sassicaia 2015, he read the article, in which his father was referred to variously as a "heartless retail magnate," "high-street clothing oligarch" and "billionaire love-rat" who had "cruelly abandoned his lover and their child."

Well, thought Miles, once he had recovered from the initial shock, aided by a fortifying third glass of wine, there goes the old man's chance of being recognised on the New Year's Honour's List.

215

CHAPTER THIRTY-TWO

Bristol, 13 March 2020

Rhiannon Barthélemy's day had begun badly and was about to take a turn for the positively surreal.

It was twelve days since she had left her digs in Warwick and moved back temporarily to her mother's to feed the cats, and, incidentally, contemplate her future.

Early that morning, however, she had received a phone call which, in a matter of seconds, had changed that future from an exciting adventure full of infinite possibilities, challenges and encounters, into a bleak wilderness of uncertainty, confusion and – worse than that – boredom.

For Amandine, her contact at Passeport numérique, the NGO she was due to volunteer for in Cambodia in just over a week, had informed her that, amid growing concerns about the coronavirus pandemic and the distinct possibility of imminent travel restrictions to and from Asia, they had decided to cancel all volunteer programmes for the 'foreseeable future' – an expression which, in the current context, struck Rhiannon as something of an oxymoron.

She was no fool: she had half-expected such an outcome, but had nevertheless been hoping against hope that somehow her trip could go ahead as planned. For the alternative – that she had potentially jeopardised her future and thrown away a year of her life for nothing – was too dreadful to contemplate.

After sounding the death knell to Rhiannon's future plans, Amandine had valiantly attempted to console her by saying that if she was still interested in lending her time and skills to their organisation, there were a number of other ways she could contribute that did not involve travelling. Rhiannon had thanked her listlessly and hung up. Sitting up in bed, she swore out loud, causing the skittish Tim, who, as usual, had slept curled up at the foot of the bed, to leap down and scuttle away. With an effort of will, she fought back burning tears of frustration and tried to focus on the contingency plan she had vaguely imagined but never really thought she would have to implement: she would go to Paris, stay at her father's, catch up with her old crowd. She could get some sort of job – bar work, perhaps. Or she could help out her father in the bookshop. It would be all right. It would be… different, but not a disaster. For heaven's sake, she scolded herself: she was a healthy, educated young woman living in one of the richest countries in the world. Her lot was not to be pitied.

Fired by this newfound resolve and optimism, she kicked off the sheets and wandered into the kitchen. Having made herself a caffe latte with her mother's machine she shook pellets into the cats' food bowls.

The cats.

'Bollocks!' She cried, and, turning to the two animals as they buried their faces in the food: 'What the hell am I going to do with you guys when I'm Paris?'

For her mother, who had originally been due to come home from Italy three days ago, had called on the morning of her planned departure to say that her return had been delayed by some vague, unspecified issue with the airline and she would therefore be extending her stay for a few days or so.

The neighbours. Of course! Her mother was apparently on good terms with the elderly lady next door – what was her name again? Willis? Wilson? She had chatted occasionally to Rhiannon over the garden wall since she had moved in.

She would simply ask her – Wellesley! That was it! Like the Duke of Wellington – she would ask Mrs Wellesley next door to pop in and feed the cats every day. Not one to procrastinate, she decided to do so right away. Returning to the spare bedroom to pull on jeans and a long-sleeved T-shirt, she scooped up the keys, pushed her feet into trainers without tying the laces and opened the front door.

Had she been of a more fanciful turn of mind, her first thought might have been that she had opened the door into an alternative universe, some bizarre parallel world.

For outside the front door, spilling over the pavement into the road, was what appeared to be a crowd of reporters.

She froze and stared.

'Marnie?' Someone asked as a flashbulb exploded.

'What the fuck…?' she muttered under her breath.

'Marnie Wade?' someone else called out.

'No… I'm her daughter. What's this about?'

Someone in the crowd murmured: 'The granddaughter!'

And then: 'Did you know your grandfather was Nigel Lovelace?'

'What? Who the hell is Nigel Lovelace?'

The cameras continued, clicking away relentlessly. She was assailed with questions from all sides:

'Where's Marnie? Is she after his money? Did you know your mum was adopted?'

She slammed the front door and staggered backwards. Inside the house, she drew the blinds with shaking hands and picked up her mobile. Her mother answered after two rings.

'What's up, Pussycat?'

'What the *fuck* is going on?' she shrieked.

'What? What's the matter?'

'There's a pack of journalists outside the house, that's what. Something about someone called Lovelace being your real Dad?'

She heard her mother sigh. 'God, the press knows about that? I mean… *how*, and why would they even care?'

'Then it's *true*? Why didn't you tell me you'd tracked down your birth father?'

'Well, I was going to, of course, but I wanted to do it in person, face to face, and you've been going through so much lately. I'm sorry…' Marnie told her about her discovery on MyRoots and the subsequent meeting with Dinah. While she did so, she looked at news sites on Amedeo's iPad. A few of the scandal rags and one or two tabloids had picked up the story.

'Look, I don't understand how they found out, but I'll look into it… I'm sorry you had to find out this way, but it's really no big deal. My father, as it turns out, is something of a minor celebrity, a billionaire, he used to own various high street clothing chains. But, listen, this story will soon fizzle out, believe me: it's tomorrow's fish and chip wrapping.' (At this point, she had to explain the expression, Rhiannon having been born long after fish and chip shops stopped serving their fare in old newspapers for health and safety reasons.) 'It'll be eclipsed by some story about a minor Tory backbencher getting caught cruising for cock on Hampstead Heath. Or coronavirus news. If there's one thing to be said about a global pandemic, it's that it puts things into perspective.'

'Yeah, well tell that to the pack of wolves outside,' Rhiannon muttered glumly. 'When are you coming home, Mum?'

'Ah, about that…' Marnie then proceeded to recount the events of the past three days and the real reason for her delayed return. On the morning of the ninth of March, Amedeo had awoken feeling decidedly worse. In addition to the throbbing head, he complained of aching muscles. Marnie had found a digital thermometer in his bathroom cabinet and taken his temperature: thirty-nine point two.

'Right,' she said. 'That settles it. I'm not leaving.'

He raised his head wearily from the pillow, half-squinting up at her. 'What? Don't be silly, I'll be OK. And besides, the way things are going here, if you don't get your flight today, you might not get back at all.' Indeed, the museum closures of the previous day had been closely followed by restaurants and bars that very evening.

Marnie had shaken her head dismissively as she bustled around him, pouring water, administering aspirin, fetching a flannel from the bathroom and soaking it in cold water to place on his burning brow.

'Nonsense,' she said briskly. 'They'll have to let nationals return home at some point. And besides, there's no way I'm leaving you all alone in your state. It's unthinkable.'

'*Ma, dai…*' he began.

The similarity in pronunciation between this last word and the English word meaning to cease to live sent a chill through her as she thought of the ever-growing number of fatalities. She pulled herself together and, forcing herself to sound brisk and matter-of-fact, said:

'I'm going to look after you and that's final.'

'But you'll get sick. I mean, if it is… what we think it is, you will catch it too…'

'Bit late to worry about that,' she said simply, removing the wet flannel from his forehead and dabbing his cheeks with it. 'Even assuming I did abandon you to your fate, when I got to Malpensa, they'd probably take my temperature or test me or something and I might not be able to get on the flight. But that's all moot: I'm not leaving you until you get better – which you will,' she added, with an assurance she did not quite feel. 'You're young and strong and healthy.'

Too weary to protest further, he nodded weakly and closed his eyes.

Marnie had then ordered some groceries online and spent the rest of the day checking her emails and making phone calls – to her parents, Guy, Rhiannon, Val. Only to this last person did she tell the truth about Amedeo's illness; she made up the excuse of problems with the airline to avoid alarming her parents and daughter.

After going onto the British Airways website to change her flight to a week later, she spent the rest of the day reading and checking on Amedeo, who slept for most of the day. In the evening she made penne with olive oil, garlic and chilli flakes, took one bowl up to him and put another on a tray with a glass of Il Bruciato and sat in front of the television with her supper. As she was finishing her pasta, Giuseppe Conte appeared on the screen and began gravely addressing the nation. She did not catch all the details but understood the gist: borders closing, everything closing, stay at home. She picked up her phone and consulted various English-speaking news sites to confirm her suspicions. The word lockdown, which would soon become part of everyday parlance, was at the time barely used by, or even known to members of the general public.

Rhiannon was understandably alarmed at hearing her mother was not only marooned in Europe's coronavirus hotspot, but self-isolating with a probable patient.

'Please don't worry, lovey,' Marnie assured her. 'You understand why I can't just leave him, don't you?'

'Of course. But please be careful. We're hearing terrible things about Italy over here. It sounds like full-on zombie apocalypse.'

'Pretty much. But I promise you, I'll just keep an eye on him until he gets better and then I'll be on the first flight back. In the meantime, he's in his room and doesn't leave it, we each have our own bathroom; I'm anti-baccing to within an inch of my life; I only pop in to bring him his meals and check on him. But tell me, how are things over there? What's happening with your trip?'

'I spoke to the woman from Passeport numérique this morning. It's off.'

'Oh, no... Look, I know you must be disappointed but honestly, with everything that's going on you don't want to be going to South-East Asia right now.' She paused for a moment then asked tentatively: 'It might not be too late to go back to Warwick and complete the rest of the year.'

After a few seconds' silence, Rhiannon said: 'You know, that actually never occurred to me. Ever since I left and made my other plans, I've turned that whole page in my head – for this year at least. And now, even though it turns out I can't go, I can't just turn back. Do you see what I mean?'

'Of course. Look, just think about it, will you? I'm sure they'll be very understanding at Warwick. I mean, if you did decide to go back up.'

'All right. I'll think about it.'

Marnie changed the subject. 'How are the cats?'

At that point, Rhiannon burst out laughing: the relief at the abrupt switch to a reassuringly mundane topic – one entirely unrelated to illness, death, scandal, her ruined plans and the momentous decision she would have to make soon – was overwhelming.

And then the laughter dissolved into tears.

'Oh, Mum,' she wailed. 'It's such a fucking mess!'

'Don't cry, my Honey Bee,' Marnie said soothingly. 'I know it's a mess, but you'll figure it out. You're a brave, clever, resourceful, beautiful young woman. And this will all pass, I promise.' Reassured that her daughter had calmed down, she continued: 'Now, really: tell me about the cats. How are they doing?'

Rhiannon sniffed. 'Fine. Although, actually, Roger was pining the first few days you were away – and no, I didn't say anything at the time because I didn't want to worry you.' She added tartly: 'Sound familiar? Anyway, she's better now, back on her food. Tim's her usual self: skittish and paranoid and in her own world. She brought in a sparrow yesterday. And no, I didn't punish her for following her natural, primal instincts. You're just used to that ridiculous, pampered, overbred show cat. This is what *real* mogs do.'

Their conversation having ended on this more levitous note, Rhiannon hung up. Peering through the blinds, she saw that the reporters were still lurking; their presence had also apparently caused some of the residents of Dowry Square to emerge from their houses and investigate.

'Fuck's sake…' she muttered and withdrew to the sofa with her laptop. After spending half an hour Googling Nigel Lovelace, she picked up her phone and speed-dialled a number.

'Hi. It's me. Listen, I need another favour.'

⋈⬚⋈

After Marnie had finished speaking to her daughter, she took a few deep breaths until the feeling of nausea abated then dialled Dinah Lovelace's number.

'Hello? Marnie?' the voice on the other end was faint, strained, showing none of the ebullience and confidence of their last meeting.

It took another deep breath for Marnie to control her anger:

'Please tell me this isn't your doing.'

'I swear it isn't! I would never do that to… well, to any of us. Not even to spite Pa. I don't understand what happened. The press are here.'

'Yes, they're at my house too.'

'Oh, no! How awful for you.'

Touched by Dinah's concern for her, despite her own situation which must surely be infinitely worse, Marnie softened.

'It's all right. I'm not actually there, I'm still stuck in Italy, but my daughter is. Anyway… what the *hell* happened?'

'I have no idea, truly. It's pretty grim here: Ma's devastated – we had to give her a Valium; she's resting now. Pa's furious, needless to say. He's absolutely convinced I was the leak, threatened to cut me off and everything. Portia's supposedly dealing with the press – she handles Pa's PR. She's sided with him – as usual – and has sent me to Coventry too.'

'I'm sorry,' said Marnie sincerely, 'I can only imagine. Is there anything I can do? I would offer you my place in Bristol to escape to but that would be a case of out of the frying pan and into the… well, slightly smaller frying pan.'

'That's awfully nice of you, but in any case, I can't run away, not yet. If nothing else, I have to look after Ma. She won't let Pa near her at the moment, which is understandable under the circs. I'll try and find out how the story got out. I mean if you didn't tell them and I didn't…'

'Maybe some business rival of your father's?' Marnie suggested.

'What, like his arch-enemy, the loathsome Sir Philip?' Dinah began to laugh. 'I'm sorry, I'm not making fun of you. I know I shouldn't be laughing at all right now, but I can't help it. It's nerves, mostly, although speaking to you has cheered me up a bit. Oh, God, did you see the article in *The Sun*? It's wildly inaccurate: according to them, Cordelia is a "renowned cellist" – she is neither, in point of fact – and I'm studying *PPE* at *Oxford*, for God's sake!'

Well, think yourself lucky you're not a "50-year-old unemployed divorcee," Marnie wanted to say, but desisted.

'Look, I'd better go,' said Dinah. 'I'll try and find out what happened and let you know as soon as I do.'

As soon as Marnie hung up, her phone rang. It was Val.

'Who would have thought Marnie's Great Matter would make the headlines?'

'Hmmm. Thank God it's just as a minor piece tucked away on page seven of a few crappy tabloids.'

'Yes, it is surprising the story hasn't been picked up by any of the broadsheets,' Val observed drily. 'Are you OK?'

'I'm fine, although Rhiannon has reporters camped outside the house.'

'Oh, poor love. Does she want to escape here?'

'She might do, I'll mention it to her. Thanks.'

'How are things out there?'

'Not great, but OK. Amedeo's still pretty much the same.' She sighed. 'So, which article did you see?'

'The Sun.'

'Ah. Well, thank you for not mentioning "50-year-old unemployed divorcee."'

'It's an outrage,' said Val, gently mocking. 'Will you sue for libel?'

'"50-year-old unemployed divorcee,"' Marnie repeated. 'Fuck me. And the worst thing is, it's technically true – apart from the age, of course. Fifty! *Bastards*.'

'Well, yes, *technically*, but they could have put a more positive spin on it, like: "budding entrepreneur in the prime of her life," or "former executive at a multinational tech company" – albeit one which has since fallen into disgrace and near bankruptcy.'

'Entrepreneur,' repeated Marnie drily. 'Hmm: the founder of a company that's barely got off its feet before a major health crisis sweeps the globe, making international travel highly unlikely for the foreseeable future and thus destroying the whole fucking point of the business.'

'Oh, dear. I see my pep talk hasn't really had the desired effect. Joly's so much better that this sort of thing.'

'How is he? And the kids?'

'Joly is fine, as busy as ever at work, and all is much the same as ever in the Weird and Wonderful World of Josh. Medora, on the other hand, has lately been spending an inordinate amount of time working herself into a vortex of angst trying to interpret some boy's use of a certain emoji. I did attempt to introduce a little rationalism and perspective, pointing out that perhaps the breadth and complexity of human emotion cannot be adequately expressed by a collection of yellow, spherical, digitally-generated icons. She then flew into a rage and told me I was a Luddite and didn't understand anything about dating in the digital age.'

'Well, she does have a point,' Marnie conceded. 'About millennial courtship rituals, I mean. Right-swiping on Tinder is about as alien to us as... I don't know, going to see the village matchmaker.'

'Oh, I know. And I wasn't bothered about the Luddite remark. It makes a change from "crypto-Facist" or "unwoke." And frankly, I was pleasantly surprised she knew what a Luddite was.'

Marnie laughed. They chatted for a few minutes more, then Marnie hung up and steeled herself for the next telephone conversation she knew she would have to make: Deirdre. She knew she had to call her.

But to say what? To explain? How could she? She still had no idea how the story had come out, although she kept gravitating towards the inescapable conclusion that it was the result of her attempts to locate her birth father: joining MyRoots, getting in touch with Dinah. God, could someone have hacked into MyRoots? It was unthinkable, and yet...

Stop, she told herself firmly. Don't disappear down the rabbit-hole of rampant, baseless speculation. *O, that way madness lies...*

If nothing else, she wanted Deirdre to know it was not she, Marnie, who had informed the press. Then she remembered she didn't have her phone number: she had deleted it from her contacts years ago, and did not have access to their written correspondence here. And of course, the woman was not on social media or even email.

Dave, she thought. He can get in touch with her via his mother or aunt – Deirdre's cousins.

She called Dave's number and immediately got his voicemail. After leaving a vague, non-committal message, she went upstairs to check on Amedeo.

Over the next few days, Amedeo's condition varied little: he was feverish and tired and had a dry, hacking cough, the likes of which Marnie had not heard since the infant Rhiannon had suffered from bronchiolitis. She went into his room several times a day to refill his water jug, air the room by opening the sliding door to the balcony, bring him bowls of soup she made from frozen vegetables: she had run out of fresh produce on the second day of his illness and supermarkets were struggling to cope with the spike in demand for home deliveries.

Aside from caring for Amedeo, she strove to establish a daily routine of sorts, involving morning yoga sessions on the terrace and early-evening video calls with Rhiannon, Val and her parents. She finished *Framley Parsonage* and wished she had brought more books with her. She watched the rolling news, listened to music, napped. She was also obliged to do regular loads of laundry to make the limited wardrobe and half a dozen bras and pairs of pants she had brought with her last for weeks. She never ventured outside the apartment building.

One morning, just over a week after Amedeo had fallen ill, she awoke just before dawn after an extremely short night and went downstairs to make tea. Shortly afterwards, she dozed off on the sofa, and was then awoken with a start by noises from the kitchen.

'Amedeo?'

He stood in the doorway, a glass of water in his hand.

'Marnie Wade, lying on my sofa in a silk nightdress,' he said dreamily. 'Did I die from this thing and go to heaven?'

CHAPTER THIRTY-THREE

Dublin, 12 March 2020

The same day as Amedeo arose, Lazarus-like, from his sickbed, nearly two thousand kilometres away, Clare Mullan went to hospital – not as a patient, but to see some of her colleagues at Tallaght. Her friend Diana, the Paediatric Registrar, had asked her to pop in for coffee and a chat sometime and Clare, bored to tears during the last few weeks of maternity leave, jumped at the chance. She also had an ulterior motive in visiting her place of work: not renowned for her ability to relinquish control easily, she was also intending to check up on the woman who had taken over from her as Ward Sister.

After catching up on ward gossip with Diana over a cup of decaf, saying a quick hello to her replacement and trying to ascertain from her maddingly reticent nurses how their new boss was acquitting herself, Clare left the hospital. Then, just as she was getting into her car, she saw Dave's cousin emerging from a gleaming, new-looking SUV with a baby carrier. She had not seen her for a couple of years, but she was still the same: rail-thin, impeccably groomed and tailored – although she did look a little pale and drawn. No doubt the infant was keeping her up at night.

Clare called out the other woman's name as she approached her.

Méabh, who had been fussing over the baby, looked up abruptly.

'Clare?' She gave a tired smile. 'My goodness, it's been ages! How are you?' she nodded to Clare's swollen belly. 'Any day now, isn't it?'

Clare nodded. 'It's actually a few days overdue.' She looked at the baby carrier. 'So, who's this, then?'

'*This*,' Méabh said, her face lighting up with evident pride, 'is Olivia.'

'I had no idea you and Sheridan had...'

'We didn't,' said Méabh, rearranging the baby's blanket. 'We're actually splitting up. I'm adopting Olivia alone. Well, that is, she's been placed in my care while Tusla process my adoption request.'

'Oh. Really? Dave never said. Anyway, that's great, good for you.' She paused. 'So, Tusla let you foster her in the meantime? I thought the fostering and adoption process was much longer and more complicated.'

Méabh looked up warily from the baby carrier. 'Ah, yes… well, it can be…' she said slowly, 'but she's actually family. A blood relative, I mean. I'm applying to adopt her as a member of her extended family. The mother was having difficulties and asked me to take her and has agreed to let me apply to adopt her.'

'Oh, grand. Anyone I know?'

Méabh looked alarmed. 'What?'

'The family member.'

'Oh, no,' she replied quickly. 'It's… a cousin on Daddy's side.'

'Ah. Speaking of your Dad, Méabh, I was sorry to hear…'

'Thank you,' she said gently. 'I got your card, it was very thoughtful.'

The conversation having apparently reached its limits, Méabh nodded towards the hospital building. 'I'd better be getting on, so…'

'Of course! Stupid question given we're in a hospital carpark, but is everything OK?' Clare nodded to the baby.

'I don't know, but I'm awfully worried. She keeps throwing up her milk. I couldn't get hold of my paediatrician so I was bringing her to the A&E.'

Clare nodded. 'Sounds like reflux. It's extremely common in newborns. Do you mind if I have a look?' ventured Clare.

'Oh… of course, I didn't think… Please! Be my guest.' She placed the car seat on the bonnet of her Range Rover and Clare peered inside.

'Hello, wee girl,' she said in a gentle, soothing tone. 'Are we having trouble keeping our milk down now?'

She placed a hand on the infant's head. 'No fever.'

Méabh confirmed. 'No, I take her temperature regularly, it's normal.'

'Any blood in the vomit?'

Méabh looked aghast. 'God, no!'

'Diarrhoea? Blood in the stools?'

'No, nothing like that. But she cries an awful lot after she's been sick.'

'Yes, that'll be the acid burning her poor wee oesophagus and throat.' Her hands moved down to the child's abdomen. 'Her tummy isn't swollen or distended.' She looked up. 'Yep, looks like a classic case of common or garden reflux. It's very common and nothing to worry about.'

Méabh closed her eyes and placed a hand on Olivia's head. 'Oh, thank God,' she sighed. 'Are you sure? I'm sorry, you must think me a complete neurotic.'

Clare smiled. 'You sound like a normal, concerned new Mum to me.'

'What can I do for her?'

'Nowadays, they only prescribe medicine in severe cases – which this doesn't look like. Try feeding her less and more often, thickening the feed, and make sure you burp her frequently. If her temperature goes over thirty-eight, or if she starts showing any of the other symptoms I mentioned, then call your paediatrician or bring her back here.'

After Méabh had thanked her effusively, the two women parted.

Looking at her watch, Clare decided to drive straight to Dave's to pick up Declan. Just over half an hour later she knocked on the door of the flat in St Stephen's Green. Dave opened the door with his shirt sleeves rolled up and a towel over his shoulder.

'I know I'm a bit early,' she said.

'No worries, although we were just finishing bath-time.'

'Oh, you get back to him, I'll just…'

He nodded absently and returned to the bathroom; Clare walked through to the kitchen-diner and heaved herself onto a stool at the breakfast bar.

After a few minutes, Dave's mobile, which was on the bar, beeped.

She tried to ignore it, to resist the temptation. But old marital habits die hard.

Peering at the phone, she saw 'Mam.' *Surprise, surprise*, she thought wryly.

But then another name caught her eye: Méabh. Two missed calls – not fifteen minutes ago – and she had left a message.

Some irrepressible surge of curiosity, combined with a sense that something was not quite right, compelled her to listen to the voicemail.

'Dave, it's Méabh. Listen, I just ran in to Clare. I told her about Olivia – about the adoption, I mean, not about you, obviously. Look, I'm a lousy liar; I said she was my cousin's. Anyway, you should probably have a story ready in case she asks about her.'

She replaced the mobile on the bar, forcing herself to breathe deeply.

Just then Dave came into the room carrying a giggling Declan in a fireman's lift. The little boy was clad in a blue towelling bathrobe, his skin pink and clean, his freshly towelled hair dishevelled.

'Mammy!' he cried out in delight.

'Hello, sweetheart.' She turned to Dave and asked coldly. 'Who's Olivia?'

After a moment's hesitation, Dave deposited Declan on the floor and asked him to run along to his room and get dressed on his own like a big boy. Once he had scampered off to his room, Dave turned to his ex.

'She's the baby my cousin Méabh's looking to adopt,' he said cautiously. 'Why?'

'Who's her mother?'

Dave shrugged and stared at the floor. 'I dunno.'

'*Who's her mother*?' Clare repeated icily.

'Well... it's Tina, but–'

'That scrubber from the Black Horse?!'

Dave nodded.

'So, how is her baby related to your cousin then?'

Dave sighed. 'Technically, she isn't, only–'

'She said she was adopting her as a family member,' said Clare slowly, 'now, if Tina's the mother, Méabh can only be related to the baby through the father. Now, who do we know of in your family who was shagging Tina, hmmm?'

He pushed a hand through his hair nervously. 'Jesus, Clare, I know how it sounds, but it's not what you think, OK? Let me explain...'

Clare had climbed down from the stool now and was standing facing him.

'You bastard, you had a *kid* with her and didn't tell me?' Her horror increased as she quickly did the mental arithmetic: 'The baby looks about eight weeks old, which means you got her pregnant just a couple of months before *our* baby was conceived?'

'No! I swear, look, just calm down...'

'You fucking lech!' she hissed, shaking her head. 'And your cousin's going to bring her up, and she and our kid will grow up together and play together, not knowing they're half-siblings? How could you? How *could* –'

She stooped and looked down as amniotic fluid trickled down her legs and splashed onto the parquet floor.

'Fuck...' she muttered.

Dave stared in disbelief at the puddle at her feet. 'Christ, is it coming?'

Clare leaned back against the stool and clutched her belly.

'Not Christ, but we'd better get to the hospital all the same.'

'Fuck…' muttered Dave. 'OK, it's OK… Breathe. Come over here and sit down for a second.' He led her over to one of the leather armchairs in the living area, (first laying down the towel he had been using on Declan's hair), then grabbed his mobile from the breakfast bar.

'Lucy? It's Dave Mullan from number fourteen. Listen, it's time, it's happening. Could you come over right away and watch Declan for a bit? Yeah, just for an hour or so until my Mam can pick him up. Grand, see you soon.' He hung up, went into his bedroom, and just as he was emerging carrying a leather holdall which had been packed and ready for the past month, the doorbell rang. He let in a plump, fresh-faced teenager with frizzy brown hair wearing ripped jeans and a pink T-shirt.

'Hi, Lucy, thanks for this. He's in his room getting dressed, come through.'

Blushing deeply, the girl followed him, ignoring Clare. Having explained to his son that his parents had to go and welcome his little brother or sister into the world and his Nanna was coming to fetch him soon, Dave ruffled the boy's damp hair and hurried back to Clare.

Holles Street was mercifully only a five-minute drive away. On the way, Dave instructed Google to call his mother, whom he apprised of the situation and dispatched to his house to pick up her grandson.

It was a good thing he was being a model of calm and capability for Clare, usually a rational person as well as a healthcare professional and already a mother-of-one, was working her way into a frenzy of anguish – not helped by her recent discovery and the conversation with Dave. She was thus allowing dark, ugly thoughts to invade her, nightmare scenarios: she suddenly thought back to when she was training as a nurse years ago, and cared for extremely premature babies who were born addicted to heroin. She thought of stillbirths, babies born with hideous deformities. And then there was this damned virus! Just the day before it had claimed its first fatality in Ireland, and the WHO had officially declared it a pandemic; that very morning, Varadkar had announced that schools were closing.

She couldn't bring a life into this chaos.

As she was wheeled into the labour room, Dave clutching her hand, she began to cry.

Four hours later, she was delivered of a healthy, blue-eyed, dark-haired 3.9-kg boy. Dave had been present throughout the birth and cut the umbilical cord.

Afterwards, as Clare lay exhausted against the pillows, the little larva squirming against her breast and suckling hungrily, Dave, on the edge of the bed, stroked her forehead and said:

'Are we still going with Lorcan?'

She nodded wearily. 'Although, between you and me, I'm glad it's not a girl because I've totally gone off Caitlin and my brain can't cope with making any decisions right now.'

229

'Lorcan it is then. Did you know it means "little fierce one?"'

'No, I didn't,' croaked Clare and smiled weakly.

Then, emboldened by joy and pride at the birth of his new son, and taking advantage of the present situation – for, aside from deep sleep and death, post-partum exhaustion was possibly the only state in which Clare would be incapable of arguing with him – he continued:

'Listen. I know this isn't the time – or maybe it is – but you have to know the truth. I swear on Lorcan's head Tina's kid isn't mine: I've got a paternity test to prove it. Méabh just asked me to say I was the Dad to fast-track her adoption application.'

Clare looked up from the baby, whom she had just transferred to her other breast, and nodded weakly.

'All right. I believe you. I don't want to fight, not now. I'm too knackered.' She stroked the black silky head at her breast. 'But then, I'm guessing that's precisely why you chose to tell me this now.'

Damn her, he thought. And more fool him for letting himself forget – even for a moment – how well she knew him.

'Well, I...' he began awkwardly. She turned to him and, craning her neck up towards him, silenced him with a long kiss. 'Shut up,' she said gently. 'Let's just enjoy this moment, can we?'

And so they remained in companiable silence, until they both fell asleep.

About half an hour later, Dave awoke and, after gently extricating himself from the sleeping mother and baby, slipped out. He was about to unlock his car, which he had parked on Merrion Square, when, on an impulse, he stuffed some more coins into the meter and set off on foot back to St Stephen's Green. On the way, he called his mother and Clare's, then Clodagh.

Had they been privy to it, most people who knew Dave well would have guessed – correctly – that his decision two months ago to comply with Méabh's request and claim paternity for Olivia was not motivated by altruism. Indeed, they would have assumed that, at best, he had simply weighed up the benefits of such a decision to those directly concerned against the inconvenience to himself and grudgingly given his consent; or, at worst, that he was intending at some later date to call in a favour from his cousin – free consultations for some future speech disorder that might afflict one of his children, perhaps, or potential business contacts from her vast network of acquaintances among Dublin's elite.

Only one or two people, however, would have deduced the true reason, namely that Clodagh was one of the few people in the world whose good opinion, if he did not actively seek it, Dave would certainly hate to lose. That comment of hers about advising Clare to abort had particularly stung. The gratification he had subsequently felt had thus derived solely from his sister's approval, and not from Méabh's effusive and heartfelt gratitude, nor from the prospect of a successful adoption application and its benefits for both adoptive mother and child (for he still harboured strong reservations about this, but had resolved forever to hold his peace on the subject).

Having informed Clodagh of Lorcan's birth, vital statistics, and his and Clare's wellbeing, and received in return effusive expressions of joy and assurances to pass the news on to the other Mullan siblings, Dave arrived back at the flat. He had a shower, made himself scrambled eggs on toast and a strong, sugary cup of tea, and, sitting on the sofa, began checking through the many emails and texts he had received over the past few hours. He saw Marnie had called that morning, but didn't listen to the message and made a mental note to call her back some time. Then, having posted a message and photo of mother and baby on his Facebook, he stretched out on the sofa and fell into a deep, contented sleep.

CHAPTER THIRTY-FOUR

Monza, 26 March 2020

A kaleidoscope of assorted Italian landscapes whirled haphazardly through her mind: endless expanses of stone pines and Lombardy poplars rolled past then merged into the narrow dingy streets of Naples' Quartieri Spagnoli; amid the laundry on the washing lines between the derelict facades hung her wedding dress.

The urban scene then gave way to a deserted beach with blinding white sand.

She was Caravaggio in his wretched final hours, staggering along the shore in Porto Ercole trying desperately to retrieve the felucca that bore his lost paintings so he could return to Rome and give them to Cardinal Scipione Borghese in exchange for the long-awaited papal pardon for the murder of Ranuccio Tomassoni.

Still weakened and half-blinded from the savage beating he had received months before in Naples, further diminished by his recent imprisonment and the days of walking all the way from Palo Laziale, scorched by the merciless, blistering sun, he finally succumbed: to fatigue, to the elements, to despair. Despair at the futility of his quest, of his life. He sank to his knees and the scorching sand rose up to swallow him…

Someone was picking him up now, dusting the sand from his face: he was saved!

But the paintings… where were the paintings?

His saviour said nothing but simply brought a bottle of water to his cracked lips; he coughed and spluttered.

'OK, *tranquilla…*'

And then she realised: her saviour was Amedeo!

She was lying on sweat-soaked sheets; he refilled the glass of water and handed it to her. She gulped it down and fell back onto the pillows, exhausted by the effort of drinking.

She was in bed in Amedeo's guest room. He was sitting on the edge of the bed, looking tired but otherwise well; the colour was restored to his cheeks. He was smiling.

'*Ciao, ma dame aux camélias.* How are you feeling?'

232

'I don't… how long have I been…?'

'In this state? Nearly three days. You had a very high fever, then you seemed… delirious. I was worried so I called my uncle who was a doctor but he said as long as you didn't appear to have breathing troubles, just to keep you at home and make sure you drank fluids and rested.' He placed a cool dry hand on her forehead and sighed with relief. 'Your fever has broken.' He paused and then said: 'What paintings?'

Seeing her puzzled expression; he explained: 'just now; you were saying something about paintings; "where are the paintings?"'

'Oh… never mind.' Her memory came back slowly. 'How are *you*?'

'Absolutely fine now. Completely recovered; just tired.'

'Good. Did you get your sense of taste and smell back?'

'I never lost them. That was just you.'

'Oh, right. It's strange, I don't remember them saying anything on the news about that being a symptom.'

He shrugged. 'Well, I guess they are still learning about the virus. It's completely new.' He stood up. 'Now, what can I get you? Are you ready to eat something? See if your sense of taste has returned?'

'I don't know… I guess I could try and eat something.'

'Good girl. I've made mushroom risotto.'

'I could also really do with a shower too.'

'Of course. Take your time and just come down when you're ready. Here, let me help you.' Putting the jug and glass back down on the bedside table, he slipped his arm around her as she slowly got to her feet. When they reached the bathroom door, she laughed awkwardly and said, 'Thanks, I think I'll manage from now.'

'Oh, of course,' he muttered, blushing, and made a swift retreat from the room.

She stripped off her pyjamas, stepped into the shower and as she turned on the water, a wave of dizziness enveloped her. She sat down on the floor of the shower just before her knees buckled and let the hot water beat down on her.

When she emerged from the bathroom fifteen minutes later, she found that the bed had already been stripped of the soiled sheets and made up with fresh ones. She slipped on a clean T-shirt and her jeans and went downstairs where she received immediate and glorious confirmation of the return of her olfactory faculties as the scent of truffle oil wafted from the kitchen.

He looked up from a large bowl in which he was tossing salad.

233

'Ah, good. Come and sit down.' She obliged as he served up the risotto.

'Thank you, this looks… and *smells* wonderful.'

He selected a bottle of red wine from the rack and began opening it.

'Would you like some?'

'I don't know if I should, but do you know what? I would really love a glass.'

She tasted a forkful of risotto. It was divine: rich, smooth, perfectly *al dente*.

'Mmm… You know, of all the symptoms – the aches, the fever – for me, the worst was not being able to *taste* things! If I can't taste food, I may as well be fucking dead.' A hand shot up to her mouth. 'God, I shouldn't say things like that, not now, with so many people dying … What is the death toll at the moment, by the way?'

Amedeo shook his head and filled her wine glass. 'I have no idea. I've stopped watching the news. I can't take it anymore.'

She nodded and raised her glass. 'Well, here's to the living.'

After the meal, having been banished from the kitchen and forbidden from performing any domestic tasks, Marnie curled up on the sofa with her second glass of Monte Solaio listening to the CD of Verdi's *Requiem* that Amedeo had put on. Leaning back on the cushions, she closed her eyes and sighed contentedly: fortified by the shower and food, pleasantly numbed by the wine, soothed by the music, she let her mind drift back to the events of the past week.

After eight days, Amedeo had begun to show signs of recovery; there had then followed a brief, twenty-four-hour period during which they had both enjoyed good health, before Marnie herself fell ill. Her symptoms were similar to his, if not identical: she too had a temperature and headache, but no cough or sore throat, although she was afflicted by the much-lamented loss of taste and smell. And the *tiredness*: the terrible, bone-wrenching exhaustion, the likes of which she had not experienced since the first trimester of her pregnancy or the weeks after giving birth.

The last few days of her illness were a blur to her, but she had evidently spent them squirming around in her damp sheets, moaning and drifting in and out of consciousness.

Some time later, she opened her eyes just as Amedeo was gently prising the empty wineglass out of her hand.

'I wasn't really asleep,' she said, sitting up on the sofa.

'Maybe, but you will be soon. Believe me, you'll feel tired for days.'

She nodded and, accepting his outstretched hand, rose. A thought suddenly occurred to her, causing her to gasp.

'God, my phone! Where's my phone?'

234

Amedeo unplugged the device from a socket near the kitchen doorway and handed it to her.

'Here. I switched it off while you were…incapacitated.'

'I've got to call people, family… They'll have been worried sick!'

'*Tranquilla…* I found your daughter on Instagram a couple of days ago and updated her.'

Already frantically texting, she nodded distractedly and bid him goodnight.

Climbing the stairs and brushing her teeth seemed like Herculean feats: she collapsed face-forward onto the bed and was asleep almost instantly.

That night she dreamt that Luc caught the virus and died, and the first she heard of it was when his first wife Philippine called her to ask for information she needed to submit a claim for her share of his pension.

◁◫▷

Paris, 26 March 2020

'If they don't have *magret de canard*, what shall I get for your curry tonight?'

Luc shrugged. 'We can't be too fussy: after all, as Macron keeps telling us, it's wartime. My grandparents ate rodents in World War Two; during the *Commune de Paris*, people ate elephants and other animals from the zoo, and you're worrying about not finding duck breasts?' He sighed: '*C'est terrible, les problèmes de petits bourgeois…*' Then, seeing Rhiannon's impatient expression, he abandoned his facetious, laconic register and said:

'Chicken thighs will be fine. Or pork loin.'

Nodding, she finished the shopping list then grabbed a new permission slip from a pile on top of the printer and hastily filled it out, ticking the 'shopping for essentials' box and signing it. She then placed the form, shopping list and her ID card into one pocket, her credit card and store card in the other, grabbed her phone, pulled on the face mask she had made out of an old pillowcase, and, with a grimace, reluctantly took the handle of the old-lady wheeled shopping trolley. As much as she detested it, she was forced to admit it was practical for people like them who had no car and couldn't go to the big hypermarkets on the outskirts of town to do a big weekly shop. For even though they had not succumbed to the frenzied panic-buying that so many had indulged in of late, they tried to make sure they made no more than one or two weekly visits to the local supermarket.

'Bon courage, ma chérie,' said Luc.

She nodded grimly and set out.

On this particular occasion, the supermarket excursion turned out to be relatively painless: she had only to queue outside for forty-five minutes, and when she finally made it inside, as usual it was incredibly fast, due to the fact that the store only let in about seven customers at a time. There were very few empty shelves this time, except – as usual – the flour section. Ever since lockdown had begun, people had been baking as if it was the end of the world – which, according to some professional Jesus-freak she had read about a week or so before in the *Washington Post* – it was not. Indeed, this self-proclaimed authority on biblical prophecies – whom Rhiannon had immediately dismissed as a lunatic – had quoted from Revelations, assuring readers that none of the very distinctive harbingers of Judgement Day – such as earthquakes, pestilence, famines and the rebuilding of the temple in Jerusalem – had yet occurred. Odd, Rhiannon had reflected sardonically, that coronavirus did not qualify as pestilence.

Since lockdown had begun, Rhiannon had begun following the news meticulously and regularly: the rolling news was on at home for hours every day, and she scoured the online French- and English-speaking media. In addition to keeping her abreast of the evolution of the health crisis worldwide, it provided material for the blog she had started writing daily and religiously ever since France had gone into lockdown on 17 March.

Her purchases completed, she let herself into her father's flat, put the groceries away and washed her hands. A What'sApp from Val asked if she had heard from Marnie, to which she replied in the negative, adding a disappointed face emoji for emphasis.

The last ten days had been a whirlwind of surreal, unprecedented events, punctuated by occasional flashes of panic and the odd burst of elation. The day the press had thronged in Dowry Square (her mother had been right: they had soon grown weary and moved on to the next story, that of a Cabinet Minister who had suspected coronavirus), Rhiannon had decided, in light of the total collapse of her travel plans, to follow her mother's advice and try to return to Warwick for the rest of the academic year after her brief hiatus. To achieve this, she had once again enlisted the help of Gulliver, who, still penitent about his inconstancy, had been only too glad to assist and had contacted the Head of Department, Professor Latimer, to arrange for her readmission. Two days later – the last day of the spring term – he had called her to announce that she was allowed to return for the summer term. *God knows how he wangled that,* she had thought, but did not ask, merely thanking him.

That same day, she had received a call from her mother, informing her that her friend had recovered but that she too had possibly come down with the virus now. Marnie had done her best to assuage her daughter's anxiety, insisting that she felt a bit off-colour, although nothing worse than a bad cold, but that her symptoms – be they of Covid 19 or merely a cough and cold – would prevent her from being able to board a flight home. She assured Rhiannon that she was being taken good care of by Amedeo and would keep her informed.

Rhiannon's next decision was to spend a week or two of the Easter holidays with her father in Paris and, having arranged for the amiable Mrs Wellesley next door to feed Tim and Roger during her absence and stocked up on cat food, she had booked her Eurostar ticket.

The next morning, she caught the train to London, got the Tube from Paddington to St Pancras and caught the 12:42 to Paris, arriving just before four. Luc had met her at the Gare du Nord and after dropping her suitcase off at the flat he said he had to go and vote in the municipal elections. It was a fine sunny day and Rhiannon decided to accompany him. At the polling station – the local primary school – everyone was masked, and bottles of hand-sanitiser stood on various tables.

Then the following evening, Monday 16 March, a grave-faced President Macron had addressed the nation and issued the stay-at-home order, effective as of the following day.

'Looks like we're stuck with each other,' Luc said lightly.

'No!' Rhiannon had wailed, then, seeing the expression of good-natured mock offense on her father's face, explained: 'No, I mean… what about college? What about Mum's cats? Christ, what about *Mum*? Poor thing, she's ill, and whenever she makes it back to Bristol, she'll come back to an empty house.'

Luc shrugged. 'Well, then, just go back to England, *mon lapin*. Tomorrow morning, before the drawbridge goes up.'

Rhiannon called her mother, who had assured her that it would make no difference to her, Marnie, where Rhiannon spent the next few weeks: the Italian lockdown and her illness would mean she was unlikely to return home for a while. It made no sense for Luc and Rhiannon to be alone on different sides of the Channel, so why not hole up together?

Rhiannon had then telephoned Mrs Wellesley to explain the situation, and the neighbour expressed her sympathy, saying she would be only too pleased to look after the cats for as long as was required. As for returning to Warwick, universities in the United Kingdom announced they were closing three days later.

And so it was that Rhiannon and her father settled into a harmonious cohabitation in the two-bedroom, sixty-square-meter flat near the Gare de l'Est Luc had lived in since the divorce. Aside from selling the odd book online, he spent his days reading, going for walks (within the one-kilometre radius and one-hour time limit imposed by French law), and playing online chess and strategy games. He also spent one whole day in his empty bookshop waxing the parquet floor – a task he had been putting off for months.

Rhiannon, meanwhile, wrote her blog, *Notes from the Bunker, or Living in Lockdown* and caught up on the coursework she had missed during her brief absence from Warwick. She also went for walks in the park, FaceTimed with friends, her grandparents, and Marnie, and baked.

After spending their days thus, each with their own separate occupations, father and daughter reunited each evening to share a meal they took turns in preparing, and watch a classic film.

After this evening's programme of Luc's fiery Thai red curry with duck followed by Marcel Carné's *Les Visiteurs du Soir*, Rhiannon opened her laptop, went into the dashboard of her blog app, and wrote:

26th March – Day 10

Greetings, Bunkerites!

On the news today, I see the Americas' two most dangerous morons, Bolsonaro and Trump, are still going down the blissful ignorance route. Trump has the patience of a kid on Christmas Eve, and the attention span of a fruit fly: he's bored, can't we talk about something else?

Prince Charles has tested positive. God, that man will do anything to get out of being king.

I took the trusty granny cart out for a spin this morning. Didn't have to queue so long this time. Has anyone else noticed how, since lockdown, people out and about not only avoid each other physically, but also tend to avoid eye contact too? As if we'll turn each other to stone.

Spoke to an old school friend today. He self-evacuated to his mum's place in Brittany after Macron's announcement. Lots of people have fled to the country since lockdown began, hoping to find some corona-free, Arcadian utopia. Anyway, he told me that two cars with Paris licence plates were burned by locals in the village yesterday. Anti-Parisian hate crime is a common phenomenon in some areas of provincial France, and it has escalated since the advent of coronavirus: they're of course blaming us dirty, pox-ridden city-dwellers for infecting the countryside. It turns out one of the car owners in question was a local doctor, Breton born

238

and bred, who has a flat in Paris, where he bought the car, and the other was a local pensioner who happened to have bought a car from someone in the Paris area and hadn't got around to changing the number plates. Well done, angry pitchfork-wielding peasants: you sure showed them!

Macron gave a rather rousing speech this evening: his rhetoric was a little less hawkish and alarmist than his initial address ten days ago: he called for people to pull together and unite against the common enemy. Toothless car-burners in Brittany: I hope you were watching.

On a more personal – and worrying note – my Mum is still stranded in Italy, with suspected Covid, and the last I heard of her was three days ago. The friend she's staying with DMd me on Instagram the day before yesterday saying she's got a fever and when she isn't asleep she's a bit dizzy and incoherent but that her breathing seems normal and he's keeping a close eye on her. But still, I can't help thinking... No! I can't let myself go down that road: I have to believe she'll be all right.

Until tomorrow; and in the meantime: stay in, stay safe, stay sane.

Just as she hit 'Publish post,' her phone rang and, seeing the name that appeared on the screen, she gave a little cry of relief as she snatched it up.

'*Mum!* Thank God.'

CHAPTER THIRTY-FIVE

Monza, 27 March 2020

When Amedeo had made that remark a couple of weeks before about his delight at seeing her on his sofa in her night attire, Marnie had ignored it – mainly because her surprise and relief at seeing him up and apparently healed had immediately chased away all other thoughts.

When her thoughts briefly drifted back to it later that evening as she was preparing some lentils for their dinner, she had attributed his uncharacteristic display of flirtatiousness to the elation of recovery, telling herself that his return to health, after seemingly endless days and nights of suffering filled with bleak thoughts of oblivion and mortality, had momentarily galvanised and emboldened him.

Within twenty-four hours, she had fallen ill and remained bedridden for a fortnight. But shortly after she had recovered, she began thinking about it again, although, by that time, Amedeo had reverted to his old self: diffident, respectful, gentlemanly.

Yet in Marnie's mind, a seed had been planted. She had been given a glimpse into that parallel universe in which she and Amedeo were not friends, not colleagues, not anything indefinable or ambiguous: for the first time, she began seriously considering him as a potential lover.

After all, in many ways, this was a parallel universe. The circumstances were so strange, so bewildering, so utterly unprecedented. The mainstays of her existence, the pillars on which she had relied throughout her adult life – her home, her career, her family, some degree of certainty about the future – all these had been swept away by the events of the past few months: her redundancy, the pandemic, lockdown, and her subsequent forced cohabitation with Amedeo. Her world had suddenly become extremely small, and in it there were just she and he, together, whilst outside chaos and uncertainty reigned and disease and death raged. Time had both stood still and was hurtling mercilessly on towards blackness and confusion and finally, nothing.

But after a few days, her initial anxiety and trepidation at the disappearance of her usual reference points – those things which had hitherto given meaning and structure to her life – gave way to an eerie sense of relief and even a giddying euphoria. For now there were no constraints, only infinite freedom and possibilities.

And they were *survivors*. They had nursed each other through sickness and together had emerged relatively unscathed. Did not that mean something?

Over the next few days, they each settled back into their respective routines, Amedeo spending long days in front of his laptop, giving pro bono training sessions and advice to teachers and school heads on how to make the transition to a distance learning model in the wake of school closures, and doing consulting work for clients to pay the bills, whilst Marnie, having regretfully resigned herself to putting Bacchus & Minerva on hold, had finally grimly consented to take on the odd freelance translation (though not from DigInnova).

But the seed refused to go away. Occasionally she would look up from her laptop at his face, grave with concentration, usually too absorbed to notice her newfound interest in him.

One evening after dinner – Amedeo's *pasta al pomodoro* followed by fruit and chocolate – they were comfortably ensconced on the sofa with the remains of a bottle of Primitivo listening to Bach's harpsicord concertos, when Marnie asked:

'How long have we known each other? Twelve years?'

'Fifteen years this month.'

'*Really*? Christ. OK, so, we've known each other all this time, and yet this is the first time we've spent so much time together – certainly the first time we've really spent more than a few hours alone together.'

He listened attentively and nodded but said nothing.

'Well, these past few weeks have been very… intense. Intimate, even. I feel as though our relationship has been tested, pushed to new limits by circumstances and… well, we passed! We got through it, and after everything we've been through, I still really like being around you.' She looked at him expectantly.

He smiled and patted her hand. 'I like being around you too,' he said softly, yet there was something guarded in his voice, in his manner.

She poured herself some more wine and continued.

'Well, I just feel as though we've crossed a line. And I don't want to go back to the way things were, the way… we were.'

He remained silent, his expression as inscrutable as ever. She leaned across the sofa and kissed him lightly on the mouth.

She had imagined this moment many times in the past few days; but never, in any scenario, had she foreseen this particular outcome. He pulled back.

The expression on his face was not one of repulsion or offense or embarrassment. He looked merely very grave and sad.

She looked at the floor, her face burning. When she spoke, her voice was hoarse and cracked. 'What is it?'

'I'm sorry…' he stood up. 'Look, I won't say I'm not flattered, but I can't help wondering if you're not just… trying this on, like a dress in a shop. It's true, our time here together the last few weeks has been strange, like a different world, unreal. But, see, it is real life. It's *my* life. We're not in a laboratory, you can't try *us* out as an experiment. Because we're not clones or avatars of Amedeo and Marnie –' at this point, he must have seen a flicker of amusement or surprise in her eyes for he looked at the floor and muttered: 'yes, sorry, I like science fiction. The point is, I'm the real, the *only* Amedeo, and you're the only Marnie! You can't just see what it's like to be with me and then if you don't like it, forget it; put the dress back and walk out of the shop.' His voice remained even, with no edge of bitterness, but his breathing had quickened and he was clenching and unclenching his right fist. His gaze was intense and piercing.

'If anything happens between us,' he continued, 'then the next day or the day after you just fly back to your real life and put this all behind you, write it off as an unfortunate incident – a failed experiment – something you want to forget, along with the lockdown and checkpoints and facemasks and everything else – then I don't think I will be able to bear it. You said just now you didn't want to go back to the way we were; but I could! As far as I'm concerned, it's still not too late. I'd be more than happy to go on as before, to continue sharing what we've shared all these years.' He turned away. 'But if things go further and then you decide it's not what you want –'

Marnie stood up.

'It's all right, I get it,' she said coolly. 'I'm sorry. You're right, it's not too late; let's just forget this ever happened.' With that she swept past him and up the stairs to her room. Ignoring him as he called after her, she closed the door and lay down fully clothed on the bed, mortified.

The next day he was his usual courteous, affable self. Marnie, however, still smarting from the previous evening's humiliation, was cool and subdued. She spent the morning working in her room but around noon realised she was being absurdly childish and went downstairs. However, they exchanged few words that afternoon, and when Amedeo had concluded his last conference call and invited her to join him on the terrace for *aperitivo*, as they did most evenings, she declined. He poured himself a glass of wine then, putting the glass down, walked over to the sofa where Marnie was feigning absorption in an Excel spreadsheet.

'You're still upset about what happened last night,' he said gently. 'I'm sorry I hurt you. But please, talk to me.'

After a few seconds, she closed her laptop and looked at him.

'It's not because you rejected me.'

'All right. What then?'

She leapt to her feet. 'Is that what you *think* of me?' she cried. 'After all the years we've known each other, you really think I'm that fickle and heartless and shallow? That I see *this–*' she made a vague sweeping gesture with her hand, indicating him and herself and the room – 'as my personal fucking *chemistry set*?'

'No, I didn't mean…'

'Do you know how hard it was for me last night? I thought –'

'You *thought*,' he said mildly, 'that because I'd been fantasising about that moment for years that I'd just jump at the chance, that I'd be grateful.'

Her face was suffused with a burning flush. 'Fuck you,' she said and stalked towards the staircase.

He moved quickly, intercepting her and standing at the foot of the stairs, blocking her way. She didn't move but stared at him defiantly. Then he grabbed her face with both hands and kissed her passionately. For a few moments she stood still, her arms by her side, limp and passive, then her arms moved up around him, pulling her towards him, letting him pin her against the wall with his body. After a few minutes she pushed him gently away and beckoned him upstairs.

It was not how she had imagined it; *he* was nothing like she had imagined. Usually so diffident, occasionally even gauche, in bed he was playful, confident, enterprising. He also had astonishing stamina, she noted.

Some hours later, as they lay in bed, she asked him:

'All those years ago, when I was still with Luc. What if, one night when we were at one of those work conferences, I'd turned up at your door and… offered myself to you. What would you have done?'

He shrugged. 'Probably nothing.'

She stared at him. 'What? We're at a hotel, I knock on your door, walk in, strip off in front of you…'

He smiled and shook his head. 'First of all, you would never have done that. And second of all, if you had, then you wouldn't be the person I thought you were and I couldn't love you.'

Seeing her look of incredulity, he laughed. 'I'm sorry, *tesoro*: I'm forever failing to live up to your image of a typical Italian man.'

She shook her head in disbelief. 'You are. I was just getting used to the idea of your not being a practising Catholic, your integrity in all matters financial and fiscal – seriously, you've never tried to get out of paying taxes?' He smiled and shook his head. 'And now, it turns out you're *morally opposed to adultery*? I'm surprised they haven't taken away your passport.'

Marnie never slept in the guest room again. Then, a few days later, at dusk, as they lay spent amid the damp, twisted sheets, Amedeo said idly:

'Are you happy, *tesoro*? Can I get you anything?'

She sighed. 'Well, since you ask…' She rolled over onto her stomach and contemplated him seriously. 'You're not going to like it.'

He shrugged. 'Try me.'

'Well, I could *murder* a piece of pecorino, or some carpaccio. I'm sorry. I can't help it.'

Instead of expressing horror, disapproval or disgust, he merely said – with a slightly complacent air:

'Do you know what the word 'barbarian' means in Mandarin? "He who drinks milk and eats raw meat." They were, of course, referring to the Mongols.'

Marnie propped herself up on her elbow and glared at him. 'Your point being?' she deadpanned. 'And FYI, vegan proselytising is *not* an aphrodisiac.'

He laughed.

'I *am* hungry, though,' she continued. 'Let's go downstairs and cook something – anything – even… quinoa or spelt or fucking alfalfa – and bring it back to bed.'

He stared at her, horrified.

'*Eat* –' he said, then, as if they were in a crack den or a morgue: '*here*?'

'You *never* eat in bed? Not even breakfast?'

He shook his head vigorously.

She sighed and put her arms around his neck.

'My poor darling! What a sad, deprived life you've had. I have so much to teach you.'

As the days went by, they became more intrepid and began venturing beyond the confines of the master bedroom for their sexual encounters. There was a – not entirely successful – episode on the dining room table, then one afternoon they coupled feverishly on the desk in

Amedeo's home office. Marnie had first, however, had to overcome her qualms about performing with the young Amedeo staring out at them from the photograph.

'It's… sick,' she said, shrinking from the boy's opaque, brown-eyed stare. 'It'd feel like I was corrupting a child. Can't you just put it face down?'

'No, no,' he protested, kissing her neck. 'On the contrary: we'll be giving my young self a valuable life lesson: for this is proof that patience and perseverance eventually pay off.'

CHAPTER THIRTY-SIX

Raddington Hall had been the seat of the Claybourne family since 1523. After the original Tudor edifice was destroyed by fire in 1645, Thomas, fourth Viscount Claybourne commissioned a disciple of Inigo Jones named Joshua Vetcher to design a new house in the Palladian style. Building was completed in 1658, but the family spent most of its time at their townhouse in London, the Viscountess professing to loathe the country – until 1665, when the Great Plague caused the household, which included four children and an extensive retinue of servants, to flee town and repair to Raddington.

Similarly, three hundred and fifty-five years later, another outbreak of disease – less lethal, yet far greater in its geographical reach – caused the current proprietors of Raddington Hall to abandon their London home and take up permanent residence there. The Lovelace family group, however, was considerably smaller than that of the Claybournes, consisting only of Nigel and his eldest daughter Portia – Cordelia and her mother having elected to remain in Eaton Square for the duration of the lockdown. As for Dinah, following growing hostilities within the family in the wake of that rather unfortunate incident involving the press, she had packed her bags and gone to her partner Nell's place in Hackney. Less than a week later when Boris Johnson issued the stay-at-home order, Dinah's friend Rollo, the sculptor, called Dinah from his parents' cottage in Somerset inviting her and Nell to spend lockdown in the West Country with him and his girlfriend Tasha, an offer both women had accepted with alacrity.

Another notable way in which the Lovelace party at Raddington differed from the Claybourne household was the complete absence of any domestic staff. For much to Portia's chagrin and incomprehension, both Mrs Fisk, the cook and housekeeper and Mrs Vaughan who came once a week to do the rough had declared themselves unavailable to wait on the Lovelaces whilst the stay-at-home order was in place. Only Jack Garrod, the groundsman-cum-handyman, had agreed to continue tending the garden.

'How can they leave us in the lurch like this?' Portia had wondered indignantly as they unloaded their luggage from the Range Rover four days before.

'Well,' said Nigel mildly, 'I do believe it has something to do with the government edict requiring people to stay at home.'

'Yes, I *am* aware of the current situation, thank you, Daddy,' she replied patiently, 'but as I understood it, certain workers are exempt from that rule, on account of their being indispensable. Doctors, teachers, firemen… Surely Mrs F and the old woman from the village come under that category? I mean, we can't possibly be expected to run a place like this *by ourselves*!'

For a moment Nigel had paused, a suitcase in one hand and his laptop bag in the other, and stared at his daughter, searching the dark brown eyes for traces of humour or irony. But there were none; he saw nothing in her expression but total earnestness and genuine outrage.

Sighing inwardly, he hoisted the laptop bag over his shoulder and began dragging the suitcase up the steps to the pillared, pediment-topped portico.

The house had at least been immaculately clean and tidy – although it was not to remain so for long – Mrs Fisk having come in the day before to prepare the place for their arrival. The central heating was on, there were fresh sheets on the beds and flowers in the bowls and vases. She had also stocked the fridge and larder with some basic foodstuffs, although there remained the considerable problem of how to turn the produce into something resembling an actual meal. For neither Portia nor Nigel had ever acquired even a rudimentary grasp of the culinary arts: at home meals had always been provided by Venetia, a cordon bleu cook and accomplished hostess, except for the larger receptions, for which she procured the services of caterers.

Fortunately, Portia had had the foresight to bring a hamper from Fortnum's – not one of their off-the-shelf ones, but a custom-made one she had ordered specially, lovingly and painstakingly filling it with all her father's favourites: there were two game pies, a whole, oven-ready beef Wellington (the only item requiring any cooking), a jar of Piccadilly Piccalilli, one of Gentleman's Relish and one of venison rillettes, a potted Stilton, a Dundee cake, a fruit cake and a box of rose and violet dark chocolate creams. There was also a bottle of Aberlour A Bunadh, but no wine: the cellar of Raddington was always well-stocked.

Once they had finished unpacking, Portia settled in the drawing room with her laptop and spent the rest of the afternoon working, whilst Nigel went for a walk around the estate. As he reached the woods which stretched from the end of the lawn to the edge of the estate, he turned and looked back at the house. With its rigid lines and uncompromising symmetry, he had always thought it a tad austere: personally, he would have preferred something Gothic Revival, along the lines of Tyntesfield in Somerset, with its bewitching myriad of turrets and gables.

But Venetia, who was looking to acquire a property to rival Vanborough, the De La Pole family seat which her elder brother Piers had inherited, had vetoed that idea, deeming Gothic Revival vulgar and *nouveau riche*; after all, she had argued, was not the man who had built Tyntesfield an *arriviste* who had made his fortune importing bird excrement? She rested her case.

It was just before six when he returned to the house. As he passed the drawing room, he heard Portia cursing to herself. He knocked once and walked in.

'Everything all right, old girl?'

She was scowling at her laptop screen. 'I forgot how damned slow the Internet is here,' she muttered. 'Honestly, it's *ridiculous* fibre broadband hasn't made it to this backwater yet.'

Anyone would think she was talking about electricity or running water, he thought irritably. But once again, he checked his impatience and changed the subject:

'Just had a look at the kitchen garden. Looks like Jack's been keeping it up nicely; the sprouting broccoli and parsnips are ready for harvesting, and we can sow some carrots, onions and spuds next.'

This comment was met with an utterly blank look: the idea of growing one's own vegetables was clearly as outlandish to her as fashioning a wardrobe out of old curtains. Outside of wartime, such economy and self-sufficiency may be a necessity among the lower classes, but for people of their social standing and means it merely smacked of eccentricity.

'Whatever you think, Daddy,' she said distractedly, and returned to her press release.

'Right,' he said awkwardly, 'I'll let you get on.' After withdrawing he had walked through to the kitchen where he grabbed the bottle of Aberlour from the hamper and taken it into the study.

That had been four days ago, and father and daughter had since established a semblance of routine for their rural exile. Portia got up at seven every morning and went for a jog around the estate, then showered and spent the rest of the day working, sometimes in the drawing room, other times, weather permitting, taking her laptop out onto the terrace or into the conservatory. One of her few clients, a hotel chain, which she had landed largely through her father's influence and contacts – had asked her to draw up and implement a crisis communication plan in the wake of the pandemic. Nigel, for his part, arose between eight and nine, breakfasted alone in the kitchen, then spent the morning in the study, writing emails, making calls, generally tending to business relating to Bennett's and the various other company boards on which he served. He also telephoned Fawley Manor to check on the Major's progress. Their few experiments with FaceTime had not been a success, the Major clearly uncomfortable and suspicious of the technology, so Nigel had reverted to the telephone, making daily calls to the nurses who occasionally put the Major on the phone, depending on his mood and degree of lucidity.

At around one o'clock Nigel made himself a sandwich, retired to his room for a nap and spent the remainder of the afternoon walking around the grounds. At around six he retreated to his study where he drank whiskey and listened to records until seven-thirty or eight when they had dinner – the only meal of the day of which Portia partook, which explained how she maintained her rail-thin physique – either at the kitchen table or on trays in the drawing room in front of the television. Neither of them had even entered the cavernous dining room since their arrival.

And now, for the fifth evening in a row, Nigel closed the study door behind him and poured himself a whiskey, sloshing an extra finger in as he had a vague notion it was Friday. He then lit the fire he had laid in the grate the night before (it wasn't really cold enough, especially with the heating on, but Nigel did love an open fire), put a Dinah Washington LP on and settled in his favourite armchair by the hearth.

The heat of the fire, the warmth of the whiskey as it coursed through him and the beguiling tones of the divine Dinah soothed him and he closed his eyes.

Over the years, he had built up an impressive collection of vinyl recordings of his favourite jazz and blues divas: Dinah Washington, Billie Holiday, Ella Fitzgerald. Yet the pleasure he experienced when listening to them was invariably accompanied by a little thrill of guilt – similar to that, he imagined, someone raised by devotees of the Temperance movement must feel each time he or she imbibed strong liquor. For when Nigel was growing up, such music had been forbidden by his father: on one memorable occasion, a fourteen-year-old Nigel had been listening to Sarah Vaughan in his room when the Major had burst in and, clamouring that there would be no listening to 'screeching Negresses' under his roof, snatched the offending record off the turntable and smashed it underfoot.

It was therefore with a perverse delight and rebelliousness that, some forty years later, Nigel had named his beloved youngest daughter after one such 'screeching Negress' – not that the Major suspected, though: he had probably assumed she had been named for the cat in *Alice in Wonderland*. Yet it remained for Nigel a source of gratification – all the more so as, of the manifold children he had sired, Dinah was the only one whose name he had been allowed to choose: Barbara had insisted on naming Miles after her little brother who had died of diphtheria

249

as a toddler, and Venetia had unilaterally decided on Shakespearean names for her first two. Indeed, if it had been up to her, Dinah would have been a Nerissa or a Viola; but for once, Nigel had put his foot down.

And to think that little harpy had turned around and stabbed him in the back, running to the press to blab about Deirdre's kid, despite her previous assurances of discretion! Worse still, she had not even had the courage to own up to it, vehemently denying any involvement in the matter, right up until the day she had stormed out and gone to shack up with that girl.

Of course, the revelations had been something of a shock to Venetia – that was to be expected. But he could not account for her excessive reaction: her continued frostiness with him, her withdrawal of all physical affection, the denial of his conjugal rights. She had even gone so far as to move into her separate bedroom, a room she had only occupied three times in all their years of marriage, during the last months of each of her pregnancies. In the four days since he and Portia had left town, he had spoken to his wife only once, a brief, lukewarm exchange during which she had inquired about his health and asked if he was eating properly.

Cordelia, meanwhile, had unequivocally sided with her mother and all but sent her father to Coventry. Speaking of names, he reflected bitterly, she should have been christened Regan or Goneril, for all the filial loyalty she had shown him.

Portia alone had stood by him. He was forced to admit that she had been his rock throughout this disaster: comforting him, supporting him, handling the press. It was she who had suggested they come to Raddington for the lockdown, insisting that Venetia probably just 'needed some space' and was sure to come round eventually.

And yet, here, alone in the vast study at Raddington, a second glass of whiskey in his hand, he forced himself to acknowledge the shameful truth. For all Portia's kindness, for all her unstinting loyalty and devotion, he did not love or even like her any better. Far from endearing her to him, her attentions merely irritated him, stifled him, and reminded him all the more acutely and painfully of the absence of the two women he missed so dreadfully.

Damn it, he scolded himself: it wasn't fair. He couldn't resent Portia merely for not being her mother or her youngest sister. And the depressing truth was that since Venetia's cooling towards him and Dinah's defection, she was the only human being to whom he could now turn for affection or compassion. He therefore resolved to be kinder to her, to fight against his natural instinct to reject her.

As if on cue, there was a knock on the door and her sleek dark head appeared from behind it.

'Ready for dinner?' she asked cheerfully. 'There's the last of the game pie and I've made mashed potatoes.' It was rather pathetic, the inordinate pride she so obviously felt at this culinary achievement. She blushed. 'Mrs F showed me how on Skype.'

'Sounds lovely, old girl,' he said, with forced heartiness. 'In half an hour maybe?' he raised his tumbler. 'Thought I'd have another quick one first.'

'Of course! Take your time,' she said.

One notable advantage she had over Venetia, he conceded as she scuttled back to the kitchen, was that she never nagged him about his alcohol intake, nor indeed attempted to thwart him in any of his indulgences or habits. In fact, with a bit of luck, he might just be allowed to dissolve into a drunken stupor every night and perhaps, eventually – for his third whiskey was making him morose – drink himself to death.

⋈⫴⋈

Down the hall in the kitchen, Portia finished laying the table and sliced up the remainder of the game pie. She opened the bottle of wine she had selected earlier from the cellar – at random, as usual, for her oenological knowledge was virtually non-existent and she never drank alcohol of any kind (the calories!) – and began carefully decanting it as she had seen her father do on countless occasions. The potatoes could go in the Aga until he was ready to eat.

As an afterthought, she decided to make a salad to go with it, for it occurred to her that they had consumed almost no fresh fruit or vegetables since their arrival and she was worried they would get gout or scurvy or something. As she sliced up cucumber, she recalled, with a certain degree of satisfaction, the events of the past few weeks.

As scoops went, the story about Daddy having a secret illegitimate daughter was not exactly Watergate, or the *News of the World* phone-hacking business; it wasn't even a Parliamentary Expenses scandal. And yet, it had immeasurably changed her life for the better.

Unlike these other cataclysmic revelations, however, the facts had not been obtained using sophisticated technical gadgets, by wiretapping or hacking into computers, but by the simple, time-honoured – albeit rather base – expedient of eavesdropping. For Portia had been watching her little sister ever since she had come home unannounced from Cambridge that night.

In point of fact, she had been watching her since she was born.

Cordelia she had never perceived as a serious threat or rival. Of course, there had been the inevitable initial jealousy when she was born and Portia was no longer the only child. But Mrs Purves, the nanny, and then Magda, the au pair, had done their best to ensure that the elder child was not neglected in favour of her infant sister. As for her parents, her mother spent approximately an hour a day interacting with the girls and occasionally had the hired help briefly parade them in front of her cocktail or dinner party guests before dispatching them back up to the nursery, and Daddy had always shown the same indifference to Cordelia as he had to her elder sister.

This did not surprise Portia. Indeed, as far as she could see, there was nothing inherently lovable or remarkable about Cordelia: certainly not her looks, vastly inferior to her own (everyone said so). As for her musical talent, it was merely freakish, an aberration: where *had* she got it from? As far as Portia could tell, Mummy had never shown any aptitude or interest in that area, and Daddy was completely tone-deaf. Consequently, neither of her parents saw any intrinsic value in Cordelia's abilities, beyond the prestige they conferred on her and, by extension, them. To Portia's mind, the only merit of her sister's musical accomplishments was that they provided an explanation, if not a justification, for her personality – the famous 'artistic temperament' – which, as far as Portia could see, was simply a euphemism for capriciousness and a propensity for tantrum throwing and attention seeking.

Then, when Portia was about to start prep school and Cordelia was five, Mummy became pregnant again (this was hardly surprising: Daddy was always pawing her). Dinah came along, and everything changed.

As a baby, she did not appear to draw his interest or attention any more than had her sisters before her: clearly he had no time for infants. Yet once Dinah began talking, became an actual *person*, he seemed enchanted, bewitched. He actually seemed to delight in her company, devoting hours to her recreation and education, something he had never done with either of her sisters (although, in the case of Cordelia, she spent every free minute practising and had no other outside interests whatsoever). He taught Dinah to play chess – something he had once attempted with Portia, but had soon given up in exasperation. At the time, Portia had not been particularly aggrieved by his impatience, nor at her own ineptness, for she had quickly dismissed chess as a game for plain, unpopular girls.

But when she saw him playing with Dinah years later, witnessed their closeness, their connivance, she had felt jealousy well up inside her like acid, coursing through her body, rising in her throat like bile, choking her.

252

And it wasn't just the chess (or, when Dinah was slightly older, poker): he used to come up to the nursery and read to her: C.S. Lewis, Tolkien. Their conversations were peppered with references and quotations from these works, they even gave each other pet names after the characters. They lived in their own secret little world for two, one which excluded the rest of the family. Until, that is, Dinah was seven, when Mummy herself became jealous and sent her off to prep school a year early (she was on the Board of Governors and pulled some strings, claiming that her youngest child was something of a genius). And unlike Portia and Cordelia, who had attended day schools in London until they were eleven, Dinah was sent to prep school as a boarder.

By this time Portia was fifteen and realised that a change of tactic was in order: having failed to endear herself to Nigel with her unfailing obedience, her impeccable behaviour and her respectable – if unremarkable – academic achievements, she decided to attract his attention through bad behaviour. Thus, she began to neglect her schoolwork, became insolent with her teachers and housemistress, and one night, sneaked out of her dormitory and went to the pet shed, on whose sawdust-strewn floor she lost her virginity to one of the assistant cooks, a strapping nineteen-year-old lad from the village. This incident and the discovery thereof resulted in the young man's prompt dismissal and should also have led to Portia's expulsion, had her parents not offered to fund a brand-new science block for the school.

Although this tactic failed as far as grabbing Nigel's attention was concerned, the discovery of sex was a significant revelation for Portia – not so much for the sensual gratification it afforded her, for this varied considerably from one partner to another – but for the sense of *power*, of feeling wanted. Over the next few years there were many more sexual encounters with boys – more village boys, pupils from the boys' schools with whom her school organised balls and socials, friends' brothers – and later, men, starting with her A-level chemistry teacher.

But nothing ever quite matched the *frisson* of that first experience in the pet shed with the kitchen hand: the combination of the illicit nature of their meeting, the difference in their social standing (Portia had not read *Lady Chatterley's Lover* but knew the story), the sordidness of the setting and the boy's dexterousness was intoxicating. She could still remember the frowsty darkness of the shed, the moon casting a thin shaft of pale light across the rows of hamster cages and rabbit hutches as he bade her sit on the crudely-hewn workbench then pulled off her pants and knelt on the floor and brought his mouth to her. The delicious thrill of pain and pleasure that ensued, for as she climaxed, she gripped the edge of the workbench, driving splinters into the palms of her hands and under her fingernails. The rancid odours of rodent droppings and decaying fruit and vegetable mingled with the earthy aromas of sawdust, plywood and straw and the tang of the boy's cheap after-shave. After pleasuring her on the workbench, he had helped her down and, on the denim jacket he had thrown down on the floor, had proceeded to deflower her.

Meanwhile, the years passed, and her father's attachment to his plump little *wunderkind* showed no signs of waning. Indeed, nothing seemed to lower her in his esteem: not her puerile dabbling in Trotskyism; not her constant lecturing and hectoring him about everything from voting Tory to eating meat to his fleet of planet-polluting sport cars; not her sexual preferences, which she had never had the decency even to attempt to hide.

As for Dinah's dazzling academic prowess – skipping a year in school, getting a scholarship, then winning a place at Cambridge – Portia was astute enough to see that, whilst this was a source of pride and gratification to her father, it was not what endeared her to him the most. For while he clearly valued and respected Dinah's intelligence, her quick mind and lively conversation, he had no more admiration for intellectual pursuits and academic distinction than he had for Cordelia's musical gift – and for the same reasons: because he himself was devoid of such achievements (for although Daddy was obviously terribly clever, he had apparently been a bit of a dunce at school).

Whatever the reason, the maddening fact remained that Nigel continued to worship Dinah – that fat, Lefty lesbian! – and ignore Portia – although, there had been a glimmer of hope four years ago when he had hired her as Communications Director for Bennet's. She was thrilled and had thrown herself into the job, working tirelessly; for, in addition to the privilege of working so closely with her father and having the opportunity to earn his respect and pride, she was well aware that, career-wise, it was a huge step up for her, her professional experience having hitherto consisted of two years in a junior position with a minor PR agency. Yet, as satisfied as her father seemed with her substantial efforts, he was extremely demanding and rarely forthcoming with praise – although, he was like that with all his employees.

Still, Portia soldiered on, drawing some gratification from the knowledge that she was of use to him, that he *needed* her. When he had stepped down as chairman of Bennet's two years ago, she had handed in her notice and offered herself as his personal PR Rep. As this role had not turned out to be as time-consuming – nor as lucrative – as her job with Bennet's, she also did some freelance brand consultancy work on the side.

Meanwhile, she watched Dinah, waiting for her to slip up, to do something that would finally knock her fat bottom off that pedestal Daddy placed her on. She read Dinah's emails, painstakingly tracked her social media activity in the hope of uncovering some potentially illicit or dubious affiliations (more dubious, that is, than her Trotskyite pals, but Daddy knew about them), scoured her own vast network of contacts around town in search of rumours or scandal about her sister. But there was nothing. The girl seemed to be the only person in London who had no secrets, no double life: she was entirely transparent and genuine. It was baffling, absurd.

And then, two weeks ago, there had finally been a breakthrough: Dinah had come home for the weekend, apparently on a whim, and gone out on the Saturday evening. When she got back an hour or so later, she had gone straight into Daddy's study and closed the door. Portia had then hurried barefoot down the stairs and listened at the study door.

What she had learned had shocked her: she had run back upstairs before Dinah had emerged from the study and retired to her room where she had lain down for half an hour, stunned.

But then, as she regained her composure, a plan had begun to form in her mind. She had started by Googling this Wade woman, finding her to be a complete nonentity, a middle-aged woman with an unremarkable career living in *Bristol*, of all places (to Portia, who had grown up in Belgravia and the Suffolk countryside, holidaying in St Barts, Klosters and Tuscany, Bristol may as well have been the Outer Hebrides or the *favelas* of Rio de Janeiro).

Then she had bided her time, waiting for the propitious moment, one when her revelations would have the most devastating impact: her father was due to receive some award for services to the retail industry the following week, and the next day her mother was due to host a luncheon for one of her more high-profile charities. This is when she had struck. With her PR experience and connections, she had of course known exactly how to feed the story.

Her objective had been threefold: to punish her father for his indifference all these years; to incriminate Dinah, thus ousting her from her long-held position as favourite daughter; and, lastly, in the manner of the arsonist who turns fireman, her deft handling of the media fallout was intended, in addition to earning her father's eternal gratitude, to win her the adulation and respect of her mother, Cordelia, and indeed, everyone in their social circle.

Even the pandemic and the ensuing stay-at-home order, to which most people had reacted with dread and horror, had been yet another opportunity that she had turned to her advantage: she had suggested Raddington as a more pleasant and wholesome venue for their isolation, knowing full well that the newly formed anti-Nigel faction – namely Mummy and Cordelia – would refuse to accompany them. Portia had once again stepped in to save the day, tentatively advising Daddy that a little time apart from Mummy might be just what they both needed.

And now, here they were, just the two of them, and for the first time ever, he was completely and utterly dependent on her!

Just then, her father shuffled into the room. She leapt to her feet and took the mashed potatoes out of the Aga. When she returned, he was standing at the head of the table, surveying the food and wine with bloodshot, rheumy eyes.

Ah, bless him, she thought, her heart swelling with love. *Look how moved he is!*

CHAPTER THIRTY-SEVEN

Dublin, 27 March 2020

'The whole world is suffering during this pandemic, and Ireland is no different. What happens now is up to each one of us. Show your support to our healthcare staff.

Show your support for everyone who is working in essential services or looking after our vulnerable citizens. Show that you care for your families and friends.

Stay at home.'

'Fuck!' Dave switched off the TV and hurled the remote onto the sofa with such force that it bounced onto the floor with a clatter and the batteries fell out of their chamber.

'Daddy, you said a bad word again,' chided a little voice.

Dave spun round to see Declan standing in the doorway.

'Hey! What are you doing? Back to bed, now!'

Having successfully dispatched his son back to his room, he continued to curse, albeit more quietly, as the full implications of the Taoiseach's speech began to sink in. The logistics were already complicated for his expanding yet fractured family: for the first week after Clare had gone home with baby Lorcan, Dave had temporarily moved back into the house in Killiney to help out. But after a week, with tempers frayed all round, Clare had suggested that perhaps it was time for Dave to return to his flat: something about 'boundaries' not being clear – whatever the fuck that meant. She had, however, accepted his offer to have Declan for a few days.

On the professional side of things, working from home wasn't a problem for him; but how were he and Clare going to organise things with the kids?

He dialled Clare's number.

'Yes?' She sounded exhausted.

'Were you watching that? Varadkar?'

'No, I was just putting Lorcan down. Why, what's happened?'

'We're going into fuckin' lockdown, as of midnight!'

She appeared far calmer than he. 'Well, we knew it was coming sooner or later. At the hospital, they've been saying–'

'Yeah, yeah,' he said dismissively. 'The point is, what are we going to do? About us? I mean, he said it's just for a fortnight for now but it could go on for months for all we know and there's no way I'm spending lockdown without my boys.'

A few seconds' silence on the other end, then Clare said:

'Are you suggesting we move back in together for lockdown? I mean, you move back in here?'

'Well, what was your plan? That you stay on your own with the kids? Or we stay as we are now – you alone with Lorcan and me with Declan? You want to split this family up?'

'Jesus, Dave, don't be so bloody dramatic,' she said wearily. 'I don't *have* a plan: I only found out five seconds ago.' She sighed. 'Of course, I don't want to deprive you of the kids, or them of you, but it's a big decision. I mean, we need to be sure there are…'

'Boundaries, yeah, so you said a few days ago,' he said drily. 'Look, I know it's not ideal and it won't be simple, but we can work something out. And the kids need us; they need us both.'

'I don't know. I need to think about it.'

'Well, OK but we don't have much time, we have to –' He was interrupted by the sound of a wailing infant in the background.

'I've got to see to him,' she said. 'Look, I'll call you back, OK?'

'OK, but –'

The line went dead. He swore again. There she was again, with her boundaries and her rules. He got up and took a bottle of Stella from the fridge. Just as he was opening it, his phone rang again. Rushing across the room to pick it up, he saw, with a rush of disappointment, his cousin's name on the screen.

'Hi, Méabh. What's up?'

'Hello, Dave. Is this a bad time.'

No, it's just the end of the fuckin' world, he wanted to say.

'No, everything's grand. What can I do you for?'

'Well, I assume you heard about the stay-at-home order and I was wondering what your plans were – for you and Clare and the boys.'

'Oh, that…' he muttered. 'Well, since you ask, I was hoping to move back to Killiney so we could both be with the kids, but…well, let's just say Clare doesn't seem too keen. She thinks it would be confusing for Declan and awkward for us…I dunno.'

'I see. Listen, I don't mean to pry or seem high-handed, but I have a proposal for you that might put a different light on things for you – and Clare.'

Dave took a gulp of lager and sat down. 'I'm listening.'

✄

Monza, 30 March 2020

They spent the next few days in almost perfect symbiosis, cocooned, sheltered from the outside world. They ate and drank and made love and slept and occasionally worked. After a while, they retreated even further from reality by shunning television and news sites: nothing intruded on their idyll.

Until one day, inevitably, it did.

They had been entwined asleep when Marnie received the call from Dave informing her of Deirdre's death. Her initial feeling of detachment upon receiving this information soon gave way to a hollow despair, in the background of which lurked an indefinable sense of guilt. Not guilt at having rejected Deirdre all those years ago, or for not having rushed to her bedside to hold her hand during her final hours.

But when she recalled that wretched news story, she thought: *she'll have thought* I *did that. She would have died thinking I set out to shame her ex-lover, destroy his reputation.* Was that why she had refused to reveal Nigel's identity in the first place? Had she assumed Marnie was going to make trouble?

With this thought, her guilt hardened into an irrational resentment, and when she finally began to cry, they were tears of bitterness and frustration, not of sorrow.

Pulling herself together, she picked up her phone. Luc's gentle, reassuringly familiar voice and words of comfort during their brief exchange earlier that morning had been of some solace, but she had a sudden yearning to speak to Guy. He did not pick up but called back half an hour later, apologising and saying he had been somewhere in the grounds in the digger doing something – digging, presumably.

'Deirdre, my birth mother, is dead,' she said flatly.

He sounded genuinely sad for her. 'Oh, no, I'm so sorry, Marn. I can only imagine how you feel. You must be devastated.'

She swallowed her irritation. *Clearly, you can't imagine*, she thought. For he was just projecting how he would feel, if he were she and Vince or Heidi had just died.

But then, she reflected, what did she expect? She knew how he felt – how he had always felt – about the whole situation. So, she simply listened to his effusions of sympathy, his compassion for a sorrow she did not feel, accepted them and thanked him. When he asked her if she intended to attend the funeral, she was grateful of the excuse of the pandemic and lockdown and closed borders, as this conveniently saved them from an otherwise inevitable argument.

But once she had hung up, she said out loud: 'Of course I'm not going! Why would I go? She meant nothing to me and I meant nothing to her.'

When Amedeo appeared just before ten, flustered at having overslept, he found her sitting on the sofa staring blankly at the television.

'Amore, che cos'è successo?' he asked, his dark eyes full of concern.

She told him, and his reaction was exactly what she had hoped for; he simply nodded and said: 'I see. That must feel...' he shrugged. 'I don't know how that must feel. How does it?' She merely sighed wearily and shook her head in response.

'OK. Forget what you're feeling right now. Can you tell me what you're *thinking*?'

She looked at him. 'Are you sure you want to know? It's rather... twisted, not to mention melodramatic and incredibly self-indulgent.'

'All of which are qualities I like about you,' he said.

She laughed weakly. 'OK. You asked for it. I'm thinking,' she said slowly, about what it would be like if I had never existed. I mean, if Deirdre hadn't had any religious or ethical concerns about aborting and had got rid of me.'

Instead of looking shocked or bewildered, he merely nodded thoughtfully.

'So, like in that Capra film – what's it called? About the guy who lives his whole life in a small town and gets married and has loads of children and goes bankrupt and tries to kill himself...'

'It's a Wonderful Life,' she nodded. 'Exactly. But in this scenario, it's abortion instead of suicide.'

'OK. Well, from what you've told me about your... the woman who has just died, and the relationship she had with your... I mean...'

'It's fine, you can say mother and father, I won't burst into flames.'

'Well, I meant to say, it probably wouldn't have made much difference to your parents' relationship or lives. I mean, he still wouldn't have stayed with her; he would have eventually

260

left her and gone back to his wife anyway – maybe a bit later than he did, but he wouldn't have loved your mother and she would still have been heartbroken when he left her – baby or no baby. She probably wouldn't have had any children with anyone else; I mean, you said she never had any others after you, right? And she didn't sound like a very maternal person.'

She said nothing but nodded, still staring distractedly at the television screen.

He continued. 'OK, let's move on to the other people in your life. This young woman, your half-sister?'

'Dinah.'

'Dinah. It sounds as though you get on well, you've established a bond of sorts with her?'

She shrugged. 'I suppose so. Yeah; she seems like a nice kid. I like her. Actually, she and my cousin Dave are literally the only reasons I don't regret tracing my birth parents.'

'And she likes you, it seems. Didn't you say she's not close to her other siblings?'

A nod of assent.

'Well, without you, she may never have developed a significant, fulfilling relationship with a sibling! That's something.' He added, although without a trace of self-pity: 'That's something I've never had.' She turned to look at him and felt a rush of tenderness.

'OK,' she said, curling up and placing her head in his lap. 'Go on.'

'Well, I can't speak for your ex-husband,' he said, stroking her hair. 'Maybe you should ask him. But as for your daughter, obviously she would not have been born. Your ex might have had kids with another woman but those children wouldn't be half you. As for your actual parents, they would probably have adopted someone else; Guy would have had another sibling. Yes, I think I know what you're thinking: he may have had a greater affinity with this brother or sister, had more things in common. But that doesn't mean he would have *loved* them more.'

He paused, and gently lifting her head from his lap, got up and went into the kitchen where he began boiling water for his tea and spooning coffee into the moka pot Marnie had insisted on ordering from Amazon the week before.

'Let's talk about your friends now,' he called over the breakfast bar. 'The famous Val, for example. You're very close, you have been since school, no? You have always been each other's rock.'

She nodded and lay on her back. 'Boarding school does that to you. You form very close, intense friendships. It's more than friendship: you become everything to each other, substitutes for the people on the outside: parents, siblings, lovers…' She rolled over onto her stomach again and looked up at him. 'Not in our case, I hasten to add. Sorry to ruin your little fantasy, sweetness. But it does happen, a lot. It's only natural.' After a while she shook her head. 'Yeah, but so what? If I hadn't been around, Val would have found what we had with someone else, someone from the rest of our gang. Bryony, Sam, Lakshme.'

'Maybe, maybe not.' He turned to put the coffee pot on the stove and walked back over to the sofa. 'But it wouldn't have been the same, because it wouldn't have been with you.'

'I suppose. Actually,' she said, 'there is something: one significant, tangible way in which I may have done some good, actually made a difference in life. I mean, it's not quite on a par with George Bailey saving his little brother from the frozen river, but…' She sat up.

'You could say I was instrumental in saving Val from getting into a number of drunken scrapes when we were young. I prevented her having several car crashes, possibly stopped her getting date-raped a couple of times – and on one occasion, actual random stranger-raped.' She shuddered at the memory, then took the cup of the coffee he brought her. 'Thanks, you're a sweetheart.

'You see, you wouldn't think it to see Val now, with her lawyer husband and her PTA meetings and her house in Hampstead – OK, West Hampstead, but still – but she used to be a Wild Child. I mean, she was always a party girl, but there was one particular period, when her parents had split up and her Dad remarried this woman she didn't get on with, and she went off the rails a bit. There was suddenly a reckless, self-destructive streak to her partying: really hard drinking, coke, blokes. The number of times I confiscated her car keys at parties – when I was pretty pissed up myself – because she was about to drive herself home or to some pub or another party. And I stopped her copping off with quite a few dodgy-looking blokes when she was completely off her face; random guys we met in clubs and stuff. One time she was just going to get into a car full of blokes and go back to a party at their place! God, I was scared she was going to get gang-raped and left for dead. I literally had to pull her back, force her to get into a cab with me. I put her to bed loads of times too, undressed her, put her in the recovery position.'

She looked at Amedeo over the rim of her coffee cup. 'But then, it's nothing much,' she said dismissively. 'I mean, nothing no one else would have done. God, I think I'm grasping at straws, trying to convince myself my life means something, that I've had any sort of impact on those around me during my forty-odd years on this earth.' She smiled ruefully at him. 'I told you it was self-indulgent.'

'*Tesoro mio*,' he said gently and took her in his arms. 'Please don't be stupid. From what I know about you, I have no doubt you are a wonderful daughter and friend and mother, and were a good wife to Luc. And now, I would advise you to cease dwelling on this maudlin idea as, apart from being a pointless speculation, it's clearly not making you feel good, and I for one would rather not think about this sad, Marnie-less parallel universe you speak of.'

262

She laughed and kissed him and thanked him and told him to ignore her in her present st. of mind. Feeling, however, that she needed further consolation, Amedeo suddenly put on his face mask and walked out of the front door. When he returned around ten minutes later, he was holding a large chopping board covered with a tea towel.

'What's that?' Marnie asked.

'Just some little treats for you,' he said and, placing the chopping board on the breakfast bar, removed the tea towel with a flourish.

Marnie gasped in delight: for there before her was an assortment of cheeses and cold meats: a wedge of pecorino, a nub of *mozzarella di bufala*, a few slices of *prosciutto crudo*, and a ramakin dish containing what looked like 'nduja.

'Oh, my God! Animal flesh and dairy products!' she exclaimed, clasping her hands together. 'Did you just go scrounging to your neighbours for these?'

He nodded.

They had lunch on the terrace under a pale, veiled sunshine, Marnie sampling the neighbours' delicious, forbidden offerings whilst Amedeo ate marinated aubergines and made a good attempt at disguising his distaste and moral outrage. In the afternoon, Amedeo hosted another webinar whilst Marnie applied herself to translating from Italian to English a short story for children written by a writer friend of her Italian teacher. As children's stories went it was rather bleak: it was the tale of a little girl and a cat, at the end of which the child died of coronavirus. In the interests of international solidarity and doing her bit for the Cause (and because it was the closest thing to a literary translation she had done since her Masters), she had offered to do the work pro bono. At six o'clock, having reached what she deemed a good place to stop for the day, she was shutting down her laptop when her phone rang. It was Luc.

'Oh, hi again,' she said. 'Is something wrong? Is it Rhiannon?'

'No, she's absolutely fine. I was just checking in, seeing if you were OK after this morning.'

'Thank you. I'm fine. I mean, I disappeared down a rabbit-hole for a bit, but I'm OK now.'

'Ah. Is this the kind of rabbit-hole where you look for all the possible ways in which something could be your fault, or the one where you go in for existential hypothesising of the 'what if' variety?'

'No one likes a know-all, Luc,' she said sullenly.

'You should know; you hardly have any friends except Val.'

'True.' She sighed. 'OK, if you must know, it was mostly the latter.'

'Ah! And may I know what particular hypothetical situation you were contemplating, and no doubt, agonising over?'

She told him.

'I see,' he said. 'Well, for what it's worth, for my part, I wouldn't have gone back to Gabrielle or Philippine and I definitely wouldn't have had children if I hadn't met you.' It was unsentimental, a simple, bald statement of fact.

'I did wonder.'

'You must know that. We talked about it at the time… Anyway. The point is, Rhiannon wouldn't have been born; my parents would not have been grandparents, and thus,' he added, with mock pomposity, 'the great name of Barthélemy would, alas, have died with me.'

She was touched and amused and knew it would have been churlish to point out that, as he had not been blessed with a son, the said great name, by which Marnie had gone for over a decade, was doomed to extinction anyway.

She thanked him warmly and hung up.

Just then Amedeo came downstairs, his working day over.

'God, I thought that would never end! I can't bear to look at another screen. *Please* can we have our *aperitivo* now?'

'Sure, but I think I'll have a mineral water. All this good living and sedentary lifestyle is beginning to take its toll on my waistline.'

He shrugged. 'As you wish, but as for sedentary, you could go out jogging, you know. Just because I've become a semi-hermit and borderline agoraphobic, it doesn't mean you have to.'

'You're right. And perhaps we should have a sort of wake for Deirdre.'

'That's the spirit! Now, what can I get you?'

'I'll do it. Campari for you?' She knelt down on the floor by the drinks cabinet, and was dismayed by the paucity of its contents: God, did the man never entertain? Even by a hermit's standards, it was spartan: in addition to the bottle of Campari, a third of which remained, she found an inch or two of vodka, half a bottle of Grappa and an ancient, sealed bottle of Benedictine.

'We really need to stock up. I'll order some supplies.'

'Really?' he said, joining her on the floor and peering inside the cupboard. 'Is it really worth getting some poor bastard to risk his life and come out in the middle of a pandemic, just because we absolutely *have* to have some vermouth to make our Negronis? Not to mention the carbon footprint –' He glanced sideways and saw her slightly irritated expression.

'Sorry, am I being pontifical?'

'Just a tad. But you're right, of course. I felt bad for that guy from Amazon who came the other day to deliver my coffee pot. He stood right at the opposite end of the landing and kicked the package across the floor at me; he barely even looked me in the eye. OK, fine, we'll make do with what we have, be creative.'

Thus, within ten minutes, while Amedeo sipped his Campari on the rocks, Marnie was savouring a cocktail of her own invention: an ounce and a half of vodka, an ounce and a half of lemon juice and one ounce of Benedictine, served in a lemon juice and sugar-rimmed glass.

'I'm calling it a Rasputin,' she said, licking sugar from her lips.

Amedeo eyed her thoughtfully for a few moments then said: 'Got it. Vodka, Russia, Benedictine, monks.'

'My clever darling.' She raised her glass. 'To Deirdre.'

'To you, *tesoro*.'

They didn't make love that night but lay in each other's arms and talked long into the night.

'You know,' he said at one point. 'Rather than thinking about what might or might not have happened if Deirdre hadn't given birth to you, focus on what actually did happen: she *did* have you, and she gave you up for adoption.'

'Thanks for the update.'

He nudged her gently in the ribs. 'Let me finish. I wanted to say: tell me all the ways – both positive and negative – in which being adopted has affected you, shaped you.'

She thought for a few moments then said:

'Well, first of all, it's not so much the fact of being adopted by Mum and Dad as being abandoned by Deirdre in the first place. I mean, I'm pretty sure I wouldn't feel the same way if I'd been adopted because I'd been orphaned as a baby. The abandonment issue is key.' She turned on to her side. 'Now as for how that affected me, influenced me, the bad stuff is easy: my neediness and abandonment issues, the kind of toxic relationships I used to get involved in. Also, when Guy and I were kids, I got the distinct impression our grandparents – my mum's parents especially – didn't like us as much as their other grandchildren. I mean, they were perfectly nice to us, but there was just *something*, something about the way they looked at us sometimes, they just seemed... I don't know, *wary* of us and a bit cold, compared to how they were with my cousins. At the time I didn't know what to make of it but with hindsight, I think it was the adoption thing.'

'You think they didn't think of you as their real grandchildren?'

'That, and I also think they felt there was a stigma attached to adoption. No one in the family had ever adopted before. I suppose there was a stigma about infertility, too: I imagine my mum's parents blamed my father for it, whereas my paternal grandmother thought it was my mum's fault: "there's never been any of that sort of thing on our side of the family," that kind of thing. I know: I'm speculating and extrapolating. But they definitely thought of us as freaks. I mean, in many ways we *are* different from my cousins: I was always a bookworm as a kid, unlike my girl cousins who were tree-climbing tomboy-types, and I went to live abroad after I graduated, whereas everyone else has always lived within a ten-mile radius of their hometown; and Guy with his ambitiousness, his business ventures and success and money. But I think they attributed it to the adoption: we were different because we *weren't really one of them*. We were like –'

'The cuckoos in the nest,' finished Amedeo.

She looked surprised. 'Yes. Exactly.'

He laughed ruefully. 'I know what that feels like. And what about the positive things?'

She thought for a few moments and said:

'I think it made me a good mother. I mean, I don't know if I have been a good mum to Rhiannon, but I know I was the best one I could possibly be. Because… because, what my mum and Deirdre went through – the choices they made, and the ones they didn't even have – that meant I didn't take anything for granted. I didn't take fertility and being able to be a mother for granted, because my adoptive parents tried to conceive for years and couldn't and then went through the whole adoption process – twice. I didn't take parenthood lightly, nor see it as burden because unlike Luc's parents, I live in an age and a country where women have the right to plan parenthood and, unlike Deirdre, I wasn't crippled by misguided religious principles. I was aware of the freedoms and privileges I had, the choices I had, and the responsibilities that came with them. For years, I chose not to have kids, until I met Luc, and then when I was ready, I chose to get pregnant, and I was lucky: I did, pretty quickly. And once I had Rhiannon, I realised I had something my mothers didn't have: a child I had given birth to, a child I had chosen to have and to keep. So there was no excuse to be anything but the best mother I could possibly be.'

This talk of birth and babies made her think suddenly of Dave, and she recalled with a pang of regret her curtness with him that morning when he had called about Deirdre: she hadn't even asked after Clare and the new baby. She resolved to call him first thing in the morning.

Stroking Amedeo's chest absent-mindedly she asked him: 'Does any of that make sense?'

'Yes, it does. You know, I –' He was interrupted by Marnie's phone vibrating.

'Sorry,' she said picking it up. 'Let me just…'

It was an email: the name of the sender was vaguely familiar, yet she could not remen. where she had seen it: Miles Halliwell.

CHAPTER THIRTY-EIGHT

Paris, 31 March 2020

Day 34

My post-bunker bucket list

Swim in the ocean. Swim anywhere, for that matter.

While away an hour in the Louvre, the Tate Modern, the Prado.

Wake up one morning and not know where I am.

Sit on a café terrace and watch the world go by.

Kiss a total stranger (OK: perhaps this one should go on my Parallel Universe bucket list).

Eat a meal that was not prepared in my kitchen.

Drink a cocktail I didn't mix myself from what I happen to find at the back of the drinks cabinet/fridge.

Have a reason to wear heels, make-up, jewellery. For that matter, a reason to wax.

See an unfamiliar view from the window.

Get lost down a side street in a strange city.

Hear some live music played by proper musicians.

Have a massage.

Hear an unfamiliar language spoken around me.

But...

In the meantime, I will lie on the balcony, feel the sunshine on my skin, close my eyes and imagine I'm somewhere else, just for a while.

It's at times like this that I'm thankful (and finally understand why) that, in addition to taking photos and videos when I'm travelling, I also make audio recordings on my phone. So, instead of listening to music now as I lie on the balcony, I can dip into my audio library and go on a trip around the world. Let me see... I have the bells of Como Cathedral; waves crashing onto the beach then hissing over the pebbles and back out to sea at Lymbrook-on-Sea; a priest chanting prayers at the Basilica di San Nicola in Bari; the throbbing and squawking of hundreds of birds and insects during an evening walk through the jungle in the backwaters of Kerala; a DJ set at Sa Trinxa Beach Club in Ibiza.

I invite my fellow Bunkerites to go on a similar voyage through their imagination and memories every now and then.

Because it's not about pining or wallowing in nostalgia: just enjoying the memory of weird and wonderful things we've seen and done before – and will do again, one day.

◌◌◌

Monza, 3 April 2020

It was nine-thirty and Marnie was sitting on the terrace in her pyjamas drinking espresso and doing her morning international Covid news roundup. Beginning with *Le Monde*'s website, she read that hospitals in the Greater Paris area were continuing to struggle with the number of cases and Orly Airport, which had closed a few days before, was now being used as an emergency transfer centre, with aircraft commandeered by the healthcare services to fly patients out from Paris to hospitals in less affected areas of the country. She glanced at some of the other headlines then went to *The Independent*. In China, some Americans had hijacked a shipment of surgical masks ordered by the French: they had apparently turned up at the airport just as the plane was about to take off for France, paid well over the asking price and had the masks sent to the States instead. Clearly, she thought grimly, it's every country for itself.

Only a visit to *La Repubblica* offered some light-hearted relief and hope – surprisingly, given the alarming contagion rate and death toll in the country: a middle-aged couple in Rome had just got married in a deconsecrated church. They had evidently not wished to wait until the health crisis was over to take vows. There was a photo of the happy couple, he in a suit, she in a fuchsia dress and black shawl, both with masks, their eyes crinkling with irrepressible joy (it irritated Marnie when people said the problem with masks was that they prevented one from being able to read people's expressions). She forwarded the link to Rhiannon with the message:

Idea for today's post? and, remembering she hadn't had a chance to read her daughter's blog the night before, decided to remedy this. The title of the previous day's post was particularly arresting:

Black holes and glaciers and turbulent priests – oh my!

Taking another sip of coffee, she read:

This morning I read about two interesting scientific discoveries in The Independent. *I don't usually make a beeline for the science section of any newspaper, but at the moment my faith in the wonders of science is helping me get through this. These are the stories that caught my attention:*

NASA and ESA have found a black hole, something they're calling (rather alarmingly), a 'cosmic killer,' which will apparently explain lots of hitherto inexplicable phenomena. It's an 'intermediate' mass – a mid-sized black hole, which is only 50,000 the mass of the Sun. At times like this I wish I knew more about physics, because my ignorance in the field is just making this all sound very scary.

UK and American scientists have found lead deposits trapped in a 72-metre-long ice core in a glacier in the Swiss-Italian Alps that sheds light on historic events in 12th-century England. The lead was carried by winds from lead mines in the North of England and has been preserved in the ice for centuries. Apparently, they can actually see in the ice the rising and falling levels of lead pollution over the years, which dovetail historical records and thus show a correlation between political and economic events and lead production. For example, there was a surge in the years after Henry II had Thomas à Becket assassinated in 1170 because Pope Alexander III excommunicated him for it, and in an attempt to get back into the Pope's good books, Henry had lots of monasteries built (lead was used in roofs and stained-glass windows).

I found this interesting in itself, but also in the light of the current situation: a lot has been said since the pandemic broke out about the butterfly effect and chaos theory, how everything's connected, how our actions have unimaginable and far-reaching consequences. It's one thing that a spat between the king and the church could have not only economic and political implications but environmental ones; but that traces of these consequences could be found in a glacier 900 years later and 1000 km away?! This is sending my little grey cells into a tailspin.

Marnie smiled, finished her coffee, and stepped back into the flat. Amedeo had been videoconferencing with some people from the Monza town council since eight o'clock and had back-to-back meetings and training sessions all day. Marnie, for her part, had planned to spend the morning doing a final review of her translation of the Italian coronavirus fable. Much to her irritation, Fabio, the author, had asked a 'friend' of his – not a translator nor even a native English-speaker – to review her translation and this person had made some 'suggestions.' During her fifteen years at DigInnova, she had become accustomed to being second-guessed by people not qualified to do so, something which had never failed to annoy her. But it was rather depressing to discover that people could be just as high-handed and presumptuous when one was doing their translations for free as when one was paid.

Just after noon she sent back the translation to Fabio, having accepted some of the 'suggestions' and politely but firmly rejecting others. She then made herself a sandwich of hummus and rocket and settled back in front of her laptop for the series of Zoom video chat sessions she had scheduled.

The first of these was with Mrs Wellesley to check in with Tim and Roger, then with her daughter. Mrs Wellesley gave Marnie a brief update on the gossip in Dowry Square: Ralph from the flat upstairs from Marnie had come down with suspected Covid and was self-isolating in the guest bedroom, according to his wife, and the young couple who had moved into one of the basement flats on the other side of the square a few months ago had been arguing frequently and noisily and the police had been called out on one occasion. She then turned her phone camera to show Roger, curled up asleep in her favourite spot on the living room sofa, and Tim, who was out in the yard, predatorily eyeing a starling perched on the railings. Clearly, the feline status quo had not altered one iota and all was as it should be.

Rhiannon, on the other hand, was somewhat subdued, and looked pale and drawn.

'Papa's ill,' she blurted.

Marnie made an effort to sound calm. 'OK... What are his symptoms?'

'He's got a sore throat.'

'Nothing else? No temperature? Aching muscles? Difficulty breathing?'

Rhiannon shook her head. 'No, just the throat. Oh, God, Mum, what if he *does* have it? They say people with asthma are particularly vulnerable and are more likely to –'

'You can't think like that,' Marnie said gently but firmly. 'From the sounds of it, there's nothing as yet to suggest it's anything more than a common cold. If the symptoms get worse, call the doctor. But in the meantime, just to be on the safe side, make sure he keeps to his room, and keep an eye on him.'

She nodded dolefully but said nothing.

'Lovey, he'll be all right.'

With a surge of love and compassion, Marnie was suddenly reminded of a holiday the three of them had taken in Andalusia a decade ago: it was unbearably hot – in the upper forties – and one evening in Cordoba they were walking back to the hotel after grazing on *salmorejo* and *croquetas* at a bar and Luc, having rather ill-advisedly taken three glasses of sangria (for regular cannabis consumer though he was, where alcohol was concerned he was practically abstemious), succumbed to the heat and fainted in the street. The ten-year-old Rhiannon had promptly burst into tears, confessing later to Marnie that she had been convinced her father was dead. Luc had soon recovered, thanks in part to the swift intervention of a gallant, dapper gentleman in his sixties who had witnessed the incident and come running to their assistance, helping Marnie escort Luc back to their hotel. Once in the air-conditioned comfort of their room, Marnie had got him to drink almost a litre of water before dragging him, grey-faced, into the shower. Within twenty minutes, he was much better, but since then Rhiannon had consistently worked herself into a frenzy of anguish at the slightest indication of any physical weakness or ill health in her father.

Deciding a change of the subject was in order, she said with slightly forced joviality: 'I'm enjoying your blog.'

'Yeah? Thanks. And thanks for the link you sent me; I Google Translated it. I actually might use the wedding photo for today's post; I'm a bit low on ideas.'

'You're welcome! Glad I could help and provide you with some, er… click fodder, or whatever it is.'

'Click *bait*,' corrected Rhiannon, adding irritably, 'but you knew that: you're just showing off. Even you're not *that* much of a Luddite.'

'Thanks very much, I'm sure,' said Marnie tartly. 'Quite a compliment coming from you.'

Rhiannon smiled sheepishly. 'Sorry I'm being such a bitch. I'm just worried about papa. Now, what about you: when are you going home? How are things going with Amedeo?'

After answering both questions vaguely and with a certain degree of circumspection – in the case of the former, because she genuinely did not know exactly when international travel would be feasible, and in the latter, because she did not yet feel like disclosing the recent developments in her and Amedeo's relationship – Marnie reiterated her reassurance as to the state of Luc's health and hung up. She had just enough time to make a pot of peppermint tea before logging on for her three o'clock Zoom session with Dave.

He looked tired, but otherwise as handsome as ever. He was wearing a white T-shirt and sitting on a sofa in a plush, comfortable-looking – and to Marnie, unfamiliar – setting.

'Where are you?' she asked? 'That's not your flat.'

'We've relocated,' he said rather grandly, grinning.

He proceeded to tell her how his cousin Méabh, who, in addition to fostering baby Olivia, was also in the process of divorcing her husband, had invited him and Clare and the children to leave Dublin for lockdown and join her in the country. Méabh and her estranged husband – who was evidently as rich as Croesus – owned a substantial property portfolio, including a sprawling country manor in County Waterford, and Méabh intended to get the most out of their various homes before they inevitably sold them and split the proceeds. To that end, a week before the Taoiseach had issued the stay-at-home order, Méabh, the baby, and her mother – Dave's aunt – had already gone to Galloways, as the country manor was called, for a break, and had subsequently decided to stay there for the duration of lockdown. Given the spaciousness of the property – for in addition to the vast main house, there were also various outbuildings on the estate, all of which had been converted into guest accommodation – his generous cousin wanted to share it with as many of her family members as possible, hence the invitation she had extended to Dave and Clare, as well as other members of her extended family.

'I've just sent you the listing for the place,' he said. 'Check it out.'

Clicking on the link in the message, Marnie saw a page from an estate agent's website depicting an aerial view of a pale yellow, slate-roofed, two-storey nineteenth-century manor house.

Galloways, Portlaw, Co. Waterford. A magnificent estate overlooking the River Suir with a private situation.

250 Ac (101.17 Ha)

Guide price: €3,250,000 (£ 2,807,353).

'Christ,' said Marnie. 'You jammy bastard.'

He chuckled. 'Not so shabby being part of this family after all, is it? And I'm even jammier than you think: I've managed to sublet my flat in Dublin to a bloke from work who's having problems with his missus and was about to throw himself into the Liffey at the prospect of being holed up with her for the duration.' He added virtuously: 'I'm only charging him a nominal rent, naturally.'

Marnie read out loud from the listing: *"'Key features include 3 reception rooms, 6 bedrooms, a 13th-Century Castle, fishing lodge: 5 bedrooms (all en suite), walled garden including gardener's cottage, equestrian facilities including 8 loose boxes, polo field and club, hunter trial course"* – fuck me.'

'Yeah, I gotta admit that as arks go, it's a pretty deluxe one. Méabh and the baby and my auntie and Mam are all up at the main house but we've got the fishing lodge all to ourselves. My cousin Fionn and his girlfriend have got the gardener's cottage. My sister Clodagh was asked to join us but she's a nurse so she's got to stay in Dublin for work.'

'The fishing lodge…' said Marnie, as she scrolled through the photos on the website on her phone. 'Is that that row of granite cottages there?'

'That's us.'

'And God, what's that ruin near it?' Standing a little way behind the fishing lodge, on the banks of the river, was a stone tower, possibly the keep of a medieval castle.

'I'll show you,' said Dave. Rising from the sofa, he walked through open French windows out onto a lawn which stretched down to the banks of the river, and then Marnie saw the stone tower looming above.

'Very nice,' she said. 'I hope you'll spare a thought for me in a week or so when I'm back in my little basement flat in Bristol.' (Was it her imagination or did Amedeo, who had just come downstairs to make some tea during a brief break between two meetings, look a little crestfallen at this last remark?)

'How are Clare and the kids?' she asked, turning back to her screen.

'Grand.' He turned his iPad to show a woman in her thirties with short strawberry-blond hair and freckles wearing a long black skirt and Aran sweater sitting on a rug on the lawn with an infant lying in her lap. She looked up briefly, shielding her eyes from the sun with her hand, then smiled and waved shyly. A few meters behind them, a little boy was flying a kite.

So this was Clare, Marnie thought. Somehow she was not quite as she had imagined. She immediately realised why: she had expected Dave's wife to be stunning, a raving beauty with head-turning, film-star looks, whereas this woman was merely pretty in a fresh, wholesome way, with nice skin and a good figure. Then, with a flash of shame at her presumptuousness and superficiality, Marnie watched as the other woman got up and, still cradling the baby in the crook of one arm, she helped the elder boy manipulate his kite with the other. She noted the intelligent eyes and the way Clare moved as she tended to her children that suggested a

274

certain grace, a quiet strength and capability, an innate motherliness, all of which would certainly be reassuring and attractive to a man-child like Dave.

'That's wonderful, Dave,' she said. 'I'm so happy for you.'

'Cheers.' Looking around and lowering his voice slightly as he walked back towards the house, he continued: 'We're taking it slowly for the minute, Clare and me. I'm in one of the guest bedrooms. But we'll see. It's great for the kids, though. So,' he asked, resuming his usual casually jocular tone, 'what about you: how's Italy? Any craic? I mean, apart from martial law and mass graves and rampant looting.'

'David,' she asked sternly, 'Have you been watching *Contagion?*'

Her next virtual meeting was with Dinah, who was in Somerset with her girlfriend and some friends. She looked well and seemed happy to speak to Marnie, cheerfully assuring her she was an avid reader of her niece's blog.

In the course of their conversation, Marnie mentioned Deirdre's death.

'Oh, I'm sorry, Marnie,' she said. And then: 'I wonder if Pa knows? Would it be all right if I told him?'

Marnie said as far as she was concerned it was fine, although privately she thought the news would be met with indifference by their father. They finished their conversation with Dinah securing Marnie's assurance that she would give her a comprehensive debrief of her next video call that very evening.

For the call in question was with the man called Miles Halliwell who had emailed her a few days before. He had introduced himself, saying he was a journalist, based in Milan, and that he wished to speak to her on a rather 'delicate matter' – but not, he reassured her, in his capacity as a journalist. It concerned an article that had appeared in the British media a few weeks before claiming that a man called Nigel Halliwell was her biological father. Halliwell went on to say that he wished to speak to her on this matter – one in which, he said, she and he had 'converging interests.' Was there any way she would agree to a video chat with him sometime? Marnie, intrigued, had agreed. She was ninety-percent certain what these 'converging interests' were, but did not mention them in her brief reply; instead, she forwarded the email to Dinah, adding above the message: *Our older brother?*

But of course it was he. Dinah had said Nigel Lovelace's first-born was called Miles; that he had a different surname meant nothing – Dinah had also said he and his father were estranged, which would explain why he chose not to bear his name. Sure enough, a quick look at Lovelace's Wikipedia entry informed Marnie that his first wife was a certain Barbara Halliwell. Marnie felt her heart begin to race: another sibling was reaching out to her, and this one lived just a few kilometres from where she now was! Dinah had almost immediately sent an exuberant confirmation of Marnie's suspicions:

Yes, that's him! Oh, you have to meet him! I wish I could join you guys. Will you at least tell him you and I are in touch and that I've always wanted to meet him?

And now it was with a thrill of anticipation tinged with apprehension that Marnie clicked on the link in the Zoom invitation and waited for the meeting to begin. She was presently informed that the host had not yet logged in. Fifteen minutes past and still nothing. She messaged the number he had put in his email asking if everything was all right; no reply, and she saw from the two grey ticks in What'sApp that he had not yet picked up the message. She got up, went to the kitchen, helped herself to a slice of the vegan orange and olive oil cake Amedeo had baked the day before, (penance for the cheese and salami lapse, she thought grimly), and when she returned to her laptop saw that her host had still failed to appear. After emailing him to say she hoped he was all right and suggesting they reschedule, she finally closed the app and switched off her computer.

ᛝ

San Raffaele Hospital, Milan

It was eight-fifteen in the evening and Doctor Michelangelo Bellavia had just begun his second shift. He was bone-tired, having snatched just a two-hour nap in the on-call room between the two twelve-hour shifts. Still, this inadequate repose in a cramped bunk was almost preferable to the last time he had returned home to Legnano, two days ago, for a proper sleep. For as he parked the car then crossed the street to his house, thinking longingly of his comfortable king-size bed, of the crisp, snowy-white Egyptian cotton sheets and memory form mattress, he looked up and saw the message pinned to his front door:

'Move into a hotel – for the sake of your neighbours.'

Dumbfounded, he slowly pulled down the sheet of paper – at least, he reflected bitterly, his public-spirited neighbours had had the decency not to deface his home with spray-paint – and glanced about him at the deserted street. Which one of you selfish, cowardly, ungrateful *stronzi*, he wondered, were responsible for this? Was it an impulsive act or had they been plotting against him for a while? Dazed with tiredness and shock, he had let himself into the house and plodded upstairs to his bedroom where, despite his fatigue, he had lain awake for hours.

In addition to the sleep deprivation which was no longer the exception but the rule, a state he was dully resigned to, he had not had sexual intercourse for weeks – something he was far less accustomed to. For Greta, his former paramour, had refused to go near him since the pandemic had begun due to his daily exposure to risk in the course of his profession, and, astonishingly, had even issued him with what was arguably history's most ill-advised ultimatum since that made by Austro-Hungary to Serbia in the July Crisis of 1914: either he quit his job and, provided he test negative for the virus, they could resume their cohabitation – or their relationship was over.

Was it conceivable that the poor deluded woman thought for *one minute* that, faced with the choice between saving lives and masturbating on the one hand, and fucking her and thus renouncing his vocation and letting down his colleagues and patients on the other, he would decide on the latter? For if she did, it meant that she had not only grossly overestimated both his attachment to her and her own charms and sexual artistry, but, worse still, she also clearly viewed him as being weak-willed, priapic, devoid of professional integrity and possessed of an utterly demented sense of priorities. It was grotesque, laughable! It was no more of a dilemma than was deciding between dining on prime rib from the local organic butcher or eating rotting human organs from the hospital waste bin. All in all, it had been the easiest and most liberating break-up of his life. In fact, he was already considering possible replacements for recreational sex (Virginia, the new anaesthesiologist, for example, was a most promising candidate).

But now, as he stumbled, still thick with slumber, into the Intensive Care Unit, his thoughts of Greta and Virginia and his mutinous neighbours were immediately and brutally chased away by the daily reality of the constant and continually rising influx of patients, of the alarming shortage of beds and staff and PPEs (the shipment of face masks that had finally arrived from China the day before had turned out to be faulty and promptly been recalled).

Wearily, Dr Amato Fontana gave the handover, mechanically thrusting a clipboard at him: his first patient was a man in his forties – an Englishman – who had been admitted to hospital the day before and just been transferred to intensive care with acute respiratory failure. Bellavia glanced dejectedly at the notes and turned his attention to the patient.

CHAPTER THIRTY-NINE

Milan Malpensa Airport, 15 April 2020

'Traffic was good,' observed Marnie as Amedeo turned the car into the airport carpark. 'One of the advantages of lockdown, eh?'

He smiled politely and nodded. Their conversation throughout the forty-five-minute drive had been stilted to say the least: after Marnie's valiant attempts at cheeriness and small-talk had been consistently met with polite monosyllables, she had eventually given up and resigned herself to sitting in awkward, gloomy silence.

The decision to return finally home and the necessary logistics measures had been taken a week before, and for the next three days, they had discussed little else. Amedeo's attempts at dissuasion were always gentle and well-reasoned, never underpinned with self-pity or anger or emotional blackmail. But they were persistent and constant, varying only in the arguments and tactics employed. His initial, practical objection, on the grounds of the travel restrictions in place, had been swiftly and easily countered:

'I'm a British national returning home,' Marnie had said patiently. 'They'll just take my temperature at the airport before I get on the plane.'

'But why go back now?' he had wanted to know.

This had been four days ago; they were in his bedroom as Marnie packed.

'Come on. You know why. I need to look after my cats. I need to wear something other than the five tops, two dresses and single pair of jeans I've been wearing out for the past six weeks. I need to be in my own environment again; I need to be able to eat meat and cheese and drink caffe latte whenever I want without feeling guilty. I need to go *home*.'

'You could eat meat here, I don't mind,' he said unconvincingly. 'And there's plenty of room here, isn't there? And yet, you want to go rushing back to your tiny underground flat –'

'Hey.' she said sharply. 'It's *my* tiny underground flat: I paid for it, I decorated it, it's mine – and I love it.' She continued, more coolly and not without dignity: 'And your pity is not only patronising but entirely misplaced: millions of people all over the world would give their right arm to live in my 'tiny underground flat.' Entire families are crowded into places smaller than mine, with no running water…'

He raised a hand: 'All right, I'm sorry.' Staring down at the floor, he continued quietly: 'I'm sure your place is lovely. It's just that… well, I don't have a good experience of long-distance relationships. They just don't work.'

'For lovesick teenagers!' she had protested, exasperated suddenly. 'For people who need to live in each other's pockets, who require constant reassurance of the other's undying devotion and unwavering fidelity! But you and I, we're old and set in our ways. We're independent, self-reliant. I've already been married once and you're an old bachelor. And besides,' she said, getting up and going into the bathroom, 'the alternative is logistically unfeasible.' She stood in the bathroom doorway for a moment, sponge bag in her hand. 'I mean, I defy you to find a greater Italophile than I. But never in a *million years* would I contemplate actually living here all year-round.'

He looked surprised. 'Really? Why ever not?'

'Seriously?' she laughed sardonically, tossing the sponge bag into the suitcase. 'OK… where do I start?' She began counting on her fingers: 'Your bureaucracy, your healthcare system, the pervasive, deep-rooted Catholicism,' (at this point she referred to a newspaper article she had read two years before about a pregnant woman in the Veneto region, a married mother of two in her early forties, who had wished to terminate the pregnancy and had had to apply to twenty-three hospitals and clinics before one had finally agreed to perform the procedure – the other establishments' refusal being ostensibly due to lack of beds, staff or time).

'And please note,' she concluded, 'that I haven't even mentioned the omnipresent influence of the mafia and the systemic corruption in this country.'

He had momentarily abandoned the topic and descended quietly to the kitchen to prepare dinner: *carciofi alla giudia* (his mother's recipe), followed by tagliatelle with pistachio pesto accompanied by a bottle of Il Bruciato. (If this was another tactic, Marnie later pondered as she savoured the succulent crispy artichokes, the delicious nutty pasta and the heavenly wine – that of forcing her to become a gastronomic refugee – it could just about work.)

Then, as they were clearing the plates away, Amedeo suddenly said:

'I could come to the UK.'

Marnie, who was in the process of loading the dishwasher, stood up and stared at him. 'What?'

'Well, your moving to Italy isn't the only solution, is it?'

'You? Live in England?'

279

He shrugged. 'Why not? I did it once before.'

'What? Oh,' she continued dismissively, 'you mean, that time you spent a few weeks in the eighties living in a squat in London?' She sighed and continued, more gently, 'I appreciate the sacrifice you're willing to make – even though I didn't and wouldn't ask to you make it. But it's a huge decision, and one that shouldn't be made impulsively and when you're feeling sad about my leaving.'

'It's not,' he protested, 'I've been thinking about it for a while.'

'Really? Well, even so… Uprooting your whole life isn't the same thing as doing a moonlight flit when you're a teenager just to piss your Dad off and then spending your days busking and your nights trying to shag English girls.'

'Evidently, I no longer need to try too hard in *that* department,' he observed tartly.

'Fuck off,' she said, hurling a tea-towel at his head. 'OK, well, *well done*, but what about my cats? I have two of them, remember? One of which is a long-haired breed. You know those white fluffy cats you see in ads for high-end cat food? That's my Roger.'

His spontaneous reaction, with its involuntary grimace of revulsion, made her laugh:

'Che orrore!'

'Just my luck!' she laughed. 'God, why do I always fall for cat haters?'

His response to this epithet was equally amusing in its histrionic excessiveness, although this time it was not repugnance but profound offense and moral outrage that moved him:

'I could never hate cats or any other creature,' he said indignantly. 'I'm an animal lover, a Pacifist. It's just… my allergies…'

'All right, all right, Saint Francis of bloody Assisi, calm down,' she muttered. 'Christ. You vegans. *"I'm an animal lover, a pacifist,"* as if the rest of us were a horde of bat-head-biting, kitten-drowning, baby seal-clubbing barbarians.'

Mercifully, Amedeo had the good grace to burst out laughing at this. For, despite his high principles, he was invariably saved from sanctimony by his good nature and self-deprecating humour. His reaction also had a humbling effect on Marnie, making her ashamed of her own ill-tempered, unfair comments, and she laughed in turn and threw her arms around him.

That had been four days before, and Amedeo had not raised the subject of their moving in together since. She assumed he had finally admitted defeat.

Then, sometime in the middle of the night before her departure, she awoke with a start. The initial sense of panic that had seized her soon subsided into a dull pang of despondency and – as she looked down at Amedeo sleeping peacefully beside her – guilt.

For she realised now that, despite her protestations about independence and the impracticalities of relocating to Italy, it was the idea of Amedeo and her that was unfeasible. Ever since she had booked her flight back home, she had tried to imagine their continuing as lovers – she back in the UK, he remaining here, both resuming their lives outside the bubble they had inhabited over the past couple of weeks – tried, and failed.

She slipped out of bed, pulled on her bathrobe and tiptoed downstairs. She put the kettle on, and, standing facing the kettle, both hands gripping the counter-top, leaned forward and said under her breath: '*fuck*!'

How the *hell* was she going to break it to him? He would conclude that she was behaving exactly as he had predicted: she had tried him out, decided he was not quite for her after all and wanted to be rid of him. She had callously toyed with his emotions and then cast him aside. She was heartless and capricious. With a sardonic laugh she thought suddenly of *Rigoletto: 'la donna è mobile.'* That's what he would think.

And yet it wasn't that. She had cherished those days and nights of perfect harmony, total intimacy, had yearned for him in those few hours a day during which they were briefly physically separated – and then only by a few meters – and each occupied by matters other than each other.

But such symbiosis is invariably fragile and transient. And now she imagined dashing back and forth to Monza every few weeks, drinking her coffee and tea black, feigning enjoyment of quinoa, trying to load the dishwasher the way he liked (oh, yes, she had noticed that muscle in his face twitch each time she attempted to undertake this task). And then his visits to Bristol. She began to see her flat as he surely would: despite her tasteful décor, comfortable appointments and respectable – if not obsessive – efforts at cleaning, it would inevitably appear cluttered, sordid and tainted with animal flesh compared with his impossibly neat, sanitised, Spartan bachelor's cell. She imagined his sneezing and wheezing until she shut Roger and Tim out in the yard; of their passionate embraces at airport arrival and departure gates. It all seemed absurd, grotesque, a mockery of what they had shared these past few weeks.

She was not so vain and deluded as to believe he would be irretrievably heartbroken and swear off women forever. But the esteem he had always held her in would be lost forever.

The kettle boiled, she made her tea and took it over to the sofa where she curled up and eventually fell asleep.

A few hours later, Amedeo awoke and came downstairs. Upon seeing Marnie asleep on the sofa, a half-drunk cup of tea on the coffee table beside her, his first thought was to wonder how long she had been there; his second was that he would not be able to carry out his intended plan to unload and reload the dishwasher lest she wake up and see him. Indeed, having hitherto successfully hidden his disapproval of her technique by sneaking back downstairs last thing at night or first thing in the morning before she rose to rearrange the crockery and cutlery to his satisfaction, it would be a pity to disillusion and offend her now – today, on her last day.

Having resigned himself to leaving the dishwasher in its current state of apocalyptic disarray for the time being, he emptied and refilled the kettle and switched it on for his fennel *tisana*. Turning back to contemplate Marnie's sleeping form on the sofa, he sighed heavily as he attempted to explain that tiny coil of doubt that had emerged from somewhere in the back of his mind a few days ago and had been growing ever since.

For as they had begun gradually to emerge from their blissful amorous daze and contemplate the future, he wondered if it had not all been a kind of voluptuous *folie à deux*, and that the delusion was now beginning to dissipate. Furthermore, he could not escape the feeling that he had somehow won her by default. True, it was she who had initiated things, and she had been neither drunk nor on the rebound that first night. But she had not been in her normal state – who was in these strange times?

Lately his old friend Max's words had been echoing in his head: it had been a couple of months ago when they had met for drinks; Amedeo had recently returned from his business trip to Paris and was recounting his dinner with Marnie. Max had put down his bottle of beer on the bar, looked his friend in the eyes and said:

'Look, if something was going to happen with you two, it would have happened by now. It's not meant to be. Move on.'

And yet, it *had* happened – finally! But he knew now it would not have had circumstances been different; if the pandemic hadn't broken out and she hadn't ended up stranded with him.

How could he share these thoughts and misgivings with her now, after that preposterous speech he had made that night when she had first kissed him – how he cringed at the memory! What a pompous ass he had been, what a diva! She would think him a scoundrel, and – to his mind, even worse than that – she would think him inconsistent, inconstant, a hypocrite.

He gazed now at the first rays of morning sunlight illuminating the creamy skin on her bare shoulder where her bathrobe had fallen away. It didn't help that he still desired her as ardently as ever; but he resisted the urge to go to her, to kiss her and stroke that shoulder and went back upstairs to shower and dress.

The drive to Malpensa later that day was grim. She chattered constantly, apparently undaunted by his lack of response. Her laboured attempts at conversation were all the more painful to him as they reminded him cruelly of the easy companionable silence they had previously enjoyed. Indeed, years ago during a DigInnova seminar in Lisbon when they were walking back to the hotel together one evening after dinner and he had apologised for his taciturnity, it had been she who had smiled, and, squeezing his hand, assured him that the ability to lapse into occasional bouts of congenial, unapologetic silence was a mark of true closeness and compatibility. A cliché, but true.

And now look at us, he thought dejectedly, as he steered the car into the airport carpark.

And then, as they were in the lift that bore them from the carpark to the departure lounge, she turned to him and smiled ruefully, and he knew. He knew *she* knew what he was feeling, that she felt the same. He was equally certain that she would not say anything, would not voice her own doubts, any more than he would.

They checked the monitor for her departure gate, then, overwhelmed with relief and love, he insisted on walking her as far as the security checkpoint, where he clasped her to him, kissed her – once on each cheek and then gently on the lips – told her he loved her and wished her a good flight.

Moments later, as Marnie placed her bag in the tray, pushed the tray onto the conveyor belt and submitted her boarding pass for inspection, she reflected with relief, contentment – and just the merest, fleeting twinge of nostalgia – on the three words he had just spoken to her. For after the '*ti amo*' he had whispered urgently in her ear almost every night for the past three weeks, he had reverted to their usual '*ti voglio bene.*' Not for the first time, she marvelled that the Italian language marked this distinction between passionate, romantic love and every other kind – filial, parental, amicable.

As she retrieved her bag, belt and phone from the tray on the other side of the security gate, she noticed she had received a text:

Val says you're better and heading back to the UK. Glad to hear it. My mate at the National Gallery is giving an online talk on Dürer on Tuesday evening; if you fancy it I thought we could sign up for it, then maybe have a Zoom chat afterwards and you could trash his lecture? Or just tell me about your Italian adventures and near-death experience. Have a safe journey, take care, Ben.

She smiled but did not reply, resolving to do so later. Suddenly the very idea of making any sort of plans for the future – even for Tuesday (when was that? Two days away?) seemed a Herculean feat. She was overwhelmed by emotion and fatigue and an almost physical longing for home.

I will go home, she thought: feed the cats, make myself something to eat (God bless Mrs Wellesley for popping in yesterday to fill her fridge!), and go to bed. Just the prospect of sleeping – alone! – in her own bed that night brought forth a deep sigh of pleasurable anticipation.

And that is it, she thought. That will do. For now.

EPILOGUE

Bristol

Marnie returned to her cats and her compact, lower ground-floor garden flat in Bristol.

Once borders opened and international travel resumed a few months later, she was able to organise Bacchus & Minerva's maiden Caravaggio Experience. The trip went smoothly on the whole and her first clients, a group of retired American academics, left positive reviews. A few more bookings for the Caravaggio tour began to arrive, followed by some for the Impressionist Experience in France and the Bristol Art Experience.

She had a few video chats with Ben Balakrishnan during lockdown and made tentative plans to have dinner with him when she was next in town.

Monza

Amedeo continued his consulting and voluntary work and finally launched his digital transformation startup in May 2020: shrewdly riding the 'new normal' wave, he specialised in change management, helping organisations adjust their strategy and company culture in light of the global health crisis. He farmed out all the translations – Italian to English and French – for his business (website, apps, marketing collateral, etc) to Marnie, which had paid her bills between her Bacchus & Minerva bookings.

Paris

Despite his daughter's concerns, Luc made a swift recovery from what was apparently a common cold. After months of lockdown his bookshop suffered considerable losses which were only partially offset by online sales. However, he managed to remain afloat, thanks to a few unexpected and exceedingly lucrative sales he made of some rare works to a collector.

Rhiannon remained with him in Paris until July then returned to the UK, where she spent two weeks with her mother in Bristol, during which she met a (young, single) fellow revolutionary called Zach at a local SWP branch meeting. She went camping with him in the Black Mountains before returning to Warwick to resume her degree course.

Milan/Bristol

After their missed video call that day, Marnie made several attempts to contact Miles. Then, a week after she returned to the UK, she received an email from a certain Luca Casaluci Bellini informing her that Miles Halliwell had died from Covid 19 on 5 April. Before he became ill, Miles had told his friend that he had contacted Marnie and even forwarded him the thread of their brief email exchange, which is how Luca had come to have Marnie's address. Miles had been taken to San Raffaele Hospital on 30 March – the day he and Marnie were due to meet online. It is hard to mourn someone one has never known; nonetheless, news of his passing filled her with sadness and regret at having so narrowly missed the opportunity to meet her half-brother.

Luca, on the other hand, bitterly mourned his friend. Having recovered from his bout of suspected Covid 19, he reconciled with his parents and remained at the family home throughout lockdown. He remained convinced that Miles's death was due to some negligence on the part of the over-worked hospital staff (for, statistically, as a fifty-year-old with no underlying health conditions, Miles was three times as likely to die in a road accident than from the virus) and instructed his family's team of lawyers to take appropriate steps. Miles's colleagues at *La Repubblica* published a touching and laudatory obituary of their colleague and friend.

Miles was survived by his mother Barbara, his estranged father Nigel, the four half-sisters he never knew, and his grandfather, the Major, who celebrated his hundredth birthday on 15 May 2020. The telegram from the Queen had pride of place on the mantelpiece of the drawing room at Fawley House.

Dublin/Portlaw

The Kavanaugh-Mullan-O'Neill ménage in County Waterford was on the whole a harmonious one: Galloways afforded more than sufficient space – and boundaries – for the various members of the extended family to coexist peaceably and productively. Up at the main house, Aiofe and Patricia ran the household between them with an almost intimidating efficiency, cooking, cleaning and minding Olivia while Méabh was working. Méabh, incidentally, had halved her workload since she began fostering but continued to see some clients via video-conferencing. Tusla eventually approved her adoption of Olivia.

In early May, Dave moved into the master bedroom at the fishing lodge. Neither he nor Clare was under any illusions about the reasons for the arrangement, being essentially a convenient and effective way of providing a stable family environment for their sons and fulfilling their parental obligations, whilst satisfying their sexual needs. There was no question of immediately cancelling the divorce proceedings (the process for dissolving a marriage in the Republic of Ireland being so protracted that there would be ample time for them to change their minds several times over), nor renewing their marital vows. They decided to take things one day at a time. (Or as Dave put it with his customary, inimitable eloquence: 'don't get excited, mind: this isn't fuckin' *Friends,* and we're not fuckin' Ross and Rachel').

Whatever the outcome of their marriage, however, Dave decided that, once hospitals began to resume non-emergency procedures after the Covid curve was flattened, he would undergo a vasectomy.

At the beginning of June, Tina Mooney discovered she was pregnant with her new boyfriend Brendan's child. She decided to keep this one.

London/Suffolk

Nigel stayed at Raddington with Portia whilst Venetia and Cordelia remained in London. He learned of his son's death from his first wife Barbara. As for his current wife, Venetia De La Pole was a throwback to a time when women of a certain class considered divorce as a stigma and a failure, and therefore had no intention of formally ending her marriage. However, she expressed a wish that she and her husband continue to lead separate lives after lockdown – a situation which is immeasurably easier when one owns several spacious houses than when limited to a single, one-bedroom flat.

As a result of this series of setbacks in his private life, Nigel became increasingly morose and drank ever more heavily. His relationship with his eldest daughter deteriorated, a situation which was hardly improved by his discovery that it was she, not Dinah, who had been responsible for disclosing Marnie's existence to the media. A friend of Nigel's, the former CEO of a merchant bank, the breadth and extent of whose contacts in the worlds of business and politics were exceeded only by his socialite wife's network of spies and gossips, called Nigel one day saying there had been rumours around town that Portia was the source of the leak. He

287

immediately confronted Portia and, in those few seconds that elapsed between his making the accusation and her response, he had seen from her expression that the rumours were perfectly well-founded. After a brief, half-hearted attempt at denial, Portia confessed and promptly launched into an impassioned, ill-advised defence of her actions, bemoaning Nigel's years of neglect, his blatant favouritism of her youngest sister, and the inevitable distress and resentment this had bred in her, Portia. Alas, far from eliciting her father's sympathy, such an argument, in both its content and form, only served to make her fall even further in his estimation, demonstrating as it did qualities which Nigel Lovelace particularly despised: cowardice, self-pity, an inability to own up to one's mistakes and shortcomings. They agreed that Portia would move out of Raddington Hall as soon as lockdown was over.

During one of their video calls towards the end of what turned out to be the first of several lockdowns, Dinah apprised Marnie of these new developments in the Lovelace family, of Portia's fall from grace and her own vindication. Marnie, who could only imagine the atmosphere at Raddington, said it put her in the mind of Maria Rushworth and Mrs Norris at the end of *Mansfield Park*, during whose exile and forced cohabitation, 'their tempers became their mutual punishment.' Dinah reflected wryly that the scenario was probably more Sartrean than Austenean: *'l'enfer, c'est les autres.'*

Regarding Portia's treachery, Dinah never retaliated against her sister, nor even confronted her about it. That said, Portia's behaviour – and her family's initial acceptance of Dinah's guilt – certainly made it easier for Dinah to distance herself from her parents and two sisters. She did, however, remain in regular contact with her half-sister and travelled to Bristol in the summer to stay with Marnie and meet her niece Rhiannon, who was briefly at home between various travels.

Nigel never attempted to get in touch with Marnie, nor she with him.

Extract from Rhiannon's blog

Today is the last day of lockdown, which means that as of tomorrow, I'll be able to venture outside and sit in a park or a pub garden with members of one other household. Woohoo! #SmallMercies #ScaleDownYourExpectations.

Over the past few months, pundits and lay people like myself have been constantly speculating on when this crisis will really be over. Personally, I'm confident it won't be too long: this time next year, we'll be looking back at all this as though it were a bad time, a dystopian interlude from which we finally emerged.

But the more I think about it, the more I arrive at the inescapable conclusion that it's not so much when will we get out of this, but what will we learn from it? Will we come out of it as more selfless, considerate, resilient, responsible citizens of the world?

Or will we all just revert to being a bunch of snivelling, entitled, navel-gazing, earth-raping, rapacious shopaholics?

Either way... I can't wait to find out.

Printed in Great Britain
by Amazon